DAUGHTERS

OF

DARKNESS

STORIES

MY SON WOULD NOT STOP CRYING

E. Z. Morgan

My son would not stop crying.

I sat in the living room alone. The house seemed to shift at every scream he would bellow from his room. I tried to close my eyes and center myself. Crying was normal. I knew this might happen when I became a mother. People warn you about the hard times, but you can never really know until it happens to you. I managed two deep breaths before the wailing started again.

The sound was a cheese grater against my eardrum. It was something about the high-pitched nature of the crying. So damn desperate. So needy. I was no longer an individual person. I was the host for this fucking parasite. This disgusting mess of cells that nearly tore me apart when I gave birth to him.

I loved him once. I really did. I tried so hard to do right by him. I let him sleep in my bed. I rocked him back and forth, his heavy skull pressed against my neck like a noose. He puked everywhere. His insides were always on my clothes or on the floor. Nothing felt clean.

The screaming continued and I turned the TV on as a distraction. I didn't watch the DVD again. Instead I found some cartoons. I turned the volume all the way up. Maybe the squeaky voices of the animated animals would drown out his goddamn bellowing. But it only made the worse. The lady mouse on TV smiled and did a little dance while the boy animals watched and clapped. I turned it off.

Suddenly there was a knock on the door. I froze. Even though I despised his crying, I didn't want to go check on my son. And I didn't want anyone else to either. I just wanted him to rot in his room and cry until his feeble vocal chords crumbled.

But it might be the cops. I couldn't hide for long. By neglecting his cries I might have made the situation worse. That fucking bastard. That useless waste of an egg and sperm.

I got up slowly, smoothing my housedress as I rose. I walked to the door. With a deep breath, I checked the peephole. It wasn't the cops! It was Arianna, home from school!

I must have lost track of the time.

I enthusiastically opened the door and took her in my arms. She felt so good. So alive and healthy. She stepped back and dropped her backpack off her shoulder. "Why was the door locked?"

"Just for safety, baby," I told her sweetly. "Now there's something I need to tell you."

"What?" She looked worried. Poor girl.

"Let's go upstairs." I took her hand in mine. My son's screams were quieter now, but still very audible. Arianna seemed scared. Her little fingers held on so tight. We climbed the stairs and walked towards my son's room.

Arianna stopped. "I don't want to go in there," she murmured.

"Don't worry baby," I said softly, petting her black curls. "You won't ever have to after today."

"I guess. Okay," she replied, squeezing my hand again.

We entered the musty room. Bottles of beer scattered the floor like cockroaches. On the bed lay my son, covered in his own blood. The shotgun blast to the stomach had revealed his intestines, but hadn't killed him. He looked up at us with nearly dead eyes. His arms held his organs inside his body. His toes were cut off, lined up neatly on the bedside table. His voice was close to death. "I'm sorry," he whispered.

A grin spread across my face. Arianna did not seem scared anymore. She looked at me and smiled. "Did you do this, Nana?"

I kissed her forehead. "I saw the video your dad made. What he did to you was not your fault. I knew he had to pay for what he did." The crying had almost completely ended. It was just small whimpers now. "He will never hurt you again."

5

Motherhood is not always easy. Sometimes you have to do things that hurt your child.

On the flip side, being a grandmother is simple. Arianna is the only good thing that that worthless, disgusting mass of flesh ever did for the world. I intend to keep her safe.

THE LETTER

Sandra Varela

Hi,

The first time I saw you, I was surprised I could see you. You had a small turtle in your hands. You kept calling it Michelangelo, which I assumed was a nod to the Ninja Turtles. You tossed your long, brown hair behind your back and knelt down to place the turtle on the ground. You were excited to see it wobbling on the grass. It reminded me of my cat, and how I used to play with him when I was your age.

I witnessed your entire childhood from my small *window*. Your first ride on a bicycle. Your first day of school. Your first real friend Brenda. Your first day of middle school and the cute uniform you got to wear. The time you won the science fair and you brought home a trophy shaped like a cell. You were such a happy girl.

I saw you grow older. Your body changing. You grew taller, your body slimmer, your face as beautiful as ever. I witnessed as others started to notice you in a different way. The stares from the jealous girls. The googly eyes from the young boys. As all this happened before my eyes, I noticed myself changing too. I got older. I got weaker. I got disillusioned. Bruised. I lost my will to escape my painful life. All I had was this *window* to your life to keep me going. I lived my days through yours. Watching you was enough entertainment for me. You couldn't know the different ways you saved me from bad thoughts, bad days, and all the pain I had been suffering from.

I saw the day that handsome young man came to pick you up in a red convertible. Your mother wasn't happy about it, but she knew she had no choice. You had to start spreading your wings at some point. You left in a gorgeous floral dress that matched the summer's flowers. You came back late that night. You had a stuffed bear and some leftover cotton candy. I imagined you had gone to the fair. I imagined all the rides you must have gone on, all the fun that must have been for you. I was so happy that you had enjoyed your first date. And then came the magical kiss. He leaned in, blushing, and kissed you. Your cheeks were so red that I instantly knew I had witnessed your first kiss. I closed my eyes, imagining what that must have felt like. For *one* second, I imagined it had been me wearing that dress, smiling so big, with butterflies in my belly and a kiss on my lips. But I was happy for you.

I wanted to thank you for allowing me to live again. For allowing me to dream again. I wanted to thank you, but just couldn't bring myself to you. I couldn't go talk to you. I didn't know how. If only you knew about my *window*.

And then, one day, I heard him talking about you. The man I live with. He noticed you. I heard him complaining about how pretty girls like you shouldn't show off their legs like that. The moment he mentioned your legs, I knew it was over. I knew you would become his next trophy. I had to keep you away from him. This was my chance to thank you. I couldn't let you turn into me.

I had been lucky. I don't know why he liked me this much. Other girls came and went, never to return. And yet, amidst all the years, he always kept me down here. I think it's because he saw that I still had a light in me. Because I had *you*. All the other girls died long before he killed them. I could tell that they were already dead in their eyes long before he viciously murdered them in front of me, showing off his skill.

But not me. You kept me going. I had my little *window*. A little crack high up on the wall of this basement I call home. He didn't like that he couldn't break me down. He didn't know about the little crack. So he kept me to see how long I could stay like this. It is a sick game... that I've been winning thanks to you.

But then he noticed you. And I knew, I knew what fate awaited you if he laid his monstrous hands on you. Whatever strength I have left, I've collected it and prepared myself to finally do something about it.

9

I want to thank you. Because if you're reading this letter, it means I did it. I gathered my courage, packed it neatly into action, and went through with my plan to escape once and for all. I will make him believe I've died. I don't know if it'll work. But if it does, he will reach to pick me up. I'll immediately kick him as hard as I can where it'll hurt the most. *As hard as I can*. I will then steal his keys and run as fast as I can and drop this letter off in your mailbox. I have a feeling he will chase me and get a hold of me eventually because I am weak... I'm very weak. Battered. There is barely a human left in this body of mine. But if that is the case, I've been prepared to leave this world for a long time. I doubt anyone will hear or see me. This street is so desolate. You're the only life here it seems sometimes. But so long as you get this letter, I know that I did my part and that you'll be safe.

Monsters are real. This one is named Ryan Morehouse. He is your front door neighbor. I have been kept captive in his basement for a very long time. I've lost track of the years but I believe I must be in my late twenties by now. I was fifteen when he first brought me here. My parents must have looked for me. Please don't tell them about me. I don't want them to know about the tortures he put me through. I don't want them to see me broken down this way. I just want you to report him to the police. His evil nature and depraved mind can only be stopped if he is caught behind bars.

They will find bodies dangling in the walls of the basement. I've learned to live with the smell by now but they will notice it the second they step down here. There are a lot of young girls in the walls of my room down here. Tell them to treat them delicately. They were good girls. They've been my companions. My friends.

Most of all, I want to thank you. You're the only thing that kept me going. You were my light. And now, I'm escaping thanks to you. Escaping this awful room. Escaping this awful life. Even if it means I finally get to die.

With love,

The girl who watched you grow up

THE WOMAN UPSTAIRS

R. R. Smith

She wears heels like my mother. I hear her click-clacking across my ceiling at night. I don't know when she sleeps because it seems like she's always up there, walking back and forth. I told my parents about her once when I was younger. Mom made an angry face, and Dad plopped down on the sofa like he was tired. I never mentioned it again.

I like the sound. I try to imagine the woman upstairs and what she thinks about that makes her pace all day. Maybe she just likes the clicking sound as much as I do. Sometimes when I can't sleep I follow the sound of her footsteps on the ceiling with my eyes. What kind of room was up there? An office? A bedroom like mine?

I used to dream about going upstairs to visit her. I'd knock on her door and when she opened it I would say, "Hi. I live in the bedroom below you." She would smile and say, "I know." Then she'd let me in for a cup of hot chocolate. We haven't met yet, but I just know we would be friends.

***

13

Tonight, Mom and Dad are fighting in the kitchen. Mom's stopped yelling, and Dad's saying all kind of stupid things to fill the silence. I decide to take my homework to my room, even though it means I won't be able to ask mom for help. Even with the door shut I can hear Dad's urgent whispers. I don't have to look to know that Mom is sitting up tall at the kitchen table looking at the wall.

Click-clack. Click-clack.

I time my breath to the footsteps above me. What is she like? Does she have a family? Do they fight like mine? Is she any good at math homework?

After a while my door opens, and Mom slips into my room. I know she's going to say something about how parents fight sometimes and that doesn't mean they don't love each other; I've heard it a thousand times. But she doesn't. She looks up. Before I can ask what she wants, she takes a step back into the hall, gaze fixed on the ceiling.

"Mom?" I ask, but she doesn't speak. She just stands there with wide dark eyes looking up toward the light.

Click-clack. Click-clack. Click-clack. Click-clack.

"Mom?" I say louder and she jumps like I startled her, finally looking at me. "Mom are you okay?" The footsteps above us pause and in that moment of silence Mom lurches forward, wrapping her fingers around my arm like a claw.

14

"Mom!" I cry and pull against her grip.

Click-clack. Click-clack. Click-clack.

She freezes, and I feel her heart beating like a drum through her clenched hand.

Click-clack. Click-clack. Click-clack. Click-clack.

I stare. What is wrong with her? Is she angry with me? Did I do something wrong? I look to her for answers, but her eyes aren't on me, they're stuck staring at the ceiling as if pulled tightly upward by invisible strings.

Click-clack. Click-clack. Click-clack. Click-clack. Click-clack.

"Honey?" Dad calls from down the hall with obvious concern. He pokes his head inside and sees Mom still frozen in an awkward lunge with fingers like a vice around my arm.

"Honey?" His voice is soothing now. She seems to hear him.

I look up, trying to see what's caught her attention so completely, and I see I little red stain I'd never noticed before. I watch mesmerized as it grows from the size of a dime to a creeping, blossoming blotch as big as my bed. The ceiling sags under the liquid weight and a single drop pools from its center, falling neatly onto Mom's hand. She doesn't notice the drop.

"You…" Her voice shakes. She isn't talking to me. With effort, she lets me go. She stands, but it looks difficult, like she has to think hard about each muscle and limb before pulling it carefully back into place.

"Okay. It's okay." Dad croons and takes Mom's shoulders. "It's alright. Let's get you to bed. Some rest is just what you need, doesn't that sound nice?"

"Dad?" I call after him, but he turns and puts a finger to his lips. I nod.

He leads her down the hall but from the kitchen I hear Mom speak again.

I look up at the ceiling, worried the red drops will stain my sheets, but the ceiling is perfectly white. The stain is gone. I shiver.

"You said you took care of it."

"Honey, I did. I swear."

"You swear?" Glass shatters, and Dad shouts a protest.

"I kept my end of the deal! I kept my promise!" More shattering glass. "I have to remember her every single day, but I've done my very best. After everything you did, I thought you could get at least one thing right!"

"I took care of it." His voice is low now. Mom says something I can't make out, and I hear crunching as I Dad walks over the broken glass. "I'll prove it to you." He says. "Stay here. I'll be back."

"As if I'd trust you to tell me the truth." Mom says with a hiss. "I'll go."

There is a moment of silence. My heart pounds, and I lean forward.

"I'll take care of it." Dad signs and I know somehow he's talking about me.

"You'd better." The front door opens and shuts.

I stand and walk to the hall to peak around the corner.

"Dad?" He's sweeping up white pieces of broken glass. "What going on? Is Mom okay?"

He pinches the bridge of his nose and his eyes scrunch together.

"She'll be fine." He balances the broom against the edge of the counter. "Come here, kid."

I follow him to the sofa, carefully avoiding the sparkling glass pieces on the ground.

"Your mother will be fine." He repeats and leans back into the sofa, stretching his legs out in front of him. "This is my fault."

He pauses to give me a chance to speak, but I don't know what to say.

He continues. "A long time ago I did something that hurt your mother. Not physically, but it hurt her trust in me. Sometimes certain things will remind her about that time in our lives and all the old hurt and emotions come rushing back to her again."

He turns to me. "You didn't do anything wrong, don't worry. And she'll really be fine, I promise. I'm sorry if she scared you."

She had scared me. I look down at my hands folded in my lap. "What did you do?"

Dad leans forward, resting his elbows on his knees, his hands hanging limply between his legs. He looks at the floor, the dark TV, and then his hands.

"I fell in love with another woman. I never stopped loving your Mom, but I fell in love with another woman too and I lied about it. She's gone now."

I want to ask what he means, but he looks so sad. Dad loved another woman? Another woman like Mom?

"Will Mom do that again?" I ask, unable to forget the way her eyes looked.

"I don't think so." Dad says. "I expect as soon as Mom comes back we can forget the whole thing. I just didn't want you to feel like it was your fault, or that you'd done anything wrong. Okay, kid? This is not your fault."

I nod, but I don't feel like I understand.

Dad ruffles my hair and I smile. The front door opens and Mom sweeps inside, locking the door behind her.

"Well?" Dad stands. He looks worried.

"A lovely old woman moved in. She looks to be about 90 and had three cats that I could see. She wanted me to stay for tea."

Dad raises an eyebrow and Mom shakes her head. She suddenly looks very tired.

"It wasn't her. Of course it wasn't. I don't know what I was thinking. I must have been hearing things. I guess work is taking more out of me than I thought."

He exhales and moves towards Mom, taking her in his arms.

"Everything is fine" He says and pulls her close. "Just like I promised."

What Mom said surprises me. If an old lady is living upstairs where does the sound of clicking heels come from? Is there someone living with her?

I think Mom might apologize for before, but she doesn't. She asks me about my homework and ends up helping me with my math after all.

***

I don't think about it much anymore. Mom seems fine now, and I haven't asked Dad anymore questions. Everything seems

19

normal, except for the woman upstairs. She walks around more quickly now, like she's angry or nervous. I hope she's okay.

I finish up my homework and put all the papers in a pile at the end of the kitchen table for Mom to check later. I slide off the chair and take a towel from the dryer on my way to the bathroom.

Dad's watching TV and Mom's reading a book. Sometimes, if I get in the shower with them noticing, I can sit in the hot water for a long time before they yell at me for wasting water. I slip into the bathroom, turn on the water, and brush my teeth while I wait for the shower to get hot. When the mirror fogs up I leave my clothes on the floor and step into the tub.

I scrub my hair and face and turn the temperature up hotter. The water pools around my feet and climbs slowly up my ankles. The sound changes from water hitting porcelain to water hitting water, and I realize the drain must have clogged. I open my eyes and squint against the soap.

The water around my ankles is red. I freeze, water pouring down my back and around the sides of my face. The red around my ankles sloshes back and forth, syrupy and dark. Chunks of something soft float in the thick soup. One of them touches me.

I throw up onto the shower curtain, and the vomit mixes with the warm blood. I feel it between my toes. I gasp, and the gasp becomes a scream. I pull hard on the shower curtain, trying to get away but afraid to move my feet. I don't want the pink things to touch me. The rings of the curtain snap against my weight and I fall halfway out of the tub to the floor, flinging a splash of blood against the walls and all over my legs.

Dad bursts through the door and runs to my side, pulling me against him. I'm wet and dripping.

"Kid! Are you hurt? What happened?" He holds my head against his chest. I'm shaking and I can seem to stop. The shower is still on and the steam wafts out the open door.

"Honey?" He calls down the hall for Mom.

I can't look at the tub. I can't. I can smell it, a metal rotting smell like old food and pennies. It's drying on my skin, caking in a ring around my ankles. I close my eyes, but I can still see chunks of meat splashing around in a red stained tub. Can't he smell it too? Can't he see it?

Click-clack. Click-clack. Click-clack.

I've never heard the footsteps above the bathroom before. The familiar rhythmic sound seems to sink down deep into my chest and calm the frantic beating of my heart.

"What happened?" Mom asks from the door.

"I think she fell." Dad says.

They're both here with me. I can look if they're both here. I pull my head away from Dad's chest and turn back to the tub with my eyes shut tight. I have to see.

21

Water streams down from the shower curtain into a clean white tub. The shower curtain is halfway torn from the pole, but the blood is gone. The smell is gone.

Mom hurries over to turn off the water and places a towel around my shoulders.

"What happened?" She asks again as Dad helps me to my feet. I hold onto him tightly.

"Did you slip?" Dad asks.

I shake my head. "No. I mean yes, but—" Mom fluffs the towel around my arms to warm me and combs through my wet hair with her fingers.

"I saw blood." I tell them. My voice sounds small and far away. "I looked down and there was blood everywhere and I got scared and I fell."

They exchange a look and my eyes fill with hot tears. "You have to believe me. Please believe me!" I throw my arms around Dad and sob.

"Hey." He says, patting my back. "Hey, it's okay. We believe you."

"You do?" I'm surprised.

"Of course." He nods. "We didn't raise a liar. Of course we believe you." Relieved, fresh sobs come up from my chest.

Mom leads us to my room and helps me into a clean pair of pajamas. The three of us squish onto my bed and, pressed

22

between the two of them, I can almost pretend it didn't happen. I can almost believe it wasn't real.

For once, I don't hear the footsteps. I think I'm glad.

I expect them to leave but they stay with me, holding me close, keeping me safe. I close my eyes and start to drift away. The last thing I hear before I fall asleep is something Mom says quietly to Dad, so quietly I'm not sure I heard it at all.

"So that's how you did it."

***

The bars of a crib make it hard to see. I recognize Mom and Dad in the living room. They're fighting again, yelling at each other and waving their hands in the air. There's another woman too. She's holding a big blanket around herself like she is cold.

She moves towards Mom. Her hand is stretched out. She looks sad. Mom shouts and shoves the woman away. Dad tries to catch her, but the blanket slips out of his hands. She falls. Her head hits the corner of the coffee table with a loud crack. The room is quiet.

***

"Breakfast is ready." Dad says through the open door. The smell of bacon is obvious but strange. Dad has never made us breakfast before.

I rub my eyes and crawl out of bed, making my way down the hall. Mom leaves her room at the same time and she looks as confused as I am.

"Wow." She looks around the kitchen. "Oh my God, are those flowers?"

"Lilies." Dad grins. "Your favorite."

Mom and I sit down at the table. I can't see her because the flowers are in the way. Dad throws a cloth over his shoulder and loads up three huge plates of breakfast food.

"One for you," he sets a plate in front of me, "one for you," and one in front of Mom, "and one for me."

I look down at the feast. There is a small mountain of bacon, pancakes, and scrambled eggs.

"What's the occasion?" Mom asks.

"Do I need an occasion to cook for my family?" Dad laughs. "Oh, I almost forgot!" He leaps from the table back to the fridge and returns with orange juice and syrup. He hums to himself as he pours syrup over everything on his plate. I take a tentative bite of my pancakes. Mom doesn't move. She's looking at Dad.

Click-clack. Click-clack. Click-clack.

My eyes dart to Mom, afraid the sound will set her off again. She doesn't seem to hear it. This time it's Dad who looks up at the ceiling, still smiling with a mouth full of syrupy eggs.

"Can I have some hot chocolate?" I ask hopefully.

"You know you don't need that much sugar." Mom reaches for the orange juice. She's still watching Dad, and she knocks over the vase of flowers.

"Shit." She stands and moves everyone's food out of the way. "Michael, I'm so sorry." She busies herself with paper towels, but Dad doesn't seem bothered. In fact, he laughs. His laughter is big and booming and… wrong.

"It's no problem. Accidents happen." He winks at me. "Don't they, Honey?"

She freezes mid-wipe.

Click-clack. Click-clack. Click-clack. Click-clack.

"Good thing I made plenty of bacon!" He leans back with another full-bellied laugh. I feel sick.

***

Click-clack. Click-clack. Click-clack.

The sound startles me out of a doze.

Click-clack. Click-clack. Click-clack. Click-clack.

25

Her footsteps are hurried and sharp. I look at the clock. It's two in the morning. The front door opens and quietly clicks shut. All my senses sharpen, and I listen to heavy footsteps walk down the hall and out of my range of hearing.

I think about moving to the living room so he'll see me when I walk in the door, but I worry Mom will catch me and make me go back to bed — or worse, ask me what I'm doing.

Click-clack. Click—

She stops.

I inhale quietly, a vague sense of fear building in my stomach. She's waiting for something.

A door creaks above me. I know what I will hear before it happens.

The thud of heavy work boots slowly crosses the floor. The woman upstairs takes a few steps back, then moves forward. The heavy stomping rushes towards her and the sound of footsteps is replaced by the sound of squeaking springs and a rhythmic scraping of furniture on the floor. From somewhere in the room above me a baby starts to cry.

I can't move. I want to rush out of the room, to cover my ears, to run to my mother. I want to go to sleep and forget my suspicions and fears. But my eyes are frozen, stuck fast to the dark ceiling while I listen.

It is a long time before the sound of the front door breaks the spell. The woman upstairs is still.

I leap out of bed, limbs singing with sudden energy. I have to catch him. I have to see.

I peak around the door frame into the hall. The coast is clear. I creep forward in socked feet, hardly daring to breathe. I don't want him to see me.

The kitchen lights are off but by craning my neck around the corner I can just see the front door. Dad is there. His back is to me. He's locking the front door behind him. Something is wrong.

He turns to face the kitchen and I clamp my hand over my mouth to quiet a gasp. It's too dark to make out color, but I know somehow the dark stain covering him from head to toe is a deep and sticky red.

He sighs and rubs his eyes with the palm of his hand. The action leaves long, clotted smears on his face. He doesn't see me.

I spin on my heels and fly back to my room, terrified he might find me awake. In my panic I knock my elbow painfully against the door frame. I inhale through clenched teeth and throw myself into bed, determined not to cry.

"Kid?" He calls down the hall. My heart slams against my chest like it's trying to break through the cage of my ribs.

The thump of his boots draws closer. I pull the covers over my head.

He flicks on the hall light and I can almost see his silhouette in the doorway through my sheets. He steps inside and I can smell the blood that covers him. I hear it squishing in his boots with every step.

His weight presses heavily on my side as he sits down with a long low sigh. I feel his hand rest heavy on my shoulder, and the blanket grows wet and warm around him. The coppery-blood smell fills my nose and I fight the need to gag.

He pats my head gently, and then he's gone.

I don't dare to move. If I can smell the blood, feel it drying in sticky patches on my blankets, I know it isn't safe. It will disappear again the way it did on the ceiling and in the shower, but I know that until then I am in danger. I don't believe Dad will hurt me, but I can't trust him when he's covered in that thick, malicious blood.

I wait beneath the blankets and breathe through my mouth to avoid the smell. Dad walks down the hall, and his bedroom door opens and shuts. I shift uncomfortably as my blankets begin to crust and harden. *When will it go away?*

Click-clack. Click-clack. Click-clack. Click-clack. Click-clack.

The footsteps are a frenzy.

28

Click-clack. Click-clack. Click-clack. Click-clack. Click-clack. Click-clack. Click-clack. Click-clack.

A scream from the bedroom rips me out of bed.

"I did what you asked!" Dad shouts and Mom comes flying into the living room. I bolt from my bed and down the hall towards them. Blood is smeared on Mom's white pajama pants. It covers her hands.

She stares at her fingers, mouth gaping wide, and screams again.

Click-clack. Click-clack. Click-clack. Click-clack. Click-clack. Click-clack.

The footsteps echo above the living room and Mom covers her ears, groaning loudly. Her eyes dart back and forth, wild and feverish.

Dad stumbles from the bedroom, leaving streaks on the walls as he drags himself forward.

"I did what you asked." He whines and reaches for her. "I cleaned up your mess."

I dart behind the kitchen island, afraid of them both, afraid of the blood.

Click-clack. Click-clack. Click-clack. Click-clack. Click-clack.

Mom jerks at the sound of the footsteps and shrieks. She snatches the lamp off the nearest side table and throws it at the ceiling, only managing to strike the living room wall. Glass shatters and she howls. I pull my knees tight to my chest and shut my eyes.

"I didn't ask you to bring her child back with you! I didn't ask you to make me raise it!" Something heavy falls to the floor with the sound of splintering rood. "I asked you to get rid of the body, but you fucked that up too. She's still up there, mocking me! You ruined us, Michael." She's sobs. "Whose blood is that?"

"I did what you asked." Dad mumbles. "I took care of her."

The front door opens and shuts with a terrible crash.

I raise myself on shaky legs to peak over the counter. Dad is on the couch, the blood dried and cracked on his skin. The blood is real this time. I back away from him. The blood is real. What did he do?

I rush to the front door and throw myself into the hall.

A trail of smudged brown leads out the door from where Dad returned tonight. I follow it. I know Mom did the same.

The blood splatter leads me to the stairwell. As I climb the amount of blood increases from brown smeared boot prints to large splotches, and then to smeary puddles that have not quite dried. They reflect the florescent lights with a sickly, deep red.

I follow, leaping over and around each wet spot until I see it. At the end of a long red hall the trail stops at the door to the apartment above ours.

I hurry down the hall, but it feels like the air has turned thick. I move forward, but the air presses heavy on my lungs. I need to find Mom. I need to see. From behind the door someone screams. It sounds so far away.

The sound seems to echo down the hall, bouncing off the walls, coming from behind every door. It's Mom. I know then what she found in that apartment. I know what Dad did to the old lady who lived there. I know what he did to the woman he fell in love with. *She's gone,* he told me. He killed them both.

I slam against the door and tear at the knob with trembling hands. It won't budge. I yell, mouth pressed to the wood, and beat at the door with both fists, but I can't hear my own voice anymore. All I can hear is Mom's scream.

The light next to me flickers and then rights itself with a buzz.

The lock clicks and the door opens.

My eyes clamp shut, afraid of what is beyond the door, afraid of what Mom found, afraid she'll have the same look in her eyes that she did when she first heard the footsteps. But I have to see.

I open my eyes.

It's her. She looks exactly the way I thought she would. Her hair falls to her shoulder in gentle waves and her eyes are blue

31

and kind. I understand now how Dad had fallen in love with the woman upstairs. I think I love her too.

"I live in the bedroom below you." The words tumble out of my mouth.

"I know." She smiles. I feel the warmth of that smile and all the bad things seem to melt away. There was something I was afraid of, something from before… but I guess it wasn't very important.

She opens the door wider and I am drawn into the light of her apartment. "Would you like some hot chocolate?"

I take her outstretched hand. We haven't met yet, but somehow I just know we're going to be the best of friends.

SECURITY QUESTIONS

Blair Daniels

"What's your name?"

"Adam Lu. I want to close my American Express Gold Card," I said hurriedly into the phone. The train left in twenty minutes. But I needed to get the account closed, before they charged me that damn annual fee.

"Okay, we just need to verify your identity," the woman said. "I'm going to ask you a few security questions, okay?"

"Okay."

"What's your current address?"

"XX Hyacinth Court."

"And what's your mother's maiden name?"

"Greenberg."

"Thank you for that, Mr. Lu. We just need to ask you a few more questions to verify you. First, which of the following addresses have you lived at? [redacted] Maple Avenue, [redacted] Emory Circle, [redacted] 5th Street, or none of the above?"

"None of the above." Oh, *these* security questions. The weird multiple-choice ones, that you didn't actually ever pick. I sighed into the phone and checked the clock. 8:12... sixteen minutes to go.

"Okay. What security system do you use, or have you used in the past? ADT, Ring Alarm, Adobe, or none of the above?"

"None of the above."

A pause. I heard what sounded like papers shuffling on the other end. Then: "How tall are you? Five-nine, six feet, or –"

"Five seven. Listen, how many questions are you going to ask me? I just want to close my account. I have to catch a train."

"Okay. One last question," the woman said. Her voice took on a smooth, soft quality. As if she were smiling on the other end. "Are you a gun owner?"

"Uh, no."

"Thank you! We've verified your identity." Her voice grew suddenly chipper. Excited.

"Okay. So I'd like to close my account," I said. 8:21. *Dammit, I'm going to miss it.*

"That's not possible, Mr. Lu."

"You can't cancel my card? Why not?"

A pause. "I can't cancel your account, Mr. Lu, because I don't work for American Express."

"...What?"

"It's a common mistake, Mr. Lu. American Express is 528-4800; you dialed 529-4800."

"I don't... I don't understand."

"Do you know how many people misdial American Express's phone number? Hundreds. Per day. And those people tend to be just what we're looking for -- wealthy, dumb."

"I don't –"

"They'll be there in a minute. You can make it easy on yourself, and leave the house... or you can stay and fight. But I don't think the odds are good, Mr. Lu. They have guns... and you don't."

A pause. Then her peppy voice continued: "Anything else I can help you with, Mr. Lu?"

"I –"

"Thank you for calling! We *do* hope you have a wonderful day."

Click.

I pulled the phone away from my ear.

Just in time to see a shadow flit across the curtains.

"Hello?" I called. I took a step back, heart beginning to pound. "Hello?"

Thump, thump.

And then a man.

Just a glimpse of him, running by. Wearing all black, complete with a cap over his head. Dashing madly past my window.

35

I backed away.

Click, click.

The locks turned and clicked. *Thump, thump.* Heavy footsteps at the back door.

I turned on my heel and ran. Threw open the front door, ran as fast as I could through the front yard. Until the cold stung my lungs and my legs were weak.

Then I pulled out my phone and called the police.

***

They came too late.

The house was ransacked. I was missing my TV, almost a thousand dollars in cash, and my iPad. I reported it all to the officers and told them about the phone number. But when we called it, we only heard:

Beep, beep, beep! The number you have dialed is no longer in service.

They left. Then I sat in silence, my mind reeling.

Then I got on my computer – an old, half-broken thing, no wonder it wasn't stolen – and wrote this post.

To warn you.

There are hundreds of different ways you could misdial 528-4800. Whoever these people are jump from number to number, pretending to be American Express. They ask "security questions" to get information out of you. To rob you blind... or worse.

Don't fall for it.

Next time you pick up the phone...

Don't answer any strange security questions.

OCEAN WATER

Adelaide Hagen

Even in the pool water and sweltering heat, her lips remained a vibrant red.

I knew it was creepy to watch my neighbor swimming, but I just didn't know how to talk to her. She climbed up on the side of the pool for a rest, singing something sweet but muffled as she combed her fingers through her hair. I didn't even know if she was into girls or not.

With a creak, I pushed the window open a little to hear her singing.

"It's a fine day…" I couldn't quite make out all the words.

Her eyes caught mine and I leapt back from the window. She must have seen me. My heart pounded painfully in my chest. In a moment of bravery, or maybe just panic, I decided that talking to her was the only way to redeem myself.

Just a pep talk later, I found myself hiding behind the fence and trying to think of something to say. Finally I decided that I would ask her about her water-proof makeup. Or maybe not, that might sound weird.

Frustrated, I decided to just pop my head up over the fence and say the first thing that came to mind. I soon found that the fence was higher than I had anticipated.

With my face scrunched between two fence posts, I said the first thing that came to mind, maybe a little louder than necessary;

"Hey! I like the day out!"

What I meant to say was either "I like your makeup." or "beautiful day out", however my indecision led to this mess. I was ready to run back inside and never come out again, but then she laughed. It sounded like music.

"I like the day out too" She said. I could feel the blood rush to my ears. She must have noticed I was blushing.

"Do you wanna come hang out in the pool?"

Not wanting to say something embarrassing I nodded energetically, which was probably a lot worse. Then I dashed inside to get my swimsuit.

When I walked around to her yard, she was nowhere to be found.

"Don't go in the pool yet! I'm getting drinks." She yelled from inside the house.

I sat down on a lawn chair. The sun was fierce and I realized I wasn't wearing sunscreen. Ten minutes passed I began to sweat profusely. Surely she wouldn't mind if I just dipped my toes in.

I sat down at the side the pool and carefully dipped one leg in. It was cold, more so than swimming pools generally are. Considering the weather, this was a welcome anomaly. Without thinking I slid into the pool entirely.

The water was extremely cold, and a shiver ran down my spine. It smelled strange too, like salt. I kicked my legs to stay afloat while I rubbed some warmth into my cold arms. Something touched my foot. Something like seaweed.

I tore my leg away, though it got entangled in the stuff. I gave it another, more violent, tug and finally tore it free. Flailing about in a panic, I pulled myself up onto the tiled poolside.

Shivering with both cold and fear, I pulled the strange tendrils off of my leg. They were dark and stringy. With a jolt I recognized what it was. Human hair.

I looked into the pool. Nothing was there.

With disgust I peeled the slimy strands off my skin and tossed it them the grass. Then she returned with two glasses of lemonade.

"I thought I told you not to go into the pool..." Her voice had a beautiful sing-song quality even when she was mad.

"I, uh..."

Her demeanor softened. She set down the lemonade on the table.

"It's okay, if you want to go into the pool now we can go into the pool." She began climbing into the water. I didn't want to go into the pool anymore, but I also didn't want to be rude.

The water was just as cold as ever. She led me to the middle, where it was the deepest. I was never great at swimming, and as I struggled to stay afloat the water surged into my nose and mouth. It tasted salty. Like ocean water.

"Let's try to swim down and touch the bottom." She suggested. I didn't like the idea, but went along with it anyway.

I swam down, my lungs burning. Something bumped into me. Despite the stinging I opened my eyes.

A pair of cold, dead eyes stared back at me. I yelped, letting my breath escape in a rush of bubbles. I kept my eyes open as I tore through the water. The water seemed infinite, definitely beyond the proportions of the swimming pool. All around me dead bodies were suspended and upright under the surface. Some had pieces missing, as though something had been eating them.

Something wrapped around my leg, and it definitely wasn't hair this time. I looked down and saw her, unnaturally red lips pulled back in a mocking smile, revealing a row of sharp teeth not unlike those of an anglerfish.

I struggled weakly. My vision became blotchy and blurred. I could see the surface above me. Human forms bobbed up and down, dark and shapeless in the infinite water.

In one last effort, I kicked as hard as my oxygen-starved muscles would allow. For a moment her grip slackened and I swam frantically.

When I finally broke through the surface the atmosphere was strangely calm. I heard the hum of lawnmowers in the distance as I desperately sucked air back into my lungs. My arms were shaking as I pulled myself out of the pool.

I looked back into the water. Nothing was there.

Now, as I'm sitting here writing this, I can still hear her singing her siren song.

ABOUT A GIRL

Charlotte O'Farrell

The world ends with trumpets. They drilled that into us at that ghastly Sunday School my parents insisted I attend. Trumpets signal the beginning of the end, then everything goes to shit. Me? I think if the world ends with trumpets, it had better be reborn with guitars.

That was the whole reason Tanya and Bianca came round that night, you see. We'd started a band. It was all strictly forbidden, of course. Our parents and our school would've crucified us for it. Their little sweet 16 year old princesses playing rock songs in a group called Satanic Sacrifice? We'd have been grounded for a year. My parents didn't even know I'd taught myself guitar. I hid it under my bed and practiced when they were out which, with their careers, was basically always. Those times saved me though. Bianca was the best singer, so that was her job. She could write good songs too, if a bit on the goth side for my liking. Tanya had a snazzy keyboard and could put a backing track on that sounded enough like drums for the songs to work. Her parents were slightly less psychotic than ours, so they let her bring it along to our "group study sessions." They thought it was a way to de-stress after

43

heavy exam revision. I think her mum was a psychologist or something. In any case, we loved it. Looking back we must have sounded pretty terrible, but playing with the band was the only time I felt really alive in those years.

It could so easily have been different that night, you know. I play it over again in my head daily. It was snowing, so the Christmas party my parents were going to could easily have been cancelled. Bianca texted me an hour before they were due to leave – "Harriet, we still on? x" – and I was watching them as they watched the snow. For my dad missing the company Christmas party was a worse fate than careering off the road into a tree, so of course they braved it anyway. As I watched their Jaguar edge cautiously out of our drive I felt such a buzz – a whole night of freedom awaited! They wouldn't be back until mid-morning, so we could have an all night jam session if we wanted.

Tanya got dropped off by her family's driver. She only did it to show off – everyone knew she was the richest girl in school – but I wondered how she kept him quiet about her escapades. She'd sold the "study session" lie to her parents this time and had a cover story for the keyboard, but surely the chauffeur knew it was bullshit from all those times he picked her up from the park, high, at 2am? Maybe he just wasn't paid enough to care.

She burst in without knocking and threw her school bag full of textbooks on the floor, not to be looked at or thought about until the next morning.

"It's fucking freezing!" she announced, which I'd kind of guessed from the snow I could see from the window.

Bianca didn't arrive until half an hour later. She'd had to walk the mile and a half from town, per usual, which wasn't ideal in this weather. I can picture her now in her black gothic gear – though not the makeup, thankfully – but with purple, flowery wellington boots. Became quite famous afterwards, those boots, didn't they? Every newspaper article seemed to mention them. Maybe it was a case of it being too weird a detail to miss out. The banality of evil, or something.

Bianca had some new songs to try, and we spent about an hour running through them. They weren't her best, but there was a pleasing "fuck the patriarchy" theme in them, which made a pleasing change from a lot of her early, whiny stuff.

We just weren't clicking though. I kept messing up simple chords. I think Bianca might have been getting a cold, or at least wasn't sounding right after her trek through the snow. It didn't take long for us to put our instruments down and start raiding my parents' alcohol cupboard (cliché sleepover behaviour, I know. Luckily for me, they never kept track of what they had).

"I did have one cool idea," Tanya said. "I brought something along that might save tonight from just being another drunken film night."

She went to her bag. In my head this is where I wish, in that desperate, changing-the-past sort of fantasy way, that something different had happened. That she'd pulled out Travel Monopoly or something. But, as we all know, it was a Ouija board.

"I thought we could use it to summon...him." The hushed reverence with which she spoke the pronoun left us in no doubt who Tanya meant. The thought of Kurt Cobain himself, our collective and long dead hero, materialising in my kitchen was a bit unsettling, but I was intrigued. In our defence we were sixteen.

Nirvana symbolised everything our humdrum, controlled lives were not back then. There was something deeper than just the usual love story between suburban teens and dead rock stars. We flattered ourselves that Nirvana was one of our "influences", though even then we must have realised on some level that we sounded nothing like them.

In any case, we decided to summon the master of rock. Dimmed the lights. Lit some candles. We started to move the planchette across the board in little circles. A couple of times someone pressed it too hard with their fingers and it shot across the room, and Tanya started to get quite cross with Bianca over it.

"Kurt, we summon you," I said, in my best spooky, talking to the dead voice. "Are you there?"

Instantly there was a gust of wind through the kitchen. It was as if a door had blown open. All of us jumped backwards, breaking the circle. I screamed. Can you blame us? There was a fucking gust of wind - in the *kitchen*!

The lights flickered.

"I think he's here!" screamed Bianca, sounding more scared and shocked than pleased with our apparently successful disturbing of the dead.

The whole thing lasted a couple of seconds. It was so quick that if there had been only me, on my own, I would've assumed it was some kind of hallucination. Straight away it was back to normal – three teenage girls, staring at each other in wide-eyed horror, standing three paces back from the kitchen table. None of us spoke for a few seconds.

"Kurt...Kurt, is that you?" said Tanya. Her voice sounded quieter and more timid than I'd ever heard it before.

There was a tiny scratching sound from the table. Terrified we crept forward inch-by-inch, until the table was in view. The planchette had moved itself across the board and was now resting on the "NO" answer.

I wish I could say that we were all brave and calm, and knew exactly what to do, but we did what I think a lot of people would resort to: ran into the lounge and huddled under cushions. Looking back, I'm not sure why we thought cushions would be any kind of defence against demons, or whatever weird thing we feared we'd invited into our lives. The human mind is a strange and wonderful thing and it's never more creative than when it's dreaming up strategies for wishful thinking.

We were probably there fifteen minutes, not even daring to speak. As our heart rates slowly returned to normal, we listened out for any noises coming from the kitchen. There was nothing.

"I think it's safe to go back," I said eventually, my voice sounding high and unfamiliar.

"Go back? What the fuck?! Let's just grab our stuff and run!" spat Tanya.

"Agreed," Bianca chipped in. "No way I'm going back there."

I felt a stab of annoyance.

"Run where, exactly?" I said. "In case you hadn't noticed it's the storm of the century outside." A bit of an exaggeration, but not entirely; the snow was getting thicker all the time. "And anyway, this is my house. What do I tell my parents? 'Sorry

Mum, sorry Dad, we can't go back to our house. I summoned a fucking demon and it's his place now'."

"Well you go in first then!" snapped Bianca. I opened my mouth to protest but couldn't think of anything to say. One of us had to be first.

I looked around the room for some kind of weapon. There was nothing but a crucifix my parents insisted on having on the wall caught my eye. I grabbed it, pushing aside the atheism I'd professed since age twelve. Any port in a storm, eh?

We clung to one another as we edged across the corridor to the kitchen. I saw the board on the table, sitting quite still now, and shuddered. I held the crucifix in front of me, arms stretched out fully.

After what seemed like an age, we reached the table. The planchette still sat on "NO", where we'd left it – or rather, where it had left itself. Otherwise the kitchen looked normal, completely fine, and there were no ghostly, indoor winds. I let out a low sigh of relief.

It was the wishful thinking thing again. Deep down, we all knew exactly what we had seen, but since we seemed to get away with it, we were all keen – too keen – to rewrite it as some silly quirk of our imaginations, getting carried away with themselves. I'll always wonder what would have happened if I'd taken Tanya and Bianca's advice and we'd all just run out into the snow and stayed elsewhere. Would it have caught up with us anyway?

As it happened, we packed the Ouija board away and tried to get on with the night, trying our best to paper over the uneasiness we all felt. We put a film on (I was paying such little attention I don't even remember what it was), but none of us were concentrating, and every time there was a small noise from inside the house we all jumped. We decided to play some music instead. Maybe the loud noise would keep our thoughts off darker things. We went to my bedroom to get away from the kitchen.

By the end of the first song we were at each other's throats.

"For fuck's sake!" Tanya shouted when Bianca made a mistake. This got to Bianca, who shouted back that we all messed up now and again, and what were rehearsals for anyway. Tanya screamed something about how it sucked having to work with amateurs and did a dramatic flounce out to the landing. Bianca followed her, pointing a finger and screaming.

That's when it happened. To this day, I can see it as if it was playing out right in front of me. I was following behind my shouting friends, trying to diffuse their argument but not being heard above the sounds of them screaming at each other. Then my guitar – which I'd left sitting on my bed – flew with devastating force over our heads and smashed Tanya across the face. She stumbled backwards, grabbed the bannister to steady herself. The guitar, which had hovered next to her after the first blow, reared back as if held by huge, invisible hands, and mercilessly flung itself again at her head. There was a sickening crack; I think it was her jaw breaking. She spun around, arms open wide, and fell down the stairs. Thud after disgusting, gut-wrenching thud. She came to a stop at the bottom. The guitar flew down beside her and shattered on the tile floor next to her perfectly still body.

It took me a moment to realise Bianca was hitting me. She'd lunged at me in shock and confusion, banging her fists on my shoulders.

"What did you do?!" she was screaming. "What the fuck did you do!"

I grabbed her wrists to restrain her.

"I didn't touch her! It went at her by itself!"

She got off me and ran down the stairs, hopping over Tanya's body and running for the door. I wasn't far behind her. I stopped by Tanya, reached down and checked for a pulse in her neck.

I looked up from my dead friend just in time to see what happened to Bianca. She very nearly made it. She was by the door, reaching for the handle, about to run out into "the storm of the century" in nothing but her normal clothes and socks. I recognised the long knife flying from the kitchen with the same inhuman speed and strength that the guitar had, but only had time to get out a weak "No!" before it plunged into her throat.

I'll never forget the gurgling sound she made as she dropped to her knees. From behind, I saw a fountain of blood splatter my front door.

The knife turned around in the air and plunged itself again and again into her back and neck. She fell to the ground front-first, and she made disgusting noises that sounded something like attempts to scream.

I ran towards the scene of the murder. I reached up and tried to grab the knife. The first couple of attempts failed, and I sliced two of my fingers. White hot pain shot down my arms, but adrenaline was pumping through my veins by now and I ignored it. Finally, when the knife was sticking into her back, I got a grasp on the handle and pulled it out. It stuck a bit and took all my strength to wrench it out, so it must have gone deep.

The next thing I remember I was in the snow, knife still in hand. My own blood from my injured fingers mixed with the huge splatters on my clothes from Bianca. I'm not sure how long I stood there before my parents drew up, having left the party early because of the worsening weather conditions. What a sight they must have seen.

With shaking hands, I held the knife towards them. Neither of them took it, so I dropped it in the snow. I don't remember anything they said to me, but by the time the police arrived I had my father's jacket wrapped around me. A sudden realisation hit me: my guitar, smashed though it was, was still lying next to Tanya's crumpled form at the bottom of our stairs. Having taken great pains to hide it from them for so long, it seemed a shame they would find out this way.

"I've got a confession to make," I said quietly. They both leaned in, horror and shock and disbelief on their faces. "Mum, Dad…I've started a band."

***

I can see you're a bit disappointed. You wanted me to change my story, to 'confess'. It would have made a great 'ten years since those notorious murders' exclusive for you, but I'll have to disappoint you.

I know how it makes me sound. But if I was making it up, surely I would have made up a masked intruder? Someone who broke in, killed my friends, left me for dead and then escaped into the snowy night? They declared me sane – after hundreds of evaluations and a number of heated arguments between psychiatrists with differing opinions – but the horrified faces of the jury as I told my story at the murder trial suggested they had a different opinion. At least they didn't set me loose into the arms of the screaming mob that built up outside the court every day. I think they would have done worse things to me than whatever the...being...did to Tanya and Bianca.

It was the boots thing that did for me. See, when I was standing outside our house, dripping my friend's blood into the snow in front of my shell-shocked parents, I was wearing Bianca's purple, floral wellington boots. People pointed out that if I was fresh from grabbing the knife off the invisible force killing my friend, putting on boots would be the last thing on my mind. And I can only say: fair point. I don't remember putting them on. I don't remember pausing to do anything at the door, except run out screaming. Perhaps it was the dark being's final act of malice – do something that catches me out and sentences me to spend the rest of my life being studied, poked, and prodded in an asylum.

They tell us not to say "asylum." It's a "recovery clinic", but naturally, one that's got armed guards on every wing.

Ten years has given me a long time to think. Most of my family and friends don't believe me. In their situation, would I believe me? I don't know, but what I lack in real company I make up for in honest-to-God fan mail. I wanted to be in a badass, notorious rock band. I achieved notoriety, and it pays well. I'm a cult figure, and people write to me from all over all the time. I get death threats, but I also get weekly marriage proposals. Might say yes to one, one day, just for something to do.

I've come to terms with what they call my crimes, as far as I can, but one thing troubles me. It keeps me awake at night. We broke the circle around that Ouija board, and we all paid with our lives in one way or another. We never closed it again, or performed any sort of rite to even attempt to. We didn't get a chance.

Whatever manner of thing we dragged out of the bowels of Hell, and into this world, is still here.

EEVIE

Gabie Rivera

Hi everyone my name is Ava Wayne and today I am eight years old :) . I was eight yesterday for the first time but now I am even older! I got to use my mom's computer today (but shhh don't tell her!). Last night when my dad came home from work he brought me a big chocolate cake with vanilla frosting that had my name on it and I got to blow out the candles. I didn't even have to eat dinner first! It was the best day even though I didn't have a party.

It doesn't matter though because I've never had a party before. My mom and dad say that I'm not allowed because we can't have any other people in the house. They lie and tell me that it's because we live too far away but I know that it is because of my friend Eevie who lives with us. Eevie looks exactly like me and we are like sisters. She is not really my sister though, we just say that.

Eevie can do this really cool trick where she can move my arms and say things in my voice. Sometimes it is a little bit annoying but she's my friend so it's okay. My mom and dad don't like Eevie though and this makes her very mad.

My mom says that Eevie needs help and we have to see someone for her. I don't know what she means, but Eevie says that my mom is a liar and I don't like telling Eevie that she is wrong. My dad gets really mad and yells at Eevie to stop and to shut up and leave me alone but that just makes her more mad. I've tried to tell him to stop but he doesn't listen.

Yesterday when my dad brought home the cake he asked me if I liked it and I told him yes and that Eevie liked it too. He got really mad but my mom told him that it was not the time and he didn't say anything about her.

When they lit the candles and told me to make a wish I didn't know what to wish for. I kind of wanted some new paints so that I could make more paintings for my room, but I also wanted a puppy or some new toys. Mostly I wanted to wish for Eevie to stay but Eevie thought that was a stupid wish because she says she's always going to be with me forever so I didn't wish for that.

I asked Eevie what else I should wish for and my dad got really mad and told me to just make a wish already because this was none of Eevies business. That made me a little bit sad because it was Eevies business and she was with us and that was rude of him to yell at her like that. My mom said it was okay but dad said that it was not normal. Eevie was also getting mad because dad said she wasn't normal. Everyone was just mad mad mad and I almost cried but then Eevie told me to just make my wish because she would make any of my wishes come true.

I thought about it really hard but then mom told me to hurry up or else the cake was going to get ruined so I finally decided to wish for my parents to leave Eevie alone and be nice to her. Then I blew out the candles and my mom clapped but I could tell that my dad was still mad.

We ate cake anyway but I didn't ask if Eevie could have some because it was finally a good time. We finished the ENTIRE cake all by ourselves and I was even allowed to have TWO WHOLE PIECES. It was awesome.

Last night I had a really scary nightmare that I stabbed my mom and my dad in their bed when they were asleep. It was really scary and I woke up and cried but I don't think they heard me because no one came to check on me. Only Eevie was there and she said it was okay.

When it was morning I got up but my mom didn't make any breakfast and she didn't answer when I was yelling for her. Eevie says that they are still asleep and that I shouldn't go up to their room so I didn't.

Eevie helped me to make breakfast. She showed me how to make a burrito with eggs and some chicken that she bought. It was really messy because Eevie said that it was fresh meat that had just been killed. I already know that they kill animals for food because my grandpa has a farm and I had seen them make a turkey before so I knew that it was very messy.

After I ate Eevie said that we could watch tv. She said that I didn't even have to clean up because mom and dad weren't going to even see it. She told me that she made my wish come true and that they weren't going to be mad at us anymore and they weren't going to yell at us either. Eevie says that now we can do whatever we want.

I had ice cream and I watched cartoons all morning instead of going to school and when the phone rang and the school called Eevie talked to them and she sounded just like my mom! She told them that I was sick and the lady believed her! It was so fun and I didn't even know that she could do that!

Eevie let me use my moms laptop because she says she knows the password. She told me I could write on here like a diary and post it so other people could read it! Isn't that so cool? I wonder who is reading this haha :).

Eevie just made me lunch and it was a sandwich with meat again. I don't eat this much meat because my mom likes for me to eat my veggies but Eevie says that mom is not the boss anymore so I can eat whatever I want. I had a lot of chips and my tummy started to hurt and I really wanted my mom but Eevie said that it was okay and she could make it feel better.

Eevie told me to take a nap and so I did but I had another scary dream that I was cutting up mom and dad because Eevie was making me. When I woke up Eevie said it was just a dream because mom and dad were still asleep upstairs. I want to go and see them but Eevie says I can't or else it will ruin the wish and we will get in big trouble for making a mess and eating junk.

I think I'm going to go play hide-and-seek with Eevie now. :)

Love, Ava <3

WEIRD CHURCH

Jennifer Winters

"What the actual hell?" I had said or thought this at least fifty times in the last twenty-four hours. This time, it was the Check Engine light that prompted the profanity. I mentally tallied the concrete expenses for the month, and tried to figure out how I would cover any potential car repairs. Maybe I could sub at my teaching job. The flu was hitting the department hard this semester, with professors out for days at a time. Of course, how would I fit and subbing in with my schedule at Job #2? Or what if I caught the flu and missed work? Shit! I hadn't even thought of that. Or what if the boys get sick and I have to stay with them? Screw it. Their dad could stay with them. He has sick days and mostly works on the computer, which he can do at home. I miss work, I get docked. Such is the life of a single parent.

I was winding up my second year of being a divorced mom. Everything pretty much sucked that particular semester. Being a teacher, I tend to think in semesters. My part time job teaching drama at the community college down the street had been enough, financially speaking, until the divorce, four semesters ago.

My rapid descent into singlehood and financial turmoil started the night I found my husband in the half-bath of the basement at two in the morning, frantically trying to scrub glitter and lipstick off of his face, chest, and crotch. His similarly stained clothing was on the floor around him; an empty condom wrapper in the pocket. He swore that he didn't know what the wrapper was doing there, although he didn't even bother to try to explain away the glitter and lipstick. He had told me that he was going to be very late that night at the office, which was technically true, as the truck stop/strip club just across the county line is called "The Office."

I actually went to The Office, hoping that, maybe, it wasn't as bad as I'd imagined. It was worse. My husband had insisted that he just went in for a soda because he felt like his blood sugar had dropped, and that he'd had his back to the stage, when he was set upon by dancers who forced him out of most of his clothes in an effort to humiliate him. In reality, the place was so small and the seats arranged so that everyone faces the stage. As for being "forced" into the glitter-smeared ordeal he described, it became obvious very quickly that such services must be negotiated and paid for, first, then enjoyed in one of the converted bathroom stalls creatively labeled as the "Fantasy Cubicles." As I made my way out the door, almost in a panic after realizing that two of the bored-looking dancers on the small stage were my students, I found myself bumping into my husband. He was walking in, alone, his front shirt pocket bulging with what must have been a folded stack of singles. Dumbass.

The divorce came and went quickly, leaving me with the house, half the retirement fund, and two years of the maximum child support possible in Maryland, soon to cease when my twin boys graduate from high school. In a moment of ill-advised pride, I declined to request alimony. What the hell was I thinking? I have an MFA in theatre and no full time job prospects. I could try to get a job in a professional theatre in Baltimore or DC. The problem is that I don't like theatre. I was burned out on it by the time I finished my master's almost twenty years ago. At this time, I was paying the bills by working two part-time jobs teaching at the community college next to my neighborhood, and another small four-year college about thirty miles away. I also had a third part-time job reading shitty romance stories of the shiny Mormon vampire ilk for an online magazine and then passing the least horrible ones on to the editor.

My own romantic life since the divorce has been pretty nightmarish in its own right. After Dumbass moved out, I went through a period of hating all men, other than my dad and sons. I took as much pleasure in shooting down date requests as I did getting asked. I finally got lonely and horny enough to start seeing the manager of the bookstore at the college farthest away from my house. I liked the distance. It was a good buffer zone. In reality, it worked well with my boys being with Dumbass most weekends. Nobody had to meet anyone. After a few months, I finally slept with my gentleman friend. The sex was pretty good. At least, it was different from sex with Dumbass, as our lovemaking had been reduced to two or three basic templates. After another month or two, Bookstore Manager and I exchanged the three words that it seemed we should at that point. I guess I really did love Bookstore Manager, but that all came crashing down last week, when, in the middle of a post-coital cuddle, he kissed my forehead and said, "It means so much to me that you love me and stand by me while I decide if I'm going to reunite with my ex-wife."

So, that was life. Top if off with the Check Engine light, and there I was, midway through my forty-five minute commute. It was a sunny day, and I really was enjoying my drive through the bucolic Maryland backroads, at least until the damned light killed my mojo. The route was only five-minutes longer than going on the highway, and the views were lovely, even in winter. My routine was to take the backroads and listen to podcasts as I drove. This morning, I decided to try another small backroad that, according to the GPS, would only add another minute or two to my commute, and went right through two farms, one of which was the oldest in the county. I love old houses and barns, so I took the route. My GPS reconfigured my path to work, and, sure enough, it only added a minute to the time.

The farms were a dud, with shiny new barns and vinyl siding covering the farmhouses. Just past them, I saw a white structure on a hill so steep that it looked like a man-made mound. It was a church. A sweet little white-framed church, with stained-glass windows and a steeple that may have been the slightest bit crooked. I hadn't been to church in years, and even though I never considered whether or not I was a believer or agnostic, I loved old churches. The new churches look like gymnasiums or warehouses. I slowed a bit to take in the sight of the old-fashioned country church on the hill, thinking that I should stop and take a picture of it, sometime. The sign at the end of the long gravel drive from the road to the church read, "Allegiance Church." Underneath that, neat purple lettering said, "Big problems? Big God!" No service times were listed, nor any other information. I sped up and headed on to work.

That afternoon as I drove back home via the same backroads route, I noticed that someone had placed a sign with stenciled lettering next to the church's main sign: "Tuesday

Prayer 9:30 AM." Fat lot of good that does me, I thought, driving on. Some of us have to work for a living.

I only had my long commute two days a week, Tuesday and Thursday, and I made sure to pass by the sweet little church each leg of the trip. By the time I passed it going home on Thursday of the next week, I felt a sad little tugging at my heart. It might be kind of nice to go to a prayer meeting. I wouldn't have to listen to a sermon or sit through any ceremonies, probably. Maybe a good prayer service would give me some positive energy to deal with mounting bills, teenage kids, my worsening carpal tunnel syndrome, budget cuts in the theatre department at Job #2 . . . Big problems? Yep, I got'em.

The next Tuesday morning, I headed to Job #2. As I passed the little church, I muttered, "Damn, I wish I could stop by today, if for nothing else to see the inside."

When I neared the college, I was hit with a feeling of total disorientation. The parking lot was all but empty, save for some trucks from the local utility company. As I pulled over onto the shoulder, I took my phone out of the pocket on my jacket. I'd forgotten to turn it on. When it powered up I saw that the college had sent out an alert in the wee hours of the morning advising that the campus would be closed due to a broken water main. I figured up how much gas I'd wasted by driving to the college as I turned around to go home. Oh well, I thought, at least it'll give me time to finish the notes on the romance short story I'd been assigned to read by the e-zine, written by an obvious virgin and possible psychopath who thinks women can orgasm from stimulation of the toes.

As I drove, it occurred to me that I would be passing by the church right around 9:30. My heart actually began to beat faster at the thought of attending the prayer meeting. I'd love to see the inside of that church, I thought, and, hell yes, I could use some good mojo. The sign announcing the meeting had still been there when I'd passed by that morning, so I decided to attend the prayer meeting.

When I drove up the long driveway to the parking lot at the top of the hill, I thought that the prayer meeting may have been cancelled. Mine was the only car. As I deliberated on whether or not I should get out of the car and see what was up, another car pulled up beside mine. I glanced over and recognized another professor from the college. A communications instructor, if I recalled correctly, thinking back to the time we'd met at a faculty professional development workshop. She stared at the church for a moment, and then looked over at me. She smiled warmly and raised a hand.

We got out of our cars and greeted each other. Sandy, I remembered just in time. Her name was Sandy.

"Is this your church?" We said the words at the same time, then laughed.

"No," she said. "I've never even heard of the denomination. I'm just curious. I haven't been to church in a long time, but I really want to see the inside."

"Me, too!" I said. "I pass by here on my commute."

She asked where I commuted from and I told her. Her eyebrows raised when I told her that it's thirty miles one way. "Did you go to campus today?" she asked.

"Yep. I didn't see the alert."

My colleague laughed, and said, "Well, I guess that's a sign that you were meant to be here today."

When I asked her where she lived, she pointed over her shoulder and said that her house was only about half a mile from the church. The church building had been in disrepair for as long as she could remember, when, out of the blue, she drove by one day to see it with new windows, a new paint job, and new occupants. We puzzled over the name of the church, and then agreed that we could Google it after the praying. I walked into the church feeling strangely happy, like maybe I was going to have an actual post-divorce friend in my colleague.

My first impression of the church was that they must have cleaned the hardware store out of white paint. The walls, pews, and ceiling were all a brilliant white. In the pews were red velvet cushions that matched the shade of the red carpet that ran along the aisle through the two rows of pews. A few people already sat in the pews close to the front, and a few others milled about, chatting in stage whispers. As I looked around, I noticed that the stained glass windows that I saw from the outside were an illusion. There were no actual windows, just bright, white walls.

"Hi!" The greeting was as much of a bright shock as the glossy white paint of the church's interior. Sandy and I were facing a woman about our own age, her long blonde hair pulled back into a ponytail that hung to her waist. She wore no makeup and a long denim skirt. She was very pretty, with smooth skin, perfect apple cheeks, and brilliant blue eyes. I could feel her warmth immediately, although there was something strange about her eyes that I couldn't put my finger on. Maybe I just wasn't used to seeing women without mascara.

The woman went on, "I'm Jessica, but everyone calls me Jessie. Are you here for prayer service?"

Sandy and I both said, "Yes," at the same time, and then the three of us laughed.

"Well, you're welcome here. Thanks for coming in," said Jessie. Her smile was infectious. I felt myself relaxing, truly feeling like she was genuinely happy to see us.

Sandy piped in, "Uh. If you don't mind, I'm going to sit close to the back. First time shyness." I told her that I'd sit with her.

"That's fine," Jessie said. "No worries and no pressure. Our God is big enough to hear you from the back row."

She turned and went back to the front as Sandy and I slid into the back pew. I noticed that all of the women had the same look as Jessie: Long hair in ponytails or buns, long denim skirts worn with long-sleeved blouses. The men all wore jeans with button-down shirts. None of them had any facial hair and their hair was worn very short. Most of the folks turned around and gave Sandy and me a friendly wave or a nod and a smile.

The front of the church had no pulpit or podium, nor did I see a piano or organ. There was, however, a baptistery at the front of the room, the kind used for baptism by immersion, like we'd had at the Primitive Baptist church where I went as a kid.

Suddenly, someone spoke from their pew, without standing up or turning around. "Let us pray . . . Ask what you will, but ask in wisdom. Our God is a big god. Great and glorious!"

"Great and glorious," suddenly brought an image of Toad in Toad Hall into my mind, and I stifled a giggle. I bit my lip and tried to act like an adult.

A low humming began, vocalizing with no words. The voices formed a tight chord with at least eight parts. The singing undulated, gradually filling the room with its wordless tune. The effect was immediate. Without realizing what I was doing, I closed my eyes. The vocalizing wrapped itself around me, seeming to lift me up and carry me along with it. I didn't try to sing along, I just drifted, feeling peaceful for the first time in two years. I wondered if Sandy was experiencing the same thing.

After a few minutes, I suppose, I became aware of people speaking. I could only hear snippets, here and there . . .

"thank you for sending . . ."

"more blessings . . ."

"baptize whom you will . . ."

"health and love . . ."

The words and the harmony of the wordless song took me higher, deeper. I was floating over the pews. I was hovering over the members of the church. I was one of them! I was drifting over to the baptistery. I saw it in my head. There was no water, just a small door in the floor, like the door to an old-fashioned cellar. Peace. I felt such a warm peace. Then . . .

"YOUR MAMA'S ON THE PHONE! YOUR MAMA'S CALLING YOU!"

My mother's personal ringtone snapped me back to where I was: the sweet little church with the white walls and red pew-cushions.

"Fuck!" I said before I realized I was speaking out loud. Sandy, looking like she was suddenly waking up from a deep sleep, jumped slightly in her seat and glared at me. I dug for my phone in my purse, not finding it until the joke ringtone had cycled through twice. I mouthed "sorry" to the church goers who were now looking back at us with confused and irritated expressions. Sandy and I both slid out of the pew, taking the cushion with us and clumsily having to put it back in its place, and scuttled out the door of the church. Jessie was right behind us.

I looked back and forth at Jessie and Sandy, who looked at me and then each other. Jessie spoke first. I closed my eyes, expecting to be asked not to ever come back.

"Shit!" Jessie exclaimed, bending over with laughter. "That was the funniest goddamned thing I've ever seen!"

Now, at this point it may seem odd that I wasn't freaked out by effect the churchgoers' vocalizing had on me. There's a simple explanation. I was born and raised in the Smoky Mountains of East Tennessee. We went to the Primitive Baptist church, which was larger and more sedate than many of the churches in the area. Our services were orderly and quiet, with no instrumental music and, since we were "no-heller" Primitive Baptists, our preachers never delivered any hellfire and damnation sermons. We did have beautiful acapella "shaped note" singing, though, with layered, tight harmonies that could be as moving as a full orchestra. That said, many of my friends and cousins went to the types of churches that the Appalachians are known for. I used to go with them, mostly for entertainment, and I did see some antics! People spoke in tongues, danced; fell to the floor in religious ecstasy. And, yep, some of the churches did "take up the serpent" occasionally in order to prove their faith, although visitors like myself were not allowed to attend when they were handling snakes. I knew perfectly well what it was like to get caught up in religious theatrics. That was what I considered religion at that point: theatre. No harm in taking in a show, right?

Sandy and I laughed over my embarrassing incident at lunch a couple of days later at work. We were both surprised at Jessie's profanity, given her appearance and obvious active role in the church. We had discovered in our half-hour of conversation with her outside the church after my phone rang that she peppered most of her language with expressions that would make a sailor forget his name. As for her appearance, I was familiar with certain denominations that had similar dress codes, again, thanks to my Appalachian home, where the super-religious roam free. Sandy had had a similar experience to mine during the prayer service, and, while neither of us was convinced that what we'd felt was anything supernatural, we both felt happier and less stressed than we had before we'd gone. Maybe their strange singing worked like music therapy or meditation.

As we parted ways at the end of our lunch, Sandy asked me if I noticed Jessie's eyes. I told her that I thought there was something a bit strange about them, as pretty as they were. As she pushed her chair under the table, Sandy said, "Eyelashes. She didn't have any eyelashes."

I ran into Sandy the next Tuesday morning in the faculty parking lot. She was heading to her car as I was walking away from mine.

"What's up?" I asked.

"Class was cancelled! The instructor, moi, has a pressing appointment."

"Everything okay?" I asked.

"Yep," Sandy chirped. "I'm going to church!"

Sandy explained that she was intrigued by the hypnotic effect that the church had on both of us. She wanted to see if it would happen again.

"Also," she said. "I want to ask what they meant by that skin thing."

I asked her what she meant.

"I could hear them praying. A few of them said something about a god with skin," she said.

Again, having been raised a Primitive Baptist, I knew what she was talking about. I told her about a story I'd heard a preacher tell during children's church. He'd said that a little boy was afraid at night, and he called his mom to his room, terrified and certain that there were monsters under his bed. His mom had told him not to be scared, because God was with him. The little boy looked all around, pointing out that he couldn't see any gods in the room. His mom told him that God was invisible, and the little boy replied that he wanted a god with skin! The preacher went on to explain to us kids that Jesus is our God, with skin.

Satisfied, Sandy got in her car and, with a friendly wave, drove away. I found out from someone in her department that she called in sick the rest of the week.

If the rest of the week was trying, the weekend was terrible. Dumbass was being, well, a dumbass. The boys were with me for the weekend, and they went back and forth between arguing with each other or teaming up on me with their teen angst. I had insomnia for two nights, largely because of the horrible romance stories I was reading for the e-zine. By the time Monday rolled around, I headed back to Job #1 a virtual zombie.

I managed to get through Monday by showing videos in class and ordering pizza for dinner. By bedtime I had already sent emails to my students at Job #2, letting them know that class was cancelled the next day. I was just too damned spent to work.

I woke up an hour later than usual on Tuesday, thanks to my sons picking up on my stress and getting themselves up and off to school. Sandy texted me while I was having my third cup of coffee. "Come to church! This is BIG!"

The first thing that I noticed when I pulled into the church parking space was that there were more cars. Attendance must be picking up, I thought, as I looked around for Sandy's car. There it was, but it looked a bit off, like the color had changed. I walked over to the car, and realized what it was that made the car look ever so slightly different. Pollen. Sandy's car was covered in a thick layer of the yellow-green pollen so common in central Maryland. It looked as if it had a week's worth covering the silver paint and windows.

I looked up to see Sandy and Jessie walking down the steps of the church towards me. Only it wasn't Jessie, but another woman who looked eerily similar, with her long blonde hair pulled back and a long denim skirt. Sandy was wearing the same clothes she'd been wearing the last week. As she drew closer, I saw that she wasn't wearing any makeup, and her hair was natty and dark from going unwashed. Yellow sweat stains were under her arms. She and the woman reached me, and Sandy drew me into a hug. I smelled that her breath was sour as coddled milk, and she carried with her a damp cloud of body odor.

"Jesus, Sandy!" I gasped and pulled away.

The Jessie look-alike laughed. "Oh, honey. We don't do Jesus here!"

Before I knew it, I was back inside the church, seated on a red pew cushion beside Sandy.

I leaned over to Sandy, who was looking expectantly to the front of the church. "Sandy, what's going on? Where have you been? I thought you were home sick last week. Are you okay?"

"I'm fine! This is big, hon! Big! He answers prayers. He answered my prayers. I have to figure out how it works." Sandy turned to me, breathing from a mouth that obviously hadn't seen a toothbrush in days. "Oh, it feels so good when he listens. It feels so, so good!"

I looked around. "Where's Jessie?"

Sandy met my gaze, but said nothing.

"She was baptized!" A voice chimed from behind me. I looked. It was the woman who looked so much like Jessie. "It was time for baptism, and she was baptized." Her smile was pure happiness. Her eyes gleamed. Eyes without a single eyelash.

I looked towards the front of the church. Along with the denim and button-down regulars, there were several people who weren't following the dress code. Some looked around as if they were only seeing the inside of the church today. Others greeted the regulars with hugs and handshakes. Aside from the windowless walls, it looked very much like any small country church, just before service.

"Ask what you will, but wisely," I heard Sandy mutter. I turned to her. She took my hand, "It's big. I can't figure out the eyelash thing, and it looks like the fingernails fall out, too. On some people, at least. He answers prayers, but don't ask for too much. It seems to all depend on asking for the right things. Not too much."

I looked over my shoulder. The door of the church seemed very, very far away. What was I feeling in that moment? Fear, yes. But also, an excitement. Big problems? Bigger God. I'd had such a terrible weekend. I remembered the peace I'd felt the last time I was at the church. It would be so nice to feel it again. To be carried by the wordless music made by voices. Even if it was just a form of sound meditation and not connecting with a deity, it would feel so very good.

"Let us pray. Ask what you will, but with wisdom. Our God is a big god."

The voices joined to make their harmonies. I closed my eyes. I floated. My troubled mind calmed in seconds. The shell of stress and bitterness that had enclosed me for so long broke away, melted, turned to nothing. The music of the voices was a warm, liquid river, and I was being carried.

I prayed. My job. My boys' college applications. My car! My carpal tunnel syndrome! For Dumbass to be really sorry for what he did! For Bookstore Manager to realize what he lost and weep. To always say the right thing at the right time! For flat abdominals and for my skin to be smooth!

The prayers went on and on as I floated on that warm, gentle river.

"Stop!!" Sandy's voice brought me back to the red pew cushion. She leaned towards me, taking my hand, and whispered. "Pray wisely. Not too much. He's a big god. So big. And once you ask, you can't take it back."

Her eyes bore into mine. She had no eyelashes.

I looked around. The singing continued, as did the prayers.

"health for my family . . ."

"justice . . ."

"oh, god of skin . . ."

"revenge . . ."

"payback . . ."

God *of* skin. Not a god with skin.

I looked around the room; tried to take everything in, even as the river of voices reached inside of me, attempting to take me back into its embrace. The button-down and denim crew, vocalizing, shuddered and reached their arms up and out. None of them seemed to have eyelashes. I noticed that a number of fingers on their outstretched hands lacked fingernails, the patches of skin pink and shiny. The other visitors sat on the pews, eyes closed, jaws slack, swaying and mumbling what I could only guess were prayers.

One of the men whom I assumed to be a member because of his clothing stopped vocalizing and walked over to the baptistery. He opened a small door that I hadn't noticed before next to the baptistery and disappeared behind it. A moment later he was walking down what I guessed to be steps into the baptistery, which was obviously empty of water. He bent over, then stood up again, as if he were opening a door in the floor. I remembered the image of the door on the floor of the empty baptistery that I'd imagined during my first visit to the church. The man stopped, and looked, lovingly and with a sad smile, towards the people vocalizing in the sanctuary. A clump of his hair fell out of his scalp and onto his shoulder. He descended, as if walking down steps in the floor.

"Jessie was baptized . . ."

The river of voices began to overtake me again, the warmth and peace pulling me under.

God of skin.

Big god.

Great and Glorious Toad!

Who, or what, the hell were we praying to? Why did it feel so good?

Just then, I heard my own voice: "Dumbass calling. Dumbass calling. Dumbass calling."

I'd forgotten to silence my phone, again. I had recorded the phrase myself as my husband's ringtone. The call from Dumbass snapped me back to myself. It was like suddenly falling out of a swing. Boom! Back on the ground. Everyone stopped singing.

This is the part of the story where I, broken out of the spell of the hypnotic vocalizations of the church members, would have attempted to run out of the church, pursued by the members of a cult who would catch me and attempt to throw me down into a pit under the baptistery. That, however, didn't happen. Instead, I stood up, grabbed my purse, and calmly walked out of the church while digging for my phone. I quickly tried to coax Sandy to come with me before I stepped into the aisle, but she was still under the spell of the wordless song, eyes closed, oblivious. Nobody pursued me. A few people gave me knowing looks, and I even got a friendly wave from a couple of the button-down and denim crew.

The only troubling event during my departure occurred just as I stepped out into the sunshine. The woman who had greeted me with Sandy, the one who looked so much like Jessie, was standing by the door. As I passed her she said, matter-of-factly, "You asked for too much. You can't un-ask. You can't go far enough away. God is bigger."

That was it. Nobody attempted to follow me. Nobody called, texted, or sent cryptic, disturbing letters. I was extremely nervous for a couple of weeks, and I did have some hellacious nightmares. That singing hypnosis, or whatever they were doing at that church, stayed under my skin for a good while. As for Sandy, she came back to work for another week or two, then resigned. She had stopped taking my calls or answering emails by that point. I asked some of the folks in her department if they knew anything about where she was going or why she left, but nobody seemed to know anything, only that she had gone. Yeah, it was a cult.

I searched for the Allegiance Church on the internet several times, but never found any significant information on it, other than a listing for a couple of congregations in Rhode Island. One day, I got my nerve up to drive by. The church was still there, but the sign was gone. I drove away, glancing at the rearview mirror. As I drove, I caught a glimpse in the mirror of what may have been a large warehouse or barn at the base of the backside of the steep hill where the church sat. I'd never noticed it before, although I don't know how, given its size.

The semester ended, and things actually started to look up. My second cousin passed away, which was bad, but she left some money for the boys; enough, in fact, for both of them to go to the university of their choice. Bookstore Manager began calling again, and we started over. He said that he must have been crazy to consider going back to his ex-wife. He took me to Aruba for vacation, and it was amazing. I was offered a full time position at the closer community college after applying and nailing the interview. No more patching part-time jobs together! I lost twenty pounds over the summer and feel great. Dumbass and I have established a kind of truce bordering on civility, although not civil enough for me to stop calling him Dumbass. Best of all, I no longer have to read crappy romance or commute to Job #2, which means that there's no chance that I might encounter the little white church.

And so, here I am, ready to begin another semester after taking off for the whole summer. My boys are settled at a university close enough that they're home most weekends. Today, I'm driving to campus on an alternate route. I start professional development today for my new position, and I'll be on the other side of campus from where I usually work. I slow down almost to a stop to check my GPS, a bit confused as to where I am. According to the GPS, I should be reaching the rear campus parking lot in thirty seconds. I look up.

I'm rolling to a stop in front of a small church. The church is tiny, but an enclosed exterior corridor on the rear connects it to a huge warehouse type building, at least two football fields in size. A modern, digital sign spells out the message: "Big problems? Bigger God!"

The letters fade, and then more letters light up on the sign:

"Allegiance Church"

The sign changes again:

"Forget about God? Our God will come to you."

WHY I REGRET GETTING GLASSES

K. J. McDonald

"I have to tell you something," I said. "And you're probably not going to believe me."

"Okay," she said. "Try me."

"Do you remember this morning when Sophie's picture fell under my desk?" I turned my glasses in my hands as I spoke.

…

I'm nearsighted, so my new glasses didn't make a big difference when I first sat in my cubicle at work. That is, until I stooped down to retrieve a pen I dropped. I saw a watercolor ship, painted on wrinkled notebook paper and torn on one corner: child's work. I figured it belonged to Amanda in the next cubicle, who was always taping her daughter's latest art to her desk.

I reached for it. My fingers brushed the space where it should be and felt only the cheap carpet. I took off my glasses – they were still throwing my depth perception off a bit – and looked again. No ship. I put them back on, and there it was. I tried to grab it again, but though it looked like my hand was right on it I could only feel the carpet still. I took the glasses off again. This time I stood up and took several steps back from the desk, scanning the floor for the picture. Nothing. I put the glasses back on, and there it was.

"Hey, Alex!" Amanda called as she approached her desk. "Love the glasses!"

"Thanks," I said. I smiled. She smiled. Heat rushed to my face. I really like Amanda. I forgot all about the ship for a moment.

I took the glasses off and rubbed my eyes as I sat down again. I could hear Amanda typing away next door. Then I heard a rustle of paper, and felt something brush my leg. I looked down, and there was the painting of the ship right next to my foot.

"Pst! Alex, can you hand me that?" Amanda said.

"Sure." I frowned and reached for the painting again. The paper crinkled under my fingertips. I pushed my chair out and leaned around the cubicle, holding out the picture.

"Nice piece," I said.

She smiled, "Thanks, it's an original."

"An original Sophie watercolor? Wow!"

She laughed. "She's with her dad this week. Drinks tonight?"

"Sounds like a plan."

"Great! You want to pick me up around 8ish?"

"Yes, I do."

...

"Yeah, sure I do." Amanda said.

"Do you remember how, when you were walking to your desk, I was standing in front of mine looking at the floor?"

"Yeah, I remember." She said, smiling a little.

"I was standing like that because I was looking for the picture. I saw it under my desk before you got to yours."

"But it didn't fall down there until later, Alex." No smile, not anymore.

"I know. But I could see it there, before it fell, but only with my glasses on."

"I'm not sure I see where you're going with this."

"Okay," I said, taking a deep breath. "Do you remember at lunch, when I said I had a paper cut on my finger, but you said you didn't see it?"

...

"What are you doing?" Amanda asked from across the table. "Rolling a booger?"

"Yep," I said and flicked my fingers in her direction.

"Really, Alex!" she laughed, dodging the imaginary projectile.

"No, just got a gnarly paper cut. Funny, didn't even feel it when it happened. Look, I can make it talk." I extended my hand and manipulated the skin to make the little wound open and close. "Hey there, Amanda," I said in a shrill voice.

"Oh, my god," she laughed, "How old are you, five?"

"Five and a half, actually."

"I don't see any papercut by the way, you hypochondriac."

"Yeah? Maybe you need glasses."

"Yeah? Let me see your finger."

I extended my hand and she took it. She squeezed my fingertip. "That hurt?"

"No."

"That's because there's no cut, you dork."

I took my glasses off and looked again. She was right, no cut. Put the glasses back on, and there it was: a slender fissure, pink in the middle.

…

"Yeah, I remember."

"Well, look," I said, extending my hand to show her the little cut.

"Okay, I see. You did cut your finger."

"Yeah, after lunch."

"So you're saying…"

"At lunch I hadn't cut my finger, yet, but I could see the cut with my glasses on."

"But not with your glasses off."

"Right."

"So you're saying that you can see the future with your glasses?" She couldn't have looked more incredulous.

"I guess that's what I'm saying, yeah."

"And you're telling me this because?"

"Because when I put my glasses on and I look at you," I said, as I put the glasses on again, "You're dead."

Amanda stared at me blankly for a moment, and then burst out laughing. She leaned over her knees and I felt all the blood drain from my face when I saw the gaping, pulpy crater in the back of her head. "Did you really stage the whole papercut thing at lunch just to play this…" she stopped in the middle of her sentence, when she saw the look on my face. "Oh, God." She said. "You're either really serious, or you're a really good actor."

"It's the first option, I'm afraid."

"Alex," she said arms crossed and leaning away, "I just…I don't know what to say about all that. Maybe you're just really tired, or stressed or something, and…"

"Why don't you put them on?"

"What?"

"Why don't you put my glasses on and have a look in the mirror?"

I took them off and held them out to her. She looked at them, but didn't take them.

"C'mon, Amanda," I said. "Won't hurt anything. And, if you don't see anything, then I'll go home and go to bed…and probably make an appointment or two in the morning."

89

"Okay," she said, taking the glasses. "But please note: I do not believe you. I think you're playing a prank. So, technically, this is me humoring you...not falling for your prank, okay?" She laughed nervously and headed to the bathroom. I followed.

I stood just outside the door and watched her lift the glasses to her face. She leaned in close to the mirror, and quickly yanked them off again. "Oh, my God," she groaned.

"Take a look at the back of your head," I said.

She put the glasses on again and took a hand mirror from the counter. "Oh. Oh, Jesus," she whimpered, running her hand along the back of her head.

"You see it too?" I asked.

"Mm-hm."

She handed my glasses back with a shaking hand. "What are we going to do?" she asked.

"Well, we planned on going out for drinks. Maybe, if we stay in, it will change what is going to happen."

"Yeah, yeah...Great idea. We're going to just stay here where it's safe. Okay. Am I still dead?"

I put the glasses on and nodded grimly.

"Well, okay then," she said, laughing humorlessly. "So that's not it. We have to change something else. What else?"

"Well, how do you think that happens to the back of your head?"

"I don't fucking know! It looks like someone bashed it in!"

"Maybe a break in? Maybe we should leave here?"

"What if it's a car accident?"

"We could walk."

"If we walk, anything could happen."

"Well, we're just standing here and you're still dead so I'd say we'd better do something."

"Okay, you're right. We need to do something. Let's go to my sister's. She's close, and she's not home but I have a key."

She must have asked me, "Did it change yet?" half a dozen times on the short walk to her sister's building. It didn't. She was beginning to get hysterical, and a storm was kicking up too. The howling wind and thunder didn't help the mood. By the time we reached the top of the stairs on her sister's floor she was crying. "Am I still dead?" she whispered shrilly. Her lips were swollen and bloody, her eyes glassy and unseeing.

"Let's just go inside. Maybe that will change it," I said without much conviction.

Her hands were shaking so badly that she dropped the keys twice. Then, suddenly, she was still. She eyed me like a cornered animal.

"What is it?" I asked.

"What if..." she sputtered, "What if it's *you*?"

"Me?" I asked. "Amanda, I would never..." I began, but she was already backing away from me towards the stairs, like prey ready to bolt. I realized what was about to happen at the very last instant. I screamed her name and lunged for her, reaching, but I was too late. It happened too fast.

Someone, some child – perhaps even Sophie – had left a bouncy ball near the stairs. A gust of wind caught it just as Amanda was about to turn and run. It rolled under her errant heel and she stumbled backwards, eyes wide, arms grasping at nothing.

The world moved in slow motion as I stumbled towards the stairs and peeked over the edge. A halo of blood was spreading around her head at the bottom.

I guess she was right. In a way, it was me.

A FAT GIRL'S REVENGE

Gemma Stovell

I've always been on the heavy side. Not *obese*, mind you, but definitely not slim either. I blame it on slow metabolism – and my love of cooking. My dream is to become a professional chef, and my specialties are anything heavy with carbohydrates – or sugar.

Of course, being chubby definitely has its downsides. In a society where women are expected to be thin, I've gotten endless snide remarks from classmates, teachers, salespeople at clothing stores, and even strangers on the street. Most of the time, I just fire back with an equally scathing insult, or simply give them my meanest glare and walk away. Sometimes, however, when someone goes the extra mile to be *extra* cruel, I'll bring out the big guns.

Donna learned that the hard way.

My single father met her when I was fourteen, and they quickly fell in love. Donna was divorced, and had two sons, Wyatt and Milo, aged twelve and thirteen, respectively. The boys were both pretty good kids, and I considered that a small miracle, given the woman who had brought them into the world.

93

Donna was a massive bitch. Shrewish, entitled, and superficial, with a stick up her ass the size of Australia. She made my life unbearable. Her whiny voice gave me massive headaches, and it bothered me how overbearing she was to her children. But most of all, I *hated* her comments about my weight.

It seemed Donna hated fat people. She hated a *lot* of people, it seemed (Catholics, Jews, Muslims, Asians, blacks, homosexuals, Hispanics, interracial couples), but fat people were near the top of the list. Never once did Donna pass up a chance to berate or belittle me for my size.

I think you should get rid of those jeans, she would say. *They only accentuate your thick thighs.*

Or

Are those CHIPS you're eating? Jesus, Katie, you're already fat enough! Why don't you try a salad for a change?

Or

Oh, Katie. You'd be so beautiful if you could just lose a few pounds.

Or

Good God, girl! You're STOMACH is bigger than your BREASTS! What a disgrace!

You get the idea.

Donna was smart enough to avoid insulting me in front of Dad, but every now and then, she would slip up. When that

94

happened, Dad would tell her to back off, but leave it at that. He was a passive guy, the kind who preferred not to make waves. Donna knew this, and it gave her the idea that she could get away with anything.

Naturally, the constant mockery did quite the number on my self-esteem. Before I had generally been accepting of my body, flaws and all. Now, whenever I looked in the mirror, all I saw was a fat, ugly girl. I saw someone weak, someone who lacked self-control, and had let herself become unsightly. I hated Donna, with her svelte frame and totally flat stomach. I knew I shouldn't let her get to me. But when you're a teenage girl, all it takes is one person to destroy your self-esteem.

A year passed. I turned fifteen, and Dad proposed to Donna. I met a boy named Erik, and we started dating. In spite of my weight I've never had trouble attracting boys; I guess I'm lucky I have a pretty face. Anyway, after we'd been together for about two weeks I brought Erik home to meet my family.

Dad and Donna were both there, as well as Wyatt and Milo. I made spaghetti bolognese, caesar salad, and tiramisu for dessert. Donna greeted Erik politely, and the dinner was delicious. It wasn't until I served the tiramisu that things went sour.

"Make sure you serve yourself a *small* piece, Katie," said Donna, in a voice as sickly sweet as cough syrup. "You don't want to add extra pounds to your hips. I don't think *Erik* would like that very much."

The shocked silence that followed was the most painful of my life. I just *stood* there, serving platter in my hands, my mouth hanging open. Dad, who'd already drank three glasses of wine, snorted and swatted Donna's arm playfully. Wyatt and Milo just stared down at their plates, and Erik looked like he didn't know whether to leave the table or pass out from embarrassment.

Donna just smirked and took a sip of wine. I knew she had planned this all along, and in that moment, I hated her more than I'd ever hated *anyone* in my life.

That night I sobbed into my pillow, so humiliated that I just wanted to die. I was convinced Erik would never speak to me again. Worse, Dad and Donna would be getting *married* soon, making that bitch officially a part of the family.

I couldn't let Donna get away with this. I *had* to do something. I had to return the humiliation, the cruelty, tenfold so that Donna would never make fun of my weight again.

By the time the sun rose, chasing away the shadows and lighting up the sky with brilliant shades of red and pink, I had come to a decision.

I knew what I had to do.

***

It couldn't happen right away, of course. I had to wait a few months, until Dad and Donna got married. They had chosen Mexico as their honeymoon destination. Donna may have looked down on the country's people, but the thought of spending two weeks in paradise was appealing to her nonetheless.

"Make sure you take care of the house," Donna told me before she and Dad left. "Oh, and please *try* to lose some weight while we're gone."

"No problem," I said, smiling.

At the end of the first week everything was ready. The pills I'd ordered off the black market had arrived, and were safely hidden away in the pockets of an old coat I never wore. Now, all I had to do was wait.

On the day Dad and Donna were due to fly back to Canada I baked cookies: chocolate chip for Dad, oatmeal raisin for Donna. I dropped four little white pills into the oatmeal raisin batter, then presented the cookies to my parents when they got home.

Donna, freshly tanned with golden highlights in her long brown hair, pursed her lips disapprovingly. "I see you haven't lost weight."

I shrugged it off and handed her a cookie. "It's a new recipe," I said. "I want you to test it."

She took a bite and smiled. "These are very good, Katie! Still, that doesn't excuse your lack of self-control."

"Now, now," said Dad. I wished he'd say *Don't you DARE talk to my daughter like that, you bitch!* but I knew he wouldn't. He loved Donna too much.

It wasn't long before Donna began to lose weight.

At first it wasn't even noticeable, but since Donna was already very slender there were only so many pounds she could shed before it became obvious. She was also having stomach cramps, and her mystery illness had her so preoccupied that she forgot to make fun of my weight.

I would slip the pills into her food whenever I had a chance. In total I had two hundred of those little white capsules, but I didn't intend to use *all* of them. My goal wasn't to *kill* Donna, after all, I just wanted to teach her a lesson.

After a month Donna had become a shriveled husk of a woman. Her eyes had retreated an inch into their sockets, her cheek bones that bulged against the skin. She had a xylophone of protruding ribs, and twig-like arms and legs. She was in constant pain, and had made an appointment with a gastroenterologist. My conscience had begun to creep back, and

I decided it was time to stop. My revenge had gone on long enough.

But I couldn't resist slipping one last pill into her oatmeal one morning.

When I came home from school that afternoon I found Donna lying on the couch, curled up under a blanket, a damp cloth draped across her sweaty forehead. "Ugh," she groaned. "I feel *terrible*, Katie."

"I'm sorry to hear that, Donna."

"I hope this doctor can find out what's wrong with me. If I get any skinnier, I'll blow away in the wind."

"Can I make you some tea?"

"That would be wonderful, honey. Add whole milk." She gave a strained smile. "Maybe I should start eating like *you*. It might help me gain some weight."

I waited until she'd rolled over before flipping her off and heading into the kitchen.

While I waited for the water to boil Donna dragged herself off the couch, and stumbled to the bathroom. Exactly four minutes and twenty seconds later I heard her scream.

It was the scream of a dying woman, of someone being gutted alive. Another shriek shredded the air as I ran down the hall and threw myself against the locked bathroom door.

"Donna!" I yelled. "What's the matter?"

"Worms!" she wailed. "Oh, Jesus! Oh, my God! Worms! Oh God, I'm dying!"

I grabbed a butter knife from the kitchen and forced the door open. Donna stood over the toilet, her sweat pants crumpled around her ankles. Her bony legs shook as she stared in horror at the long, segmented white worms dangling between her thighs.

"Holy shit!" I exclaimed.

Donna screeched and began to pull at the vile parasites. A couple of them split in two, and the severed halves hit the tiled floor with a grotesque *splat.* Poor Donna was practically hyperventilating by this point. She shoved past me and headed for the phone, the worms trailing behind her like streamers. They looked an awful lot like linguine noodles.

Weak from sickness and her own terror, Donna collapsed before she could make it to the phone. Her head bounced off the marble counter, and she hit the floor hard, streaming blood everywhere. I wrapped the wound with a dish towel and dialled 911. "Come quick," I pleaded. "She's in bad shape."

When the ambulance arrived, I put on a show of being genuinely concerned. One of the paramedics took one look at the worms and vomited into the sink. They loaded Donna onto a stretcher, carried her to the vehicle, and sped off, sirens screaming.

I watched the ambulance disappear around a corner, burning rubber on the way to the hospital, and I let a malicious smile creep slowly across my face.

***

Donna believed she'd contracted the tapeworms in Mexico. "Those fools don't know anything about food safety!" she spat. "I doubt the cooks even wash their hands before going into work!"

The Mexico theory seemed most likely, so the doctors didn't question it. They simply prescribed Donna some anti-parasitic drugs, stitched up her head, and sent her home after a night of observation. I flushed the remainder of the pills down the toilet.

Donna made a full recovery. She was still an insufferable bitch, but she never commented on my weight again. I think part of her suspected me, but she was too cowardly to confront me.

I felt guilty for putting her in the hospital, of course, but my plan had gone perfectly.

You see, I had bought those pills knowing very well that they contained tapeworm eggs. I had planted them in Donna's food, knowing the nasty creatures would hatch and grow inside her. And I knew Donna would probably blame the food she'd eaten in Mexico, so that I wouldn't get caught.

Donna sealed her fate that night she mocked me in front of Erik (whom, by the way, I'm still dating). Heck, she sealed her fate the first time she ever hurt me. Donna believed she could get away with anything. I proved her wrong, in the most twisted way possible.

Take it from me: you do *not* want to fall victim to a fat girl's revenge.

I WAS HIRED TO MURDER MYSELF

Thamires Luppi

I have always enjoyed killing, and I blame it on my farm childhood.

Calling it a farm is a big stretch. I grew up in a shack on a rural area, having only my father and sister around. He never mistreated us, but he was stiff and relentless in his beliefs. For him there was no such thing as male or female, everyone under his roof was, by default, a hunter.

Back when we were really young he would leave us home alone for hours and hours. He first took me hunting when I was 3. I never thought rabbits and squirrels were cute – they were always prey.

I first hunted a deer when I was 10. I was limber, and had developed a strong body. Danna was never a huntress, but she was great at hiding so she hid at first. Dad was angry, but I hunted so well that I did more than enough for both of us. Besides, Danna was good enough to manage catching smaller animals. She was outstanding at fishing with her own hands due to her quietness.

But she never enjoyed any of it.

103

Dad died when I was 13. He was caught by a bear, and kept screaming "Shoot it! Shoot it, you fucking bitch!" I only had 2 bullets left, and I was too worried, so the first missed and the second wasn't enough to take down the bear. Danna grabbed my hand and we ran like the wind.

I'm honestly not sad for my father's last words to me. He was desperate, and being eaten alive, after all. I forgave him in a heartbeat. Who I never was able to forgive was myself, for failing Dad.

We were taken to a foster family after that. Danna soon adapted to having a normal life, and she clearly was held dear by the couple. I am grateful to them for having a comfy bed, and for finally learning how to write and read, but I kept to myself at home. I missed killing things.

I went hunting alone every day. The first time my family was impressed by my ability, but the second time my foster mother cried about "the poor ducky." The third time my foster father begged me to give what I hunted to someone else.

I started selling it. I made some nice cash, and gave everything to my sister's college fund. She was smart, and needed the money after all. I just needed to smell the delicious bitterness of fresh blood.

By the time I was 18 I married the sweetest man. It was crazy how we balanced each other's personality, him being always so calm and gleeful. Thom was 15 years older than me and a merchant, selling a myriad of things in our small town. He sometimes sold parts of my hunting; the meat, the fur, the heads as prizes.

We were happy. We lived for 5 great years together until he was shot in a robbery.

From that moment on a burning rage lived inside of me. The eagerness to kill took over. I didn't know how to manage a shop, so I asked my husband's brother Stu to take his place in management; but Stu was a drunkard and a buffoon, and soon the shop bankrupted. I was left with nothing.

When I learned about...certain shady parts of the internet, I finally realized I could sell my services and satiate my ever-growing bloodlust.

I'm famous now – I mean, my work name is. Nobody knows my face, nobody knows I'm even a woman. My body is small and strong, perfect for sneaking in. I look trustworthy enough for my prey to take me to dinner. Sometimes it's too easy.

I have built a name between politicians, and rich, cheated wives love me. Of course my clients are not always from the highest social standings, and they try to bargain a lot. It's not unusual that some broken-ass guy asks me to murder his rich father/uncle and get paid after I do the job, when he gets his inheritance. I just laugh at their faces and tell them to fuck off before I murder them instead.

Until the day my intuition – no, my instincts – told me to keep talking to the guy after he told me his conditions of payment.

"I will inherit some money" he wrote "but the thing is, I used to have a brother. He's dead now. No kids. But I talked to my attorney and he told me his widow will get half of my money. So I want to eliminate her."

"Sure, just send me her info" I replied for the first time. I knew this story. I didn't want to be paranoid and think it was me; I just felt sorry for the poor woman, and maybe would fuck up the guy.

But it was me. My brother-in-law, who was constantly helped by me and my husband after losing everything in gambling over and over, who ruined our store and I never said a thing, wanted to kill me. No, worse than that, he wanted to hire someone else to kill me, because his coward ass couldn't even do it.

I took the job. The next day I went to see my sister Danna, and asked her something no twin sister should ask the other – can you die in my place?

***

When I take a job I will finish it, no matter what it takes, so I sent my client a picture of my dead victim, my sister. I was famous for this modus operandi.

As I said, Danna ain't a huntress. She's a great hider. So, after I forged her death and gave Stu a false sense of safeness, he found my sister, characterized as me, at his dirty apartment.

"D-D-Dora, what are you doing here?" he was stuttering and sweating.

"Just came by to talk a little about the inheritance we're about to get", my sister calmly said, perfectly mimicking my voice and intonation.

Stu never knew I had a sister because she lived far away during her graduation. Both me and my husband always kept to ourselves and never had a wedding party, so our families didn't know each other very well.

"Inheritance? I don't know what you're talking about," he made a poor attempt at lying.

"Why don't you ask the hitman you hired, Stu?" she asked, as I came from behind him, wearing the exact same clothes as her. I gotta admit it was so much fun to stage this.

When he turned to look at me, Stu was pale, and I'm pretty sure he pissed himself.

"W-w-what is going on? What kind of joke is this?"

That's all he could say before I gagged him.

"It's your fault that my husband was shot, isn't it?" I stabbed him once. I knew very well how to lethally stab someone only once, making a cleaner death, but it wouldn't happen this time. "You fucking deadbeat. Your damn loan sharks broke in the store and killed him. You let the store go bankrupt because you were fucking terrified of staying there."

He shook his head desperately, trying to deny it, but his eyes told the truth. I never fully realized it until that instant. It was a moment of clarity, and I hated his guts even more.

Both me and my sister did what we were best at. She hid, not wanting to see the bloodbath I was about to cause, and I stabbed and stabbed and stabbed.

When the body was found the police immediately arrested Stu's loan shark. They were investigating him for a long time, and they just needed one more move to make theirs. They confirmed my suspicious about the loan shark killing my husband.

I noticed that, with the closure, my bloodlust diminished. I still go hunting most weekends, but I'm done with killing people. Nothing can bring Thom back, but I can move forward, learn new things, and work with something else. I still have a lot to live for.

So let me give you an advice: if you're thinking about hiring a hitman, don't. The best one went out of business.

NIGHTMARE AMONG THE STARS

Blair Daniels

We were 100,000 miles away from Earth when we heard it.

Claaaang.

A metallic clank, reverberating through the cabin. Coming from the outside, as if something just hit the side of the spacecraft.

"Did we just hit something?" I asked.

"No, Captain. Radar's clear," Alex replied from the console.

"Is Davis out there, fixing something?"

"What did I do?" Davis asked. He was crouched near the floor, picking up a piece of freeze-dried ice cream.

"Nothing." I shook my head. The possibilities ran through my head. Likely -- a small rock or debris. Unlikely -- a tentacled alien eating our ship. Of course, that's still what I pictured.

Claaaaang.

My heart began to race. I glanced out the window -- an endless black sea of stars. The same night sky I gazed up at from my grandpa's pickup in Texas, as a kid. The same night sky I danced under, kissed Gavin under, looked up at when I was sad. Sometimes I imagined someone was watching me from the indigo sky. Someone up among the stars.

Now it looked so different. As if someone had broken the sky itself, jumbled up all the pieces, and put them back together again.

Claaaang.

"I'm going to see what's going on out there." I got up from my seat and walked over to the row of suits hanging in the corner.

"What if it's dangerous? Shouldn't one of us go?" Alex asked.

"If a Captain isn't willing to go down with her ship, what good is she?" I replied as I zipped it up.

Their voices snapped into muffled tones. It was like plunging underwater.

I walked out of the cabin and down the hallway. It was dark, only lit by a stripe of green LEDs running down the wall. The airlock -- and the door to the outside -- lay just ahead.

Claaaang.

It was louder, now. Or was it just amplified by the silence of the hallway, the lack of Alex's and Davis's useless blabbering?

Claaaang.

111

I stepped into the airlock. Hissing sounds erupted around me. *Beep, beep!* I swung the door open. I reached for one of the rungs attached to the outside of the ship, and pulled myself out.

There it was. Space. In my entire career, I'd only set foot outside the cabin and experienced space a few times in my life. It was hard for me to look into the darkness, and imagine how what lived in the dark spaces between the stars. Alien life, or nothing at all.

The second one scares me more.

I clung to the side of the spaceship, climbing up the rungs. The noise had stopped now. No *clanks*, no *clangs*, no *thumps*.

What I saw matched the silence; the exterior of the ship was empty. No tentacled aliens, no twenty-eyed spider men, no gelatinous slug creatures.

Claaaang!

The noise reverberated in the metal underneath me. The vibrations coursed through the rungs, through my gloved hands.

It was coming from the other side of the ship.

My heart plummeted. *There's something out here. Banging on the side of the ship. There are no rocks, no debris...nothing that could possibly be making that noise.* My mind filled with Cthulhu-like monstrosities, clinging to our little spaceship. Banging at the hull.

Looking for a way in.

Slowly, I reached for the next rung. And the next. I slowly climbed around the side of the ship, feeling the tug of space at my back. One misstep, and I could be floating out here forever.

I reached for the next rung and pulled myself over. That's when I saw it.

Not an alien. Not a monster.

A person.

Clinging to the side of the ship. Head turned away from me. He took a step, and his foot collided with the metal.

Claaaang.

I pressed the radio button on my chest. "Alex? Davis? There's someone out here. Do you hear me? There's someone out here!"

"What are you talking about?"

"There's another astronaut out here."

A dry chuckle crackled through the other end. "You stole some of Davis's DMT, didn't you? You little fox."

"No! Listen Alex, there is someone out here!"

Shit.

He heard me.

The astronaut turned around. His pitch-black visor stared blankly at me -- curiously. Then he took a step forward.

"He's coming towards me! Shit, Alex!?"

"Then get back inside!"

The astronaut reached for another rung and pulled himself forward. *Claaaang.*

I scrambled away. My hands slipped clumsily over the rungs, pulling myself towards the door. It looked so far away -- nearly on the other side of the ship. Each of his steps reverberated through the metal, vibrating every bone in my body.

My hand fell on the handle. I yanked it open and darted into the airlock. I punched the button -- *hisssssss.* The air started to fill the room.

Claaaang.

He stared in at me through the tiny window in the door. The black, endless void of his visor stared back. No details, no face even remotely discernible.

The handle jiggled.

No. He's going to open the door. He's going to open the door and drag me back out --

Beep, beep!

I grabbed the interior handle and swung it forward, then I ran down the dark hallway. The green lights streaked by me like stars. I swung the cabin door open and clicked the lock.

"Go!" I screamed.

"What?"

114

"He was trying to get in -- if you engage the thrusters, he'll fall off --"

"Okay, okay. Calm down." Alex's fingers skimmed the controls. *Click* -- he wrenched the stick down.

Nothing happened.

Alex's eyes went wide. "Uh, I'm not sure what..." He grabbed the stick and pulled it down, again.

Still nothing.

"They're not working." Alex's fingers punched at the buttons, his eyes growing wider every second. "Nothing's working. The thrusters -- the engine -- none of it's working!"

"Let me try!" Davis shouted, pushing Alex aside.

But nothing happened.

Claaaang!

The metallic clank echoed through the ship.

From the inside, this time.

PICKY

B. R. Jewett

Many of us tout family dinners as a bright spot of our childhoods, a cherished gathering of loved ones setting aside time to laugh over home-cooked food crafted from recipes dating back decades.

At our house, my family was content with any meal that didn't include a screaming match.

Almost every night our kitchen turned into a battlefield. My siblings watched in awe as I pushed away almost anything set in front of me, proclaiming I wouldn't eat it.

Fish? It better come fried enough to taste like chicken. Salad? Why don't you go find some rabbits to feed that trash to, and I'll wait here. Macaroni and cheese? I hope you're cooking original Kraft because the other varieties with different-shaped noodles taste weird.

Yes, I was a little terror. Eventually my parents stopped trying to introduce new foods to my diet. They surrendered, opting to work around my pickiness rather than incite me.

My friends took up the charge once we were old enough to eat out at restaurants by ourselves. I couldn't escape a meal at the local diner without a jab for ordering a plain cheeseburger or chicken strips for the millionth time.

"I like what I like and that's it," became the constant response to the teasing.

Everything changed when I went off to college. The endless options presented by the dining centers opened my palate to a whole new world. Everything was buffet style, and I could try anything with little consequence. And, it turns out, there's a lot of good food in the world.

My mom nearly fell on the floor one weekend I came home to visit and suggested she make tacos for supper.

The list of foods I liked greatly expanded during those years, but still remained more reserved than the average adult.

It wasn't a problem until Joey. We met through the magical portal of Tinder, and bonded over our mutual love of science fiction and disdain for politics. His cubicle-bound job as a software engineer played foil to my career as a wildlife biologist.

By some favor of fate the restaurant he picked for our first date didn't betray my finicky eating habits, and neither did the one after that.

For date three he asked to cook me dinner at my place. I obliged, and started looking forward to it. My enthusiasm for the evening waned once I realized Joey never told me what he planned to make. My concern grew when he walked in with two full grocery bags and shooed me to the living room.

"It's a surprise," was the only phrase I could coax from him.

Defeated, I sat on the couch and awaited the mystery entrée. Grotesque possibilities floated through my head, and I tried prepare for the worst. If there's one thing you get used to as a picky eater, it's coming up with polite refusals and convincing excuses. If those fail you, well, there's always the napkin in the lap trick.

"Come and get it!"

Four of my least favorite words.

I willed myself from the couch and eased over to the kitchen table, trying to keep a pleasant look on my face as I awaited the unveiling.

"Voila!" Joey declared, sweeping he arms over the spread on the table. A fillet of baked salmon floated on a bed of rice, while a pile of seasoned asparagus rested nearby on the plate. It looked like a meal fit for a magazine.

I suppressed a gag.

"Looks... great!"

I took my seat across from him at the table, my stomach already clenched and my throat tightening at the sight of the seafood dish. The fork slid easily through the fish, clinking as it hit the plate. Slowly my hand raised the morsel to my face, while my brain tried to find an exit strategy.

Joey stared, a big, dopey grin plastered on his face. The napkin trick would be impossible.

I felt the salmon land on my tongue. I held it there as my lips met on the fork prongs, trying to figure out how to swallow the abomination of flesh. In that moment I hated Joey. Why couldn't he ask me what I liked instead of showing up with fish?

I took a breath through my nose, my eyes fixed on the plate in front of me. The moving air accentuated the revolting taste of fish.

The first gag might not have been noticeable if my dining companion had fixed his attention on his own meal. The reflex jerked my head slightly forward and widened my eyes.

"Uh, Val? You okay?"

A flying piece of salmon answered the question. It rocketed from my mouth, propelled by a fit of coughing. The chunk bounced once, and came to a rest in the middle of the table.

After taking a deep breath I guzzled the glass of water near my plate. It only took a moment for the horror on Joey's face to shift to annoyance.

"So, I take it you don't like fish," he said, the tone eerily similar to one my own mother employed many times when she sought to keep herself from unloading on me for leaving something uneaten once again.

"No," I sputtered. "I don't. What kind of guy makes a girl dinner and doesn't ask what she likes?"

The question hung in the air for a beat, giving me time to cross my arms and glare. Joey stared back, his face betraying no thoughts or emotions. The left corner of his lip twitched, then he sighed.

"I guess you're right. How rude of me. A gentleman should never assume what a lady would like to eat. How about I pack this up in tupperware, run it to my place, and grab us a pizza on the way back?"

The idea of placing that meal in my tupperware almost made me balk at the offer, but compromise is key to any good relationship. Or so we're told.

"Yes, that sounds great. Thank you, sorry to be a pain."

Awkward silence filled the apartment for a moment. Then Joey rose and began clearing the plates. I retreated to the bathroom to brush my teeth and get the taste of fish out of my mouth. Joey was just about to leave as I stepped out of the bathroom.

"Just so there are no more mishaps, what kind of pizza would you like?" he asked from the entryway.

"Pepperoni is fine."

"As you wish."

In the time Joey was out, I reflected on the dinner. Hopefully I hadn't bruised his pride too badly. I appreciated the effort he went though, but why not just ask me what I eat to save himself the wasted effort?

Dwelling on it would only prolong my unhappiness, so I put on my best smile and greeted Joey enthusiastically when he arrived with a pizza in hand. As a surprise he had also picked up a bottle of red wine. I preferred white, but still downed a glass, trying to limit how neurotic my pickiness made me look.

The sound of my wine glass tipping over on the coffee table is the last thing I remember. Blackness gave way to the soggy feeling of warm drool on a pillow. My brain fought through a cloud while a sharp pain bloomed in my mouth, pulsing in tandem with my heartbeat.

I heaved, more viscous drool escaping my mouth before a breath drew a wave of it into my throat. The liquid cut off airflow, and racking coughs jerked my head into the pillow and amplified the intensity of the pain

Through the haze I tried to command my tongue to circle my mouth in hopes of locating the source of pain.

I found it.

The paramedics arrived to find me alone in my bedroom, blood running down my chin. The police followed them into my apartment, and before I was wheeled me out on a stretcher I watched an officer pick up a note on my kitchen table.

He read it and ran to the paramedic standing near my head. She scanned it and frantically gestured for her partner to start moving.

The contents wouldn't be revealed to me until another police officer visited me in the hospital a few hours later after an unsuccessful emergency surgery. He asked a few questions, and scanned my answers after I wrote them on a piece of notebook paper. I jotted down a question of my own, and he presented me with a copy of the note.

"Valerie,

Sorry about dinner. I'm sure it's tough being a picky eater so I thought I'd help you out. And don't bother looking for your tongue. Consider it the last unpleasant thing you'll ever have to taste.

HUSH, LITTLE BABY

Kitty Olsen

Dear Diary,

We're going on a vacation! I'm really surprised because daddy said we didn't have the money for a summer vacation this year, but he came home today and told me and mommy to start packing. I don't know where we're going yet, but I can't wait.

I filled my suitcase to the brim with my clothes. Daddy hasn't said how long we'll be gone yet, I wonder if we're going to see grandma and grandpa down in Florida? I hope so! They promised the next time I came down they'd take me to Disney World. I've always wanted to go.

Mommy's really tired so I'm trying to help her pack, but she keeps saying 'don't worry' and sends me back to my room. I wonder if the baby will be born in Florida?

Gotta go, dad's coming down the hall, he really wants to get going!

Bethany

~

Dear Diary,

123

We're on the road! Boy, we packed a lot of stuff into the van. Dad's put on my favorite playlist so we can sing Let It Go on the way to Disney World. He hasn't said that's where we're going yet, but I just know it! Why else would we pack so much?

I get to take up the whole back seat, when it's nighttime dad usually lets me unbuckle so I can sleep. It's always so hard sleeping in the car though. I hope mom doesn't need to puke. When she first told me that I was getting a little brother or sister, she was non-stop barfing! Blegh! Barf is gross!

Oh, I think we're meeting with Uncle Harry and our cousins on the way down too. I hope Uncle Harry brings his camper. We're not allowed to stay in it while it's moving, but maybe if I ask reeeaaallly nicely…

Bethany

~

Dear Diary,

I get to stay in the camper!

It was getting really dark by the time we met up with Uncle Harry. Traffic was really bad today and dad had to keep turning off Frozen so he could check on the radio. I dunno why, I think he wanted to hear the traffic reports.

For some reason Auntie Debbie isn't here. I tried to ask Uncle Harry why she wasn't but he seemed grumpy so I just played Go Fish with Kevin and Macey. Kevin didn't even call it a baby game this time, so that was fun.

Macey said she thinks her mommy was working at the hospital when it was time to go. That's really sad. She's gonna miss Mickey Mouse.

Bethany

~

Dear Diary,

Ugh! I'm so BORED! We've been on the road for two days and I'm already so bored, bored, bored.

I think Uncle Harry's sad about something. He keeps crying at night and not looking at Macey. Whenever I get carsick and try to look out the window when we've stopped he snaps at me to keep the blinds shut.

Kevin's sad too. He's pretending like he's not crying but I can hear him in the bathroom sometimes. I think he really misses his mom. Macey misses her too but she's not crying.

I don't wanna play more Go-Fish but there's no INTERNET out here so I can't watch anything on YouTube. This is gonna be a loooong trip.

Bethany

~

Dear Diary,

I think I saw someone who was really sick today.

We were stopped at a gas station to load up on snacks, I think we were the only ones there cuz I didn't see anyone else. I was playing Barbies with Macey just outside the camper and we were pretending to be dragon riders when I heard something. I looked up and I saw a lady walking up.

She didn't look very good, her skin was all gross and her eyes were leaking green and white goo, sorta like whenever I have a cut that gets infected. She looked really scary. I yelled for Kevin and he poked his head out to see her getting closer.

I think he was scared.

He grabbed me by the hair and Macey too, pulling us in and yelling to his dad that one of 'them' was out there. I dropped my Barbie and asked Kevin to go get it because I didn't want to see that ucky lady anymore, but he told me to shut up.

He must've felt bad because after his dad came back, he went and got my doll. I don't know what happened to that lady, but she was gone. I think Uncle Harry told her to go away.

Bethany

~

Dear Diary,
We're not going to Disney World.

Daddy held a 'pow-wow' when we stopped for the night to tell us why we were on vacation. It's not really a vacation. People are getting really sick and they're becoming very dangerous. If we're too loud, they'll come and they'll hurt us. The sick people are attracted to noise and they're very dangerous. They could get us sick too. I don't wanna get sick so I wanna be quiet.

Aunt Debbie died. That's why Kevin and Uncle Harry have been so sad. They told me and Macey at the same time. One of the sick people hurt her really badly while she was at work. She's in heaven now with Great Aunt Julia and my dog Bucket. I'm gonna miss Aunt Debbie. She always liked singing in the car with us, even though she sung really badly.

Macey cried until she fell asleep. I haven't cried yet. I feel really sad, but I can't cry. I hope I'm not broken.

Bethany

~

Dear Diary,

I'm not broken, it just took a while. I was eating breakfast with Kevin and Macey when I started bawling my eyes out. I'm never ever ever going to see Aunt Debbie again. She's not gonna get to see Mommy's baby. And I'm scared that I'll get sick too and hurt Macey and Kevin and Mommy.

127

Macey hugged me better and told me that I wasn't everever gonna get sick, we have her daddy and my daddy and they'll make sure we're safe. That made me feel better.

I think Mommy's scared about the baby. We can't go to a hospital so she can have it. I hope she'll be okay.

Bethany

~

Dear Diary,

Mommy's having the baby right now!!!! Ahhhhhhh!!!!

She's hurting really badly but she's trying not to scream so the 'zombies' (that's what Kevin says they are) don't find us. I feel really bad for her.

I gotta stay in the truck right now. I'm keeping a look out for zombies with Macey and Kevin! Haven't seen any though. Just a lot of empty road and no cars. It's super quiet.

Take that back- mommy just screamed. Kevin has his dad's gun in his hand and he's looking scared.

I'm a little scared too but I know we'll be okay.

Bethany

~

Dear Diary,

I have a little brother. I'm so happy. We're all really happy.

He's so tiny and bald! He's got like maybe five hairs on his head, and dad told me to stop exaggerating but it's true! I love him so much. I want him to be safe and I promised mommy that I'll do my best to make sure he's happy. Mommy's tired but she smiled so wide when I said that.

My brother's named Nathan. I love him so, so much.

Bethany

~

Dear Diary,

It's been a crazy few days. Nathan really likes to cry a lot. Dad says I wasn't this fussy, but I think he's stressed out. We've seen a lot more zombies lately now that we're getting closer to a town and they can hear Nathan crying.

Uncle Harry and Dad go out when they start getting too close to bash in their heads with a baseball bat. It's a lot quieter than the gun, which can only be used in emergencies. I'm not allowed to look outside when they're getting rid of the zombies, but sometimes I take a peek.

I always knew my daddy was strong.

Ugh, Nathan's crying again. Mommy says he's having trouble 'latching'. I don't know what that means, but I'm gonna have a headache if Nathan keeps crying.

Bethany

~

Dear Diary,

Uncle Harry, Daddy, and Kevin are going into town. They have to get baby supplies. Mom is letting me and Macey take care of Nathan while she's lookout. I get to be a babysitter for my own brother!

Macey doesn't like holding him, she says he kinda stinks but I love holding him. He's so still and he just looks at me and I love it so much. Because he loves me too.

It's getting dark. I hope Daddy gets home soon.

Bethany

~

Dear Diary,

It's been two days. Daddy and everyone else isn't back yet. Mommy's really scared. She's tried calling them a few times but they don't pick up, it just rings out. She's crying.

I'm so scared that my daddy's dead.

Nathan needs to stop crying. The zombies are getting closer. And Mommy isn't strong enough to use the bat to bash in their heads.

Bethany

~

Dear Diary,

Daddy's back! Everyone's okay! And they brought back SO MUCH STUFF! I get to have potato chips at dinner tonight, I'm so excited.

Kevin told me what happened. Apparently they got cornered in a building and had to wait for the right moment to book it. It was so scary, he said, but it sounds exciting! I'm glad everyone's not hurt though. Nathan's a lot happier that daddy's back too, I think.

I can't wait for potato chips. I have to wait until Daddy and Uncle Harry clear away the zombies though. No dinner until we're safe.

Bethany

~

Dear Diary,

We didn't have dinner last night. Uncle Harry's dead.

He got torn to pieces in front of the camper. We thought the zombies were all gone but they weren't and Uncle Harry was heading on back when they all attacked him at once and they bit his neck and there was so much blood and it was so so horrible… there was nothing Daddy could do.

We all cried last night as we drove away. We couldn't even bury him. We had to leave him behind.

Macey and Kevin don't have a mommy or a daddy anymore. I don't have an uncle anymore. Daddy doesn't have a brother anymore.

I wish we were going to Disney instead.

Bethany

~

Dear Diary,

Mommy says that Nathan has a colic. I think that just means he cries a lot.

Kevin's teaching me and Macey how to drive the camper. He no longer teases us or calls our dolls stupid. He makes sure we have plenty to eat and reminds us to be quiet.

I keep waking up in the night crying. Kevin once had to smush a pillow into my face to keep me quiet because he couldn't wake me up. I can't stop thinking about Uncle Harry. How much it hurt when the zombies ate him.

Why is this happening to us? And why can't Nathan stop CRYING?

Bethany

~

Dear Diary,

Mommy and Daddy are going to get more supplies. Nathan needs more formula and diapers. Kevin is going to keep look out while they're gone, Macey and I are going to watch the baby.

He won't stop crying. We're trying SO HARD but he won't be quiet. We're trying to feed him but he won't eat, and he won't nap, and his diaper's clean, and I don't know what to DO. I keep asking Kevin but he doesn't know either.

I heard Daddy tell Kevin if they're not back in two days we have to leave.

I hope Daddy comes back in time.

Bethany

~

Dear Diary,

I'm a murderer.

I killed Nathan.

It was an accident! The zombies were getting close, Kevin was in the front with his bat prepped and Nathan just wouldn't stop CRYING! Macey was crying too, she was so scared they were gonna get inside to get to the noise and then the zombies would eat us all up. I didn't know what to do, so I decided to make Nathan quieter by covering his face with a pillow.

It worked. He stopped crying. But when I took the pillow away his lips were blue and he wasn't breathing. I tried to wake him up but he wouldn't wake up. I shouted for Kevin and he tried to wake Nathan up but he couldn't.

I killed my own little brother. I'm so sorry Nathan. It wasn't your fault you were colic-y. But it is my fault for not being able to help you.

Bethany

~

Dear Diary,

We had a funeral for Nathan today. I wasn't allowed to be a part of it, I had to stay in the trailer.

Mommy hit me when she found out what happened. Kevin tried to take the blame but I couldn't let him do that. It wouldn't be fair. I killed Nathan. Not Kevin.

Mommy hates me now. Whenever I say something she tells me to shut up. She hates me. I hate me too.

I think Macey hates me too. She doesn't want to play with me anymore. Daddy just makes sure I eat, even though I don't want to. He doesn't talk to me.

I think the only person who likes me now is Kevin. After dark I'll sneak out and put my favorite doll on Nathan's grave. So he isn't alone when we leave.

Bethany

~

Dear Diary,

Mommy isn't doing well. She keeps snapping and yelling at everyone, even though Daddy has to remind her that she has to be quiet or the zombies will get us.

Last night I woke up and she was standing over my bed. I sat up and asked why she was up. She just glared and stomped back to bed and started crying again.

I just make things worse by being here.

Bethany

~

Dear Diary,

I think Mommy tried to kill me today.

I was washing up at a creek we stopped by when my head was shoved down below the water. I couldn't breathe. I tried to scream but I just got a mouthful of mud. I thought I was going to drown.

Then I was let go and I popped back up so I could scream.

Mommy was being dragged away by Kevin, Kevin was calling her a lot of mean words I can't repeat but I can write down- 'bitch' was one of them. He called her a bitch a lot. Mommy just cried and screamed nonsense, so we had to get out of there quickly so the zombies couldn't find us.

My mouth still tastes like dirt. Mommy's just sitting on the couch and staring at me. Kevin won't leave my side. I'm glad there's someone who loves me still.

Bethany

~

Dear Diary,

We're almost to Florida. Maybe we can make it to Disney after all.

Bethany

~

Dear Diary,

My parents forgot me.

We stopped at an abandoned motel. There was no one there except for a few zombies and Kevin took care of them. He's so strong. I went to sleep in a bed last night, Macey was next to me. But when I woke up this morning I was alone, with my backpack full of my favorite toys and my favorite foods.

The camper's gone.

They'll realize I'm gone soon and come back, right?

Bethany

~

Dear Diary,

It's been two days. I've spotted a few zombies but they don't come close. They don't realize I'm here, I'm excellent at being quiet.

I'm still waiting for my mom and dad. I'm searching the motel for more food so I don't go hungry. At least the sink works so I'm not thirsty.

Bethany

~

Dear Diary,

It's been five days. They have to come back soon. They have to.

Bethany

~

Dear Diary,

It's been two whole weeks. I think I found all the food that's left here. And Mommy and Daddy aren't ever coming back.

So I gotta go find them.

I packed my bag full as I could and I'm gonna start walking today. Maybe they'll still be going to Disney, and we can meet there.

I'm so sorry, Mommy and Daddy, for killing Nathan. But maybe when I find you again, you'll forgive me.

Bethany

I'M A NICE GUY

P. Oxford

The following was posted on the subreddit r/relationships:

Dear denizens of the world wide web, my cunning and guile has failed me, and I must turn to you for help. There's this girl, you see. I am a nice guy, and I try to show her that, but I do not know how to convince her that I am the one for her. If only I was better looking, but alas, that I cannot change. I need but a hint on how to proceed. I hope you will read my story, and that on of you fine internet folks will be able to help me out.

The first time I saw her was the very first chem lab of my college career. I was sitting at one of the stations all alone as the other students meandered in. Much to my chagrin, nobody sat down next to me. I have to admit that it saddened me, as I had hoped that in college I'd find my brethren. I would be recognized for my mind – nay, my genius – but it was not so. The frauds who had called themselves my high school teachers were unable to grasp the extent of my gifts. They gave me second tier grades, and thus sentenced me to a second tier school. The second tier people in this place did not recognize that they had a behemoth mind in their midst – but I digress.

I was in chem lab, and She walked in. She looked me right in the eyes and smiled. Oh, heart be still! The thought of that smile still sends the old ticker into overdrive. She walked up to the front of the class, white lab coat billowing around her like the robe of an angel. Her tight shirt strained against the size of her ample bosom, and her wide hips, perfect for childbearing, moved tantalizingly side to side. Could this lovely creature truly be our teaching assistant? She came to a halt behind the desk at the front, pulled out some papers from her bag, and shot me a nervous glance. And finally, after all the years of solitude, I knew what love was. I watched her intently as she flipped through her papers. I think that she could feel her soulmate was in the class today; why else would she keep shooting me those nervous glances every now and then, if not to ensure I was still watching her?

"All right, guys!" she said, her voice like ambrosia. "This is a chem lab, and that means that shit in here is dangerous. That means no eating and no drinking in here. There's always some idiot who thinks that doesn't apply to him, but rest assured, people use things in here that can kill you in minutes if accidentally ingested, 'kay? Hey!" she looked right at me. She was talking to me! "That means you! Cake is food too!"

I stuffed the cake into my bag. She cared about my safety! In that moment I knew it - she loved me too! I lingered after class, hoping to catch her alone, but she was gone before I had the chance. I was not fazed. I am a true romantic, not like those guys who are only after one thing, and when they don't get it right away the move on. No, I am one of the last knights in shining armour, and I had found my quest.

Being the master sleuth that I am, I was able to find her workspace in the chemistry building, and there I left a single red rose for her. Just imagining her smile when she found it kept me warm for days. Each day I left her a new rose. With my master wordsmithing skill, I crafted poems praising her lovely dark curls, her red lips, and her ample bosom. To brighten her day, I left them in her department mailbox. And every lab, I could but stare at her, waiting for her to realize I was the one.

Finally, after weeks, I could not resist any longer; I had to take our relationship to the next level. After class I found her and outed myself as her secret admirer – I even asked her to be my companion for a meal before she could respond.

My lady politely declined, and hurried out of the room. Oh, what shyness! Such an endearing quality in the human female! I vowed that I would be the one to break through her barrier of shyness, and so I posed the question again and again. Each time she gently rebuffed me, but I knew she didn't really mean it. If she wanted me to stop, would she have said no in such a polite, lovely way? Like all females she wants a dependable man, one that does not back down easily. Clearly, she was waiting for a grand romantic gesture, like in those old romantic comedies. But which gesture would be the right one for her?

When the university told me I had to leave her alone – insisting quite forcefully that I change labs – I was not deterred. The love between a student and a teacher is forever illicit; it was clear that she was afraid of our love jeopardizing her degree, her career, so I accepted her choice – even knowing she'd need neither when she became my wife.

Instead, I surreptitiously left her love notes at her home. The university did not want to give me her home address, leaving me to rely on my cunning and guile: I hid outside her office and followed her home one late evening. So unsafe, I thought when I watched her enter the ground floor apartment. Any predator could hide in the bushes and leer at her through her windows, or worse yet, simply climb in. It was my duty was to protect her! Thus, to ensure her safety, I patrolled those windows every night. I think she knew, for she left a gap in the curtains just large enough for me to watch her as she slept. My, what beauty. If she was angelic in wakefulness, it was nothing like how she looked in her sleep. So innocent. No frown marring her lovely forehead, like the one that appeared to be permanently affixed to her brow in her wakeful state. Reddit, I am not too proud to admit that I occasionally pleasured myself outside that

141

window. I believe she knew, and that she liked it. Why else not close her curtains completely?

All the while, she remained so shy. I knew I just needed to prove to her the extent of my love, and I'd break through her shyness. She tested me, again and again. When I called her phone to ask her to dine with me, she rebuffed me. When she blocked my number, I got a new phone. When she changed her number, I searched and found it. When she moved to a different apartment, all I had to do was follow her best friend around. She led me to my angel's new apartment in less than a fortnight. Our love was so all consuming to me that I neglected my coursework, and I was told to leave my academic endeavours behind. More time for her tests, proving myself as one that does not back down in the face of adversity, a true white knight. And I welcomed each new test.

At least for the better part of a year I did. But recently, dear Reddit, doubt has crept into my soul. Have I been too subtle? Now, I will not lie and say that I have much experience with the fairer sex. I have always believed in true love, and saved myself for that, but this has left me rather underdeveloped in my understanding of the workings of the female brain. I just wanted to prove how nice I am, and how much I truly care about her. So I researched the female mind, and what I found frightened me. If it is really true that women only fall for good-

142

looking men – Chads, as the good men of the internet have dubbed them – who treat them like dirt, what is a nice guy like me to do? My doubts grew. What if she is not as different from other girls as I thought? Has she been leading me on this whole time?

A few days ago I went to confront her. She refused even to open the door, she just yelled at me that I was violating her restraining order and that she would call the police if I did not go away. The police? What had I ever done except love her with a burning passion?

"If loving you is a crime, then I am guilty!" I declared, and she did not even have the decency to respond.

Reddit, I will not lie, this made me angry. After everything I had done for her, every compliment I had given her, every gift I had bought her, every sleepless night I had been standing outside her apartment just to keep her safe – this is how she repays me? She would not even give me a chance to show her how delightful our life together would be? Oh, but as I wrote that sentence I saw with complete clarity what I must do. I must *show* her how delightful our life together would be! If she just knew how nice I really am, she would love me – I am sure of it.

And I happen to have the perfect little room in my basement. If I keep her there for a few days – a week at most! – she will see how nice I am, and she will love me. So, reddit, what do you think of my plan? Do you think I found the way to my lover's heart?

~

EDIT: Oh, my heart now knows true joy! Just now the doorbell rang, and I went outside to find a small cardboard box on my front steps. Inside was a lovely chocolate cake. The best part was, literally, the icing on the cake. For on the cake, in icing, she had declared her love for me!

My love,

I didn't see what was right in front of me. This cake is an expression of my true feelings for you. Eat every crumb, and I'll know that you'll love me for the rest of your life.

Sincerely,

Your Love

Can you believe it? I am over the moon with happiness! She loves me! She took the time to bake my favourite cake, the very type I was eating when we first met, and painstakingly write a message on top of it! Of course I couldn't resist, and I ate it all. For once, the nice guy does not finish last!

~

EDIT 2: This post is already getting a lot of attention – people seem to my plan might be a tad too much, which I do not understand? – and I really wish to respond to you all with haste. I currently do not feel very well; perhaps my lady is not yet the best cook (that will change when she finds her place in our kitchen, of course). Or, it is possible that I also simply may have eaten too quickly in my excitement. Based on the initial response, it seems I will have to explain in simpler terms why I am in the right, but for that I must have all my faculties intact. So forgive me if I do not respond to your comments immediately, I think I will have to go to bed early today but I will surely get back to you tomorrow.

I'M SORRY

Aimee Sek

I watched her die.

I had never seen anyone die before. It was slow as if she was holding on to every last moment she had left and stretching out time itself just for her last breath. It wasn't peaceful. I had always heard people say that people pass peacefully. Maybe because her death was violent, or it's just something people say to make those of us still alive feel better so we can be at peace.

She screamed and choked on blood and vomit. Her body thrashed as I tried to calm her. I wasn't sure if it was her or I shaking as I held her. I wanted to keep her still. I tried holding her broken pieces together as the blood poured freely. Pieces of her were escaping, just falling off her broken bones. I remember looking at my hands and not even knowing what it was I was holding.

I didn't throw up until the paramedics came and pulled me away. I kept thinking about how the professionals threw up before I did. Was that odd? How strange the things we think about during an incident such as that. I remember feeling sad that my expensive dinner was lying all over the ground, that my wonderful exciting date with Jacob would forever be tied to this memory now, and then feeling guilty that it made me a horrible person for being worried about that when this woman's life was over.

I had just arrived home after dinner, and was having that in-love feeling where you have butterflies and feel like you could just float away. I was in my own world, thinking of our kiss, when I heard her screams. I didn't see anyone else just her behind the dumpsters near my building. I couldn't even tell she was a person at first. It was dark, with only a faint light from the building, and all I could make out was a red blob. Discarded wet trash it seemed, until she moved and cried out again and I realized…

I remember I kept wondering how anyone could have the capability to do that to another person. The violence. The damage. The pain she must have experienced. How is anyone able to cause that? It was like a pack of animals had torn her apart. So many broken bones. So many knife wounds. She was practically flayed in some places. I couldn't grasp it; it was simply beyond my understanding.

A Jane Doe, with no possible way to identify her with how she was left. No witnesses. Not a single person in the entire apartment complex said they heard anything. How that is even possible is beyond me. We live in a nice neighborhood where people call the cops if you raise your voice at your own kid. This didn't make any sense.

No, I didn't feel safe after that. No one did. No suspects. Some insane violent killer running loose. We were all terrified, and obviously I was more than a little shaken. The doctors said I had PTSD. I had been through a traumatic event. I couldn't eat. I couldn't sleep. I stopped going to work or returning calls. I didn't leave my apartment. They wanted me to see a therapist and take medication. I tried, I really did, but it wasn't helping. I just needed time, that's all. Now I know all the therapy and drugs in the world couldn't help me with this.

She whispered 'sorry' before she was gone. They told me later that it wouldn't have been possible for her to do that, so that I must have just heard sounds and imagined it. But no, I heard it as clear as possible. And those words haunt me. At the time I thought maybe she was sorry she was dying, or blamed herself for what had happened, but I know now why she was sorry. She knew. She was giving it to me, and she knew.

I can't really blame her. I was angry at first but it wasn't like she was choosing me she was just getting rid of it. Maybe it was fate, magical threads being spun so that all the events in my life would lead up to me being in that wrong place at the wrong time and being given it. Maybe it's just bad luck.

It started maybe two months after I had found her. I slipped in the shower. It was fast, nearly painless, with just a small thud. I hit my head hard. I didn't even realize I had died that time. It almost makes me want to laugh at that realization. I woke up much later and my head hurt, and I was freezing as the now-cold shower was still running over me. I felt foggy, but not too bad. I probably should have gone to the hospital, but I didn't. Depression – You don't even care if you die!

The second time I died it was worse. That's how it happens; it seems to grow stronger inside of me. Every death is worse, slower, more painful, more difficult and cruel.

I choked to death. I hadn't eaten in almost two days, so it seemed like a cruel joke. Feeling your air cut off as your panic grows is terrible, and you feel death coming. You know it is happening, and you can't stop it. It is that way most of the time, to be honest. Your last moments are filled with fear and desperation, and you feel completely helpless to stop it. It was as if death itself had its cold hands around my throat, then it goes dark.

And then I wake up hours later perfectly fine. Well, physically fine. My emotional and mental wellbeing; not so much.

At that time I still hadn't realized what was happening. I thought bad luck maybe, but why would it even cross my mind that I had died and come back?

The third time I knew something was wrong, but I was not sure what.

I went for a swim in the pool at my complex. It was an indoor pool at night so it was empty. I couldn't really take being around people. I've swam my entire life. I grew up on the beach and loved the water. It was one thing that had relaxed me. I swam for a while trying to burn off some restless energy and clear my mind, then I finally settled into a gentle float on my back while trying to be calm. When…I don't even know if I can put it into words, I felt as if something grabbed me. Not like a person or a thing, more like gravity itself. Just a force, a need, pulled me down, down, down. I struggled with every bit of strength I had in me to fight against it but I couldn't. Drowning is a terrifying and painful death. It burns your nose and lungs. It takes so much energy out of you. Somehow in the struggle you become confused on which way is up, and which is down. I've died in much worse ways since then, but this one still haunts me. Maybe because of how much I had loved the water before it betrayed me, or maybe because it was the first time I knew I had died.

When I woke up on the side of the pool I thought I was just going crazy. Bad dreams? I wasn't in denial over what I had been through with finding the woman. I was traumatized, so it made sense that my mind was giving me bad dreams.

After the fifth time I died I couldn't take it anymore. I slit my wrists. When I woke up I was alive and fine, and I didn't even have a scratch on me.

I want to say I knew what was going on then, but I didn't. I knew that my brain was saying I died, and even though these deaths felt incredibly real it wasn't possible. I was just crazy.

I think it took maybe twenty or so more deaths, some of which were self-inflicted, to just accept it. I would die, then wake back up fully alive. I never know how, or when, I will die. There doesn't seem to be any rhyme or reasoning to it, no pattern. Yet it feels intelligent, alive even. Maybe death is just fucking with me. Maybe I am a glitch in the system.

Time keeps moving forward. I am not stuck in some time loop, Groundhog Day nonsense. I don't think I am a zombie, at least not the movie version. I don't crave brains, and I have a pulse. I have tried to seek help. Obviously this sounds insane, and I couldn't just tell someone because they wouldn't believe me. I thought that if I were around others maybe I could die, then if they saw me die I wouldn't come back. How could I?

At first it stopped me. I'd die before I was able to get near anyone to see, and then when I thought I had outsmarted it…it just killed others too. A fire. I was hailed as so lucky for being the only survivor, even though I had not survived. I had just come back. I didn't try again after that. Their deaths were my fault. None of them came back to life as far as I could tell. I am just walking death.

But that is what made me realize that perhaps it was contagious. The woman, her last words an apology. I think she passed this on to me somehow. Could I do the same? Would I on accident? How did it happen, and if I knew how could I even bring myself to do this to someone else?

But dying isn't easy. Maybe the death isn't real, I'm not even sure, but it feels real. The pain and fear and helplessness are all very real.

Time went by in a blur. I lost my apartment, funny how that happens when you don't pay the rent. I have family, but they live far away and I wouldn't, couldn't, risk their lives. I sleep in my car, and there are some churches that offer food. I don't go often, or when many people are around. After a while a few kind people have helped me out with some supplies and food, they just think I am fearful of people or crowds or something. I appreciate their kindness for what it's worth. They tell me they will pray for me, and I never tell them that I don't think it will do much good.

I mostly just waited around to die. Then I would die again and again. I lost track of time, but I think it has been three years or so now. Sometimes deaths will come close together, a few days or weeks apart, other times it has been months before I would die again. Each one is worse, but every time I wake back up. That's all that is the same.

It's bad now. Well it has always been bad but now it has reached the point where I just… I just can't. Unseen hands have murdered me. Not people or beings or anything, it just happens somehow. I've been stabbed and cut and had things removed. My throat slit. My bones broken, neck snapped. I've bled to death countless ways. If the darkest, cruelest minds have imagined it then it has happened to me. It's slower now, more painful. The torture and cruelty reaches on and on, until it feels like an unending valley holding me between life and death. I long for the quick deaths of the past.

Why is death so cruel? What is the purpose?

It feels as if it is leading up to something perhaps, the pinnacle point of a divine purpose? Maybe that is just my mind trying to grasp at a reason for this. Funny how our minds try to find reason with death, I suppose. Maybe it will just make me feel better if I feel like this was done for some grand design, and not just empty and pointless. Did I suffer for something? Maybe my deaths have saved others? Maybe I am taking deaths to spare others? Am I a hero in this story?

I wish I could have been, but no, I'm afraid not. I am sadly not strong enough. I wish I could be. I understand why she did what she did, and no, I don't blame her. Maybe writing this, my last words, will help someone else and that can at least be one good thing I have done, though it won't make up for the wrong.

I'm sorry.

LESLIE

Stephanie Scissom

I don't know how long I stared at the notification on my computer before I clicked on a new private message from Leslie. In the right corner of my screen a glowing green light next to her name indicated she was online.

Leslie: 8088088088088088088088088088088808808808808...

"Who is this?" I replied.

A message bubble with a dancing ellipsis appeared.

Leslie is typing …

Leslie: 8088088088088088088088088088088808808808808...

The morning sun burned across my face as I sat at one of the little tables outside the coffee shop, but I shivered, then looked around to see if anyone was watching me. Was this was some sort of joke? No one appeared to pay me any mind.

Leslie is typing …

Leslie: 8088088088088088088088088088088808808808808...

"Who is this?" I typed again.

Had her account been hacked? Had someone found her phone? Was this her killer?

I decided on the first. But still...I couldn't simply shut the window. Not yet. All those months with no news. Gone without a trace.

Leslie is typing...

Leslie: Mo 0 s y

Mo o s y

Mo o S y

What the hell? Mossy? Moosy?

I wiped my sweaty palms on my jeans and looked around again. People were laughing, chatting, and enjoying the unseasonably warm March morning. They seemed oblivious the the fact that I was falling apart.

"What are you saying?" I typed. "Where are you?"

Leslie is typing...

Leslie: idontnoidonntnnnoidonnnnnnhhnoo

nononononnnno9-1765e808dvdsz

no hellpmehelppmehrllprmemee

Help me? My confusion turned to anger. This was someone's idea of a joke?

I typed, "What is wrong with you? It takes a sick person to do this."

I slammed my laptop shut and sat there for a moment with my eyes closed. Six months, and the loss of her still consumed me. I no longer clung to hope that Leslie was alive, and I felt ashamed of that. Now I only prayed she'd be found, and the person who'd taken her would be punished. The investigation so far had been frustrating and fruitless, and the police had spent most of their time investigating me.

My phone buzzed, delivering my second nasty surprise of the day when I looked down to see Michael Vandergriff's name on my phone. Michael was Leslie's brother. The last time I'd seen him he'd punched me in the face in the police station parking lot after the first time I'd been brought in for questioning. Still, maybe there was news.

"Hello?" I said.

"What the hell is wrong with you?" he asked. "Mom is crying."

"What are you talking about?"

"I'm talking about the message you sent her from Leslie's account. Why would you do that?"

My temper surged. "I didn't do that. I got one too and thought maybe it was you."

I sent him screenshots, and he sent me one back.

Leslie: Helo

Karen: Deacon, is this you? You're logged into Leslie's account.

Leslie: Imis$you

Leslie: Icant808808808gettout

Michael was quiet for a moment, then he said, "If you can answer her security questions, change her password. I've been trying, but I can't access it."

The thought of him hacking into her profile--deleting pictures and snooping through her private messages--bothered me. I promised I would, and disconnected the call.

Getting into her account wasn't a problem. I'd spent the last five years memorizing everything about this girl. I knew her favorite book and her favorite teacher and I sure knew her favorite pet's name. Although I hated cats, Satin and I had bonded over our mutual grief. I changed the password, then I glanced at her inbox. There was no record at all of today's messages sent to me or to her mom. They both showed last messages sent in September. I didn't know parts of messages could be erased.

I knew I should probably deactivate the account, but I couldn't do it. Instead, I found myself looking through her photo albums. Big mistake. This was the girl I loved, the one I wanted to marry. It hurt to look at her smiling face, because the last time I'd seen he she'd been beating her hands against the passenger glass of a stranger's car.

The waitress came by with my check, saving me from the black hole I was about to disappear down. I paid and went to class, and didn't think more about it until that night when I logged onto my own account. I had a new message from Leslie's account.

Leslie: icantaeseeicantseaanymorrhlpe me

The new password wasn't something even Leslie would've guessed. How was this person doing this?

My phone buzzed in my pocket and I snatched it out, anticipating another call from Michael. What I saw nearly stopped my heart.

Leslie's face popped up on my homescreen, with the caption LESLIE CALLING.

Her phone had disappeared with her. Could someone fake this? I squeaked out a hello.

Over the pop and crackle of a bad connection, I clearly heard my name.

"Deacon?"

Leslie's voice. Oh, God. She was alive!

"Leslie, baby, where are you?"

The voice on the phone screamed. One word, over and over. No! Then the call disconnected. With shaking hands, I tried to call her back. Her mom put money in her account every month to pay the phone bill, because she said she couldn't bear it to think that Leslie might somehow get access to her phone and not be able to use it, but my call went straight to voicemail.

I disconnected and jerked on some shoes. This was different. This wasn't social media. I went straight to the police department.

It was hard not to feel resentment as I sat across from the sheriff. I mean, I knew he was only doing his job, but even after I'd successfully passed the lie detector I'd still been followed and interrogated. I felt like he'd let the killer slip by because he couldn't see past me.

I told him about the messages and he frowned. "Why would someone be doing this now, after--" He checked the file in front of him and grunted. "--six months?"

I had no answer for that, but I signed a release for my phone records and he promised to trace the call and get back to me. After I left I debated calling Michael, but decided against it for now.

At home I had another message from Leslie. Again, a string of gibberish.

Leslie: 80880880880880880808808

Leslie: 9-1765 Mo 0 s y

I couldn't make any sense of it, but thought it strange that it was the same sequence of numbers. I thought about how we'd first met. We'd both had summer jobs at the hospital, dealing with medical records. She worked in the Medical records department and I was basically a gopher, someone who delivered files all over the hospital. Because of the concrete walls cell phones weren't exactly reliable, so we were supplied with these archaic, numeric beepers. She'd message me a floor and a file number and I'd retrieve them. One day, just goofing off, I'd sent her 317537 14, which--as any fifth grader could tell you--spelled Hi Leslie upside down on a calculator, or those pagers. Not much of a pick-up line, but somehow it had worked. We started messaging each other in code. Some were standard--20 for location, 411 for info, 911 for emergency come up here, 143 for I love you, 1432 for I love you, too. Some we made up. I decided to try these on her messenger.

Deacon: 20?

Leslie is typing:

Leslie: Mo o s y

Deacon: Idk what that means. 411 who is this

Leslie: 317537 . 814.

My mind raced. How would anyone except Leslie know this, especially since we hadn't used the same way of coding of our names? 814 was just my birth month and day, but it was what she'd used for my name.

Leslie is typing …

Leslie: 607

That meant I miss you. I typed back 204? (Are you okay?)

Leslie: 17

No.

She didn't type anything the rest of the night. I didn't know what to think, or do. Especially when I got a phone call from the sheriff the next day saying there was no record of any call from Leslie's line, nor any record of my phone receiving a call. But he'd seen the number in my received calls, so he didn't know yet. Maybe it was a new spoofing method he wasn't aware of, but I was beginning to think it was something else.

The day Leslie was taken we were camping. It was a normal afternoon, an activity we did frequently. She'd taken my truck to the little market down the road to get marshmallows for S'mores, while I worked on the campfire. She'd been gone long enough that I thought she should be back--the store was just a couple of miles away--when my phone rang. It was Leslie and she was upset, said some guy in a beat-up Buick had just rear ended her. She was getting out to exchange insurance info. When she told me she was less than a mile from camp I banked the fire and told her to wait on me, then I took off walking.

I hadn't gotten far when a beat up, blue Buick roared past me. What I saw would haunt me for the rest of my life. Leslie's terrified face in the passenger window, her hands beating on the glass. For a moment I froze. All I could think of was: do I chase the car, or run to my truck? Of course I couldn't catch the car, but it seemed wrong to run in the other direction. Then some common sense broke through and I called 911. The cops never spotted the car, never had any leads on it. It was like she'd vanished off the face of the Earth. If I could be honest with myself, I would admit that I don't think she lived out that day.

I still don't think she did.

That afternoon I skipped my afternoon classes and got back on my laptop. I just had the feeling something was happening and I needed to be here, something that I hadn't been able to do before.

The green light beside Leslie's name indicated she was online. I got a notification that she'd tagged herself in a location.

Briar Ridge Baptist Church.

I looked it up on a map. It was about ten miles from the campgrounds. I grabbed my keys and headed that way.

Thirty minutes later I stood in a deserted parking lot, staring at the charred remains of the church. The only thing that remained was a large sign in the front with the message: Come unto me, all ye that labour and are heavy laden, and I will give you rest. Matthew 11:28.

I felt foolish. Did I really think Leslie was sending me messages from the grave? The late afternoon sun was setting, and the streetlights began to buzz on. Across the street a neon sign from a junkyard buzzed on. It looked as old and battered as the cars it advertised. Most of the letters were burned out, but a few stood out in red.

MORTON'S JUNKYARD

Moosy.

I ran across the road. I didn't see a worker, so I just went through the gate and started walking around. I found the Buick on the second row.

The smell of decomposition hung heavy in the air, only partially masked by a stinging, chemical smell. I had the strangest feeling as I stood by that trunk, and I noticed a few things at once. The red letters of the sign, the church sign...the tag on the car across from the Buick read 9-1765.

"Can I help you?" a voice behind me asked.

When I turned, I saw his name tag and the final puzzle piece slid into place.

BOB. Bob converted to 808 on a pager.

He looked nervous, twitchy. I could only imagine what he saw written on my face. I stared at him, judging. He was taller than me, but lean. I thought I could take him. I thought--

He reached behind him and pulled a gun from the waistband of his jeans.

"How did you find me?" he asked.

"She led me here," I replied.

The look on his face--horrified, yet not surprised--made me wonder if Leslie had been haunting him as well.

He led me to a small, grimy office, took my phone from my pocket and motioned for me to sit on the concrete floor beside a big black barrel. He tossed my phone on his desk and fished a pack of cigarettes and a lighter out of his front pocket. His hand shook as he lit one.

"What did you do to her? Is she in that trunk?"

"Was," he said mildly, and rubbed his hand across his pockmarked cheek. "The weather got warmer. I moved her yesterday because of the smell." He nodded to the barrel. "You wanna know what happened to your girl? She's in there."

I thought of what she'd told me and her mother.

I can't see anymore. I can't get out.

"Now, because you just wouldn't let it go, I'm gonna have to find another barrel for you."

Music blared suddenly, scaring us both. Bob looked at the old boombox in the corner, which was blasting Conway Twitty's "I'd Love to Lay You Down."

"Not that song again!" he cried, and strode over to the corner to jerk the plug out of the wall. It died briefly, then screamed to life again. He cursed and threw it on the floor.

I noticed my phone on the desk light up. I saw the keypad for the phone pop up and the numerals 9 1 1 appear. Then the dial key flashed, like someone placed a thumb on it. Bob never noticed, he was too busy trying to smash the boombox.

I heard a murmur as the call connected and started screaming, "Help! Help me! He has a gun! His name is Bob."

Bob looked at me in utter confusion for a second. I looked away from the phone, toward the window and kept screaming. He pulled his gun and started toward me. Somehow the cord from the boombox tangled around his feet, and he crashed to the concrete.

I had just finished tying him up with the cord when the cops arrived. The truth of how I'd gotten there would've gotten me locked up in a mental ward. Instead, I told them he was the one who'd been messaging me. He lured me here and confessed. I told him where her body was, and where it had been, while Bob sat silently.

At the station he confessed to everything. From raping her while he played Conway Twitty, to strangling her and keeping her body in the back of the Buick, to being haunted by her ever since. He said he was glad to confess, and that now maybe he'd have peace. In a way he was right. Bob was found hanging in his cell that night. I wondered if he'd had help with that.

When I got home from the station, I found another message from Leslie.

Leslie: 53. 143

I typed, "You're welcome. I love you too."

A MOTHER'S CERTAINTY

Julia Smith

November 15

The rocking chair arrived yesterday, so now I can finally finish setting up the nursery. I can't believe how much earlier I'll be done with it this time. I was still working on the finishing touches for Owen's nursery right up until I left to deliver him. I guess it helps that I already had most of the big pieces of furniture. I told Hank there was a reason for saving all of Owen's baby stuff for all these years. I can't believe he tried to convince me to sell the crib a year ago. Ha! I love that man, but he never has seen the purpose of keeping things that aren't being used. At least I had the satisfaction of being right in the end.

November 23

I could not have imagined a better Thanksgiving! Owen loved being "in charge" of the desserts. I've got to thank Emily the next time I see her for the wonderful idea. It really did help keep Owen from getting underfoot while I was cooking. Instead of constantly following me around, he sat and watched the timer count down until it was time to take out the pie. He's

170

such a sweet boy. My mom managed to get the perfect picture of Owen kissing my belly, or as he calls it "giving Sarah an early kiss." He's going to be a wonderful big brother. He's just so excited. He told my parents that he was going to take her to school with him every day so she can be an "extra smart baby." I hope that attitude lasts once she gets here and he sees how much time and attention newborns actually require. God, I hope he doesn't get jealous. Maybe I should take him out and do something special before she gets here, just the two of us.

November 30

It's funny how your entire life can change in an instant. One minute, we were happily going about our lives, ready to go from a family of three to a family of four. Now...now I'm home from the hospital with no baby to hold and nobody to sleep in the world's cutest nursery. Hank had to return to work today. Not that he's been much help. Any time he sees me crying he just leaves the room. He won't talk about what happened at all. He was barely in the hospital room once they told us they could no longer find the heartbeat. I think he blames me...I know I do. She was supposed to be safe. What kind of mother can't even protect their baby in the womb? Telling Owen was a different kind of heartbreak altogether. I'm still unsure he fully comprehends. How much can a four-year-old really understand about the death of a sibling they never got to meet? This is his first experience with death, and we're totally screwing it up. I can't even talk about it without sobbing uncontrollably, and Hank won't even say her name out loud. I just wish we could go back to being a happy little family, but, right now, I feel like I'll never be happy again.

December 5

The house still isn't decorated. I know, I know, I should start. Owen loved decorating last year, but I just can't bring myself to do it. I feel like everybody else is moving on, but I am stuck. I just can't act like everything is okay. I want to scream at Hank most days now, sometimes I do. I mean we lost our baby girl. How can he just go back to work like nothing happened? He acts annoyed anytime I bring Sarah up or if I get upset. I feel like I'm constantly walking on eggshells about showing my true emotions just to make him feel more comfortable. We used to talk about everything. Communication was never an issue for us. Now that I think of it, I don't think we've ever had a fight before we lost Sarah. Now we've had several. To see the way he acts, you'd think nothing had happened at all. At least with Owen, I can understand. He's four, he can't possibly comprehend the magnitude of it all. Plus, he's got Santa to look forward to.

How could something as abstract as death compete with the certainty of Santa? He can tell I've been sad though. Yesterday, I had to go into the nursery for the first time since everything fell apart. I cried so hard, I could hardly breathe. Every emotion I'd been trying to keep down just came rushing up, all at once. I was glad that Hank wasn't here at that moment. It took a long time before I could breathe again. Owen noticed and asked why I was crying. All I could manage to tell him was that I was sad. He immediately climbed into my lap, gave me a kiss and said he loved me. Normally, that would have filled me with such joy and warmed my whole heart, but this time just made it more obvious how empty I felt. I noticed the strangest thing though. Owen's eyes were much darker than I can ever remember seeing before. I swear when I went to the hospital, they were still that warm amber color. I thought they'd stay that color forever, but now they are a dark brown, almost black. I mentioned it to Hank, Owen seems to be the only topic we really discuss anymore, but he said he hadn't noticed anything. Maybe I should bring it up next time I take Owen to the pediatrician for a checkup.

December 8

I don't even understand what just happened. It was such a nice day, warm even for Texas. I took Owen to the park in the hope that getting out of the house might do me some good. He was playing in the sandbox with another little boy while I chatted with the mom on the bench. Out of nowhere, Owen stopped digging in the sand, stood up, looked over at me, and loudly said "You aren't done burying people yet." I am afraid I might have overreacted. That other mom certainly acted like I did. You'd think hearing a child talk about burying people would warrant a reaction of some kind, but she just kept prattling on about how warm it was. It's like she didn't even notice. How, I'll never know, because Owen was so incredibly loud, louder than I've ever heard him speak before. It wasn't just the volume level of his voice that was odd either. In fact, just about everything about his voice was different. He said it with an intensity and tone that sounded more adult than a four-year-old should be able to muster. Honestly, it scared me. I know grabbing him by the shoulders and yelling at him was an overreaction, especially since he was already back to digging by the time I got over to him. But I needed to be sure he'd never say something like that again.

December 10

I'm worried about Owen. Something's not right. This is not the same sweet little boy I've loved for four years. That sounds crazy, I know, but he's just so different lately. He's been

174

turning down food, and he's always been a good eater. This morning, he got violently angry when I told him he couldn't take his tablet with him to preschool. He has never acted like that before. My nose still hurts where he headbutted me. He scratched the crap out of my arm too. Then when we were waiting in the drop off line at his school, his voice changed again. He said, "Sarah got off lucky, you're a terrible mother." It took everything I had to hold it together long enough to drop him off. I made it to the Kroger parking lot across the street and then broke down crying in my car. For a split second, I wished he could stay there at school forever. Why would he say such a hurtful thing? Could he really think I'm a terrible mother? Maybe I am, I have been distant since losing Sarah. What kind of mother wishes for their child to not come home?

December 13

How the hell am I supposed to explain this to the neighbors? I'm pretty sure Owen killed their cat. I'm not sure how or why, because I had stepped inside to grab a drink. Owen was swinging on the swing set, and I only stepped inside for a minute or two. When I came back outside, Owen wasn't on the swing anymore. He was standing near the fence, looking at something on the ground. I couldn't see what it was from the porch, but I could see the smile of his face. It was grin that seemed to stretch unnaturally wide across his face. When I got close enough to see what was on the ground, he stopped smiling and went back to the swing. I looked down and saw Tink, the neighbor's cat, lying lifeless on the ground with its head turned the wrong way. Never in a million years, would I have imagined Owen would be capable of doing something like that. Not until I saw that sick grin on his face anyway. He just looked so pleased while he was staring down at that dead cat's body. God, that look on his face chilled me to my bone. I remember a time where his smile seemed to light up my soul. It was filled with warmth and love, and you couldn't help but smile with him. This smile though, this smile just felt wrong. It was too big, too happy for such a disturbing sight. That smile will haunt my dreams. I felt nothing close to the love I used to feel looking at him in that moment. I don't think I can even try to tell the neighbors. I just don't think I could explain it, I'm not even doing it justice now. I should bury it though, it deserves more than to be in a trash bag. Yeah, I'm going to bury it by the rose bushes.

December 14

Am I losing it? I'm beginning to think I might be. This morning, while checking the mail, I saw Tink run out from under my car. At least, it looked like Tink. I don't understand how it could be though, I buried that damn cat last night after Hank went to bed. He's been sleeping in the guest room lately, so it's not like he noticed I wasn't in bed. I can still see the spot from the porch. What did I bury there if it wasn't that cat? Could it have been some stray that just looked like Tink? I tried to ask Owen about it before I dropped him off at preschool, and he just looked at me like he didn't understand. But he does, I know he does. I'm certain that whatever is happening to Owen, is responsible for this too. I still don't understand what's happened to Owen, but I know in my heart he's changed. Sometimes I catch myself thinking that it isn't Owen at all. Sure, it looks like him, it even sounds like him most of the time, but my Owen couldn't do or say the things he's said recently. It's like he's been swapped with a different child these past few weeks. Surely, that can't be possible though...right? Maybe I am losing it.

December 15

I finally got the Christmas tree put up last night. I couldn't sleep after the dream I had, so I figured I might as well do something productive. Otherwise, I would have spent all night just trying to get back to that dream. It was the kind of dream you don't want to wake up from. In the dream, I was sitting in the rocking chair in Sarah's nursery with Owen. It felt so real. He looked up at me, and his eyes were amber colored again. His smile was warm and filled me with a sense of peace and happiness I haven't felt in quite some time. He made me promise not to forget him and told me he wanted to come home now. He started crying and he hugged me tight, begging me to find him. "That's not me mommy, can't you tell?" Then I woke up. It was the most vivid dream I've ever had. I woke up confused because I was certain I was already awake. This will sound strange, but I feel like Owen, the real Owen, was trying to reach me from wherever he is. I know now, that whoever or whatever this other child is, it's not my Owen. A mother knows her child better than anybody else in the world. I knew him before he was born, he was literally part of me. It makes sense that I would be the one to know that something is wrong. Emily is supposed to come over later today. She knows me better than anybody else on the planet, well maybe other than Hank, but I don't count him anymore. Emily will understand though, she'll help me figure this whole thing out.

December 17

I just feel so utterly alone and betrayed. Emily just left. The conversation didn't go as well as I thought it would go. Not only did Emily not believe me, she told me I was crazy. I never knew she could be so closed minded. The visit started out well enough. We sat in the living room, and she filled me in on how things have been over at her house. Then I started to explain about that little boy not being Owen. At first, I think she thought I was joking, so I started telling her more and more of the details about what's happened regarding Owen. I was trying to make her understand, and then Owen used that voice again. Every time I hear it, it sends chills down my spine. A child's voice should not be able to sound so adult. Owen turned and looked at me and said, "She won't believe you, nobody will. You'll never get him back, and if you try, I'll make sure you end up all alone." A feeling of dread crept over me. He was threatening me, taunting me. I couldn't have stopped myself from screaming, even if it had occurred to me to try. I don't remember exactly what I said, but I remember repeatedly yelling at him to shut up while covering my ears. That's when Emily freaked out on me. She grabbed Owen and took him upstairs, to his room. I thought for a moment, she was going to come down and ask what the plan was, but that isn't what happened. She charged toward me like a bull seeing red. She started yelling at me that I needed to get my shit together. I tried explaining that wasn't really Owen, she knew I'd never speak to Owen like that. I told her about Owen visiting me in my dream, and she got really quiet. She asked how long I had been thinking these thoughts, and if I had any plans to act on them. Of course, I'm going to take action. My son, my real son is missing somewhere, and I don't see how she could expect me to sit here doing nothing with this information. She told me I sounded like a lunatic. I should have realized this was too much for somebody who doesn't see Owen every day to take in. I had trouble coming to terms with it, I still do occasionally. There are still moments, from time to time, where I look at him and still see him as my Owen...but then I remember that isn't him. It's not my Owen. I think, as much as I don't want to, I need to talk to Hank. I used to be able to depend on him for everything. If anybody else will ever believe me, it has to be Hank. In spite of all of our problems, I know he still loves Owen, and that he'd do anything to save him.

December 15 (10:00 pm)

He didn't believe me! I don't understand how Owen's father couldn't tell the difference between our Owen and this imposter. I think Emily called him after she left, or maybe it was that thing masquerading as Owen. Somebody convinced him I was crazy. He didn't even let me explain how I knew. The Hank I married would have believed me. Hank gave me an ultimatum tonight. Either I go with him and let him check me into a psychiatric hospital, or he'll pack up Owen's things, take him, and leave. At first, I thought maybe he was right. I agreed to go in the morning, and I had every intention of following through, but then Owen visited me in my dream again. He told me he's running out of time and that as long as that imposter was here, he'd never be allowed to return to me. I woke up and the way forward was clear. I needed to kill whoever that was pretending to be Owen. I can't let Hank commit me, and I can't let him take that child. I know I'll never get the chance to see my sweet little boy again. I already lost Sarah. I can't lose Owen too. I just don't know if I can do it on my own. Even though I know what needs to be done, it's hard to actually do it. I stood in front of the bed with a pillow ready to do it, but all I could think was how much he looks like Owen when he's sleeping. This is why I needed Hank to believe me. How can I possibly do this on my own? What if I'm wrong? I can't be though, Owen told me what needs to be done. Why does he have to look so much like him when he's sleeping? What if I kill this thing and I still don't get Owen back? Hank would never forgive me. Maybe it's too late. The only thing I know for certain is that I don't want to live in any world without my sweet baby boy in it. Maybe I should let Hank keep this monster he's so attached to, while I go back to join the real Owen without him. There's got to be a way. He

181

keeps coming to visit in my dreams, there has to be a way to stay there with him. Those visits are the happiest I've been since I lost Sarah. I know Owen told me he wanted to come back here to us, but what if it doesn't work and then I don't get the chance to join Owen? I still have those leftover pain pills from when I had my gallbladder removed last year. There should be enough to help me sleep deep enough that I will get to stay with Owen forever. Is that fair to Owen though? Shouldn't he get the chance to come back to his real life? There is an extra pillow on the floor next to Owen's bed. I could easily overpower it and hold that pillow down over its face until it can't breathe anymore. Whatever I do, I need to do it before Hank gets up. I won't get another chance. Okay...it's time to stop writing, and start what needs to be done. Don't worry baby. Mommy's going to make sure you're not alone.

THE CRYING
Alanna Robertson-Webb

Growing up in a small, rural Vermont town meant that my household didn't have a lot of money, but we still shared everything we had with our family. That included letting my aunt, uncle and cousin move in with us when they got evicted from their house. Everything was just fine, until the crying started. For two years, from age fifteen to age seventeen, I had to share a room with my little cousin Katie. It wasn't all bad, since she was close enough to my age that she wasn't a pest, but I hated the blackout curtains we had to hang so that any outside light didn't keep her up at night. I loved seeing the moonlight filter through the screen in the summer, and I missed that once Katie moved in.

It was the second year that they had been living with us when the crying began. At first I thought it was Katie sobbing quietly when she thought I was asleep, which made sense to me because she had just gotten dumped a few days before. I figured she just didn't want to talk because she was ashamed of being the one that got dumped, or she was still just too heartbroken. Over the next few weeks, however, I began realizing that it was coming from different places within our room at night. I

183

couldn't understand why Katie was continuing to cry so much, or from weird places like inside the closet sometimes. Any time I asked her about it she just looked scared, and she would shake her head nervously. I thought something else had happened between her and her ex-boyfriend, but she just wouldn't talk to me about it.

I told my mom and aunt about it one night while Katie was out at her friend Bree's house, but they just shrugged it off and said that we were going through a rough time as teens. My slightly drunk aunt joked that Katie was probably crying at night because my fashion sense was so bad, and that maybe we should try a nightlight if we were going to be babies. I ignored her, and decided that I was done with the whole situation. If she was going to keep crying then I was just going to block out the noise. Things came to a head about a month later. I was trying to sleep one night, my CD player earbuds lodged firmly in my ears, when I felt a gentle tug on my pajama top sleeve. I removed the earbuds, turning my face to Katie even though I couldn't actually see her in the darkness.

"What's up?"

Instead of an answer all I got was a sniffle, and before I knew what was happening Katie had crawled into my bed and curled up next to me. This was so out of character for her that I didn't even question it, I just gently stroked her hair. She quieted down after a bit, and I covered her with my spare blanket because she was so cold. I must have fallen asleep at some point, because I woke up to Katie moving around next to me. She leaned over, her soft whisper barely reaching my ears.

"Run! The one who got me is coming for you."

I had no idea what she meant. I felt her get off the bed, and then everything was still and silent again. I strained my eyes to make her out in the pitch-like darkness, but with the blackout curtains shut I couldn't tell where she had gone.

"Katie, who's coming? You're creeping me out. Hello?"

She never responded. A primordial growl sliced through the quiet, and white-hot pain blurred my senses. I screamed as wet, warm liquid ran down my face, and a single hand snaked its way around my throat. I tried to kick out at my attacker, but my feet didn't seem to be able to connect with anything.

The air was rapidly getting squeezed from my lungs, and no matter how hard I tried it was impossible for me to rip free from the vice-like hand. I was about to pass out when my door was flung open, and my father stood there. The invisible hand released my throat, and when my vision cleared I realized it was just my dad and I in my room. He shouted to my mom to call an ambulance, then he tried asking me what happened.

"Dad, where's Katie!? Is she okay?"

185

"She's not here. She went to a last-minute late movie with friends an hour ago, and she won't be home until tomorrow. What in Hell happened?"

I frantically begged him to search the room, but there was no one else there. The window was locked from the inside, and the closet had nothing but shoes and clothes in it. I ended up passing out from losing so much blood, and I also lost my left eye that night. The doctors tried to blame it on a mixture of sleep paralysis, nightmares and accidental self-harm, but at 120 lbs and no muscle even my normally-skeptical parents didn't believe that explanation. We moved out of that house immediately, since none of us felt comfortable there anymore. On the night I lost my eye Katie came to see me in the intensive care unit as soon as her mom picked her up, and I can still recall her tear-stained face. I was almost asleep in bed, and I remember her leaning over and whispering to me, her voice heavy with sorrow.

"I'm so sorry cuz, I wish I could have been there to help you..."

Even in my drug-induced, mostly asleep state it struck me that her whisper didn't sound at all like the one that tried to warn me about the attack. I never had another strange experience like that again, and when we moved I even got my own room. Since then I never fail to make sure there's some sort

186

of light on in the room, and I refused to hang any more dark curtains. I never did figure out who warned me, or why they did it, but I'm forever grateful to them. If they hadn't woken me when they did I believe that I would have been caught too off-guard to fight back at all, and I would have lost more than just my eye. I am so thankful to still be breathing, and I make sure to always whisper goodnight to my unseen savior.

EDGAR FALLS RUN

Katie Bennett

Nora and I were the only ones in the Edgar Falls Salon and Spa this time of night—a special, late-night appointment we'd reserved to accommodate Nora's work schedule as a nurse at the local hospital. We sat in oversized faux-leather chairs with our feet in warm, bubbling water. The single aesthetician alternated between our feet in a slow, tired-looking dance.

"A fat high school basketball coach. Whoever heard of that? I'm a joke."

"Hey, you're not just a fat high school basketball coach. You're a fat P.E. teacher, too." She shot me an impish grin.

I laughed, appreciating the fact that my friend didn't try to lie to me to make me feel better. I always could trust Nora.

I twirled my feet around in the bubbling water in the foot bath below me. I wrinkled my nose as a strong whiff of peppermint met my nose. Whoever decided that feet were supposed to smell minty? It's not like they were going into anyone's mouth. This was my first pedicure, and I found the entire ritual ridiculous and beyond pointless.

I'd invited Nora because we hadn't spoken in months, and it was the first thing that came to my mind to do that sounded like something normal women do together.

The previous evening I'd been doing one of my nightly grocery store runs for comfort food when my cart ran into something hard with a metallic clang. The force sent my midsection right into the cart's handlebar, and the liters of soda and tubs of ice cream tumbled around crazily inside the cart.

"Oof!"

I was already thinking about the curse words I wanted to use on whoever'd been rude enough to exit an aisle without looking first.

I looked up from my cart, my first thought was annoyance that now I'd have to wait even longer before opening my sodas so they wouldn't explode, and I opened my mouth to let the offender have a piece of my mind.

But when I lifted my eyes I saw Nora, my best friend. Or, rather, my *former* best friend. Before I'd gone MIA and pushed her out of my life.

"Kayla?"

Her irritated expression morphed into recognition. She shifted her weight with an awkward movement of her legs and flitted her eyes away from me, toward a stack of canned corn.

"How have you been?"

189

"Oh, fine."

I always said that when people asked that question. Nobody actually wanted the answer when you were chronically depressed.

Our conversation continued at a slow hobble, but it was an important meeting. I'd been afraid to let Nora see me like this: Fat, depressed, and boring. I'd avoided her ever since the traumatic ACL repair surgery that had left me this way. I had been conveniently "missing" her calls for months and replying with excuses to her invitations to hang out. At the end of our chat in the grocery aisle she started to roll away, and I felt something catch in my throat.

"Nora!"

My heart thudded against my rib cage.

Her cart's wheels squeaked to a halt.

"Want to hang out tomorrow?"

I was afraid she would give me a verbal slap to the face to punish me for my months of avoidance.

Instead, she gave me a small, knowing smile.

"Sure, Kay. Just tell me when and where."

Panicked, I thought of the first thing that came to mind that didn't involve physical activity.

So now we were getting our feet buffed and our nails painted, even though neither of us really cared for that sort of thing.

We had always been rough-and-tumble girls, and our friendship had been predicated on shared experiences of running, climbing, and thrill-seeking. Now that I didn't do those things anymore, it had seemed like there wasn't any reason to hang out.

As I looked at my feet I couldn't help but notice Nora's thin, toned calves out of the corner of my eye. By contrast my own legs looked bloated and disgusting. I lifted my leg in the air and let my foot come down hard, making a splash that hit Nora's legs.

She laughed.

"Kayla, it's temporary. You'll snap out of this, as soon as your leg is healed up."

She yelped as the esthetician prodded her cuticles.

"Easy on that toe, sister!"

"Yeah, when it's healed..."

I hadn't admitted yet that my doctor had cleared me for regular physical activity months ago. Every time I wanted to run, either in my students' gym class, at basketball games, or on my own time, my legs felt paralyzed, as if I'd forgotten how to move them. I wanted to run, but I couldn't. It seemed like that part of my life was over now.

It was too much to admit to my longtime friend. I'd been the one who had taken a gap year to go backpacking across Europe. I couch surfed regularly when I wanted to travel across state lines, not always making plans ahead of time. My hair, which was sporting several inches of dark roots, held evidence of pink color at the ends. In the past, I'd sported pixie cuts and other wild styles. I'd even buzzed my head once just to see what it would look like.

I hadn't ever been afraid of anything like this before.

I needed a way to change the subject, so I snatched the newspaper from the small square table that sat between our chairs. I rifled through the pages until one of the headlines caught my eye.

EDGAR FALLS WOMEN GO MISSING

"Have you heard about the Edgar Falls disappearances? Crazy stuff. Nothing like this ever happens here. Gives me the creeps."

And another good reason not to pick running back up again.

Nora scoffed.

"Yeah, for a few months there I thought *you* were one of the disappeared women."

"Ha. Ha. Not like I was recovering from surgery or anything."

"You've been 'recovering' for almost a year now."

She glared at me for a moment, but then her expression softened.

"Was the recovery too bad? For the surgery?"

I felt tears stinging my eyes at the casual way she brought it up as if we were discussing the weather. *How are the roads today? Is there much rain?* I pretended to cough to choke down the sob that wanted to come out.

To say that the subject of the surgery was a trigger would be an understatement; the subject of the surgery was a landmine.

My mind raced with anxiety and regret. I had known that meeting up with Nora would be a mistake. I wasn't ready to rejoin the regular world yet. I felt my heart rate increase, and my breathing became shallow and fast.

"Nothing worth talking about."

My heart continued to pound. I opened my phone and angled it away from Nora so she couldn't see what I was doing. I went into my phone settings and played the notification sound to make it seem like I'd received a text message.

"Oh, man."

I performed a frustrated-sounding sigh.

"What? Is that Corwin? Tell him you're busy. This is girl time."

I winced at the mention of my old boyfriend. Had it been that long since Nora and I had hung out? Did she really not know that he was gone from my life? I didn't want to correct her and get into that story on top of the panic I was already feeling.

"No. It's my mom. Kipper got out of the fence, and she can't find him anywhere. She thinks he might come back if he hears my voice. I've got to go. I love that little pain in the butt." I looked at the aesthetician, who was currently rubbing a peach-scented exfoliating scrub over my heels.

"Can I get a towel? I'm going to need to get out here."

"But you paid for a paraffin dip."

"It's okay. Just keep the extra."

"Well, I guess I'm going to get out of here too, then."

Nora didn't even attempt to conceal her irritation.

"Sorry, Nor. I just have to do this."

"Ugh. He's a farm dog, isn't he? What kind of trouble could he get into? I bet he'll be back in time for dinner."

I looked at her for a moment, and I considered coming clean about what was wrong. Her eyebrows were pressed together in a silent plea. She missed me. I was one of her closest friends, after all.

I wanted to tell her what had happened to me during my ACL surgery. Maybe I would find healing just saying the words out loud.

My mind took me back to that terrifying event as I struggled to find the words to describe what had happened during the surgery.

The fog had lifted from my mind, even though my eyes were still closed. No, that was wrong. It wasn't like a fog lifted from my brain—it was as if a curtain had been ripped down and a blinding torrent of sensation had rushed in on me all at once.

The first sensation was the pain. I felt like my entire left leg was on fire. I wanted to scream, but I found myself unable to move my vocal cords. I wanted to flinch away from the pressure and poking sensations I felt in and around my knee, but I couldn't move my muscles either.

I was paralyzed, yet fully conscious.

I heard sounds. The beeping monitors, the clinking of metal tools on rolling trays, and someone clearing their throat. I heard the middle of a conversation.

"Looking forward to the weekend?" a disembodied female voice said.

"Yeah," replied another. "I'm going to the lake with Monty."

"That's great. Hand me the gauze and that other scalpel, please?"

I tried to interject. To scream *I'm awake*, but all I couldn't even open my eyes or wiggle my toes to communicate.

I felt sharp tugging and intense pressure at my knee joint, and I wondered how long the surgery would last. I didn't know if I could last much longer, because the pain was so intense. Yet, what other choice did I have? I couldn't move. I felt sweat pooling at my armpits and I smelled the coffee breath of the person standing near my head. The smell sent a wave of nausea through me, and for a moment I hoped that I might throw up so they would know that I was awake.

"What's going on with her heart rate?" The woman said.

"Shit!" I heard someone mutter in a panicked voice. "Daniel, have you been watching that BIS monitor?"

"Crap!" another voice replied. "She was fine a minute ago."

"Fix it!" the woman commanded. "God, it's like you're fresh from school. She might be aware."

Then it had all gone black again. The next thing I'd remembered was waking up in a blue-dotted hospital gown with a large bandage on my knee.

A fresh-faced nurse with a swinging yellow ponytail skipped into my room with a clipboard and a smile, shoving a chart with cartoon faces in my face.

"Rate your pain on a scale of one to ten, please," she chirped.

My mouth was dry as sandpaper as I swallowed and pointed to the number one. I felt no pain anymore, but the memories of my wakeful period were still vivid and intense.

I thought about telling her about what had happened, but what good would it have done? What could they do now?

So I didn't tell anyone.

"Earth to Kayla!" Nora said, bringing me back to the present moment.

The aesthetician working on my feet stood, looking annoyed at the interruption in her regular routine.

Nora didn't know what I was hiding, but with the searching look she was giving me I think she knew that something was up between us. She just didn't know what.

"I don't want to get blamed if something happens to Kipper," I said, avoiding Nora's eyes. "We should do this again," I added. I gave her my best fake smile.

Nora snorted in reply. She'd never been one to hide her opinions and feelings.

I hadn't either, until the surgery.

After I put on my sandals and stood, Nora grabbed my arm.

Despite the firmness of her grasp, her face softened as she spoke.

"I know something has been up since the surgery. I don't know why, but why don't we try to do something like we used to?"

I felt a small amount of relief. She wasn't giving up on our friendship yet, even though I was acting like a complete weirdo. That was good, right?

"Yeah, we aren't really froo-froo girls, are we?"

"Hmph," said the esthetician from the floor where she was cleaning up the foot tubs and manicure accessories.

"No offense. I'll be honest—this was my first pedicure. It's not really my thing."

The subject had changed away from the surgery, and soon I'd be home and safe from questions again.

"Why don't we go running again, Kayla? Tomorrow night, just like we used to before you got injured."

All of the calmness that had been building inside me was rendered inert in an instant.

"I already told you, I can't run anymore."

"Bullshit," Nora said. Her voice was clipped and sharp, and it left no room for arguing.

"Okay, I *won't* run anymore."

I sighed, looking at the nail tech who was now impatiently tapping a finger on the countertop by the register.

"Can we finish this conversation outside?"

After we left the spa we went to the parking lot. The sun had slipped under the horizon and the street lamps came on. The lights buzzed, and one of them flickered on and off when we passed it. I felt my mood plunge as this happened, as if the world around me dimmed wherever I went. It had sure felt like that lately.

"I know I should be able to run. It's just, I can't make my legs go. Like...It's hard to explain."

"Try me."

As I gathered the words in my mind, I heard the wind whistle through the gap in the old wooden fence that surrounded the parking lot. The sound sent a shiver down my spine, despite the warmth of the summer night.

"You ever feel like you have a word on the tip of your tongue? Like you know that you know it, deep down, but some part of your brain just is blocking you so that you're helpless to remember it? And it's always a really stupid-easy word, too, right?"

"Yeah, all the time."

"Well, it's like that. Except with my legs, and running. My legs don't remember how to run."

"Hm. I'm still not sure that makes sense."

Just then a rumbling pickup truck squealed as it turned into the parking lot. It slowed as it neared us, the bright headlights making it hard to see the driver until it idled directly in front of us.

For a moment my heart stuck in my throat as it appeared that the truck was headed straight for us. I prepared my muscles to jump, but I knew I probably wouldn't be able to make myself move in time.

Thankfully the truck squealed to a stop, a mere foot away from us.

"You ladies should get home! Haven't you heard there's some loon out snatchin' women?"

"Oh, I'd like to see somebody try to nab me. How ya' doin', Abe?"

"Fine, just fine, but you won't be if you don't haul tail home. Git!"

"Thanks, Abe. Appreciate your concern. Truly."

"Y'uns better listen, or you'll be the next headline," he said, shaking his head.

Then he revved the old truck and sputtered out of the parking lot.

"Who's that?"

"My neighbor. He likes to think it's his job to make sure girls abide by curfew, even the ones in their thirties. Small towns. You never really get to grow up in some people's' eyes, I guess."

200

"Yeah. I'd had such high hopes of leaving someday, and yet after all my adventures I ended up here anyway."

"Oh, put away that tiny violin. You were always terrible at music. Now, stop changing the subject. What is this about you not remembering how to run?"

She leaned back against her SUV.

"I guess I'm also, like, scared shitless that as soon as I do I'll tear my ACL again. Or experience that pain again. Or just that *something* will happen."

"There we have it."

She grabbed my shoulders and gave me a playful shake.

"There. Now, don't you feel better?"

"Yeah."

Actually, it felt worse. I felt my face burning with embarrassment.

"Well, if you don't think you can run, let's just start with baby steps. We can walk! There's no shame in that."

She was wrong about that. Me, a former women's college basketball player who got a full ride scholarship for my physical prowess, reduced to walking for exercise. But I had already been pushing Nora away for months, so I had to give her something.

"I think I can walk."

"Atta girl!"

She whooped and whirled her fist around in the air as if she were cheering on a football team.

"We should go tomorrow at night when I get off work, and it's cool outside."

She wiped at her brow, which glistened with sweat under the street lamps.

"I swear, Edgar Falls is the frying pan of God in the summer."

"Okay. Tomorrow it is."

This felt odd and unpracticed, making social plans. I used to go out all the time, and now planning a walk felt exhausting. I was just ready for it to be over and to sink into the comfort of my bed.

"Eight o' clock, and if you find Kipper today put him in a crate before we leave for our walk. No backing out."

"Yeah, yeah."

I couldn't help but smile. Maybe things really could be normal again.

On my drive home I felt exhausted from the effort of being social. I never used to be that way, but now more than a few minutes of talking with someone left me feeling drained. I was looking forward to eating whatever my mother had cooked for dinner and then traipsing upstairs to my comfortable bed.

Instead, my mother had planned a serious discussion.

I walked into the door to the smell of rosemary and roasted chicken, and I gave Kipper a pat.

When I sat at the dinner table, I knew something was up when she put her fork down in a delicate motion and cleared her throat. She gave my father a significant glance, and he did the same.

"Kayla, honey..."

"What?"

"Your father and I love having you here, but we think maybe you'd be happier with a space of your own. You know, with some privacy for yourself and...a space of your own." She smiled brightly.

Translation: We're sick of having you here.

I swallowed, and the mashed potatoes that went down my throat felt like a hard lump of rocks all the way down.

"Yeah," I said, "just as soon as my leg is better."

I had moved back in with my parents after the surgery so they could help take care of me while I recovered. It was supposed to have been temporary. I knew that I'd overstayed my welcome, but I couldn't bring myself to go back to my empty apartment by myself. I wasn't sure what I might do.

"It's just...Well, it's been a year sweetheart..."

"Gotta' pick yourself up by your bootstraps. Get back on the horse. Stand back up after you fall. Fall down seven times, stand up eight."

His voice sounded strained, as if he realized he was drowning in clichés but was unable to stop himself. He'd always been terrible at this sort of thing. In a better mood, it would have made me laugh.

I answered them with silence.

Mother frowned at father and looked back at me, then she looked down at her plate and cut a thin slice of chicken.

"Maybe you could move in with Corwin? You two have been dating for a long time. I'm sure he'd be happy to help you out while you recovered."

My silverware clattered as I dropped the fork and knife. My hands trembled with frustration and I took a long swig from my wine glass, hoping the alcohol would quell my anger.

"There is no Corwin."

How had my mother not realized that already? He hadn't been to the house in months.

"What happened?"

Bless her heart—she looked so concerned.

I took another large swig of my wine and coughed as some of the liquid went down my windpipe. How could I tell her? How could I explain to my mother, the woman who loved me more than anyone in the world, that my longtime boyfriend had left me at the first sign of adversity? When my moods darkened, he had started ending dates early. Eventually, he stopped asking me on them. And when my waistline and thighs had grown, and grown, and grown, well then he stopped coming on dates when I'd asked *him*.

How could I tell her that I was a bad judge of character? That I'd dated someone vain and superficial? I didn't want to face that embarrassment.

"We broke up. It was months ago."

And since there was nothing else to say, I stood from the table and went to bed.

The next day I avoided my parents, leaving the house for work even earlier than usual so I wouldn't accidentally bump into them.

At school I had trouble keeping my eyes open, having slept very little the night before. I'd been thinking about what a mess I had made of my life. Most of all, I was thinking about how helpless I was to change any of it. I yawned as I watched my gym class take place from a bench. The students were in the gym doing "free time," because I was too tired to organize anything else. Free time meant they could go to one of the four corners of the gym and play either basketball, volleyball, dodgeball, or tag.

The big problem with free time days was that there would inevitably be a corner that took a rest break that turned into social time for the students. That was when I had to get up and prod them to move around and play again. Otherwise, there would be trouble. I'd waited too long to break the groups apart this time, and a small huddle of girls had gathered around someone in the dodge ball corner.

I groaned as I stood and lumbered over to the group of girls, feeling aggravated that they'd made me stand up from my comfortable spot on the bench.

The girls were chanting something, and as I got closer I was able to make the words out.

"Wendy the Weirdo! Wendy the Weirdo!"

Great, I thought, *now I had a bullying situation to deal with.*

As I approached the group the girls parted to reveal Wendy, a thirteen-year-old social outcast who was often the subject of such bullying.

"This is unacceptable behavior!" I said, huffing from the effort of walking across the gym. "Girls, go to the locker room. Now. Think about what you've done until I come to talk to you."

Wendy wiped her eyes and started to stand up, but I put out a hand in the air to stop her from leaving.

"Wendy? Are you all right?" I felt bad for Wendy. Her family life was chaotic, and she had no home to speak of. Instead, she was juggled from family member to family member, depending on who was the most stable at the time. It made her vulnerable, and the other students knew it.

"Yes, Miss Kayla."

"What happened?"

"I told them about the voices," she said, her vocal cords trembling. "What they've been saying. I wanted to warn them. We all need to be careful."

I gulped. I'd tried to refer Wendy before to a counselor for the voices she reported hearing, but nothing had helped yet.

"What are they saying, Wendy?" I had to ask, even though I knew it wasn't good to indulge her imagination.

"The possessions are starting again."

I felt a chill down my spine. Where had Wendy heard about the Edgar Falls murders of 1981? A string of murders had taken place in the town years ago when I was young. They'd found the murderer, and he spouted such nonsense about masters and dark lords that he'd been given prison for life instead of the death penalty. They'd ruled him clinically insane. He had said there were more murderers like him but had refused to give names, even for a plea bargain. He'd been killed by a fellow inmate not long after he was imprisoned.

"Wendy, go talk to Mrs. Marshall, okay?" I said, my voice slightly stern. Truth was, as sweet as Wendy was I was worried she was going to crack one day and hurt someone.

Wendy snatched my arm in a sudden movement that made me scream. She grabbed my arm tight until it hurt. My eyes went wide with fear and surprise.

"Miss Kayla! Don't go to the woods alone. Don't go anywhere alone! It's not safe."

"Let go!"

She looked stricken and shrank back into herself, assuming her usual sunken-in stance and quiet demeanor.

My voice trembled when I spoke next, relieved that she hadn't done anything worse in front of the class.

"Mrs. Marshall's office. Now. Let's go."

I walked her up to the counselor's office in silence, and as she walked in she looked back at me once with a sad frown.

"Wendy—I'm sorry. You just scared me. It's going to be okay, though, all right? You and me: We're okay. Just keep your appointments with Mrs. Marshall."

Wendy shook her head slowly and whispered under her breath.

"Be careful. Don't go out alone."

After my harrowing day at work I spent the rest of the day shopping and wandering the historic downtown district of

Edgar Falls so I wouldn't have to go home to another lecture from my parents. I bought a jagged-cut, sparkling amethyst from the new age gift shop and pocketed it to give to Nora later as a peace offering. She used to collect them. It was a little bigger than my fist, and I was barely able to fit it in my pocket. I smiled, because I knew Nora would make some kind of crude joke about my bulging pocket. It was nice to have her goofy, blunt personality in my life again.

Late at night, after Nora got off work at the hospital where she worked, she and I started on our walk. She had chosen the Edgar Falls Park, the namesake for the town, to be our hiking location. As I got out of my car and walked toward the entrance of the hiking trail I watched the wind whip the Edgar Falls Park sign. It was a cheap sign: Canvas strung with a bungee cord to two poles. The wind made it bounce in a crazy, erratic manner that disturbed me, almost as if it were trying to get my attention or trying to warn me of something.

"Is it me, or are you happy to see me?"

Nora glanced at the ridiculous swollen pocket of my jogging pants where I'd stashed the amethyst.

I jumped at her voice, having been entranced by the jumping sign.

"So happy."

I stuck my tongue out at her and twisted my face into a goofy grimace.

Her comment made me think about my pants, though, and the thought made me unhappy. I'd had to get new jogging pants just for this walk. I didn't fit in any of my size sixes anymore. The fact that I was wearing a size twelve had been embarrassing, but it was better than exercising in jeans.

The tall grass brushed our hips as we entered the forest path that we used to take almost daily, before I'd become depressed. The familiar feel of it all was comforting. I felt my mind become calm as I listened to the steady thuds of our feet hitting the ground, punctuated by the sharp crunches of plant matter. The hoot of an owl startled us both, and we giggled.

It was eerie weather, with a deep fog settling over the trees with humid air that was thick and hard to breath. Nora had a flashlight to see in the dark, but I tripped on several rocks anyway, earning me several rounds of good-natured heckling from Nora. As we continued to walk down the hiking trail the trees became thicker and closer together, and I forgot about the amethyst I wanted to give Nora because my mind was preoccupied with just breathing.

I was embarrassed by how much I huffed and puffed. Was I really that out of shape that walking wore me out?

"You take up smoking recently or something?"

I started to laugh off the comment, but then I heard a shuffling sound far off to our left. I froze.

"Nora, point your flashlight over there. I heard something."

I pointed into the darkness where I heard the sound.

"Ugh. When did you get so jumpy? It's probably just a squirrel, or a opossum or something. We're in the woods. Animals do live here, you know."

The sound repeated itself: four distinct shuffles through grass and leaves. Each one sounded louder and closer.

"There it is again."

"It's nothing."

Nora waved the flashlight around in exaggerated erratic arcs. She started walking, leaving me several yards behind her.

I stayed still, trying to listen.

"Come on, let's keep going. You're just making excuses so you can catch your—"

Nora froze with a surprised expression on her face as the light caught on a human face lurking in the darkness behind a nearby oak tree.

We both shrieked at seeing the man's face, which had a loose, odd-looking smile peering out from under a blue ball cap. The man's eyes were shrouded in the darkness and shadow of the hat's bill.

"Abe?" Nora said, her voice trembling. "W-what are you doing out here?"

Nora gasped as her flashlight flickered, then went out.

Then she screamed.

I couldn't see, because my eyes hadn't adjusted to the absence of the flashlight, but I heard more rustling and an inhuman growl come from the man.

I heard a sickening snap, and a thud. Nora was shrieking, and the man was grunting with effort.

My heart raced and my mind reeled. Was this really happening to us?

"Run, Kayla!"

Nora gasped, her voice sounding choked.

Without thinking I sprinted toward the sound of her voice. My legs were as supple as springs as I ran to my friend's aid. I flung myself to the ground where she'd dropped the flashlight, and I swung it around to where the man was wrestling Nora to the ground. I saw the scene in flashes: The blood dripping from Nora's forehead, the ugly expression on the man's face, the red scrapes on the man's forearms where Nora had scratched, hit, and bit him.

I swung the flashlight back and struck the man in the head, hoping I wouldn't miss my target in the dark, wild tangle of struggling arms and limbs.

The flashlight made contact, and I heard a sickening crunch, yet the man didn't shout or cry out. He just turned with a slow, determined resolve and grasped the flashlight in his hand. His arm was strong, much stronger than it should have been for a man of his advanced age, and he yanked it away from me, throwing the flashlight far out of reach.

I backed away, feeling helpless and wondering if this would be my last night alive.

Nora was whimpering and cradling one of her arms. It was jutting out at an odd angle, as if it had been broken.

As if things couldn't get any more bizarre or terrifying he started chanting in a low, menacing voice as he closed in on me with his hands outstretched. There was an eldritch gleam in his eyes, and the language he spoke was one I'd never heard before. The moonlight gave his sweaty skin a sickly, yellow gleam.

Even though I couldn't understand the words I knew that what I was facing was pure evil.

So I ran.

I ran, focusing on the sound of my own breathing until I settled into a familiar rhythm. My feet, my hips, and my lungs worked in a holy communion to propel me out of darkness. It all came back to me then, despite my terrible physical condition. I could hear the man keeping pace behind me, ready to pounce, but I pushed on.

Once a runner, always a runner.

Then my foot snagged a log and I tumbled onto my face.

"Obey! My master requires your life."

I flipped myself on my back and watched as he leaned in close. I waited until his hands were almost around my neck.

Then I pulled the amethyst out from my pocket and struck him in the mouth. Spittle and blood flew from the opposite side of his mouth almost immediately.

The scariest thing was that he didn't react at all. He seemed to feel no pain. His tongue worked around his mouth for a moment, and then he spat a bloody tooth onto the ground as if it were something as banal as a watermelon seed.

I reared my legs back and kicked hard on his chest with both legs, and the momentum sent him flailing away. While he was off balance I struck again with the amethyst, this time on his temple.

And again, and again.

The jagged stone drew blood wherever I struck, but he didn't scream. In the dark I saw strings of something hanging off the amethyst. It took me several moments to realize they were pieces of skin that had been scraped from his face by the blows.

He laughed.

Even as he crumpled to the ground, he continued to laugh. From this new perspective, I saw that I had left a huge dent in his head with the stone. I felt a high-pitched scream come out of my throat unbidden at the sight.

He shouldn't have been conscious with an injury like that.

As the blood slowly seeped out of the wound, he ceased chuckling for a moment, and his eyes started to droop closed.

"It won't stop. I'm only a vessel."

Then the eyes closed. They stayed closed, and I resisted the urge to keep pounding away at his lifeless body, just to be sure.

I jumped at the sound of rustling behind my shoulder.

"It's just me. I'm going to go get the flashlight. Stay put." [*voice shaking*]

After a few moments, I heard Nora scream.

I ran toward the light of the flashlight and she looked at me with a horrified expression.

"What?"

In reply, she merely pointed the flashlight at a spot on the ground. There was a dainty-looking hand peeking out from under leaves. That was when the decayed smell hit me.

I struggled to control my gag response, but I failed and had to whirl around quickly and vomit in a bush.

"I think we found the missing woman."

She put a hand on my shoulder.

"Guess we should call the police." [monotone, traumatized]

Nora pulled out her phone and started to dial.

"Nora."

I gripped her uninjured arm hard. I was seized by a strange and macabre kind of joy despite the circumstances.

"Nora, I *ran*."

"I know."

She still held her injured arm in an awkward position. The reassuring sound of her ringing phone filled the night air.

"Nora."

I held up the blood-slicked amethyst up in my trembling hand.

"I got this for you."

She gave me an unreadable look and I dropped the gore-covered rock. She let out a strange, strangled laugh and shook her head. We hugged.

We held each other, trembling with sobs and hollow laughter until the cops and the EMTs arrived.

HELL IS LIVING WITH OTHER PEOPLE

J. H. Sullivan

Communal living can be such a headache.

I live in an old mill with my friend Breanna, which was converted into a block of flats with appalling sound insulation. If you live in an apartment complex you probably know what I'm talking about. If you don't consider yourself lucky.

The stairs in my particular complex convert sound as though they're made out of tin, and there's no way to climb them quietly, which means we can hear the comings and goings of every single one of our fellow residents. It can get annoying at times, but I cope with it. That's just how it goes, living in a city and in such close quarters. You curse, take some painkillers, and move on.

My downstairs neighbour is not so forgiving.

Our flat is on the second-floor, above an *extremely* pedantic neighbour named Linda. Remember the crotchety old guy who lived downstairs in Friends? Who used to bang on the ceiling with a broom? Imagine him, but middle-aged and a woman.

I sometimes feel sorry for her, as she lives alone on the ground floor and rarely leaves the house. Brianna and I, two

217

young professional women living a rather active and social lifestyle, probably do irritate her, but it's not intentional. We go to work, we go out for dinner and drinks, etc. I'm not about to apologise for being a woman in her 20s. We try our best to be nice to her – say hi when we see her in the hall, take our shoes off to creep up the rickety stairs, play music rarely and *super* quietly. Nothing seems to budge her disdain. After a year of living above her, I've accepted she's just rude, and we're definitely not the only ones in the building who've had issues with her.

Not long after we moved in Linda started shoving notes under our front door, mostly about noise. They were awful, hastily scribbled notes, written on paper ripped haphazardly from a reporter-style notebook, but she'd always sign them 'MILLS MANAGEMENT'. It's as if she thought the threat of authority would scare us into submitting. The complaints and warnings were always hilariously vague, with random words in all capital letters:

'We have complaints of TALKING BANGING and GENERAL NOISE all weekend'

'Please keep the NOISE down'

'Stop the GENERAL NOISE'

They weren't signed, but we know they're from Linda. After the notes I visited each flat in the building to chat about any problems they may have had with us. Every single one of them answered the door and had a pleasant chat with me, and stated they had no noise complaints, except 2 – the empty flat next to ours and Linda, who has a spyhole and didn't even bother to come out. I mentioned this to Linda's next door neighbour, who scoffed.

"She'll never talk to you civilly," she told me over a cup of tea. "She's never stopped complaining to me and I've owned this flat 10 years. She's driven people out of the building. If I were you, I'd try and ignore her."

It wasn't this easy though, as we found out Linda had also been complaining to our landlord, who began threatening to take action (see also: throw us out). We discussed the issues with him, but he told us he couldn't get personally involved – we'd have to sort it out with her ourselves.

How can we do that if she refuses to talk to us?

For want of anything better to do I slipped a note under her door (see how she likes it) apologising for any distress we may have caused, and asking if she'd mind just giving us a knock if we ever bother her again so we can keep it down. I don't appreciate being hassled in my own home, no matter how hilariously ridiculous the notes are.

The noise notes stopped after this, but Linda's strange behaviour didn't. She began staring at Breanna from her window every time my friend went outside to the courtyard for a cigarette. I thought Breanna was making it up at first – being paranoid – but one night I went to sit with her anyway to make her feel better. As we were sitting and chatting I glanced over to Linda's window, and there I saw it. A pair of eyes, staring right at me, from her slatted wooden blinds.

She didn't stop at just staring at us. One particularly rainy evening I decided to store my bike in the second-floor landing area one day, as I didn't want it to get soaking wet and rust. When Brianna and I arrived back from work that day (we're both office drones, 9-5, Monday-Friday), one of 'The Notes' had been left lying on the seat:

'NO bikes allowed in hall please MOVE IT'

It was kind of annoying – it was against the wall not bothering anyone, and had only been left there a few hours – but because we didn't want any more trouble, we took it inside. One thing was bothering me about the note, though. The bike was stationed on *our* floor, behind the door to the landing area. So why had she been up there at all?

The thing that creeped me out the most happened after the bike incident.

Our flat is basically a long corridor, with the entrance at one end, the kitchen at the other, and all of the rooms (bathroom, two bedrooms, and a living room) leading off the hall to the left.

The bathroom is the first room on the left as you enter, so if you're in bed or in the living room you have to walk towards the door of the flat to get to it. At night, because the landing lights stay on constantly in our building, you can see a strip of light at the bottom of the flat's front door.

A strip of light that sometimes, when I went to the bathroom in the middle of the night, was blocked by two leg-shaped shadows.

One Monday night at about 3:30am I walked swiftly down my hall to the bathroom with my head down, trying not to look at the door. However, my morbid curiosity got the better of me. Sure enough I glanced down to see those two dark patches. My heart was beating fast, and I locked myself in the bathroom, embarrassed at my fear. Slowly, however, this began to give way to anger.

Who the hell does she think she is?

Sitting in my own bathroom in the middle of the night, shivering and afraid to walk down my own hall, I'd suddenly had enough.

Why can't I climb my own stairs at 2am without taking my shoes off?

Why can't I play music to listen to while I do the dishes?

*How is it fair that I am **literally** tiptoeing around my own home to please this woman?!*

I pay hard-earned money to live here, just like her. I am civil to her, and she treats me with no respect. We've given her many chances to resolve this, get to know us. It's been over a year.

It's about time I confront this.

I don't think she actually expected that I would open the door in the middle of the night.

I know she definitely didn't expect me to whip out my heavy, metal bike lock from behind my back, and bring it down on her head.

I took the next day off work. I needed to…let's say…get my house in order.

As I said, she never leaves the complex. She has no visitors, no job. I imagine it'll be awhile before anyone comes looking for her.

In the meantime, I'll play my music as loud as I like.

The following Monday night at about 3:30am I walked down my hall to the bathroom, glancing down at the strip of light under the door out of habit.

What?!

To my utter fucking horror, I glanced down to see those two dark shadows blocking my door. Again.

This isn't possible.

222

I locked myself in the bathroom, my terrified brain working overtime. It must be a dream. Those aren't Linda's legs. I know because I sawed them off, right above her knee joints.

So who the fuck is that?

Nearly paralyzed with fear I slowly opened the bathroom door, just enough to peek out at that strip of light. As I stared I heard a shuffling sound, and could see movement in the light of the hall.

As I stared I saw a piece of torn-off notepaper, with hastily scribbled writing, being slid under the door.

'Please STOP this GENERAL NOISE'

DEATH WITH BENEFITS

Samantha Mayotte

I sold my soul when I was twenty-three.

I don't say this to elicit any sort of pity, shock, or fear for what will happen once I die. In fact, I researched the pros and cons of my decision quite thoroughly. I was even able to add an extra five years to my bargain without sacrificing anything I'd wanted in the process. What can I say? I've always been good at negotiations.

I stood by my apartment window, a glass of my favorite merlot held loosely between the fingers of my left hand. I was watching the sunset when I heard a knock at the door, a polite rap that somehow commanded my attention. Without setting down my wine I padded across the soft carpet and threw back the deadbolt.

I knew who it was the moment I saw him. I'd never seen his face, but the pristine appearance of his well-tailored suit, and the accompanying dread that filled me, gave him away. I had to admit, his blond hair and sky-blue eyes were beautiful. Being God's favorite all those years ago had come with some lasting perks.

It was the box he held in his hands that unnerved me more than his presence. I'd seen it only once before. I knew the symbols on it were my name in some ancient language. I gestured for him to come inside. "Not what I would have expected the Prince of Darkness to look like," I said, trying to play it cool.

He let out a dry chuckle as I led him to a chair and forced myself to sit on the edge of the couch across from it. My pulse beat so fast that I worried vertigo was soon to follow. "I assure you, this meeting will have no negative impact on your contract."

His expression had changed. I never knew that the Devil would worry about something, but there it was. A faint worry, well-hidden on his face, but a glimmer shone just behind his eyes. "If I'm allowed to ask then, why have you come?" I felt myself becoming defensive, adrenaline making me stupid. "I have eight years left on my contract. I have a copy of the agreement."

"I know what your contract states, Megara. I've come because, well, I need a favor." He was almost embarrassed saying the words. "If you accept, then this is yours to keep." He gestured to the box in his lap that contained my soul.

A favor? The Devil needed a favor. "What sort of favor?" I knew better than to blindly rush into deals like this. "If it involves putting my contract in jeopardy, I'll have to pass on it."

He smiled at me then. His teeth flashed, but there was no hint of fangs or bloodstains anywhere, once again shattering the fairytales my mind conjured of Satan. "It's a simple favor, really." He tapped his fingers on the box, drawing my eyes back to it. "I need you to collect a new soul for me. She's been keeping my demons tied up for weeks. All I need is for you to get her to sign." The wine sat in my hand, untouched.

"Meet with her tonight. I'll supply you with her contract. Make any changes you see fit to it during the meeting. The only caveat to the favor is that she needs to sign tonight, or your contract remains unchanged."

Something about the agreement felt too easy. "Why ask me to do this? If your demons can't make her sign, what makes you think I can?"

"You have something my demons do not," he said.

"What's that?" Finally, I took a sip of wine from the glass in my now-shaking hand. I knew what my answer was going to be, even before he held the box out to me that contained the precious part of me that I'd given up for my wildest dreams to become reality.

"A soul."

***

As cliché as it was, the meeting had been set for a café at a crossroads. I'd read over her contract as my Lyft carried me across town. I sat in a booth, nursing a coffee and waiting for the woman to show up. When the bell over the door jingled, I glanced up. She looked nervous, her hand running through mousy brown hair. Her head frantically went from side to side before spotting me, holding a stained white mug in my hand, a manila folder sitting on the table.

She walked over and sat down without a word. A waitress quickly came over to take the woman's order. A cup of black coffee and a slice of apple pie. The waitress limped off with a small smile, appearing after what seemed like no time with a slice of pie and a coffee pot. It was only after the waitress had finished that the woman – Marlene Sanchez – looked at me. "You're not one of them, are you?"

"No, ma'am. I'm something of an...outside consultant for your specific case," I answered, glad for my ability to think on my feet. "I've read over the contract, and it seems that, well, everything should be perfectly fine. What is it that you're hesitant about?"

Marlene looked around nervously, and I noticed the cross hanging from her neck. "Are you religious, Miss Sanchez?"

She nodded. "Yes. My whole life I've been faithful to God. Until...until..." she hesitated. I nodded encouragingly. "The doctors say the radiation is no longer affecting the cancer. They say I only have six months." Her voice broke, and I felt genuinely sorry for her.

"Your contract takes care of that." I felt a twinge of guilt as I spoke; it felt wrong trying to tempt a righteous woman to sell her soul for a handful of healthy years. "You would have ten years. Perfectly healthy. Not even a head cold." I smiled, making the gesture as warm as I could. If she worried about her children, ten years was a long time to instill her values in them, and perfect health meant there would never be a day she would be unable to care for them.

She sniffled, picking up her fork and poking at the pie. She was quiet a moment as she cut a wedge and put it in her mouth. I watched her eyes water as she chewed and swallowed. "I am all my children have. I promised I would be there." A tear that had been hanging slipped down her face.

I thought for a moment. How would I be able to make this deal work for everyone? I couldn't simply extend the woman's life, not without adding something else to sweeten the pot for Lucifer. "It's clear to me that you'd like to live, but unfortunately these types of deals don't work one way; you'll have to find a middle ground, somewhere you'd be happy letting go."

She looked around, as though she were searching for the demons hiding in the corners, overseeing our meeting. I wished I could assure there we were alone, but I realized I didn't know how much scrutiny I was under. "I would be willing to leave this world tomorrow if I knew my children would be taken care of."

Depending on her feelings on the matter of 'taken care of' that arrangement may last the rest of her natural life, and then some. Time to do some digging, get to the root of what she wanted. As politely and professionally as I could I began probing her, asking small questions in a conversational tone, assessing her answers and seeing where they fit, for both her and for Lucifer.

I made a few quick notes, realizing I had no need to. Each time Marlene answered a question the notes appeared before me, allowing me time to look them over, using my own thoughts to rearrange the statements into clauses. Her wishes were understandable, as well as the fears she intimated to me. Looking at the contract before me I had a feeling it wasn't a lack of understanding and agreement on the deal that stopped her from signing before.

"Alright, Miss Sanchez. I think we've got a good deal for you. You'll remain in this world until your children are taken care of in the ways you've specified in the deal." I gave her a sweet smile as I signed all the places I had to sign before sliding the paper her way. The pen that appeared before her was an old-fashioned fountain pen. The tip, I knew, was very sharp. "I just need your signature here and here, and your initials here. In blood."

Marlene hesitated. She crossed herself, likely saying another prayer. She looked at me for reassurance, and I held my smile. When she looked like she might slide the folder back to me, I opened my mouth. "I know this is frightening, Miss Sanchez. Not long ago I was in your shoes as well. Looking for reassurance that I wasn't about to have the wool pulled over my eyes by some demon in a business suit. Just think about why you're doing this. Think of your children," As I spoke, my voice dripping with sweetness and concern, I reached my hand across the table and covered hers with it.

She looked into my eyes for a long time, as though she were trying to see through into my soul. Being used to boardrooms, and businessmen who did their best work through intimidation, I held her gaze, keeping my expression neutral. Finally she gleaned whatever it was she was looking for, and she picked up the pen, deftly pricking her finger and signing.

She slid the folder back to me and I looked at her signature a moment before closing the folder. "Of course. Always good to have someone on your side. A copy of your paperwork will be waiting for you at your house." I slid out of the booth, leaving a twenty on the table. "The coffee and pie are on me. Good luck, Miss Sanchez."

I took out my phone as I exited the café with the manila folder in my hand, though I had no need to. A car was already waiting for me and I opened the passenger door, sliding into the seat. I handed the folder to the man in the driver's seat.

Lucifer gave me a small smile, taking the folder from me. "You've done well. Not only did she sign, but she actually feels as though she's done the right thing."

"Your demons lack empathy, which is just as well for some, but people like Marlene require that human connection to feel comfortable. Maybe you need to give them some sensitivity training."

I wasn't sure I like the smirk on his face as he answered. "I'll surely consider that, Megara."

There was a certain light in his eyes I didn't quite trust, and I began questioning motives for the umpteenth time. "Why her?" I asked finally. "Why have me take her soul in exchange for my own? What was the point of all this?"

"Megara, it's not the soul that's important. It's the purity of that soul. That woman: a devout Catholic, raising her children in the light of my Father. And you, whom I'm near positive would have ended up in Hell with or without a deal." Lucifer chuckled before he finished. "A pure soul is worth much more than a tainted one."

"Then what was my soul worth to you? Your demons didn't come close to getting you a decent arrangement for me," I said haughtily. I knew I was right, too. I'd played those demons like a fiddle.

"Your soul has more value than you give me credit for, Megara." As Lucifer pulled to a stop in front of my building he looked at me once again, his eyes glowing like I'd always imagined the Devil's might. I knew dread, fear, and panic were the correct emotions I should have been feeling, but I found I was more curious than anything. What could Lucifer have possibly wanted from me? "Before you go, however, I should ask you: how would you feel about an employment opportunity?"

I couldn't help the smile that spread on my face. Still, I wasn't one to rush into an opportunity without weighing all the options. As nonchalantly as I could manage, I shrugged and met his eyes. "Depends on the benefits."

THE TRUTH ABOUT WOLVES

E. Z. Morgan

Sweat. Copper. Wind, swift and tasteless. Dirt. Rock. Blood.

Being an animal is a very different experience than being a human. When you encounter something you react instinctively, instead of logically. A river becomes a slick, moving sound. Color melts into shades of green. There is less thinking and more doing. I am a flash of orange, blurry on purpose.

Of course, I am not always an animal. Only during the day. At night I revert to my human form for a few hours. I am a woman, naked and swathed in red thick hair. In the forest, by the moss-covered boulder, I have hidden a simple shift dress. When I was little, and my mother was alive, she showed me how to transition from animal to person. It is a stressful process, but her calm words still echo in my brain as my claws become fingernails and my fangs become smooth and flat.

Deep breaths, my kit. You are loved.

The people in town call me Sionnach. They don't know the truth about me. I like it that way.

I have thought of telling Retta, but not yet. She is a redwood of a woman. Retta stands above most men and knows how it makes them feel. And likes it. She owns a pub nearby and always gives me a bowl of soup for free. Pity, maybe. She thinks I'm an orphan. I suppose I am.

The night is alive with fireflies. A coyote calls on the wind. I can still sense the rabbits in their burrows. Being human allows me to connect these ordinary things with emotions. Joy. Regret. Sadness. Beautiful feelings these be.

Retta's pub is full of rowdy patrons tonight. As usual, it is mostly men who talk with their hands, mouths full of beer and meat. I slip in unnoticed. A fire is whispering from the hearth, its warmth a gentle touch. I reach the bar and slide onto a stool.

Retta finally sees me. A knowing smile reaches her dark cheeks. "Soup for ya, girl?"

I nod, fingers drumming on the old wooden bar. The men around me seem to be getting louder and louder. Inherently, I detest noise. Such clumsy hunters they would be. If I were that loud I'd never eat.

One of the men takes the stool next to me, leaning on an elbow. "How about I buy you a drink?" He has grayish hair and blue eyes that could cut glass. Not an ugly fellow, but definitely not for me.

"I'm fine," I reply, amazed at how soft my voice sounds.

"Nah, you need a beer! Retta, grab this lady one on me." He tries to touch my shoulder but I shrug him away. "Feisty," he jokes. The other men begin to laugh at his failed attempt.

"Not feisty, just not interested." I turn away from him, hoping he will get the hint. Human men are just as clueless as any other male.

Retta brings my bowl of soup. "Mushroom and rice," she says, rolling her eyes at the man beside me. "No beef tonight, Sionnach."

"Sionnach's your name, huh? You know that's Gaelic for fox." He sounds so proud of himself, like a pup who has just learned to bark.

"And what's Gaelic for 'fuck off?'" The men laugh, but I am deep in my spoonful of liquid.

The first drop of salty soup hits my tongue, and I savor each spice. The mushroom tastes of earth. When a human eats it can be slow, tantalizing. When an animal eats it must be quick. No chance to linger, lest it be stolen from you.

I am well into my bowl when I feel the man's hand crawling down my back. "The truth about me is that you will regret saying no," he whispers.

Without thought I grab his arm and bite down, tearing whatever I can away from the bone. He screams and jumps to his feet, blood spilling onto the floor. "Bitch!" he spits, cradling his arm. The other men grow quiet. Perhaps they also smell the blood, or more likely they are in disbelief that a woman my size has teeth so strong.

Retta has a hand on her chest. I let out a long sigh. Looks like I'll have to find a new town again. Slowly I rise from the stool, wiping the blood from my face. "The truth about women is that they bite," I tell him sternly. He is silent. I turn from the scene and begin running down the street, moving swiftly and noiselessly through the night.

I feel someone behind me. Without looking I know it is the man from the bar. His breath is angry. Blood drips from his wound. I quicken my step, weaving across lawns. He keeps pace behind me. In my current form I will not be able to overpower him without a weapon, or surprise. I also don't like to call attention to myself, regardless of how much he deserves the beating.

I reach the edge of town with the man hot on my heels, but as I face the forest I smile. I can feel that familiar itch. The turning process will happen soon. My fingers twitch and tingle. My stomach feels like it's about to fly away. I stop in my tracks and turn to face the stranger.

He looks hungry. I stand firm. "You cannot chase me like prey," I call to him.

"I want you, and I will have you." He begins taking off his clothes. He is so pink and fragile.

"I am no rabbit," I say. I am moments away from the turning.

"And I am no fox." Suddenly he is hunched on all fours, screaming like a madman. I watch in horror as he transforms. There is nothing soft or brilliant about it. His bones crack. His eyes move with his elongated face. Teeth cut through gum. His grey hair spreads like a rash across his skin. This is no man.

This is now a wolf.

I have never felt fear as a human like this before. As an animal fear is everywhere, but humans have the capacity for rational thought. I yell to him, "I can outrun you! I will burrow so deep you will never find me."

My fingernails begin to grow. My teeth begin to sharpen. And I see, coming closer, the other men from the bar. They are all hungry now. Some turning, others already turned. I can feel myself slipping away to the mind of an animal.

The tallest man laughs and offers me one last call before I disappear into my real form. "Didn't you know, wolves hunt in packs?"

SANDY

Amanda Isenberg

I haven't left my house in over two years. I'm what you would call an agoraphobic. Becoming a shut in wasn't a conscious decision. At first I just timed my outings to when I knew the crowds would be thinner, then one day I decided to skip going out all together. Then another day passed, and another. Now, two years, later I'm a recluse. A hermit. I don't leave, and no one comes in.

I've adjusted pretty well though. I had my faithful dog, Sandy, by my side. Sandy is loyal and caring, and calms me when I panic. We sit on the couch together to watch movies, we sleep side by side in bed, we eat breakfast next to each other in the kitchen. Then one evening everything changed.

It was storming that night. Loud cracks of thunder boomed and streaks of lightning illuminated the sky. I sent Sandy out to use the bathroom before bed. A few moments after I let her out I heard an ear splitting peal of thunder, followed by a loud thud outside. It was silent for a beat, then I heard a loud shriek. I took a deep breath, opened the back door, and called for Sandy. She never came back.

My fear and depression deepened after Sandy went missing. I found myself completely and utterly alone. I managed to carry on for a few weeks without her, but eventually I gave up. I sat at my kitchen table with an array of pill bottles laid out before me, ready to end it all. As I reached for my glass of water I heard a sound at my back door.

It was a scratching sound. Cautiously I crossed to the door, and I was able to make out a low whimpering. I opened the door a crack. A wet nose and long, dark muzzle pushed into the open door.

"Sandy?" I called hesitantly. I opened the door a bit wider. It was her. She was soaking wet and filthy, but it was her. I crouched on the floor to take her in my arms, ad she shivered slightly against me. Warm tears ran down my face as I held my best friend in my arms.

Her ears were a bit ragged, as though they had been chewed on. She had a few barely-healed scratches and puncture wounds, and she was much, much thinner than the last time I had seen her. Strangely, she seemed a bit afraid of my touch.

She refused to eat the food I set out for her, but she did drink plenty of water. We were both tired, so we went up to bed. Sandy didn't want to get into the bed with me. Instead, she curled up in a darkened corner of my closet. I fell asleep listening to her soft snores emanating from the open closet door.

Things went on like this for several days. Sandy was skittish. She kept a bit of distance between us, and still refused to eat. One night I awoke to a sharp pain. I turned on my bedside lamp in time to see Sandy darting back into the closet. I looked down at my hand and found teeth marks on two of my fingers. Some of the marks were deep enough to break the skin and draw blood. Sandy had never tried to bite me before. Clearly I needed to work harder with her, so I resolved to redouble my efforts.

The next morning I was chopping vegetables for an omelet. Sandy was lying next to the back door when I heard her whimper. I looked up suddenly, and the knife came down on my index finger, slicing the tip clean off. In shock I stared dumbly at the blood pulsing out of the stump of my finger. I ran to the sink and pressed a towel to my finger to try and contain the blood. I turned around to find Sandy staring at my severed finger. She licked it once, then opened her mouth, picked up the finger, chewed slowly, and swallowed.

I knew my finger wouldn't stop bleeding on its own, and I knew I wasn't going to the hospital. I did the only thing I could think of: I heated up a wide kitchen knife on the stove and pressed it against the nub of my finger to cauterize the wound. I almost passed out from the pain, but when it was over the bleeding had stopped. After cleaning up the blood, and popping several pain pills, I collapsed onto my couch.

From the kitchen I heard the sound of Sandy eating from her bowl of kibble, then I heard her pad into the living room. She jumped onto the couch, laid her head in my lap, and fell asleep. When I finally went up to bed Sandy climbed in with me and curled against my side. The next morning she happily ate her breakfast and was eager for me to pet her. I finally had my old Sandy back. I barely cared about my injured finger. I was so grateful to have my best friend back to herself again.

That day, and for a few days after, Sandy followed me everywhere. Things were perfect, but by the end of the week she began withdrawing again. Eventually she was back to sleeping in the closet and refusing to eat. I needed Sandy. I needed my best friend. I couldn't make it through these long days of isolation without her. I knew what I needed to do, but it was easier said than done. Finally, late one night, I found my nerve.

I chose my sharpest knife and separated my small toe from the others. I took a deep breath, then pushed the knife into the base of the toe. It slid in easily until it hit bone. Blood welled up through the cut and began to pool on the kitchen floor. Sandy's ears perked up and she cautiously moved toward me. I took another breath and pushed down on the knife with both hands.

I heard a crunch as the blade sliced through bone. With one more small push, the knife hit the floor and my toe was severed. Blood pulsed rhythmically onto the floor. Sandy greedily ate the toe, then lapped the blood off the floor and licked at my wound. I forced myself to cauterize the wound, then cleaned the remaining blood off the floor. Sandy and I fell asleep next to each other in my bed.

It's been a month since Sandy came back. I've come to understand the pattern now. Sandy needs to eat a bit of me every fourth day in order to keep her spirits up. As long as I stick to that schedule, we are fine. Life continues as it should. Sandy is healthy and happy, and I can go on. I still have a few fingers and toes left, and I know I'll figure something out when those are gone. After all, it's a small price to pay for my best friend.

MY HUSBAND BLAMED ME

Penny Tailsup

My husband's last words were an accusation. Nathan blamed me for his death even before it happened by his own hand. Nathan had always been like that, in life and in death, always finding ways to make his mistakes someone else's fault, usually mine.

"You didn't care enough, Ivy. This is *your* fault."

Some way or another he'd twist things, until I was on my knees and begging for forgiveness. His last words were intentional, one last shot from the grave...a guarantee that I'd never be free. His death was my fault, he wouldn't let me forget it. Death guaranteed the last word, an argument won and closed forever.

We'd been in the middle of a messy divorce when it happened. Nathan kept the rent-controlled apartment...I slept on a friend's couch. To be honest I didn't care. The scratchy fibers of the couch felt like freedom, something I hadn't had for a long time.

The only real point of contention was our dog, Piper. That, and the fact that Nathan didn't *actually believe* I wanted a

245

divorce. He thought I was trying to prove a point, and while he waited for me to 'come to my senses' he used Piper as leverage. It broke my heart when he refused to let me see her. On the rare days he allowed it, Nathan was sure to remind me what an act of benevolence it was.

My threshold for his bullshit only lasted a good year and a half into our marriage before I started worrying over ways out. The prospect of divorce was enough to get the pews at church abuzz with scandal, which I desperately wanted to avoid. I procrastinated—and tolerated—until Nathan's bullshit went beyond emotional abuse and became physical.

How did I even get to that point?

My answer shouldn't come as a surprise: I rationalized the red flags. When we met, Nathan was 28 and I was 18. I'd been eager to prove I was an adult and made mistakes learning what that actually meant. Nathan was an attractive man, made even more attractive by his apparent maturity. His initial possessiveness was flattering; I didn't realize he considered me a possession until we were already married.

With a divorce already underway, I was actually happy. My life was far from perfect, but the feeling of throwing off the yoke and becoming my own person again was exhilarating. If I could walk away with only one thing, I wanted it to be Piper. Nathan refused to give up his leverage, claiming I was too irresponsible and unstable to keep her. Unwilling to let him win even one more time I planned shamelessly, intending to get my dog back at any cost.

Nathan didn't expect it, but I was equally capable of guile. I knew what he anticipated—and frankly I didn't have much pride. When I was ready to make my move I didn't hesitate to humiliate myself. I let him think he won, showing up one morning and crying on his stoop. I begged him to take me back.

"I made a mistake!" I kept my head down submissively. The theatrics were necessary; an argument at the door wouldn't resolve anything. If I showed any sign that I wasn't there for him, I'd only find myself on the wrong side of a slammed door.

Barely able to contain his smugness, Nathan let me inside. Immediately his lecturing began—he steered me into the living room almost gleefully. My future ex-husband loved being right, he loved it so much that I might've gotten off easy...if I'd really been there to reconcile.

I grabbed a handful of tissues, dabbing at my face as I continued to blubber. I had cried a lot over the years—ugly crying, not the pretty kind you see on television. My face goes bright red and puffy about ten seconds in; it's not something you can fake. Hiding my face was the only way to guarantee Nathan wouldn't catch on.

"Let's talk about what needs to change for this to happen. I'll take you back, but you're going to have to try harder." Nathan gloated, the words sounded rehearsed. He picked up a notepad with a list of demands, further proof that he'd fully expected my return. Knowing him, he'd type it up and have me sign it when he was satisfied with the 'terms'...he wouldn't let me 'pull this stunt' again.

I pretended I was too overwrought to listen. I leaned forward, burying my face in my hands with a burst of unintelligible apologies I didn't mean. Piper had already waddled over on her short, stubby legs—giving my knee a comforting lick. The corgi bought my performance as readily as Nathan did. I reached down to pet her, unable to resist; it had been too long since I'd seen her.

Nathan sighed, tossing the notepad on the coffee table with an audible *thwack*. He wasn't angry (he thought that he'd won after all) but his patience wore thin.

"I'm making us some hot chocolate." He declared, "Try to get yourself together please, this is embarrassing. I don't want the neighbors to hear you crying again." never mind that he was always the reason I cried, he added:

"You're making us both look even worse than you already have. I wish you had more self-control, but...we'll address it. Things will get better, for both of us." he said that with authority, but the corners of his mouth must have been quirked in a barely concealed smile. No matter what he said, he was delighted. I knew that without looking. I heard Nathan get up, strutting victoriously down the hall.

That was what I'd been waiting for, a moment alone.

I made my move then; scooping up Piper and heading out the front door. My friend Nadine was my waiting getaway driver, peeling off the second I jumped in the car. We escaped to a symphony of squealing tires and the accelerating rhythm of my heart.

We'd made it. I had Piper and walked out without so much as a scratch! I couldn't help but grin, hugging a bewildered, but excited, corgi to my chest. Nathan had underestimated me—victory was sweet.

***

"That was badass!" Nadine howled with laughter once I recounted the story back at her apartment. We were all safely nestled in her living room while a Netflix binge played, ignored, on the screen in front of us.

"Badass?" I snorted. "All I did was cry until he left the room—then I grabbed her and ran. There's nothing badass about that."

"Standing up to that douche canoe IS a huge accomplishment, don't try and downplay it Ivy. With all you've been through...you've got guts." Her smile was infectious. I couldn't help but smile too, though there was still a niggling worry in my stomach.

It wasn't over yet.

That night Nathan called me over and over, and when I didn't pick up he left messages. I didn't block him, I always kept his messages for court. The messages escalated from annoyance to fury—and even begging. It was shocking at first, because I'd never heard him cry before. It didn't make me happy, it made me...uncomfortable. I couldn't help but listen—driven by morbid/masochistic curiosity.

Then came the final voicemail. He was no longer crying or screaming...his words were perfectly level and assured:

"You didn't care enough, Ivy. This is *your* fault." his voice held the tone of an ultimatum, but I just laughed. He was used to making demands—he was used to me obeying. He didn't even bother following it up with a threat. For a moment, I thought I was free...his words no longer had power over me.

I didn't know that these would be his last words to me...his last words to anyone. I got the news in the morning: Nathan was dead, a self-inflicted gunshot to the head. Is it bad that my first feeling was relief?

The police deemed it a suicide in record time, thanks in part to a note he'd left me (I declined to read it). The final voicemail suddenly had an unnerving perspective; a grip I couldn't shake.

Nathan had the last word, there was nothing more I could say. I became a widow, with no need for a divorce. Dutifully, I dealt with the aftermath. I didn't smile...it wasn't a victory.

About a month after his death I moved back in to the apartment we'd shared. I was reluctant, but knew I couldn't stay on Nadine's couch forever. The old apartment was a haunting collection of bad memories, so I tried to fix that: I got rid of everything. I used my savings to buy new furniture, trying to make the apartment look and feel completely different.

It didn't work, because Nathan had never left.

I heard him. Felt him, but...I never saw him. It was enough to keep me in denial, and I fell back into a pattern of stubborn rationalizations just I had in our marriage.

At night Piper would bark at something unseen. I'd hear creaking footsteps creeping down the hall; a slow and deliberate tread, like a predator waiting to be noticed. The building must have been settling. I'd pull up the covers, trying to ignore the oppressive weight of anxiety as I curled beneath the blankets.

Denial didn't stop the footsteps from coming closer, closing in on my cowering form. At the foot of the bed I'd hear Nathan's voice; his words woven with shadows, a tapestry of woe:

251

"You didn't care enough, Ivy. This is *your* fault."

A footstep followed each syllable; the mattress warping under his weight as he climbed under the covers too. I had to be imagining things...I told myself it was the guilt, guilt I didn't even need to be feeling. I'd tell him so, a wavering whisper...but that just made him laugh with incredulity at my gall.

It was worse when he didn't laugh.

I'd feel the bite of his fingers, gripping my throat with invisible hands. I'd be paralyzed with fear, gasping for breath while his tongue would trace the contours of my body, leaving an icy trail of putrid saliva and my own cold sweat. Time always seemed the slowest then. I couldn't move, but his grip was just tight enough that I could still scream.

"You did it to yourself!" became my shrieked mantra in the middle of every night. A prayer before the sun started its descent, medication, meditation, none of it helped. I was haunted, terror lurking in every shadow and unexplained sound. I wore a necklace of fingerprints, bruises circling my neck.

My nights became increasingly difficult to explain away. I lost it when I woke up one morning to find a ring under my pillow—my wedding ring, long abandoned. The simple band was a gleaming circle of etched gold, engraved with my broken promise: '*Forever Yours*'.

I dropped it in the toilet, flushing it down with stress induced vomit—but that wasn't the end of it. The ring appeared under my pillow the very next morning, within a stinking water stain and a single dirty hand print next to where my head had been.

The next few days were a repeat of the same, with alternating methods of disposal. It didn't matter. The ring kept reappearing, until one day it wasn't under my pillow. A moment of relief was cut painfully short—*it was on my left ring finger.*

I couldn't get it off, no matter how hard I tried! Trying only made it worse, tightening until my skin began to bulge and discolor. It didn't stop, even after cutting off my circulation...The metal bit into my skin, blood seeping out and running in rivulets down my hand and arm as I tried to drive to the hospital.

The gold was unnervingly cold, even when my skin was glistening red...my wedding ring remained immaculate, gleaming without a drop. It didn't stop, even when I stopped resisting and parked my car in the middle of traffic— screaming in agony— the ring continued to chew through my finger, until it was off completely.

It was only when my finger fell off and rolled under the driver's seat that the pain went away, giving way to a tingling numbness. I finished the drive to the hospital, managing to find my lost digit...but not the ring, it was gone.

The finger couldn't be reattached. While it wasn't a life-threatening injury, the loss of my ring finger was symbolic. It was a message: I was never going to get married again, I still belonged to Nathan.

The ring did not reappear after that, but I couldn't sit still and wait for Nathan to find new ways to hurt me. I knew he would, because the more I tried to ignore him the angrier he became.

Without any other options I went to church. It seemed silly even to me, but I didn't know where else to turn. After services were over I waited patiently for the congregation to disperse. I kept my head down, not making eye contact with anyone. I didn't want my plight to become gossip, so I wouldn't speak up until everyone else had gone.

Except in passing, I'd never spoken to Father Dan. Although I faithfully attended every Sunday service, I'd never felt comfortable asking for his help directly. Of course, I probably could have used his help a long time ago...'taking responsibility' for my mistakes had not ended well.

Father Dan noticed, taking a seat beside me once the church went quiet. His eyes were warm, his face lined with years of genuine joy and sorrow; he was a man who had heard and seen it all. I'd always found him intimidating, he wasn't exactly what you pictured when you thought of a priest. He was scruffy, with calloused hands and skin that was almost perpetually sunburned...I wasn't sure how he found time to get a tan, let alone the time to overdo it!

Once I was sure we were alone I told him all that had been going on since I'd moved back into my old apartment. I didn't hold back, finding it surprisingly easy to be honest with him. I showed him my left hand, missing a finger. To my credit, I didn't even cry. To his credit he didn't interrupt me once—just listened quietly to my entire story, withholding judgment.

"This isn't your fault." He told me once he was sure I was done. I smiled wearily when he said that—it did sound a lot more convincing coming from a priest. "Where's his body?" Father Dan was getting right to business.

I was surprised, but answered that he'd been buried at Memorial Park Cemetery. I watched as he wandered over to his office, only to return moments later with a shovel and what I assumed was a very old bible.

"Father, can you explain before I get the wrong idea?" I laughed nervously, eying the shovel. He smiled, not at all surprised by my reaction. He answered decisively, speaking slowly in the scripted way people do when they've explained something a thousand times.

"His body needs to be burned." He explained, "Unfortunately, since he's buried..." he nodded towards the shovel by way of explanation. "I'll also annul the marriage." He added, "I'm assuming the courts didn't deem it necessary to issue a decree of divorce upon his death?"

"They didn't, there wasn't a need. 'Till death do us part', right?" except Nathan hadn't parted after all. I felt tears build pressure behind my eyes, but I managed to keep them in check.

"That's poetry. Death isn't an end, it's a beginning. If you were happily married, would you really want to be parted from someone just because you'd died?"

"...No." I admitted, although I considered that a big if. *If* I was happily married.

"I have the authority to annul the marriage in this case, there are special circumstances. That won't sever his connection completely, but...the cleansing fire will." I didn't pretend to understand, but I had hope. Without further argument we both made our way to Memorial Park Cemetery.

It felt like the setup to a bad joke: *A priest and a widow walk into a cemetery*...only neither of us were laughing. However, for the first time since Nathan's haunting had begun—I felt safe. Father Dan waved at the groundskeeper as we walked through the gate. The groundskeeper waved back; not batting an eye when he saw us with a shovel conspicuously in tow.

My fears that we would be caught were quickly proving unfounded. This must not have been the first time Father Dan had to perform this kind of service. It was broad daylight, but that didn't seem to be a deterrent. No one bothered us.

"Is this really okay?" I bit my lip, watching him press the shovel firmly into the dirt covering Nathan's grave. I was surprised to see a priest doing this sort of heavy labor — when I offered to help, he wouldn't have it. Father Dan was considerate of me, pausing every few minutes to offer a kind word or reassurance even when his breathing became labored from the task at hand.

"You're so comfortable at a time like this...have you done this before?" I finally felt comfortable making conversation, breaking the one-sided silence.

"Many times, unfortunately." He answered, "Don't worry, this isn't illegal. You're the widow, you have the authority to allow this. Breathe, Ivy." His smile was compassionate, his tawny eyes crinkling at the corners.

"It's just...I don't know..." But my reaction must have been common, because he was calm and patient throughout. I'd always thought Father Dan was stern and serious from where I'd sat during the Sunday services, but now I saw that I'd misjudged his character.

When the casket was unearthed he had me step into the grave, where he then read a passage from his book. All I had to do was repeat after him, with my hand placed on the dirt caked coffin—carefully enunciating every syllable, although the recitation wasn't in a language I understood.

With that I was free. It was so simple I almost wanted to laugh—a lot easier than anything I could have hoped for in a courtroom.

I kept my distance while he salted and burned the body, adding a dusting of a strange black powder from a satchel at his waist. I tried to ignore the smells and sounds of burning flesh...It wasn't pleasant, even if he'd been dead for a while.

I refused to leave, even with assurances that I didn't need to stay. I needed the closure, so I waited as the fire burned unnaturally hot and bright—watching a column of black smoke rise dramatically up into the sky, as though Nathan were giving us both the finger. The thought didn't frighten me, it made me smile.

It was only when the body was reduced to ash that I braved a look inside what was left of the coffin. I almost wasn't surprised to see two golden rings, spotless and gleaming amid the ashes. Our wedding bands. Father Dan picked them up, despite my immediate protest—having lost a finger, I was naturally reluctant to see them in anyone's hand.

"Remnants like this have their uses within the Church." He assured me, "Don't worry, without Nathan's malice tied to this Earth any longer they are rendered inert." While I didn't feel completely convinced, I decided to believe him. This wasn't the first postmortem annulment he'd performed, and I didn't even want to know what else he'd done, or how often! Some things are best left to the experts.

"So he's...?" I had a million and one questions. Father Dan predicted them, and answered before I could even find the words:

"Gone. Without a physical body or marriage to tether him, he will go where he's meant to go now. Take a shower before sunset, since you'll be cleansed as well."

The muddy priest fished through his pockets and extended a business card, pressing it gently into my hand. Confused, I glanced down to read the embossed golden print: Father Dan's Plumbing and Exorcism Services. As my eyes met his with questions, he grinned sheepishly.

"My services are primarily word of mouth, I don't advertise because I only take on special jobs."

"You're also a plumber? Is that allowed?" I wasn't that I'd cause trouble, but the question stumbled out of my mouth anyway before I could think better of it. By 'special jobs' I guessed he didn't mean clogged toilets.

"Only as an extension of my ministry." He explained, leaving it at that. He mopped at his brow with a handkerchief that had seen better days, exhausted yet exuding a sense of deep satisfaction.

"Thank you, Father." I whispered gratefully, tucking away the card. I had more questions, but I decided it was better not to ask. I already felt like I knew too much, and I didn't need or want to know anymore.

"Go home Ivy, your duty has ended here." with a final pat on my shoulder, he sent me on my way. "See you next Sunday."

The first thing I did when I got home was take a long shower, washing away the events of the day and the past few months, watching my worries wash down the drain. Nothing happened, even when the sun set. I'd grown so used to nights of terror that I didn't completely trust the peace and quiet at first, but that initial apprehension melted quickly.

As I lay down to sleep, curling up with my corgi, I murmured a quick, sincere prayer. I took comfort in the fact that Nathan was gone. Remembering Father Dan's words, I smiled: *He will go where he's meant to go now.*

Who would've thought I'd be relieved that Hell exists?

RITUAL OF THE LOST AND FOUND

E. C. Woodard

I've never believed in ghosts. Even as a teenage girl attending a slumber party I thought the ghost games my friends would get so scared of were stupid. I did have some fun volunteering to be the first person to play Bloody Mary, though. I would walk into the bathroom, say the words, and when my friends came to check on me I would burst out and scare them silly. I've always had a level head, and I knew things like the afterlife and ghosts are coping mechanisms for people who can't handle the bleak reality of the world.

When I was 19 both of my parents were killed in a car crash, and I became one of those people.

I was despondent. My parents were the last family members I had left. I was an only child, without a lot of friends, and suddenly I was totally alone in the world. I spent so much time lying despondently in my room wishing that the crash had killed me instead that I was kicked out of university for low attendance. After losing that scholarship I lost my housing, and therefore contact with what friends I had made.

In short I needed a coping mechanism.

Searching for how to get over dead relatives led me to religion websites. Religion websites led me to check out new age hippie websites. This rabbit hole eventually took me to a small website with a collection of creepy pastas and horror stories specific to my hometown. It was tiny, but active. I clicked around for a while before discovering the following:

The Ritual of the Lost and Found.

Recipe:

This ritual is not for the faint of heart. In order to collect your loved one(s) from the jaws of hades and free them from an eternity of suffering, you'll have to go to hell and back.

You will need:

- *A rope*
- *A blindfold*
- *A knife*
- *Six drops of fresh blood*
- *Three red candles*
- *Three white candles*
- *A match*
- *Pen*
- *Paper*
- *A photo of your loved one(s)*

When the clock strikes exactly midnight, you must sit down at your desk. Place the six candles in a circle around your piece of paper alternating colors. Light them all in a counterclockwise motion with one match. If your match goes out before all six are lit, you must try another night.

Once the candles are lit – write a suicide note. It can be short or long, but it must be convincing. In order for you to access hell, you see, you must declare your intention. It is said to work best if you say you simply cannot bear to live anymore without your loved one. Tear the note out. Drop your six blood drops onto the note and place it somewhere easy to find. Blow out the candles. Leave the photo near your note.

Bring the rope, blindfold, pen, paper, and knife in a bag to the corner of Maple Ave. and MLK Blvd. at 3:00 a.m. exactly. A grey Honda Civic with no license plate will pull up. Walk straight to the passenger window and knock three times. The door will unlock. Get in, and keep your eyes downcast. The man driving the car cannot harm you – he does not exist in this realm. He can frighten you but he cannot touch you. He will drive you to the entrance point to hell.

This is when the man will give you a set of clear instructions to follow. Write them down, and follow them _exactly_. If all goes well… you and your loved one(s) will make it out by 4:44 a.m.

DO NOT:

Leave evidence of this ritual on your browsing history.

Tell anyone where you are going.

Try to engage the man in conversation.

Be male. This is important – only a woman can successfully complete this ritual.

Deviate from the man's instructions in any way.

If you are going to turn back – at any time before entering hell you can close your eyes and shout 'I WISH TO RETURN HOME.' The car will screech to a halt. Get out of the car with your eyes closed. You will wake up in your own bed with nothing lost but the time you spent attempting this. Once you get into hell, however, there is no turning back.

Good luck.

With tears dripping from my eyes I wrote out a convincing suicide note. I explained that my parents were the only things keeping me on this Earth, and that I would follow them to Heaven or Hell. As I pricked my finger, and dripped six careful drops onto the paper, a few tears joined them. For a brief moment I considered making good on my note and really killing myself. After all, it was unlikely anybody would even find it or me for weeks. The temptation passed, and I decided to at least try and see this ritual through. It likely wouldn't work, and if it did…With the tentative hope of reuniting with my only family I cleared my browsing history as instructed, gathered my objects, and left.

That's how I found myself at the corner of Maple Avenue and MLK Blvd at 3:00 a.m. with a bag full of suspicious weapons. I thanked God for the late hour – it was unlikely any policeman would be patrolling this innocuous suburban neighborhood right now. Just before the clock struck 3:01 a.m. the promised grey Honda Civic pulled up.

My heart threatened to beat out of my chest. Had this actually worked? Was I going to be able to rescue my family?

Could I go to Hell and come back with the only thing that mattered?

I nervously walked up to the Honda Civic. I gathered my courage and rapped on the window three times. Just like the recipe said the door immediately unlocked, and I got inside and kept my eyes to the floor. The car took off with a loud screech, and the doors locked. This is when I snuck a peek at the driver.

He was a tower of a man – it's tough to tell while a person is sitting, but he had to be at least 6'2. He wore a dark hoodie and a black baseball cap. Scars lined his skin, and his eyes gleamed with a predatory hunger I couldn't quite name. I reminded myself that he could frighten me, but not harm or even touch me. We drove for a few minutes before the gravity of what I was doing hit me. I'm a loser dropout – I wouldn't have a chance of making it out of Hell. Disappointment coated the tense silence in the car as I shut my eyes tight. I shouted,

"I WISH TO RETURN HOME."

The driving man laughed a harsh, sandpaper laugh. I opened my eyes and looked at him in confusion. This wasn't part of the ritual.

The man winked at me. I looked him in the eyes again.

"I, I wish to return home."

The words came out a harsh whisper. The man showed no signs of stopping, or even slowing down. Panic rose in my chest as I reached to open the door handle, only to realize that there was no inside passenger door handle at all. I banged my fist on the window and screamed for help, even though there was nobody around who could hear me. I remembered the note I left to ensure that nobody would ever think of looking for me as the man pulled me back into my seat with his warm, human hand.

MOTHER-DAUGHTER BONDING

Kitty Olsen

I think most parents have a fear of not being able to bond with their child.

I was a wild child, much to my mother's chagrin. I never sat still. Everything asked of me was immediately met with a 'Why?' I never remembered to take off my shoes when I entered the house, and they were nearly always covered in dirt. On rainy days I'd play 'mad scientist' outside, meaning I'd take some of my mother's best cups and start mixing mud and leaves together, stirring them with sticks as I imagined creating terrible potions.

But I never recall having a poor relationship with my mother. Even during my frightful teenage years, my mother and I never had a serious fight. Even nowadays I'll call her asking for her advice, and usually we'll be on the phone for an hour or two talking about what's going on in our lives.

I knew I wanted a daughter, and I knew I wanted a relationship like I had with my mother. When I turned thirty-one and decided now was the time, I was artificially inseminated.

Four weeks before her due date, little Mina decided it was time for her to enter the world.

I was so pleased when the doctor said I'd had a girl, but those first few days still make me sick to think about. She was so little, and I was terrified that she wouldn't make it. But she did. She made it through just fine, and I loved my little Mina.

It was pretty clear from the early days though that Mina was going to be nothing like I was as a child.

When I had started to walk I started running the very next day, but Mina didn't want to run. She wanted to stay by my side, where she felt safe. I never had to deal with constant 'why's', she listened to what I had to say the first time. Babysitters always reported that Mina was inconsolable when I was at work. Her first day of daycare she hid under a table and cried for me. It broke my heart when the owner of the daycare called me to let me know that Mina wasn't eating lunch because she wanted to eat with Mommy. Kindergarten a few years later was not much better. The teacher nearly panicked when he couldn't find Mina, only to find her hiding behind the backpacks and asking for me.

She was what some might call clingy. But certainly, I reasoned, she would grow to stand on her own in time. She would start to crave the independence I did. But there was no sign of that. She was my little shadow, and I loved that, but I worried that she'd never be brave enough to do something on her own.

It was a strange day when I was cleaning the house and realized that Mina wasn't right behind me, playing with her own toy vacuum and mimicking my every move. I stopped vacuuming and listened carefully. Quiet.

I headed down the stairs, and was starting to worry, when I heard her voice.

"...and that...is...a...result!"

I poked my head in the kitchen to see the most welcome sight.

My little six-year-old Mina had managed to get the food coloring out of the top cupboard and had taken several of my cups, filling them each to the brim with water and dripping color inside. With the most adorable scowl she took a cup with yellow food coloring, and one with blue, mixing them together in an empty cup. She nodded slowly as the water turned a pale green, picking up a clipboard and scribbling absolute nonsense with a bright red crayon. She'd been very careful not to spill a drop, and had even taken the precaution to put newspapers all over the floor like we did whenever we colored eggs for Easter.

I cleared my throat, and Mina nearly jumped out of her skin, dropping her clipboard on the ground with a clatter. She turned around. "Mommy! I'm sorry, I should've asked!" She cried out.

I shook my head as I walked into my daughter's make believe laboratory. I should've thought of this years ago, I thought as I examined her little colorful potions. "Well, you didn't make a mess. Where did you get this idea?" I asked.

Mina shuffled her feet on the floor before shrugging. "I dunno," She muttered.

I squatted by her little table and smiled at her. "I'm not upset. I used to play potions too, but I always made such a mess. Do you want to play potions with Mommy?" Cleaning could wait, moments like this were precious and rare.

Mina gasped before she nodded, her little pigtails bouncing up and down. "I do! I wanna play potions!" She picked back up her clipboard and made some more meaningless scribbles. "Should we try to mix the green and the blue together?" She asked.

I shook my head. "I have a better idea. Come on, my little mini Mina, I want to show you something," I said. I took her hand in mind and led her to my study.

Mina's eyes nearly popped out of her head as I pulled the green book back, causing the whole bookshelf to shift and slide out of place, revealing the secret passage to the basement. "I thought you said I wasn't allowed to go down there!" She said.

"I'll make an exception, as long as you only come down here with me," I said as I walked down the stairs. Mina clung tightly to my hand as we walked into the darkness. I flicked the switch and she blinked rapidly.

"Welcome to Mommy's workshop, Mina."

I walked up to the table and pondered continuing to work on my previous project before an even better idea came to me. "Mina, drag over the stool, I want you to get a good look," I said. Mina obeyed without question, dragging along that old stool before clambering on top. "All right, you choose three things to mix together. Tell me, what do you want to pick?"

Mina looked over the many bottles and jars, chewing her bottom lip thoughtfully as she made her decision. "One of ugly dead bugs, the crushed butterfly wings, and that water that's sparkly," She said, pointing at each thing as she said it.

What good instincts. My heart swelled with pride. "Good choice. Now, when you're older, remember to put on gloves when you touch things." I pulled on my own gloves in demonstration. "Keep a steady hand, keep your mind clear, and above all - have a little fun when things get boring."

I mixed each of the reagents together in a new beaker, the bug and the wings first before pouring in the fountain water. Mina's face was full of wonder as the finished product turned a bright gold. "It's so pretty..." She reached to put her fingers in before jerking them back. "How can we test it?"

"Luckily, I have a test subject all ready."

I picked up the beaker and walked to the corner, where my subject was covered by a blanket and chained to a wall. I threw off the blanket and the man shot awake, glancing about wildly. "What's going on!? Where am I?" He said, his voice slurring together.

I gestured Mina forward. "Don't worry, he can't hurt you. Throw the potion on him, let's see what happens," I said.

Mina carefully approached, eyeing the man with concern before taking the potion. She examined it before choosing to pour it on his face. I almost giggled. "Why did you choose there?" I asked.

"Felt right." Mina stepped by my side. "Now what?"

"Watch, observe."

The golden liquid oozed over the man's nostrils and mouth as he squirmed away. It seemed to meld with his skin, and his eyes went wide as he realized he couldn't breathe. His lips and nose had successfully transmuted into gold. He thrashed wildly, actually managing to pull a hand free to claw at his face. The shock in his eyes when he realized it wasn't just a seal was almost priceless.

I escorted Mina away as his struggles lessened, the poor experiment unable to breathe. "Congratulations. Mina, you just did what took me years to figure out on my own. Your grandma didn't believe in just giving me the answer. There's more ways to accomplish gold transmutation, but that's a solid way to do it."

"I, I did good?" The little girl seemed in shock.

I knelt down and kissed the top of her head as the experiment's thrashing came to a halt.

"I'm so proud of you, my mini Mina. Just remember, this laboratory is only for me and you. Our little secret. Let's go get ice cream, this is something to celebrate."

DON'T GO INTO THE TREEHOUSE

Jess Charle

"Don't go into the treehouse." It was the first thing Maddie ever said to me.

We met on my first day of McCormick Middle School. I was new to the area, so while everyone else had the tight-knit clicks they had started in elementary school I stood alone. I watched the blurs of my happy peers swarm around me, isolating me further.

"What treehouse?" I asked, startled by the sudden interaction. My square piece of pizza hovering in front of my mouth, the lukewarm cheese coagulating into grotesque shapes.

I looked down at the thin piece of grey-white paper in my hand:

Second Period. 6th Grade Literature. Mrs. Caldwell. Room E312.

I scanned the map of the school the guidance counselor, Ms. Stein, had given me. A plastic sign with the letter "A" hung above me. Hall E didn't seem too far, but were the 300's to the right or the left?

After getting lost twice I jogged through the door of my second period English class just as the tardy bell rang. I collapsed into an empty desk, banging my elbow loudly against the metal bar of the attached desktop. I bit down on my lower lip trying to hide my pain, uncomfortably aware of the many eyes that now lay upon me.

"You just moved into 220 Hedge Road, right?" Maddie ate a french fry, her dark eyes boring into me.

A heavy-set woman in her early forties stood from the large desk at the corner of the classroom. Her thin grey hair was dyed a drastic orangey-red. Inch-long silver roots contrasted sharply with the fake color. She walked towards the front and turned to face me. Using a worn, wooden ruler she pointed to the whiteboard behind her where a meticulous seating chart had been drawn. On the square that represented the desk by the door - the desk I now sat in - was the name George Henderson in neat, red lettering.

The pizza was rubbery in my mouth. "Yeah?" I said as I tried to chew it.

My cheeks burned as I scoured the chart on the wall as fast as I could, trying to find my name. I could feel everyone judging me for being an outsider, for not knowing the particularities of Mrs. Caldwell long before graduating the 5th grade. Finally, my eyes caught it: Lindsey Graham.

Maddie nodded. "I'm your neighbor." She said without inflection. "My family lives at 218. The red house. There's a treehouse in the woods behind us. Don't go in it."

I hunched my shoulders up to my ears in an attempt to make myself as small as possible as I navigated the narrow paths to my correct seat. I sat and inhaled deeply, trying to calm myself. Or to at least look calm.

Mrs. Caldwell cleared her throat and began her introduction to 6th grade literature. The interest of my peers waned and they quickly forgot about the awkward new girl, but I could still felt eyes on me.

"Why not?" I asked.

Beside me sat a petite girl in a black shirt and baggy pants. Her eye makeup was heavy and dark, her large lips painted a dark purple. She was staring right at me. We looked at each other for a moment before she turned her face downwards to the spiral notebook in front of her. She quickly scribbled something and handed me the sheet of paper.

In looping, clumsy letters were the words: *Hi, I'm Maddie.*

I blinked, not really understanding. I looked up to see that she was staring at me again, but this time the corners of her lips were turned up into a small smile. I waved at her timidly, returning the smile as I kept reading.

It was nice to have a friend.

Because Mr. Itch lives there.

We sat at the round lunch table, the other five chairs empty. I took a sip of my chocolate milk and looked up at the bare sky above us. The clouds stood motionless. Heavy and thick. I looked around. The outdoor section of the cafeteria was far from full, the day too overcast to draw a crowd.

Maddie picked up another french fry, examined it, and then shoved it in her mouth.

"Who's Mr. Itch?" I asked, unsure whether my new friend was an appropriate choice. It figured that the only person to talk to me all day would be insane.

Maddie's eyes grew dark. "Someone bad. Someone you don't want to meet."

My mother stood at the counter chopping vegetables, not looking up as I entered.

"How was your first day of school, love? Make any new friends."

"Uh...Sort of."

She looked up me. "How does one 'sort of' make a friend?" Her rich voice was light with amusement.

"I'll let you know when I've figured it out."

Maddie and I had lunch everyday that week. She was an odd girl, but she was friendly and easy to talk to.

The brisk autumn air that Saturday was intoxicating. The air was crisp with a cool breeze. I hadn't left the house intending to defy Maddie's warning, but the sun shone through the trees that lined our backyard like guiding lights beckoning me to explore.

Looking back over my shoulder the blue-grey wood of our new home looked old and heavy, but in a comforting way. Like a grandmother waiting for me to return and tell her stories of the forest fairies. I liked our new house. It had a wisdom to it, a knowledge that only old homes can possess. I faced the woods again and stepped forward.

The red pine needles cracked and crunched beneath my boots. The woods felt deserted. Private. Hidden.

Soon I reached a small river, slightly too big to be a stream. It gurgled past me lazily. Large rocks lined its sides, but there weren't enough sticking out from the water to form stepping stones to the other side. I looked around and saw a tree trunk that had fallen across the water twenty feet from where I stood. As I approached it I realized that it was a log that had been cut in two, the halves laid side-by-side to form a narrow bridge.

I followed the tree trunk and soon stumbled into a small clearing, which sat still and silent within a thicket of thin trees. Not even a faint breeze stirred among the branches. An indistinct smell of musk hung in the air, tickling my nostrils. In the middle of the clearing stood a fat, squat tree surrounded by brown grass, though 'stood' doesn't describe it well. The tree looked as if it were crouching. Preparing for something. On it's thick branches rested an old treehouse, five or so feet above my head. The wood was stained from years of rain and snow. Slats had been nailed into the trunk, leading up to a trapdoor in the floor above.

The smell grew stronger as I approached. I reached out and stroked the tree, relishing the feeling of its surprisingly smooth bark beneath my fingertips. The musk around me was interrupted with a new smell. Something floral. Or maybe woody, I couldn't tell. A shiver ran down my spine and I slowly backed away. Something wasn't right about it.

A groaned emanated above my head. It was not the groan of weighted wood, nor that of a human. Maddie's warning echoed through my brain and I turned away from the tree, the smell of wood and earth following me as I left the clearing.

A month later I was beginning to adjust to my new life. Maddie and I started to have weekly sleepovers. Each of our homes proved to be both alien and exciting to the other. Maddie's house was pure chaos compared to the serenity of mine. As an only child my home was quiet and secure, my privacy valued as highly as my parent's. Maddie, on the other hand, was one of five children, each one louder than the previous. Maddie's youngest brothers - identical twins named Steve and Brad - made a hobby of running from one floor to the other while screaming at the top of their lungs.

At first the house was as nerve wracking as it was fascinating, but soon I was able to see the coziness of it. At dinner time all eight of us sat around the large dining room table, the home cooked meal that Maddie's mother made spread out before us. Maddie's brothers and sister would fill the air with ideas and events, troubles and successes. Maddie's mom made a point to include me, asking about my interests, what subject at school was my favorite, what subjects I hated.

I liked her mother. My mom was tall, lanky, slow speaking and methodical, with cold steel-grey eyes that scrutinized every detail. Unlike her Mrs. Harris was short and stout, quick tongued and with laughter so large it seemed to engulf her whole being. Her voice was high with constant excitement, almost in a manic frenzy. Questions and answers piled on top of each, leaving the other party little room to respond. Her eyes were a bright warm brown, the edges of which were constantly wrinkled with her wide smile. I'd answer her questions and nod at her responses and suggestions. In one breath she'd tell me how much she loved *Jane Eyre* at my age, scold Steve to stop kicking Maddie's younger sister Lana, and ask me if I was enjoying my mashed potatoes.

Maddie was the second eldest. Her brother, Tim, was five years older than us. The first time I stayed with her I couldn't help but notice how handsome he was. He had brown, subtle curls that framed his long face. Dark stubble cast a slight shadow down his strong jawline and across his high cheekbones. His brown eyes were clear and focused. They weren't the warm eyes of his mother, but were colder, revealing confidence and power. He didn't look at things, but instead stared with a great intensity as if scrutinizing everything, trying to see beneath the skin, the image, into the depth of something's essence.

I wanted him to look at me with that intent stare. I wanted him to touch me, to kiss me, to want me. But he paid little attention to me. I blamed my young age, my lack of curves, my lack of breasts. I felt ugly and young, painfully aware of my mousey hair and heavily freckled face, still round with youth.

One weekend Maddie and I spent the evening eating popcorn and Oreos while watching rom-coms with Mrs. Harris. It was unexciting, but I loved every second of it. The friendship, the comradery.

At eleven Maddie and I went to bed. It wasn't long before I heard faint snores coming from the bed where Maddie laid. I turned in my sleeping bag, unable to sleep. My mouth was dry and uncomfortable, probably from all the junk food we ate. I slowly got out up, careful not to let the nylon shell rustle with the movement, and made my way down to the kitchen.

As I passed the living room I noticed Tim sitting on the couch watching television. The room's lights were off, and the flickering screen cast blue and black shapes across his face and chest. My cheeks grew red when I realized he was wearing nothing but a pair of plaid boxers. I didn't notice I had stopped until Tim suddenly turned his head to look at me. His brown eyes drilled into mine, his face expressionless. His blank stare was penetrating.

He pushed himself up from the couch and approached me. His long limbs hung loosely, his body relaxed. Yet his gaze was firm and holding, his eyes never leaving mine. I tried to quell the tremble that threatened to run through my body. He stood tall in front of me, and I craned my neck to look up into his face as I ignored the chest hair that covered the front of his torso directly in front of me. Tim leaned towards me, and I thought I would lose control of my bladder. I wasn't ready for this. I didn't know what to do or what was going on, but I knew that the fear echoing inside of me, making my insides feel empty and far away, wasn't right. Whatever this was, this closeness, this intimacy, it wasn't healthy. It wasn't supposed to feel like this.

His lips stopped beside my ear. His breath was warm and moist against my skin, causing my flesh to prickle.

"Boo." He whispered.

I turned on my heels and ran up the stairs, taking two steps at a time. I slammed the door of Maddie's room, my heart pounding, tears forming in the corner of my eyes. Maddie groaned and turned, but did not wake up.

Curling back up into my sleeping bag, hugging my knees to my chest, I shook with the memory. A memory that both frightened and excited me.

I began to avoid Tim. Part of me was still attracted to him, even more so from our bizarre encounter, but I decided I prefered to admire him at a distance. I liked to think of him, and to mentally replay that night, but the idea of talking to him or having his eyes on me again caused my stomach to twist. He was better as a fantasy than a reality.

As the school year continued I found my heart fluttering for other boys in my grade, and even went to the school dance with Matt Rickson. Maddie and I continued to have regular sleepovers, but I was able to keep a distance from Tim.

Almost.

It was late one night, and we were watching slasher films at Maddie's. She had fallen asleep and was snoring peacefully beside me as I watched the final girl run through the woods, tripping over branches. Her white shirt was brown with mud and ripped to expose her soft flesh covered with fresh cuts.

The film ended with dawn breaking over the untamed southern landscape while our heroine - only powerful in her ability to not die - hopping into the back of a farm truck.

As the credits rolled the room fell into an uncomfortable darkness.

"Maddie?" Her snoring continued.

I heard a noise and squinted my eyes to try and see through the darkness. A light turned on down the hallway, barely illuminating the space in front of me. I stood and followed it to the kitchen. The fridge door was open.

"Mrs. Harris?"

A lanky figure stood, his cold eyes piercing me instantly. I froze. He smiled.

"Hiya Lindsey." He said, his voice dripping my name out as if it were a bloated, heavy liquid.

I swallowed. "Hi Tim."

He closed the fridge door lazily, "What are you doing up so late?"

The clock on the kitchen wall beside me read 2am. "Watching movies." I shrugged, trying to make the gesture seem nonchalant. "I'm going to head to bed now." My foot began to slide back past the kitchen barrier.

"Wait." Tim commanded. I hesitated while he walked towards me, his stare gluing my feet to the floor. He looked at me how a wolf looks at a lamb. "Do you want to hear about Mr. Itch?"

The name rang in my ear. I remembered the first conversation I ever had with Maddie, months before.

"Don't go into the treehouse."

"Why not?"

"Because Mr. Itch lives there."

I shook my head, taking a step back from Tim. He grabbed my arm. A small whimper escaped my lips and I tried to pull out of his grasp, but he tightened his hold.

"Has Maddie told you about Mr. Itch?"

I nodded, slowly.

"I bet she told you he lives in the treehouse."

I looked back down the hall towards the dark living room. I wanted to yell for help, but my throat was too tight.

Tim moved his lips to my ear and whispered, "Sometimes, Mr. Itch leaves the treehouse." His breath felt scratchy against my skin and hot tears welled in the corners of my eyes. "Mr. Itch likes little girls, and sometimes Mr. Itch leaves the treehouse to come and get them."

He pulled me against him. I felt something move by his leg, and I squirmed to get away from it. It felt like something really, really bad. Something I didn't want to touch me.

"Tim!" Maddie's voice broke through the scene, shattering the tension as if it were glass.

Tim let go, and I ran into Maddie,'s protective embrace. She glared at her brother, and I buried my head into her shoulder. I could feel Tim's heavy presence pass beside us, and I heard his footsteps grow faint as he climbed the stairs towards his room.

We only had sleepovers at my house after that.

The air hung heavy beneath dark cloud when Maddie showed up on my front porch. My mother and I greeted her warmly. It had taken some time for my mom to get used to Maddie's thick eyeliner and dark lipstick. All the studs and buckles. But she had grown to know and love the girl beneath all of the black.

We were an odd couple of sorts. I wore knit sweaters and plaid skirts, thick stockings and Mary Janes while Maddie looked like she had just stepped out of a Hot Topic after a shopping spree, but we loved each other like sisters.

One night, at one of our usual sleepovers, I awoke suddenly. My bed was warm and comfortable from my body heat. I turned, pulling the covers tight around my shoulders. I closed my eyes, determined to drift back to sleep, but something was keeping me up. Then I realized what was off in the room. I couldn't hear Maddie's heavy breathing.

I peered over the edge of the bed. Maddie's sleeping bag was empty, lying flat against the carpet. I cautiously dropped my legs to the floor and, tiptoeing to avoid making a sound, I walked into the hallway. The bathroom door was open, the light off. I continued past it and down the steps to the kitchen. Maddie wasn't there either.

Light moving beyond the small window above the sink caught my eye. A flashlight beam was dancing across the ground, bobbing steadily towards the forest. I could make out two figures behind the light. One was tall and lanky, the other short and thin.

Maddie.

I raced upstairs, still careful to not make a noise - I didn't want to get Maddie in trouble for leaving the house so late at night - and threw on a pair of jeans and some wool socks. In the mud room I stepped into a pair of old boots, grabbing a jacket from one of the hooks. A wicker basket sat in the corner of the room, full of things one might need before going outside. I reached inside and found a flashlight.

With that I was off.

The cold air pierced my naked neck and cheeks as I jogged through the now-familiar woods. I slowed only as I crossed the makeshift bridge over the creek, which gurgled and ran menacingly beneath me. My flashlight illuminated the wood before my feet, but the water beneath was black.

Running again I exploded out of the woods and into the clearing. The treehouse loomed in front of me, and I approached it for the second time. It was bigger than I remembered, the tree beneath its floor more knotted, its branches more twisted and tangled. Its trunk was thick and black. Its roots ripped through the earth around it, stretching up towards me.

A high-pitched scream filled the air, startling me into action. I recognized the voice immediately as Maddie's, and before I realized it my feet were pushing against the hard cold dirt, propelling me forward towards the treehouse.

Thrusting the flashlight into my jacket pocket I grabbed one of the pieces of wood nailed into the tree trunk, and as my hands wrapped around it a piercing chill cut into my skin. I yelped in pain, but did not let go. I reached for the next rung and my breath caught sharply as the wood seemed to cut into my hand like a knife. Pulling myself upwards was agony, but Maddie's screams kept me going.

I pushed the trapdoor of the treehouse with one hand, holding tight to the ladder to keep my balance. The door opened a crack, and then fell hard above me. It was too heavy.

Moving my feet up a rung I pushed again, this time straightening my legs to rocket all of the force I was capable of into the door. It swung up, then fell to the other side with a loud crash.

With a hand on each side of the opening I pulled my head up into the treehouse, and what I saw was a confusing mess of nightmare and reality. A stabbing pain dug into my skull as I looked at two identical rooms, each superimposed over the other. Two realities played out in front of me, both as real as the other. The closest thing I can compare it to is taking off the red and blue glasses while watching a 3D movie. My stomach twisted with the sensation, and I thought I was going to be sick both from the tableau in front of me and the sensation of two overlaid images. My eyes were unable to focus on either one.

Time felt like it was frozen as I took in both scenes, like a horror movie paused before me.

In both the interior of the treehouse looked the same. It was as if someone wanted to recreate the overkill of macabre gore you find during Halloween, but with real blood and viscera. The walls were streaked with red clumps of organic matter, many of which were pierced with splinters of bone. Raw animal pelts hung from the ceiling. Skulls were deconstructed, eye sockets and jaw bones hung together, tied with twine like repulsive windchimes. The largest one, a combination of multiple skulls, hung in the middle of the room like a gruesome mobile.

Vomit tickled my throat as I noticed the corpse of a crucified cat nailed to the far wall, its front paws stretched to either side, its back legs nailed one on top of the other. Around its head was a crown made of thorns. Trickles of blood dried from where the nails bit into the wall. The smell of wood and earth filled my nostrils, mixing with the rusty scent of blood.

I tried to focus my eyes, but the scene was too muddled. There was a muffled scream. Maddie's scream. It gave me something to focus on.

Tim was on top of Maddie, his hands around her wrists, his weight pushing her down into the wood. She wriggled beneath him, crying out in pain. Her ripped pajamas were in a pile beside her. A low grunting noise was coming from Tim as he heaved up and down. The smell of sweat mixed with the foulness of the air.

It was only a moment before my eyes rejected the sight. I inhaled sharply, terror reverberating through me as I squinted, focusing again on the image behind the image.

Tim was in the same position, his arms holding Maddie down against the dirty wooden floor. Above them was a shadow. It was shaped like a man, but it's darkness was heavy, as if made of actual matter. The silhouette was stretched upwards, its limbs elongated down towards Tim and Maddie.

The shadow, thick and viscous, began to draw forward. Maddie's body twisted, and her face distorted as she screamed again. Her voice seemed to echo against the meaty shadow. Its head came down to her mouth as the rest of the being laid over her. Tim continued to hold her down, allowing the beast to lie on top of her. The smell of cedar filled my nose, accompanied by an earthy, wet scent. It wasn't the scent of dirt, but of a burning rubber. I recognized it as tar. The scent burnt my nostrils and assaulted the back of my throat.

My head began to hurt looking at the double image and I felt nauseous. My brain spun.

I swallowed, pushing my mind forward through the haze. With a scream I lunged at Tim. Startled, he fell to the floor. Maddie was crying, blood staining her thighs. I grabbed her and pulled her back down through the trapdoor with me, collapsing as we fell to the hard ground. I heard a sickening snap as I stood, my ankle going out beneath me with a horrifying pain.

Maddie, standing naked beside me, grabbed my arm and pulled me up and over her shoulders. Using her as a support we hobbled towards my house. I turned my head to see Tim climbing down the ladder, his pants hanging loosely around his thighs as he held them up with one hand. He jumped to the ground, and I noticed that the tips of the grass were white with the first frost of the season.

I turned away from him. The creek was only a few feet away. We were slow, but steady. Tim's angry cries rose behind us, but we didn't slow.

The bridge groaned with our weight, the wood too narrow for Maddie and I to walk next to each other. We had to rotate, Maddie first. I held on to her, looking at her instead of the water beneath us. As Maddie's bare feet touched the other side I felt the tree sag behind us from additional weight.

Tim's pants were fastened around his waist again, leaving his hands unhindered. They reached for me greedily. As I screamed my good foot slipped and I fell onto the narrow bridge, hitting my tailbone hard.

With tears in my eyes I looked up at Tim, who loomed over me. His face was twisted into a deranged smile, his eyes bulging circles of white and red. His hair stuck up in odd angles, and his chest heaved with excited breath. He reached a hand down to me and I closed my eyes.

There was a dead thunk, and I opened my eyes just in time to see Tim land with a yell into the water below us. Maddie stood over me breathing hard, a large branch in her hands. She looked down at her brother with pure hatred.

She extended her hand to me and I grabbed it. Together we stumbled back home.

The next few weeks were a blur. Tim was sent to the hospital with hypothermia, and I was put in a cast for my broken ankle. Once Tim recovered he was taken into police custody. Maddie and I had to testify against him. We were forced to describe what he had done to us in all its brutal detail, but I never mentioned the black shape, the beast in the treehouse and the magic spell it had cast over my eyes and mind. The case was simple. Open and shut as they say on crime shows.

***

Maddie came to live with me and my parents after the trial. Mrs. Harris was devastated that her eldest son was sent to jail, even though his sentence was only for a few years. Maddie felt alienated from her family and her home.

I avoided discussing that night with Maddie. I wanted to ask her why she went with Tim in the first place, and I still want to ask about it, but I know it doesn't matter. All that matters is what happened in the treehouse.

I'm 16 now. Maddie tried to commit suicide last year, and is now living in a special home for troubled teens. I haven't seen her in months. My last memory is her pale face looking out at me from her window, the trademark black eyeliner and dark purple lipstick making her look like a drowned corpse under crystal waters, searching for me. Begging for help that I could never provide, for healing that could never be.

Tim was released and is living back with Mrs. Harris. He's on the sex offenders list, but it doesn't seem like enough. They say he won't come after me. They say that I'm safe.

I don't feel safe.

Since that night I dream of Mr. Itch a lot. The dark shadow beast. I see his arms reaching for me as I'm frozen to the floor in fear, unable to tear myself away. My gaze glued to his dark, faceless head. I wake up most nights screaming. My mother comes in and hugs me, hushing me and telling me it's okay, letting me calm down in her reassuring grasp.

Last night in my dream Mr. Itch bent down, his shadowy presence only inches from my face. His body was hovering just above my own, and he began changing. The slinky, wet mass shifted and morphed into a human. At first I thought I was seeing Tim, that it was those hands that will haunt me forever. Reaching, grasping, holding me down. But the face was older. Much older. The face was harsh, a thick rust-brown beard barely brushing against my chin.

It was Mr. Harris, Maddie's dad. My memories of her home came back with a new focus. A focus that included a large, portly man, face stained red with alcohol and fatty foods. His nose wide, his skin greasy. Mr. Harris. The quiet father sitting at the end of the dining room table, an open beer can beside him. The father who disappeared during Tim's trial. The father who no one's seen in years. The roofer.

The man who always smelt of cedar and tar.

SWEET TOOTH

Melody Grace

For as long as I can remember, my town has been terrorized by tourists, and the monster. Starting at a very young age, we are taught just two simple rules; avoid sweets - as it will entice the beast, and do not make friends with any visitors. They can be deceiving. While most of us heed this advice with great care, others would pay for their rebellions.

Take Tommy Jameson for instance. He was never one to listen to our elder's warnings, always telling us that they used this idea of a monster, to make us behave and eat properly. I'll admit, it made a lot of sense. Until the day Tommy brought donuts to class. He sat all the way in the back during our morning lecture, stuffing his face with the delicious jam fill desserts, as we all watched in horror.

He extended one of his powdered covered sins to Stacey, who promptly shot him a disapproving glance, before turning her back to him as she faced the front. Our teacher Ms. Raine however, occasionally gazed upon him with a fervent smile as she continued her lecture; she never did care for him much.

When class had finished, Ms. Raine asked Tommy to stay behind. We could all feel the tension as we walked out. I held my breath as I inched towards the front. I took one last glance at Tommy's arrogant expression, before Ms. Raine closed the door behind me.

The next morning, she told us that Tommy had been expelled due to his disruptive behavior, but we all knew the truth. Our suspicions were confirmed, when his body was found in the woods later that week. Well, what was left of it anyways. He had been violently ripped apart limb from limb with his vital organs missing.

All of the adults in our town would hold weekly meetings, especially after a death. I assume discussing how to contain the monster from attacking one of our own. They were never successful. When rules get broken, people get hurt.

Years went by, more people disappeared; some of them never having been reported, as it was all part of living in this God forsaken town.

When I reached the age of thirteen, I had my first run in with the monster. I was walking home from class, when a visitor approached me, asking for directions to the nearest shopping mall.

She was absolutely beautiful, with long amber hair that glowed when the sun touched it. Her voice, serenaded me in song as she repeated her question. I was hypnotized. My heart began thudding rapidly in my chest as she moved closer, and then it hit me, like a cool breeze on a hot summer day. The sickly sweet smell enveloped my whole body, leaving me stiff as a board, yet begging to follow her every move.

The woman stared at me with deep emerald eyes, enticing me, drawing me in. I took another deep inhale of her sweet scent before snapping back into reality. Adrenaline began coursing through my veins. I knew what she was, my parents had warned me about the monster's tricks. The beast came in all disguises, that's how it traps you, with its only tell being the redolence it gives off before it attacks. *Always avoid the tourists.*

I stumbled backwards, waving my arms out in front of me as I begged for it to stop. Pleading for my life. The "woman" appeared frightened at first, then stared at me with betrayal in her eyes, before bolting back towards the town. I quickly jumped to my feet, running in the other direction. Never stopping to see if she had followed.

As I reached my house, I bounded through the front door, causing my mother to drop the plate she was washing in all of the commotion. Out of breath, I began explaining my close call. She immediately yelled for my father. He came around the corner, surprise on his face, as he caught sight of my frightened expression and trembling body.

My mother glanced at him with worried eyes as my father placed his hand on my shoulder. "I think you are old enough now, son," he said, beckoning me to follow him to the kitchen table. Once we sat down, my father told me the ugly truth about our town and the ominous monster that has always tormented those who live here.

From that day forward, I was more terrified of the awful beast than I had ever been. Every tourist caused my body to tremble with anticipating desire. The scariest part; I have no preference, they all smell the same to me, all giving off the sickly sweet scent that makes my mouth water. All the while, the monster is there, taunting me with three simple words over and over inside of my head - *just one taste.*

THE LOVE SIMULATOR™

Blair Daniels

"You are so *fucking* self-righteous!"

"I'm just doing what I think is best --"

"For you, or for *us?*" I asked. "You know what? I wish -- I wish I'd married Dan instead!"

Of course I didn't mean it. Exes are always better in retrospect, eroded to perfection by the sands of time.

But it was too late. Tommy slammed the door in my face.

I plopped down on the couch, my heart pounding. After staring at the wall forever, I pulled out my computer and typed into the search bar: "what to do if you married wrong man." Hoping for a self-help article, or maybe even some sort of wikiHow on divorce.

I got something else instead.

Marriage Troubles? Try the Love Simulator™! Only $19.99!

Curious, I clicked. I half-expected a porn site -- which, honestly, would be fine by me.

But it wasn't. A page loaded up. Hot-pink Times New Roman on a black background, like some sort of '90s Geocities monstrosity.

Welcome to the Love Simulator™

Worried you'll marry the wrong person? Or that you already did? Find out below!

Below were rows. *Your name. Your love's name. Your Facebook page. Your love's Facebook page. Click here to upload photos, videos, and sound clips. Remember -- the more information you give us, the more accurate the simulation!*

It's probably nonsense. But I needed a distraction. Maybe I'd get a good laugh.

My cursor hovered over the Submit button.

Click.

The scene that loaded reminded me of the Sims, with crappier graphics. A 3D living room. Blocky armchairs with ugly brocade textures. A vase with some bubbly things that only mildly resembled flowers.

A man sat on the sofa. His face was Dan's -- but it was weirdly stretched and warped. His Facebook profile picture was a texture, mapped haphazardly to the cylindrical face.

"Hi. Kasey," an automated, stilted voice said from the speakers. "I. Love you."

Despite myself, I laughed. "Uh. Hi. I love you, too." The words felt weird on my lips when spoken to someone other than Tommy, even if it was just a computer program.

"How. Are. You. Doing?"

"Uh, not so good, Dan, to be honest."

"I'm. Sorry," the voice said. *Oh, this is kind of neat. Must have some sort of speaking recognition...and an AI...like those old AOL chat bots.* "Is it. About. The fight?"

"Uh, the fight?" I said into the microphone.

"I'm. Sorry. I fought. With you." The pixelated, still eyes from Dan's profile picture stared out at me. "I. Love you. Kasey."

"I love you too."

"Also. Also," it started, tilting its head. "I am. Not. Self, righteous like Tommy."

My blood ran cold. "Wh-what?"

"I would. Never. Slam the door. In your face."

My cursor hovered over the x. *Click, click.* The window didn't close.

"Don't. Try to. Leave." He leaned in closer with his deformed head. "You're with me. Now. Kasey."

I slammed the laptop shut.

For a second I thought I'd been successful, but then his voice came through the speakers, muffled through the plastic: "Do you. Remember. How we met?"

I nodded, scrunched into the corner of the couch. "You, uh...you stopped me on campus. I dropped my phone. You gave it back."

"Did you ever. Realize. You didn't actually. Drop your phone?"

"Uh, what do you mean?"

"I. Stole. It."

A buzzing silence filled the room. My ears rang.

"And did you. Ever realize? I wasn't. Even a student." A rustling sound from the speakers. "I worked. At the auto body shop. Next to campus."

I grabbed the laptop and threw it to the floor. Bits of glass and plastic exploded, covering the rug.

His voice continued, distorted and low:

"I wasn't. Even a student. Watched you for days. A pretty little co-ed --"

Rap, rap, rap.

Three knocks on the front door.

I bolted up. Stepped into the foyer. "Tommy -- is that you?"

No reply.

"I'm so sorry for what I said. I'm so, so sorry."

Then five words came through the heavy oak door:

"Get out of the simulation."

Click. The sound of a key fitting into the lock.

Creeeeeaaaak.

I shut my eyes and screamed. A hand grabbed my wrist, yanked me onto the porch.

"Kasey! Kasey!"

I opened my eyes.

I wasn't standing on the porch.

I was sitting in a bed, in a dim room. The damp smell of must flooded over me; a dim beeping sound came from somewhere in the shadows.

"Kasey."

I turned to see a figure in the shadows, sitting at the computer.

"I'm...back? What are you talking about?" I pulled myself up further. My forehead suddenly itched. I reached my hand up to scratch; my fingers brushed wires instead of skin.

"Yeah. I just pulled you out of the simulation."

The voice was gravelly. Low. Familiar.

No.

The man stood up and walked towards me. His large nose, short dark hair illuminated in the light.

"Dan."

He smiled. "See, I knew it wouldn't take long. You're a grass-is-greener kind of girl. You said you wished you'd married Tommy, so I gave you that. Then, only two days into the simulation, you told *him* you wish you'd married me." He broke into laughter. "Tommy *is* a self-righteous asshole, isn't he?"

My blood ran cold.

The memories flooded back in pieces. The wedding to Dan. The fight, only a few weeks after. *You're a liar and a creep. I wish I'd married Tommy!*

"What happened after that? I don't...I don't remember."

"I dragged you down here and started the simulation." He frowned. "I'm surprised you don't remember that. You were thrashing and yelling quite a bit."

My heart dropped.

Then I leapt out of the bed. Tore the wires from my forehead, ran up the stairs. I heard his yells behind me, his thundering footsteps.

I yanked the door open.

Then I disappeared into the snowy night.

KELLY

THE CULT ON ROCHESTER LANE

Kelly Childress

It started with a dumb, collectible figurine.

I was at a resale shop with my friend Aubrey when I saw it. A cutesy statue, a girl with disproportionately gigantic eyes and a bow clipped to her balloon-sized head. And there was a familiar diamond-shaped chip on her shoulder, colored in with marker.

I stared at it for a moment. Long-forgotten memories came rushing back, and I remembered how I'd felt when I knocked the collectible off Aunt Matilda's shelf: a mixture of fear, and relief that it hadn't shattered. How she'd reassured me it was all right, mistakes happen, bad things happen. All you can do is try to fix them, and try to make sure they don't happen again.

I was holding the figurine in my hand when Aubrey strolled up. "Don't tell me you're going to start collecting," she said, wrinkling her nose. "Should we get you a muumuu to go with it?"

"It's my aunt's. She loved these things. I don't know why she would sell it."

Aubrey smirked. "Maybe she got some taste."

307

Frowning, and ignoring Aubrey, I put the figurine back and made a mental note to call my aunt when I got home.

***

Hi, you've reached the voicemail of Matilda Carver. Please leave a message.

I'd called a dozen times to no avail. It wasn't like Aunt Matilda not to return calls. She loved them, even more so since she'd moved to a new neighborhood a few hours away from us.

When a week went by and neither my mom nor I could get in touch (and her local, molasses-slow police department remained unruffled by our calls), I decided I was going to drive down. The hours passed easily, and before long I was pulling into her driveway.

About a year and a half ago she'd bought a giant house. It was one of those overwhelming and haphazardly designed homes in a recently built neighborhood. Think Astroturf, blue-white sidewalks not yet stained by the elements, and the eerie absence of trees. My grandparents were poor, so as an adult Aunt Mattie had used her professional success to treat herself to finer things.

Her house lay on a large tract of land at the end of Rochester Lane. Next to it was an empty field, half-bulldozed to make way for more homes. The late afternoon sun hung in slanted lines across the concrete and dirt. There was no car in the driveway, and all the blinds were closed.

I got out and walked to the front door, trepidation creeping down my neck. Morbid thoughts of what grisly scene lay inside bloomed in my mind. I let myself in to the dark foyer, bracing myself to see a body sprawled at the bottom of the stairs, neck twisted at an unnatural angle.

There was nothing. I deactivated the alarm and shut the door. It was cool, dark and smelled very faintly of dogs and bleach. I heard jingling in the distance.

"Max?" I called. The jingling grew closer, until the familiar black-grey snout of her Labrador came zooming out of the kitchen.

A few happy yelps and licks later, Max and I explored the house. No one was there. Aunt Mattie's bed was made, clothes hung in the closets, refrigerator empty. Her car was in the garage, the keys in a bowl on the kitchen counter.

Things looked normal, and yet they weren't. So many of her things were gone and replaced with stuff I'd never seen before.

For one, all her china collectibles were gone from the house. The last time I'd visited they were all on display in her glass cabinet in the living room. Her desktop computer – the one she needed for work – was gone from her desk, replaced with a cream-colored journal and a silver fountain pen. Aunt Mattie had the sloppiest handwriting, and had taken to printing everything she needed (even grocery lists).

Instead of Aunt Mattie's oil paintings and sketches, the walls were adorned with the generic, abstract kind of art you'd see in a medical office. There were unfamiliar trinkets, like decorative gourds in the kitchen and a heavy silver clock on a table. There was some strange set of carved stone figurines nestled in her flower beds out front. If it weren't for Max, I'd have thought she'd moved.

I called Aunt Mattie's number again, feeling unsettled.

Hi, you've reached the voicemail of Matilda Carver. Please leave a message.

"Aunt Mattie. I'm, uh...I'm at your house now, with Max. Please, will you call me. Please? I'm worried."

I hung up, and the quiet of the house caused the strangeness of my situation to sink in. Unsure of what to do next I grabbed my stuff from the car, and I was in the middle of texting Mom when I heard the front door open. I dropped my phone and ran into the foyer, calling out, "Aunt Mattie?"

It wasn't her. It was a short lady I didn't recognize, her grayish-white hair coiffed in that short style sported by so many older women. When she saw me a confused smile spread across her face.

"Hello," she said. "I'm Alice, Matilda's neighbor."

"Do you know where she is?" The question had already tumbled out of my mouth before I realized I hadn't introduced myself, but I kept going anyway. "She won't answer me or my mom's calls."

"Oh, she's on a trip. Left a few days ago - said she needed to clear her head. She asked me to take care of Max while she was gone." A Milk Bone treat appeared out of her gardening apron, and she waggled it at Max, but he stayed at my side.

"Vacation? Where?"

"She didn't say, hun. Just that she needed to get away."

"You've talked to her?"

"Yes, just this morning in fact."

She waved the treat at Max once again, but he remained unimpressed, his normally wagging tail still.

There was an awkward pause as I struggled to process this information. What could have possibly upset Aunt Mattie so much that she'd just leave home and ignore us? This was the woman who Snapchatted me twenty times a day on her trip to Cabo San Lucas because she wanted to show me the ocean and the palm trees, and a couple of buff guys she met on the beach.

"Well, I'll leave you be. If you want some company come by! I'm sure everyone would love to hear from the famous Casey. She talks about you all the time."

I stretched my face into a smile that didn't reach my eyes. "Thanks. Nice to meet you."

The door shut behind her, and I was alone once again.

***

I decided to take Max on a walk to get some air. I quickly realized there wasn't much to see - all the houses were the exact same brown brick with gray stone; turrets and boxes and three-car garages stuck together randomly like Tinker Toys.

I sighed. My angry, judgmental thoughts had nothing to do with these houses, and I knew it.

As I walked I noticed a lot of the houses had decorative cornucopias on the front stoop - the same as the ones I'd noticed out front at Aunt Mattie's. At the entrance to the neighborhood there was a similar display in a concrete island filled with acrid-smelling mulch. I could tell Max needed to go, so I took him over there.

Max had just started squatting when I heard a scream. I looked up to see a man and woman running towards me.

"Stop him!" the woman shrieked. "Get away from it!"

Max whimpered and retreated behind me. Befuddled, I waved the doggie bags like a white flag. "I'm sorry, I'm sorry, OK? I'll pick it up."

I picked up Max's turds and hurried away, not in the mood to meet any more neighbors just yet. Glancing back I saw the man and woman standing in front of the cornucopia display, murmuring to each other as they made gestures at the little display with their right hands.

I was grateful to re-enter the gloomy silence of the house. I reheated some leftovers, and as I sat moodily in the empty room I gave in and called the police.

An officer told me (in a kind, but unworried tone) that they could come take a statement, but there wasn't much they could do. It wasn't illegal or strange for a person to rearrange their house, sell some old belongings, or go on vacation alone. They recommended we simply wait and ask Alice to pass along any messages in the event my aunt called again.

Before the call ended the cop encouraged me to try Ms. Alice's peanut-butter cookies.

I hung up, feeling more confused than ever. They were right - none of this was illegal, but they didn't know Aunt Mattie. She'd wanted a big house, but she'd also wanted to make it her own. She'd never changed herself for the sake of others, but now it seemed she'd traded the unapologetic person that she was for the same beige mediocrity that surrounded her.

And I won't lie - it hurt to think that she might simply not want to talk to us right now. That she was struggling with something, and didn't think we could help.

I stared at the TV for an hour or two, not really watching. When the doorbell rang I almost jumped out of my skin. Standing on the front porch was Alice, holding a plate of cookies and flanked by two strangers.

"We thought we'd be the welcome wagon," Alice beamed. I almost flinched at the saccharine-sweetness in her voice. I wasn't in the mood for visitors, but I couldn't come up with an excuse, so I let them in.

Alice had brought her husband Bill. There was also Vicki, who must have been the "overzealous HOA lady" Aunt Mattie had actually mentioned once or twice. I recognized her helmet-like blonde bouffant immediately.

When Bill spoke I recognized his voice as the cop I'd talked to earlier. "You sounded like you needed some company," he said. "I'm sorry we weren't able to help earlier." His voice was kind, but I bristled nonetheless.

***

The next hour passed awkwardly, with my discomfort multiplying every second. I felt like I was on a bed of needles as

314

I perched stiffly on Aunt Mattie's couch, a peanut butter cookie in my hand at Vicki's insistence.

At first it was the normal, forced kind of talk, not unlike the life updates I'd give my relatives at holiday parties. They asked questions while we all sipped water and ate cookies. I babbled emotionlessly in response, not really engaged, just spouting the pre-approved scripts that I knew would translate into fractals of equal non-controversy.

While we talked, I started to notice odd things from the three of them.

For example, once we sat down in the living room I noticed Vicki staring at me like a hawk. Her dark eyes crawled over my face and body like a searchlight, and I crossed my arms without realizing it.

The other thing was that, whenever possible, they would turn the conversation back to Aunt Mattie and our family, asking about our extended family, cousins, and Aunt Mattie's life before she came here. I thought that was strange - she'd lived here for over a year, yet they didn't seem to know anything about her.

The final alarm bell was when I saw Vicki was slowly running her hands over the cushions and upholstery of the couch surrounding her. When she finally stopped, she was holding what looked like a dark string, pinching it with one hand and stroking the length of it with her other thumb and forefinger. Struggling to mask my curiosity, and suspicion, I snuck a look at it when she went to take a drink of water.

It was hair - *my* hair.

It had to be. Alice, Bill, Vicki, Aunt Matilda - they all had light hair, and Max's wasn't that long. A sudden itch crept across my neck, and I scratched at it furiously.

I felt oily, sweaty, and visibly uncomfortable. I swayed in my seat, struck with unexpected exhaustion.

Before I could come up with an excuse to leave the room, Alice suddenly barked, "And what do you think you'll do after college, Casey?"

I shrank back, intimidated. "Um, I don't know, I'm only just starting to get through my gen eds and...." I trailed off and smiled, shrugging, trying to mask the unease uncoiling in my belly.

The room swam before my eyes, and I realized I was still swaying.

Drugged. The word flitted across my mind. It was like the first time I'd gotten high, and I'd felt a similar detached fogginess. It had to be. Alice had drugged me, like some kind of Betty Crocker Judas.

I sucked in gulps of air and fought off the drowsiness. Yelling something about not feeling well I stumbled to the bathroom next to the kitchen. I had the foresight to make sure the door was locked, and that the water was running full blast in the sink, before I collapsed next to the toilet. Forcing two fingers down my throat I knelt over the bowl until all the gooey, yellowish contents of my stomach had come back up.

Outside in the hallway, I heard hushed, low mumbling. The doorknob rattled. I lay down. The cool tile felt soothing against my burning, throbbing skin. If they were going to get in, I couldn't stop them. I was too late and so sleepy.

I closed my eyes, and it was only the sensation of Max's rough tongue on my cheek that brought me back.

Inch by inch I rolled over until I was sitting. There was a sharp pain from under my left buttock, and I realized my phone was in my pocket. I flipped it open and read my one notification - a text from my mom - with bleary eyes.

Honey, it doesn't make sense. FriendFinder says her phone is still in KS. I think you should leave. I'm sorry you went out there but I have a bad feeling. We can figure it out when you get home.

I shook with silent laughter at the last line, slumped up against the toilet bowl. I slapped myself a few times, and Max loitered anxiously at my feet.

I turned off the water, which was still running. Outside, I heard only silence.

Alice, or Bill or Vicki, or all three could still be outside...there was only one way for me to tell.

My eyes roamed and settled on a wooden bookend that was on a shelf above the toilet. Clutching it, I slowly opened the bathroom door and peered into the hall.

I clamped a hand over my mouth as I saw Alice standing in the dim light next to the door to the garage. To my right I could see the living room. My purse, which held my wallet and car keys, sat slouched against the coffee table.

I shut the door quietly. I got out my phone, then went to the security system app. I hit the button I was supposed to use if there were intruders in the house.

Alarms immediately blared throughout the house. I heard Alice cry out to herself in surprise; then I heard her little feet pattering down the tiled hallway to the console next to the front door. Even if she had the code I only needed a few seconds.

I lunged into the living room, kicking off hard in the opposite direction after hooking my fingers around my purse. Max followed, and we both streaked down the hallway to the garage. I clicked the lock to the vertical position on my way out. Sure, Alice could unlock it, but it might slow her down and I needed all the time I could get.

I unlocked the deadbolt and flung the door open, letting out a shriek when I saw Bill standing on the other side.

Max biting his ankle was all the distraction I needed. As Bill howled I swung the heavy bookend at his temple. It made a meaty thud and he gasped, tottering forward. I pushed him into the shelves at the opposite end of the garage and he went down hard, boxes of Christmas lights and gardening supplies showering on top of him.

My feet slammed into the pavement as I rushed to my car. I opened the door. I paused for one second to wait for Max, who jumped in ahead of me. I twisted the key in the ignition and fled the cul-de-sac, panting with fear and adrenaline. I blew through stop signs. I clipped curbs. I almost drove onto the median at one point as I zigzagged through the winding streets.

A scream erupted from my throat when I got to the neighborhood exit, only to find a wrought-iron gate in my way.

Tires screeching, I swerved to a side street and brought the car to a stop. I screamed again, and the sound trailed off to a wail. I pounded my fists against the dashboard. "God damn it!" I shouted. "God damn it, God damn it, God damn it!" Hot tears leaked down my face and I dissolved into quiet whimpering, my head cradled in my arms.

I took a deep breath, and another.

Keep breathing. Keep moving.

I slung the strap of my purse over my shoulder, locked the car, and headed for the nearest house, grateful that everything was shrouded in darkness. I thought Max would follow me, but he bolted off in another direction the moment I let him out of the car. I loitered for a moment, torn, but when he didn't come right back I resolved to keep moving. I hid behind some bushes and kept an eye on my car - half out of curiosity, wondering if I'd been followed, and half out of pure uncertainty as to what I should do next.

It wasn't long before lights illuminated my little sedan. I heard footsteps and the slamming of car doors. Shouts floated down the gently sloping lawn, the angry voices softened by the distance.

"She's not here!"

"Well, then we need to fucking find her!"

A voice I recognized as Bill's cut in as he hushed his cohorts. "Will you shut up?"

After that, it was just inaudible mumbling. As I watched the group split; a few of them got back into the car, and some others went on foot with flashlights.

My heart began to pound again, and I moved across the backyard to a different house, keeping low. I couldn't stay here, but I didn't have a plan other than 'don't get caught'.

My eyes fell on a small shed. It wouldn't do forever, but I could catch my breath and try to think of something.

I was halfway across the grass when a motion-sensor light burst to life, causing me to jump and skitter to the safe darkness. At first the door wouldn't open, and my heart jackhammered with panic, but after some wiggling it swung open.

I shut the door behind me and half-fell into some cardboard boxes. The contents jangled as I righted myself, and I decided to go through them as quietly as possible and see if I could find a weapon.

The first item I pulled from the box was so unexpected that I almost dropped it. Everything had happened so fast; the implications didn't hit me until that moment. I clamped a hand over my mouth, overcome with shuddering sobs. Hot tears leaked down my face. It was one of Aunt Mattie's china collectibles.

These fucking people. They had done something to her, maybe even killed her. They had taken her house, and quietly boxed up and sold her things.

If I wanted to survive, I needed a plan.

My mind raced as I went through the boxes. A few minutes later, I had gained a crowbar and a hair elastic. I put my hair up in a bun and called 911.

At first, the operator took down my information, but once I gave her the address, her tone changed. "Ma'am, this line is not for prank calls," she said sternly, and hung up before I could protest.

I called back, and each time I was told it was a misdemeanor to knowingly waste first responder time and resources. I had to fight to keep my voice calm on the fourth and last call, and almost threw my phone when the operator disconnected.

I sat on the ground, hugged my knees, and tried to slow my breathing. It finally dawned on me why we couldn't get the local police to do anything about Aunt Mattie. They weren't just reluctant to believe something was wrong, they were purposefully stonewalling us.

My options were running out. I needed a car, and I needed a way out of this goddamned neighborhood.

***

The sliding glass door barely made a sound as I slipped back into Aunt Mattie's house. I surveyed the dark. When I saw a figure on the stairs, I yelped and dropped the crowbar with a clatter.

The figure moved into the light. Alice approached me, her eyes huge and glimmering in the dark. "I'm so sorry, Casey. I'm sorry."

"What the fuck, Alice?" I gasped, shock turning quickly to anger. "You drugged me? What are you doing here? Why won't the police take my calls? What did you people do with my fucking aunt?"

Alice shrank back against the wall as I stormed towards her. "Casey, listen -"

"Tell me where my aunt is!" I shouted.

"I will, I will, I will, but please, you have to be quiet," Alice said, breathless and fast. "Vicki will be here soon and she's the one you have to worry about."

I stepped in close to Alice. "Talk."

Alice couldn't hold my gaze. Her voice trembled as she said, "Your aunt is dead. Vicki killed her because she couldn't control her."

I snorted. "That's fucking ridiculous."

"I'm serious," Alice said, the seriousness in her tone so great that even I had to pause. "She isn't human. She can do things, and if she has some of your hair or nails she can control you, influence you. Some people she can manipulate like puppets, some can only be compelled to do or believe or feel little things - everybody's different. Do you remember when you saw her last? Did you really want to eat those cookies? Was that itch on your neck real, or did she make you feel it?"

A barking laugh escaped my throat. My exhaustion and terror had collapsed into acidic cynicism. "*You* fed me drugged cookies, and now you're saying your neighbor is a spooky witch and you expect me to believe you."

But the seed was planted. I *hadn't* been hungry when they'd showed up, and I *had* felt a strange urge to comply whenever Vicki encouraged me to eat. I chalked it up to politeness and the general discomfort I'd felt at their visit.

Alice took a phone out of her pocket, and I recognized it as Aunt Mattie's. She unlocked it, went to the photos, pulled up an image. She guarded the screen from me for a moment, and then looked at me with a pained expression. "I can prove that I'm telling the truth about Matilda. Are you sure you want to see?"

I looked down my nose at the phone, and nodded slowly.

The image was of a bloodied, motionless woman lying in the dirt. Next to her body was a freshly dug hole, clearly her impending grave. I thought I recognized the spot as the vacant land next to Rochester Lane, the one where more houses were to be built. My eyes welled up when I recognized the face.

"No," I breathed, reaching for the phone.

Alice let me have it, and she even held me for a minute when the tears came and overwhelmed me with their darkness. I was falling and needed someone, and didn't care who.

***

I sat in the near dark, feeling oddly calm. Alice had left ten minutes ago, slipping a medallion on a chain over my head before she did. *"This will help you resist her when she tries to manipulate you. She gives them to her most trusted. I stole it from Bill."*

My face felt hot and dry, tear stains still on my cheeks. The cold metal lay heavy against my thumping heart.

I had pilfered some knives from the kitchen and hidden them in the couch cushions, keeping one to hide on me. Whatever tools and knick-knacks could be defensive - hammer, wrench, skillets - I hid.

As I was trying to find a place to hide the crowbar I heard the humming of the garage door opening. I dropped it to the carpet and hurriedly pushed it up against the dark baseboards, where it was somewhat concealed.

Vicki's dark clothes and blonde coif made it seems like she was levitating as she walked into the room. Wrinkling her nose, she switched on a light. "Isn't it a little dark in here, dear?"

I turned to face her, my hands in fists. "I prefer it that way."

She ignored me, keeping one hand in her pocket. "I'm glad you came back. I'm not sure what startled you so, but this has all been a big misunderstanding."

325

"You killing my aunt and burying her in a field was a misunderstanding?" The words fell out of my mouth before I could stop them.

Vicki paused for half a second, then started towards me again. "Take a deep breath, dear," she said, almost cooing. "Everything's okay, just listen."

I could see her hand still in her pocket, and I would have bet everything she had those strands of my fallen hair in there. I took a deep breath.

"None of us know where you aunt went. We're all very worried about her. After all, the world is a big place, and accidents happen."

Moisture stung the corners of my eyes as I thought of the chipped figurine. I remembered Aunt Mattie fixing it, telling me mistakes happen.

"Accidents do happen," I said, my voice shaking. The tears unexpectedly came back in full force. I covered my face with my hands, crying into my jacket sleeves...where I'd also concealed one of the smaller knives.

Vicki looked satisfied and stepped in close, clasping both hands at her heart. "I'm so very sorry," she said.

My heart was hammering in my chest as I gripped the cool handle.

When Vicki extended a hand to squeeze my arm I made my move. I flung my arm back, pointed the blade at Vicki's face, and swung it straight for her eye.

Vicki gasped and managed to get her other hand in the way, and the little knife went straight through her palm. A surprised screech crackled out of her throat, her prim facade gone. She pulled the knife out and threw it away.

"Stop!" she roared.

She lurched towards me, her skin turning a mottled gray. I felt a horrified chill as I noticed that - instead of red - the liquid that dripped from her hand was dark yellow.

Fuck.

"Is that any kind of response to hospitality?" she rasped.

I tried to run for the basement (the door was still unlocked) but five bony fingers clenched around my ankle and brought me to the floor. I grabbed for the crowbar, but all I succeeded in doing was knocking over an end table.

I managed to get one foot free and I kicked at Vicki with the other, but it was like my blows barely registered. She seemed almost amused - she let out a cackle before sinking her teeth into my calf. I let out a wail and fought, the wet blood allowing me to twist free of Vicki's grip.

I scrambled to my knees but Vicki was on me in an instant, pinning me to the ground on my back and squeezing my throat with both hands. She was as strong as an ox, even though she looked like she couldn't have weighed more than eight pounds. My hands scrabbled helplessly over hers.

Fuck.

Dark spots floated through my vision...but there was a light there, too. An annoyingly bright one, shining right in my eye.

Things cleared for a moment and I saw it on the floor near me: a heavy, silver clock.

I let out a sigh and slowly crawled my hand towards it, going limp and closing my eyes once I could touch it. Vicki held on for a few seconds longer, and then let me go.

Not taking in a huge breath the moment she let go was one of the hardest things I've ever done. I kept repeating to myself *two minutes, two minutes,* because I'd read somewhere that most people could hold their breath for up to two minutes. I felt like my veins were going to explode from the effort.

But I did it, and I heard Vicki stand up and go to open the basement door. That was when I grabbed the clock, and smashed it over her skull.

Hissing clouds of smoke erupted from her wound. I could feel heat coming off of it, and I dropped the clock and stumbled backwards. Vicki's body rattled and convulsed, like some unseen figure was shaking her. Rivers of yellow streamed down her face and splashed on the carpet.

Then, she just collapsed like a mannequin.

She was still alive when I kicked her down the stairs, her weak croaks crescendoing into screams when I poured gasoline on her.

I remember lighting the match, the hiss of the flame louder than Vicki's howling.

Mistakes happen, after all. All you can do is try to fix them.

And make sure they don't ever happen again.

MY BEST FRIEND

Allison Bainbridge

She's changed since she moved in with me. It's nothing too bad, though. I think it's just my influence rubbing off on her. When we first met she was a bit of a wild child – the party girl of the office. She'd be off going out every other night with colleagues or friends from outside work, and I would watch as she came in the following mornings, chatting about dancing and men and trying to cure her hangover with cups of the cheap office coffee.

She doesn't do any of that anymore.

I spent hours watching her back then. I would watch her playing solitaire on the company computer, photocopying, chatting by the coffee machine and flirting with the man at the next desk. Brad, I think his name is. It doesn't matter. I followed her on social media, careful not to like too many of her posts so that I wouldn't look like one of those creepy girls. I commented every so often on her selfies, on the rare posts about work – she was forever breaking company policy – and trying to look like I wasn't trying too hard. I was trying though, that's the thing. She's just one of those people: kind and lovely and bubbly. You can't help but adore her from the moment you meet her; I wasn't any different. She drew me in. I'd always wanted a friend like her.

It took me ages to work up the courage to approach her. I'm not ashamed of that. I know that I'm not really the type of person she'd normally hang out with. I'm too quiet, too shy. I know that. I've overheard her old friends at the office list my faults often enough. I'm the chubby, mousy girl that they ignore, unless it's time to try and get me to take on a bit of extra work for them, or unless it's time for the Christmas party. I don't really mind it, you know. I don't hate any of them. I was always a bit jealous before *she* came into my life, but never resentful. I like being useful. It's just...wanting a friend for myself wasn't too much to ask, was it? It took months of effort to get her to like me, to trust me, to want my company as much as I wanted hers. Months of sharing smiles and gossip when our lunch-breaks coincided; of quiet drinks after work and having my shoulder wept on when her endless strings of relationships failed to work out. She had terrible taste in men in those days, they always treated her so badly. I kept telling her that she needed to focus more on herself; that she would find someone who would treat her right if she only looked hard enough. I'm so glad to know that I was right, so very glad. She's much happier now – she never cries, and she's always smiling.

It took months. Over a year, actually, before she came to my flat. We had dinner. I cooked all of her favourite things and we opened a bottle of wine in front of Netflix afterwards, talking and laughing. She never wanted to leave! I know she didn't. She was so happy that evening, so relaxed. She dozed off on the sofa and I let her sleep. She moved in after that; became a totally different person. She became my best friend. She promised – she *promised* – that we'd be friends forever.

The office is a lot quieter now that she stays at home. Our home. She was missed at first, but after her letter of resignation landed on the boss's desk her absence was forgotten. People gossiped at first, of course. People don't just disappear, they said, but they didn't question her resignation. They were more disappointed that they didn't get a chance to get drunk at a leaving party than they were upset about her actually leaving. She'd developed a bit of a reputation for things like that over the years, afterall.

None of them know that we live together now. I didn't see any reason to tell them. After she posted on Facebook to let them know she was deleting her profile to distance herself from negativity on social media, I didn't see how it was any of their business. Besides, we like our privacy – just the two of us. Living together is like our little secret, like an endless sleepover. It's so much fun!

There's something special about coming home every day to see her. She's always sitting in the living room, the volume of the television turned down so low that it can barely be heard over the hum of the air conditioning and the dehumidifiers. The room is always dark. I keep the curtains closed to block out the sunlight. She used to tan herself in salons and on the beach in summer; now she knows that too much sunlight is bad for her complexion, and she appreciates the dark a lot more than she used to. I love to step up behind her as she sits, press a kiss to her cheek and hug her; run my fingers gently – so gently – through her hair.

It was her hair that caught my attention in the first place. It's so long and fine and pale...it's the kind of hair I've always wanted. She lets me style it for her now; I can brush it for hours. I'm always gentle. I feel like I have to be when it looks and feels like cobwebs against my skin.

She taught me how to do makeup before she moved in with me. In the office and online it was one of the things I always complimented her on. I'll admit, I was jealous of her skills. Now I help her with it. Not that she wears much! At least, not as much as she used to. She doesn't need to, now that she stays at home so much – she doesn't have to worry about who's looking at her or judging her. She was always so very worried about that sort of thing. Usually, it's just a bit of gloss to make her lips shimmer these days, and keep them moist in the dry air. She doesn't need to use anything else when I'm the only one to see her. I love her for who she is; she doesn't need to try and impress me. She dresses differently now too. She doesn't wear those tight suit-skirts and blouses anymore, and her high heels lie forgotten. She goes barefoot now, and those skimpy clothes have been replaced with loose satin dressing gowns. There's no point in her getting dressed up just for me, and she's so much more comfortable like this.

She's more comfortable around me too, now. You can tell because she talks less. When our relationship first began it was all about her. It was about the men who hurt her, the friends who stabbed her in the back, and the family that didn't understand her. Now she listens to me speak. She never takes her eyes off me. She never looks away or interrupts; she never looks bored. She's so unlike everyone else. She's the friend I've always wanted – always smiling, always happy to see me. She never complains, even when we fall into silence together. It's that lovely, friendly silence that you only get between two people who adore each other. Even when we don't talk she still smiles. It's the smile she reserves for me; no one else has ever seen it. Her thin lips stretched back, showing her white, white teeth.

Sometimes, over dinner, I ask her how her day has been. There's never any reply; there's no need for one. I already know how it went. It's the same every day. She sits quietly, staring blankly at the television as daytime programmes display the lives of the lowest of society for the world to see. I make sure to keep the volume low for her; low enough so that it doesn't disturb anyone.

We don't want to be disturbed, after all. No, no. We like our privacy.

We never do all that much in the evenings. We watch a little television. Sometimes I open a bottle of wine, sometimes I even pour her a glass, but she never touches it. She doesn't drink anymore. Drinking just got her hurt in the past, and it always got her the wrong kind of attention. And, well, she never seemed to really like it anyway. After all, on the first night she stayed with me she drank so quickly that she never tasted the tablets I crushed into her wine.

When I'm tired we go to bed. I push her chair into our room and lift her into our bed. She always lies still, waiting for me as I change. She doesn't ever move as I slip into bed next to her and wrap my arms around her. She's so thin now, fragile. I count her ribs through her nightdress as I fall asleep, and I caress her cold, dry skin.

There's no fear that she'll be gone when I wake up. She's my best friend, and she promised that she always will be. She'll never leave me. Never. I made sure that she'll never leave. She's mine forever.

UNDER THE BED

Shayla King

"Mommy?" came my son's cry, for the third time that night. "There's something under my bed, can you come check?" A brief pause before, "Mooom?" Ethan had been going through that phase, you know? The one every kid eventually goes through, where their imagination is at its peak and goes unchecked at night. The closet, the bed, cubby holes in the room that are too dark when the lights are off. The list of nighttime terrors goes on and varies for every kid, but for him it was under the bed. Ethan didn't have a closet and honestly, in hindsight, my husband might have done that on purpose. He was a secret genius when it came to this kind of stuff, one of the many things I'll always miss about him.

I had been watching television for the last few hours or so, when I flicked a glance over at the wall clock it read 1:12AM. It was a lot later than usual. I thought about just pretending I had fallen asleep on the couch, but I knew he would know better, somehow he always does. I muttered something definitely not PG-13 under my breath and sat with my head in my hands for a few moments. Rubbing the bridge of my nose with my thumb and index finger I heard him cry out again. "Mooooom? Please,

I can't sleep." A part of me didn't want to go, a part of me just wanted to pretend I hadn't heard it and lay down and sleep until morning. What kind of mother would I be if I didn't go though?

Slowly I lifted myself from the couch and shuffled around it, grumbling about the time to no one in particular. *It'll be like any other time you've checked his room, just get it over with.* I would tell myself. *You'll be out of there in a moment and then you can resume your pitiful existence as a couch growth.* I almost laughed at my own pessimism, but since Sam left it was all I really had. Sam's old man slippers shiff-shoffed across the floorboards as I lazily dragged my feet toward the bottom of the staircase. I gripped the end of the bannister, pulling myself up the first step before staying there for a moment. This end of the house was so quiet now, I thought, sighing loudly before taking another step upwards.

The TV light reflected harshly off of the photo frames hanging on the wall, and I shielded my eyes from the flashing colors. I remembered the day we hung them up: it was the first thing Sam wanted to do after we had them taken with the family photographers. He looked so sweet in that blue shirt, and Ethan wore this horrible overall set that his grandparents had bought him. I couldn't stand those people for the life of me. If I was

338

honest with myself I was a little glad that Sam had left, since I'd never have to deal with his parents ever again. *Good riddance.*

As I continued ascending the staircase I stumbled on my robe, which was half-falling off my shoulder and draping onto the wood. I caught myself with both hands on the bannister, the heavy odor of scotch drifting from my mouth as I sighed in relief. *Close call there, partner.* I chuckled nervously to myself...Because that's all there was anymore, and I stepped out onto the second floor. The hall in front of me was short, and Ethan's door wasn't too far from me now. I heard him start whimpering as I reached the top of the stairs, the pang in my chest reminding me that I should be quicker while the sluggishness in my legs reminding me why I couldn't. I groaned aloud and whispered that I was coming.

Running my hand along the wall I slowly staggered down the hallway, passing what used to be Sam and I's bedroom. I had long since stopped using it and now, preferring to sleep on the couch. If you could call blackout drunk 'sleep'. Sam never approved of my drinking, and I know it was just him looking out for me, but somehow it made me want to do it more. Ethan had been a short-term solution to a long-term problem, I guess. The sting in my eyes started up again and I quickly shoved my sleeve into them, wiping the tears away before they even formed. I knew I had to be strong now, but it was always so hard.

I shakily knocked on Ethan's bedroom door, which was a fraction ajar. "Ethan?" I called, my voice hoarse and broken, "I'm here, baby." I pushed the door open with my forearm and stared into the dark, my eyes since having adjusted to it. I scanned the room, from desk to toy box to dresser to bed. It was just as I remembered it being, left exactly the way he liked it. Or rather, left the way I liked it. I almost cracked a smile, remembering how Sam would haze me for being too strict about tidiness, but the stomach churning emptiness stopped me. I stared at the spot I would find Ethan, blankets up to his ears, sitting in the corner of his room against the wall. He would point downwards with so much force, and he wouldn't stop until I got onto my knees and checked it out for him. It was almost cute, seeing him so afraid of nothing, the way only a mother could find that cute.

I stood in the doorway for the 5th time that week, staring into my son's empty room, my heart full of pain and my eyes full of tears. Staring at the spot I should've found him. Listening to the chattering from under the bed.

This time, I stepped into the room.

And I closed the door behind her.

340

MY DAUGHTER IS DYING

Thamires Luppi

Tina was a good baby. Ever since she was born, other mothers watched us with envious, longing faces. She was so quiet and peaceful. She was a good sleeper who didn't mind being put in her crib, and most nights I could make it only waking up to feed her once. That was the dream of every mother and every babysitter.

She didn't mind being around other people, and never cried for me when I wasn't around. Potty training her went smoothly. Tina was the most easy-going baby, toddler and little girl I have ever met. I would add that she's also super smart and beautiful, but every mother thinks their children are. I think it's our brain deceiving us so we don't be like "Ew, 9 months and a lot of stitches for *that*? I'd better throw it in the garbage can."

Well, I would trade all of it to have a healthy daughter. I wouldn't mind one bit if she was a hysterical child, covered in snot and unable to poop by herself.

It started suddenly, as silent tragedies usually do.

I was at work when her kindergarten teacher called me. She talked in a calm, almost singing-song tone, the only one grow women who spend the whole day around little kids know.

341

"*Hiii*, Mrs. Davis, how are you doing?" after a pause for exchanging pleasantries, the teacher spoke again. "Look, Tina is being *reeeally* good as usual, but today she's a bit under the weather. We checked and she has a fever. Could you come pick her up now?"

I left in a hurry, and when I got there Tina could barely stand. I carried her in my arms to the car, unsure if I should take her to the hospital or just put her into bed with an antipyretic. Tina had never gotten sick before.

I sighed, wishing I had some help and wishing that her father hadn't left. I was so, so in love with him.

My mother lived in another town, but I decided to call her for advice. She told me to let Tina rest for today, then take her to the hospital tomorrow if she didn't get better. Pretty obvious advice, if you're not feeling overwhelmed and tired.

As I drove I started thinking about Ben. He was handsome and a sweet talker, ten years older than me. I thought we were madly in love. When he asked me to have a child with him, I was silly enough to think it was the biggest commitment a couple can make. I felt honored and blessed.

Then he got a job offer in Japan, and decided for me that I wouldn't be happy there. I assured Ben I would be happy anywhere with him. He said I couldn't leave my job (which I didn't like that much) or my mother (who I didn't see often anyway). In just one week he was gone forever.

When Tina and I got home I made us some tea, prepared a bath and put my daughter in her bed. I had a bad feeling about this, but I dismissed it as classic mother paranoia.

I slept by Tina's side in her tiny bed that night. I couldn't wait until morning to take her to the hospital. She woke up sweaty, shivering and with an ugly cough. Her lungs made a weird static noise.

"Time for some serious antibiotics", I said to calm myself.

When we got there Tina had to be immediately intubated. She could barely breathe by herself, and she was so small and fragile between the machines that kept her alive.

In the next few days things just got worse.

Her hair was rapidly falling out, hundreds of strands at time.

Her skin was so dry and sunken that she looked a thousand years old. Her eyes got milky and blind, her voice was all raspy, and her breath smelled awful. The doctors had no clue what was going on. We called specialists in infectiology from other states, other countries even. No one knew a thing, and a huge effort was made just to keep her alive the way she was, with no improvement.

343

I still had to work, so my mother came to stay with Tina at the hospital. I spent all my days crying at my desk and researching rare diseases. I posted a plea in my Facebook wall — "If you know what my daughter has, please tell me. I'm desperate," I wrote, and described all her symptoms.

A woman I didn't know, nor had in my friend list, reached out to me. Her name was Jennifer, and we had no mutual friends.

"Samara, I can't even imagine what you're going through. I need to talk about your daughter and her father, and it's really important. Can you please meet me at [coffee shop near a subway station]?"

I immediately answered yes, and we met in the same day. I had no time to think this was some scam. My guess was that she was some old friend of Ben and knew he had a disease. I was full of hope.

Jennifer was in her mid 30s — a little older than me. She was tall, pretty and looked friendly. She was already there when I arrived, and bought me a cappuccino.

"Look, Samara, you don't have to believe me. I know it's crazy, but I know what your daughter has. Will you give it a chance and listen to me?"

"I will listen to anything. I'm desperate.

"I'm Ben's ex-wife. I know you probably hate me, and think I want to harm your daughter, but I'm fucking serious. That man is a psychopath. Did he leave you when you got pregnant?"

"Yes...and no, I don't think you are a bad person."

"Well, I had to put a fucking gun in his head to get this confession. The son of a bitch made a deal with the Devil. He wanted to be attractive for longer, and promised his firstborn in exchange."

"WHAT?" I screamed. We were the only clients there. The young barista quickly looked at me, then probably remembered people scream all the time in front of him and didn't mind us much.

Jennifer gave me some much needed time to let that sink in.

"So...you guys didn't have a kid?" I asked too casually.

"Oh, *I* had a kid. Ben thought my son was his, but jokes on him - he wasn't. He started to get desperate. He begged me to have another child with him, said he would take care of everything and I wouldn't even miss it. *It*. A son or daughter of mine."

"What a monster," I mumbled.

"I obviously refused. I know it wasn't right to cheat on him and get pregnant with someone else's baby, but I had a gut feeling something was wrong. Before I got pregnant he was too intense about it, and I knew he always hated kids. I knew something shady was going on, but couldn't imagine how big it was. I thought it was some inheritance matter, you know? I'm really glad I did it, but Ben was running out of time. So he..." she hesitated for a long time, bit her lip and looked at me with eyes full of pity "Well, he started looking for someone else to bear his child. Now the Devil is claiming your daughter."

We talked for a long time, and I'd say we became good friends. After a month Tina got so much better, and was out of the hospital in no time. She's back to her old, full-of-life self now.

There's a tiny detail I'm forgetting to tell you. I took a trip to Osaka with my new bestie, and we had a little talk with the man who tried to ruin our lives. Maybe we were a little too...blunt, if you know what I mean. It was a real burst of emotions. And brains.

My life is only getting better and better. I think Satan was pleased that I sent something that belonged to him. I heard he's really warm when it comes to welcoming his deadbeat debtors.

LIFE AFTER

Candice Azalea Greene

It started the week before the Presidential election in 2016. We had just read Anne Frank's diary in school, and we were learning about the Holocaust. When I turned the page in a history book there a photo of Adolf Hitler jumped out at me. I was confused, so I raised my hand.

"Yes, Shannon?" Mrs. Rayburn, a plump, dark-skinned woman with dozens of tiny braids in her long hair, paused in her lesson to call on me.

"Is this a real picture?" I asked, unable to take my eyes off Hitler's face.

"It is."

She must have seen something in my expression, because instead of continuing the lesson she said, "Why do you ask?"

"His face... Why does he look like that?"

The visage staring up at me from the black and white photograph was hideous, as gruesome as the decaying body I had seen on a true crime TV show that my dad had made me watch.

"Oh, you mean his mustache? I guess he thought it was fashionable at the time."

Did he have a mustache? I didn't see how he could when there was hardly any skin for hair to grow.

"No, I mean his face. He looks like a monster, with one eyeball hanging out, his skin peeling away, maggots falling from—"

"That's enough."

Mrs. Rayburn's stern tone broke through my morbid fascination. With the spell lifted, I was finally able to look away. Laurie Feldman made a gagging noise next to me. I glanced at her then around at the other students. Several were pale and looked like they were going to be sick. I agreed. The photo of the man had been the most horrible thing I had ever seen in my ten years, but my teacher glared at me like I had done something very wrong.

"Hitler did some terrible things in his life. I won't deny that. But that doesn't mean you can talk gross in front of the class. Leave your imagination in your head on this one. Okay?"

I was so confused that I didn't argue, merely nodded my head, and turned back to my book. Mrs. Rayburn continued the lesson, but I didn't hear a word she said. I couldn't get over the man in the photograph. When I snuck glances at them, none of the other students seemed disturbed by the picture on the page, but they had been grossed out when I described the Hitler-monster. Why did none of them show the same revulsion now? It made no sense.

I looked down at the book again, at the monster's face. As I stared, transfixed, the photo came to life.

Pustules covered the left side of Hitler's face, trailing beneath the stiff uniform collar. Fat, white maggots writhed, gorging themselves on the desiccated flesh that remained. Bone peeked out from the right side of his jaw. A few maggots fell into the hole. The man's jaws began to work, grinding and chewing. The one eye left in his skull turned to me, and he spoke words in another language. Then he pointed at me and laughed—a low, hacking sound that made the hairs on my arms stand up.

I screamed and pushed back from my desk, falling from my chair and crawling away as fast as I could on my hands and knees.

Mrs. Rayburn wasn't happy with the disruption and gave me detention. Mom wasn't happy she had to leave work early to pick me up since I had missed the bus due to detention. I tried to explain to her what I saw, that I hadn't meant to be disruptive. The monster in the photo had scared me, and I had been trying to flee from a threat. Mom didn't buy it, and I spent the following weekend grounded and stuck doing chores inside the house.

A week later, Dad was watching a Presidential debate on TV. I happened to pass by on my way to the kitchen to see when dinner was going to be ready. One glance at the TV, and I froze. The man was talking, but I was too transfixed by the sight of his face to hear the words coming out of his mouth. He was a monster, just like Adolf Hitler.

This man's nose was missing. A blood-red snake slithered in and out of the black void. Milky white eyes stared at the camera, rooting me to the floor. Thick, bloody scabs covered every inch of the man's exposed skin above his white collar. His right ear hung from a single string of flesh, flapping around like a dead fish every time his head moved. The other ear was completely gone.

The next thing I knew Dad was shaking me. I had been rolling on the floor screaming my head off. Mom rushed into the hall, demanding to know what had happened. My mouth clamped shut, the screaming immediately cutting off. Afraid of what I would see, but needing to know if I was just seeing things, I sat up and looked at the TV. The woman was speaking now, her face perfectly normal. The man stared at the camera like he was looking directly at me. I gulped and turned to Dad.

"Do you see it?" A shaking hand pointed at the man. "Do you see the monster?"

He didn't, of course.

I didn't watch TV again until the election was over, and then I would only watch cartoons on DVD. I was afraid to watch anything with real people in it. Books with photographs of people were off limits too. I didn't want to see any more monsters.

Dad and Mom didn't know what to make of my freak out. Mom told him what had happened at school with the history book and he tried to talk to me about it. I told him what I saw, describing the monster in the book, plus the one on TV, but he didn't believe me.

The next time I saw a monster was in real life. The mall had been decorated for Christmas, and Santa was making his debut. Mom had dropped a few of my friends and I at the mall on a Saturday while she went grocery shopping.

Kodie, Manda, Jorisa, and I messed around in a few stores, played games in the arcade until we ran out of tokens, then decided to head to the food court for a slice of pizza. Santa's Workshop was on the way. As we passed it, Manda slowed to a halt to watch the kids waiting in line, a smile on her face.

"Whatcha staring at Manda?" Kodie teased. "You want to sit on Santa's lap? Wittle girlie want to ask for a baby doll for Christmas?" Kodie and Jorisa laughed, Jo slapping Kodie on the back like she had made the best joke ever.

I rolled my eyes at Manda, who happened to be on my left in front of the candy-cane-colored fence. Manda shuffled her feet, and I caught sight of the man in the fluffy red suit. My legs turned to pudding, and I staggered to the fence, knocking into Kodie on the way.

"Watch it!"

I ignored her, holding onto the fence for dear life.

Santa's face was just as monstrous as Hitler's and Trump's. Oozing, green sores covered his skin. Blood seeped from his mouth each time he asked the kids what they wanted for Christmas. A gloved hand patted and rubbed every kid's back.

"What the hell's with her?" I heard Jo ask from a thousand miles away. I was falling headlong down a dark hole. Although I could feel the wood beneath my hands, everything else faded away, tumbling faster and faster until I thought I was going to vomit. With a *crack*, the world stopped spinning.

I was staring at the Santa-monster, but he was in regular clothes. We were no longer in the mall. Squat windows high in the walls indicated we had been transported to a basement bedroom. A boy around six sat on a bed next to the Santa-monster. The monster reached out to touch the boy, rubbing his legs, back, and chest. Then he began to undress the boy.

Reality slammed back into my mind. Heaving like I had just woken from a terrible nightmare, I tore myself away from the disturbing scene that was threatening to replay in my mind, bile rising in my throat. Choking and screaming, I turned and ran face first into something solid. Arms shot out to catch me. I looked up into the concerned face of a normal-looking man.

Sounds of laughter and people talking drifted back to me. I glanced around to see we were in the mall, surrounded by families going about their weekend business. What the hell had I just seen?

"Whoa, what's the rush?"

Peeking around the man, I saw the Santa-monster staring straight at me. When he saw me looking, he put a finger to his lips and shook his head. I leaned back to my right, allowing the body in front of me to hide the monster.

"You okay?"

I looked up at the man again. He wore a black hat and coat with a star embroidered on both of them. Slowly, I shook my head, not trusting myself to speak for a moment.

"Santa is a bad man. He likes to touch little boys where their underwear covers them."

The cop's eyebrows shot up, and he turned to look at the Santa-monster. He wouldn't see what I saw. To him, Santa would look like any other man.

"I saw him with a six-year-old boy. He made the boy take off his clothes. Then they got into bed together."

The cop's grip tightened on my shoulder. I gasped in pain and tried to wriggle free. The movement broke the trance the man had been in, and he glanced down at me.

"Are you sure?" His voice was deadly calm. "You're not pranking me?"

I looked up at the cop with tears in my eyes. "I saw it. Please stop the monster before he hurts anyone else."

All hell broke loose after that. The cop radioed for backup. Santa-monster realized I had ratted him out and took off running. Angry shouts rose up wherever he went, so the cop had no problem following him through the crowd. He caught up to the monster and tackled him to the ground, pinning him in place as he handcuffed the gloved hands behind the monster's back. Children cried, and mothers screamed in protest. Backup arrived soon after to cart Santa-monster away while my friends and I were led to a mall office and our parents were called.

It quickly became evident my friends knew nothing. Their bewildered parents took them home. Mom didn't understand what the police told her. She didn't know who the Santa-monster was and insisted I didn't either.

After a lot of arguing, we were finally allowed to go home. Before we left, the police said they would be in touch. Mom dragged me from the mall, which had closed hours ago, and practically threw me in the backseat of her Kia Rio. She yelled at me the entire ride home, saying I had ruined a man's life, how disappointed she was in me, and that she couldn't understand what was happening to me.

That made two of us.

I sat outside my parents' bedroom later that night listening to them talk about what to do with me. Dad thought longer grounding and more housework would stop me from making any more accusations about people I didn't know. Mom kept saying something was going on with me, that something might be wrong medically. They argued well into the night but didn't come up with any better ideas than what Dad had suggested.

I went back to my room when I started to nod off and lay in bed wondering if Mom was right. *Was* there something wrong with me? It certainly seemed that way since I was seeing things no one else seemed to be able to see. What if I *had* ruined Santa's life for no reason? Maybe it was all in my head, and he was just a normal person.

Sleep evaded me that night, so I was up when the police officer from the mall came by the next day. They had searched Santa-monster's home after taking him into custody. Mom was horrified when he told us what they had found in the man's basement.

The police had to cut a padlock off the bedroom. Inside, they had found the boy I had seen in my vision. At least, I assumed it was the same boy. They didn't show us a picture or describe him, but I knew. Deep down, I knew what I had seen was an image from the Santa-monster's mind, a memory from yesterday morning.

Apparently, the boy I had seen in my vision wasn't the first either. Hundreds of photos of young boys lined the walls of the basement, all posing naked on the full-sized bed in the back bedroom. There were even videos of the man and the boys doing terrible things in bed together.

Mom stared at me the entire time, like I was an alien she had never seen before; Dad's hand on my knee was firm. As soon as the cop left, Dad turned to me, his mouth open like he wanted to say something. No words came out, so he shut his mouth and walked away. Mom continued to stare at me from the opposite end of the couch.

"I don't feel well. I think I'm going to lie down," I mumbled and darted for the stairs.

Shutting the bathroom door behind me, I sprang for the toilet, where my entire breakfast released itself from my roiling gut. After my stomach was empty, I splashed water on my face and stared at myself in the mirror, watching droplets slide down my cheeks like tears and fall into the sink.

Word got out at school, of course. My friends steered clear of me, and the other kids stared at me in class until the teacher told them to stop. No one could stop them at recess though. They would halt whatever they were doing to watch me walk across the school grounds.

One morning, I was running from some kids who had congregated outside a door to harass me. I ducked my head to avoid their taunts when a red-orange ball flew in front of my face. I jumped back as another slapped me on the arm. Crying out in pain, I looked around, realizing I had accidentally wandered into the path of some kids playing wall ball. That didn't stop them from throwing the balls. I had to spin and dodge to get away. Only three balls hit me—the one on my arm, another on the side of my face, and a third in the center of my back after I was clear of the wall. The recess monitor was on the playground helping a kid with a scraped knee, so she didn't see what happened to me. I turned and ran before the kids could see the tears in my eyes.

"Nark," several of them shouted.

Why didn't they understand I had stopped a man from doing horrible things?

I ran until I came to the fence at the edge of the grounds, where I collapsed behind a tree, knees scrunched to my chest. The tears couldn't be stopped; they fell until well past the tardy bell. I didn't want to return to school, didn't want to see any of my classmates ever again.

Adults called my name. Some of them even got close to the tree. I remained still and silent every time one neared my hiding place. As far as I was concerned, I was done with the lot of them. The school could catch fire, and I wouldn't care if they all burned.

Life only got harder from there. Everyone I knew was scared of me. As a result, I began to act out. I fell in with the wrong crowd and began smoking and drinking a couple years later. Monsters assaulted my vision at every turn. They were mostly in the media—on TV and in movies and photographs. Occasionally, I saw them in real life too.

Meeting a monster face to face never got easier. There was no pattern as to when I would see one. Weeks or months could go by before I would be walking in a crowd and a decaying face would suddenly leer at me. No matter how often I would mentally prepare myself, those moments always took me by surprise. I could usually suppress the scream. Jumping and running away were my typical go-to responses.

Three times in five years, I was scared so badly by a monster that I pissed myself. Each of these incidents was followed by a vision: the first of a man mutilating women's genitalia, the second of a woman murdering her husbands, and the third of a man shooting up a movie theater during a Disney movie. Only the woman had actually done the things I saw in the vision of her. The mutilator would strike soon, probably within a day, and the shooter was only a possibility. He teetered on the edge of turning into a full-blown monster, able to go either way.

There was never a cop around after that first encounter with the Santa-monster. Every other monster I ran into got away with their dark deeds. After each encounter, I fell into a deep depression, unable to get their faces or the visions out of my mind. Drugs and alcohol helped me cope, and I'd spend days in a stupor so I didn't have to feel anything.

My parents kicked me out after everything they tried to do to get me to turn my life around failed. Druggie friends let me crash on their couches, until their parents found out and sent me packing. I slept on the streets after that. When I was old enough I got part-time jobs wherever I could, usually at places that would pay me under the table so I could disappear more easily when I needed to. The last four years of my teenage life were spent so high and drunk that, to this very day, I don't remember anything but small snippets here and there.

Squatting in abandoned homes had become my regular lifestyle. I was stumbling home after a wild party one night when a man stepped into my path, seemingly out of nowhere. Swaying back and forth, I peered up at him. Even with a foggy brain, I registered what he was. While drugs could take away the memories of what I saw, they didn't stop me from seeing the monsters in the first place.

This man was actually less scary than some of the others I had seen. I had figured out how bad a monster looked depended on what tickled his sick mind. Rapists tended to look like scabby, scaly lizards. I had seen a tapeworm under a microscope once when I was still in school. Molesters usually looked like those worms, with a circular hole surrounded by hooks for a mouth. Murderers looked like reanimated corpses with severe infections.

The man standing in front of me had bulging, red eyes that looked like they were about to burst from his head. A fat, purple tongue lolled from his mouth like an elongated dog's tongue. Shattered, yellow and black teeth protruded from his mouth. His skin was the color of puke after it has been sitting in the sun for three days.

I could tell he was a smalltime offender. Grand larceny, drug dealing, and/or solicitation of minors was his vice. It was almost comical—the bug eyes and raspy breathing due to the enlarged tongue.

"Beat it." I attempted to push past him.

"Give me your wallet."

A shiny pistol appeared in front of my nose. My eyes crossed as they tried to look down one of the four barrels swimming before me. A huge part of me wished he would do it. Living had become a chore that I wasn't cut out for. I was ready to die—I craved it. My head knocked into the barrel, and I closed my eyes.

"Take it all. Please."

Being shot in the head wasn't as painful as one might think. One moment I was alive, and the next I wasn't. The agonizing part was the seconds of contemplation in between.

With eyes scrunched shut, I waited seconds, or years, for my assailant to pull the trigger. More fear and doubt encroached on my drugged mind every moment that passed and I still lived. Finally, I had to make the decision myself: Did I want to live another day—another hour—frightened beyond imagining, ashamed of what I had become, just waiting for it all to end?

My hands didn't tremble as I raised them to the gun and placed a finger over the assailant's. My resolve didn't falter as I gently squeezed the trigger. There wasn't even time to register the sound of the bullet firing before my body crumpled to the cool sidewalk.

***

The thing I miss most about living is something I had taken for granted every day.

I no longer need to eat, so food has become an all but forgotten relic of a life long gone. Clothes are irrelevant without a human body, and socialization is something I was never any good at anyway.

What I miss the most is fresh air, scents pulled on a breeze, like lilacs, ocean tang, sawdust, or baking bread. Clean, crisp air has been exchanged for the odors of sulfur, decaying bodies, and rotting peaches.

They tell me if I follow the rules long enough I'll see the world above again. They say if I perfect the techniques of torture and dismemberment I'll be given limited reign to walk amongst humans. They show me how they want me to behave every day that I escape from my confined cell by ripping my soul to shreds, by breaking my consciousness over and over.

When I become what they want me to be, then I will be free. Free to inhabit a human body and punish those who wronged me in my former life. Until then, I must be subjected to the things I saw in the visions when I was alive.

I thought Hitler and sadistic murderers were the worst, but I know now those were smalltime offenders. I bide my time, confident in the knowledge that once my consciousness is free, I can become so much more.

THE WOMAN, UNFORGETTABLE

Claudia Renée Winters

I had to say, she was the hottest woman I had ever had the pleasure of seeing at our shitty little puddle of a pool. If I had to guess her age I'd say around mid thirties, but she looked early twenties, especially with that smoking figure of hers. She was a bit on the lithe end of things, but had curves where it counted. A bright red hue of lipstick contrasted her pale skin nicely.

This woman also had an air of mystery about her--thick dark cat-eye sunglasses and a different patterned scarf obscuring her hair each time she showed up. Enough of her face was showing to deem it as gorgeous as the rest of her, but she still retained a sense of anonymity with those two things. Beastlike and elegant, under her gaze you felt like she was eyeing you in a way that indicated she could eat you up. She was the subject of many dirty daydreams of mine, but the scrawny lifeguard pretty much never gets with the hot chick, no matter how many romantic movies or pornos say otherwise.

I was perfectly content witch watching her from afar, and had plenty of opportunities to do so. She showed up rather frequently at the pool, and though it was one of many strange

364

things about her, my hormones blocked out any red flags I should have seen. My superior Diana, who was female and not at all amused with my attitude, chided me pretty much every day about the necessity of doing my job. But other than that woman showing up, it was a quiet summer.

In retrospect one of the first strange things was that, though she went to the pool almost every day, she never swam, like, ever. All she did was set herself up at the poolside in a variety of cute swimsuits that never saw a single drop of pissy chlorine water. You'd think she would at least tan--because honestly, it would have suited her well--but she sat in the shade of an umbrella the whole time, reading a book while the kids she brought along messed around.

Another oddity was how often she showed up. At least twice a week or more, which adds up pretty quickly in the long run. On the days she did show up (always ten minutes after opening), she'd let loose the kids, and they'd play for just as long as she could get away with before Diana began to walk over to her to tell them to get lost.

Her kids were pretty weird too. The boy, aged around six, was a chubby little thing, and there was something about his face that made him seem frightened of something. The girl, roughly eight years old, had a dirty matted mop on her head, and thin little legs that looked like they might collapse under her. Both looked rather terrified on that first day of the summer, looking at the pool as though it were going to hurt them. The mother coaxed them in, of course, but never entering herself. "Go on, try it," she murmured (in an enthralling voice, might I add). "It's fun." They glanced at her, unsure, but then entered.

"Mama, it's cold!" they complained.

"It'll warm up soon enough," she replied, and cracked open her thick novel to the first page.

It did warm up, of course, and as soon as it did they livened up quickly. They got even more enthusiastic when other kids and parents showed up, and suddenly they had a ton of playmates. At the end of that first long day they seemed reluctant to leave, but at the time I figured all kids are like that. Their gloomy faces lightened just a bit when she told them that, since they'd been good, they could come back very soon.

For a while I had been hoping to see her in action, gracefully and powerfully stroking her away across the pool and back. You know the reason why, of course, but it never happened. Her kids were total pros after a while though. Diana was even nice for once, and showed them how to tread water so they could extend their play to the deep end. They just got better and better, but noticeably darker too. Even I knew what it meant if you stayed in the sun too long, especially with its rays magnified by water. I couldn't muster up the courage to ask about sunscreen to this woman, so I sheepishly asked Diana to do it instead.

From what I observed the woman just nodded her head, presumably after each point Diana made, but her sly little grin was no more. It was an issue to her, and while I hoped those lovely red lips of hers would form a cute little pout the woman seemed genuinely unhappy whenever she applied sunscreen from then on, like this extra step was a disturbance to her pool ritual or something. But even that fell into the steady beat and thrum of summer, and I put that incident aside.

The next happening was quick, but disconcerting. The little girl, who was running around the pool (obviously a big no-no), ran into me while I was about to switch lifeguard duty with Diana. There was a pretty nasty bruise on her arm, just about every color of the rainbow. For once, I asked for her name. "Kayla," she said. I asked her what happened. "Kade hit me real bad." She pointed over to where her brother was floating on his back. I was disinclined to believe it, but decided not to pry. Besides, kids were getting more and more aggressive these days.

A few days after that, Diana murmured some offhand remark to me while we were closing up. "That woman has balls, taking her kids here so often. Kinda dumb, really."

"Why dumb?"

"Don't you ever look at the news, dumbfuck? Kidnapping rates are much higher these days," she hissed, shoving the gate keys into my hand. "Which means you need to stop sitting up in that glorified high chair drooling like an idiot and actually watch those kids."

"What's this all of a sudden? You jealous, Diana?"

"Piss off," she spat. "That woman is up to something, I bet. Pay attention for once, jackass." Angry, she stalked off to her car, leaving me to lock up alone.

Now, as a horny sack of shit, I have never been great with knowing which head to keep in control, which is why this is all stuff I realized in retrospect. How was I to know they'd leave one day in early August and never return? How was I to know she was going to give me that letter?

Those next few weeks, when June was reaching its peak, I was very excited indeed. She started to walk around the pool a bit more, swinging her hips in a rather seductive manner. Pretty much every man, and all of the gay chicks, couldn't help but stare. However, the only person she stared back at was me. She'd do that little finger wave towards me, and my heart would suddenly be racing. If she was close enough I could almost make out a flash of movement beneath those dark glasses--a flirtatious wink.

Diana was out for the rest of the summer, rather "conveniently", I'd like to say without it sounding too fucked up. Her replacement was a newbie, who was liking the looks of this woman as well. We did keep our eyes on her more than we should have. We were lucky nobody drowned, because honestly, since neither of us were really thinking much. She just had that much sway over our teenage minds. Just when it was on the verge of becoming an unhealthy obsession for me she was gone.

Around a week after she stopped coming with the kids, I figured that one of them got sick. After two weeks, I figured they were getting ready for school. After three, I began to feel a dull ache in my chest, worried and longing to see her one last time before I went back to school myself. About a month after that a strange letter showed up in my mailbox.

Letters were a thing of the past, but it was a welcome distraction from my newfound course loads and hours in front of thick textbooks. At least, I had hoped it would have been.

"Hey, Kiddo,

"Did you know that there is a tactic of meal preparation that involves beating a wild animal alive? It tenderizes the meat, and the fear juices, or adrenaline from those terrifying last moments supposedly creates a better tasting meat?

369

"You didn't say anything the entire summer, and that worked in my favor. I was glad strutting around like a minx was enough to distract you. The children I acquired weren't quite to my taste, but the exercise gave them quite a bit of muscle. Working out in the water does a lot more for you than if you were on land.

"I was afraid your female staff member had seen right through my intentions, so I had to take care of her at some point. Easy enough. What wasn't easy was washing out those chemicals you made me put on my children. Had I not bathed them rigorously, the sunscreen would have ruined their flavor entirely. I am a very particular woman, and the muscle mass was perfect. The tenderization process went swimmingly. It makes my blood boil to think it would all have been for naught.

"I suppose I am very lucky you were an outright fool. If it makes you feel any better, you probably would have had a shot with me if you were older."

It was signed with a lipstick kiss. Bright red.

I had a visit from the cops soon afterwards regarding this woman's case. I could not tell them anything about her, other than her general appearance and what I thought to be her height. It was then that all these details came rushing back to me at once. I told them everything I could, but it wasn't enough to find her. She'd been careful about that. No DNA could be lifted from her letter either. No fingerprints, not even saliva from the kiss.

For a brief period I was considered as a accomplice, but that theory went out the window once it became evident I really was just a stupid teenager. It haunts me, has haunted me for years, wondering about this woman's prior expertise, how she cleaned up everything so efficiently, how she developed her taste. I wondered what other kinds of intentions those sunglasses had been hiding.

I shudder to think that she has had many more "meals" since.

LIES I TELL

Whitley O'Brien

"Margaret, are you ready to begin?"

The smartly dressed detective slides into the chair across from mine in this dim little room. I thought interrogation rooms were supposed to be well lit? Shadows shroud this room like a veil.

"Margaret?" He speaks slowly, as if to a child. "Can we begin?"

"Yeah, sure. Let's begin."

He nods and looks down at the yellow legal pad in front of him, nods again and leans forward, pressing a button on the tape recorder.

"Please state your name for the record, ma'am."

"Margaret Greenwell."

"And your age as well, please." His politeness is starting to irk me.

"21." I say flatly. I've already been through this part of the process many times over.

"Ms. Greenwell, is it true that you are choosing to waive legal counsel at this time?"

"Yes, please, let's just get on with it." My cool is collapsing. I've been in and out of these bland, dingy rooms for hours. It's going on 2am and I'm ready to go to sleep.

He smiles as if he finds my forcefulness adorable. "Ok, I understand. You must be tired."

I don't dignify that with an answer. He knows I'm tired. He knows I'm mentally exhausted. That's why he's in here now to take my official statement instead of six hours ago when I might have been more alert. He thinks he can use this dirty tactic to get me to tell him something about what happened tonight that he doesn't already know.

"Could you please tell me where you were over the previous 24 hours?"

"I was at my apartment, then I was here."

"And who else was with you in your apartment?"

"Just me, my mother and my cat."

"Could you state the name of your mother?"

"Allison Moore."

"You don't have the same last name as your mother?"

I narrow my eyes. "As you know, I was adopted as a child. I bear the name of my adoptive family."

"Oh yes, that's right. My apologies." He smiles in a way that most would find friendly, but I see it for what it is. He's gloating. "At what age were you adopted? For the record?"

"I was seven when I was adopted."

"And what was your life like before you were adopted? What was your relationship with your mother like?"

"I don't know. As you doubtlessly know, I don't remember much before being adopted."

"And what precipitated the need for your adoption?"

I roll my eyes. He's so predictable. "My siblings were murdered. My mother was the only suspect."

"Care to elaborate on that?"

I sigh deeply but delve back into the story that I've told at least four people already tonight. My voice is mechanical, my words well practised by now.

"When I was 7, my mother allegedly had a break from reality brought on by severe, undiagnosed, postpartum psychosis following the birth of my baby sister, Ellie. She killed Ellie first by drowning her in the bath. She was only six months old. My little brother, Jake, walked in on her and she chased him through the house with a knife, eventually catching and killing him too. He was 5. I heard the commotion and hid in my toy chest. She had come out of her delusion before she found me. I was the only survivor."

The detective nods and makes a note on his pad. He already knows this story. He's hoping if he makes me repeat it again I'll crack and spill something new.

"But I thought you had no memory of the incident?"

"I don't, but I have read the files."

"What about your father?"

"I never knew him."

"Do you know his name? Where he's from? Anything about him?"

I shake my head and tell my first lie. It comes out smoothly. "No, I don't know anything about him. My mom was a prostitute, so he could really be anyone. Same for my siblings."

"Ok, what happened after your mother was taken into custody? What is the first thing you remember?"

"The first memory I have is meeting my adoptive mother, Cheryl Greenwell, at the group home. She was nice and pretty and she told me it was ok that I couldn't remember what happened, because we could make new memories."

"And how was your childhood? After you were adopted of course."

"It was lovely." I smile, genuinely. "I have the best family a girl could hope for. My mom and dad and my older brothers all welcomed me with open arms."

"So, there were no lasting effects from the trauma you experienced aside from the memory loss you still experience today? No hospitalizations?"

"Just one." I cross my arms over my chest. I know he is going to make me talk about it, but I'm not going to make it easier on him.

"When was this?"

"When I was 11."

"What happened?"

"I had another episode, lost six months."

He sighs, irritation creasing his face. "What caused that?" He seems to have dropped the 'we're just having a friendly chat' act and I respect him more for it.

"When I was 10 my mother sat us all down, and explained that we would be welcoming a new family member soon. We all expected her to say that she was going to be adopting a new kid, but she said she was six months pregnant."

I stop and take a sip of the warm water from the styrofoam cup I'd been given hours ago.

"We all knew she couldn't have children of her own, at least that's what she told us. That's why she adopted. I found out later that she never really gave up on the dream of bearing a child, she just quietly hid the miscarriages from us. I couldn't tell you how many. But this time she had made it farther than ever before, so she told us."

"Were you upset? Is that what led to the hospitalization?"

I roll my eyes. "Upset? We were *excited*. Especially me after I found out that it was a girl. I was tired of being the only girl. I couldn't wait to have a sister."

"You weren't worried about your parents loving you less when they had a child of their own?"

My eyes blaze, and I raise my voice for the first time since being here. "We *are* their children. Just because my brothers and I were adopted doesn't mean we aren't their children."

The detective gives no indication he even registered my outburst. "I'm lost as to how this relates to your subsequent hospitalization."

"Do you want to hear this or not?"

He raises his hands in supplication and I continue.

"Like I said, we were *all* excited about the baby. When mom went into labor less than two months later we all camped out in the hospital waiting room. My sister was born premature, so she spent a couple weeks in the hospital before coming home. She was so small and beautiful. They named her Emma.

When she came home it wasn't at all like any of us kids expected it to be. We were expecting to get to hold her and feed her and play with her all the time, but we couldn't. She was sickly from being born early, and she seemed to always be wailing. The boys stayed away as much as possible, even Dad, but I stayed with mom and Emma all the time. I was always by their side, ready to run and fetch diapers or fresh clothes when Emma inevitably spit up most of what little she'd eaten."

I stop talking, getting lost in the memory. The stuffy room, the sour smell of partially digested breast milk, my mom's gentle voice as she practically begged the baby to eat, to sleep, to stop crying. But none of that bothered me. What had bothered me was the fact that, even with all the crying and smells and lack of sleep, my mom was happier than I had ever seen her. She finally had what she'd suffered so much for. What she'd really wanted all along.

But I don't say that to the detective.

"Emma was with us for four months. Then she was gone. My last memory before everything went blank is my mom's scream waking me from sleep."

"So, Emma's death triggered another bout of memory loss and your hospitalization? What caused her death?"

I shrug and swipe at a tear. "Later, when I was more...myself again I asked to see her. I asked them to bring her to the hospital. I had forgotten she was dead. They told me it was failure to thrive, or SIDs or whatever else bullshit terms they use when what they mean is we don't know. I was in the hospital, nearly catatonic for six months after my baby sister died. I didn't even get to go to her funeral."

"That must have been difficult for you to cope with at such a young age."

"Of course, it was difficult for all of us."

He shifts in his chair and I can tell he's ready to move on. "So, were there any other instances of memory loss? Any other problems at all? How did you do in school, did you have friends?"

"What exactly does all this have to do with anything?" I'm getting fed up with telling my life story. I've been through a traumatic experience and this asshole won't let me leave. I can feel my level of irritation rising by the second.

"Just trying to get a feel for your life and the things you've been through. You can stop the interview at any time. But do know that the quicker we get through this, the quicker we can all go home."

He smiles. What he means is if I don't talk to him now, I will talk to him later. The only difference is how long he'll make me sit here in between.

"Fine. No, there were no other problems. I did well in school, rarely got into trouble and I had a few friends here and there, not too many. But hey, being unpopular isn't a crime is it?"

"Not that I'm aware of," He answers, totally serious. "How did you end up back in contact with your mother?"

Finally, he's asking the relevant questions.

"When I turned 18 I decided I was ready to know more about her. I only knew just the bare basics of the story up until then. My parents thought it would be best to shield me from the horror as much as possible considering my innate reaction to trauma. But I went behind their backs when I was officially an adult and dug into all the case files and such. I found out where birth mother was being held, and I decided to write her."

"Why would you want to speak to the woman who murdered your siblings? Weren't you horrified?" His eyes sparkle as he asks this and I get the feeling that if he had been in my shoes he would have done the same.

"You have to remember that I didn't even remember my siblings. I was detached from that horror. You might also remember that she was found incompetent to stand trial. Insane. She hadn't been in her right mind when she killed them."

"Okay, and how was your interaction with her? How was she?"

"Well, she'd spent the last decade in a mental institution so she wasn't all there. But she seemed nice, soft spoken, timid even. She was happy to hear from me and proud of how I'd grown up."

I decided not to mention that she had chosen not to return my first six letters. That when she finally wrote back she was dead set against meeting me. I had had to *beg* my own mother to see me. But eventually she began to trust me, to look forward to seeing me, to love me even.

"So, when her time at Shady Hills was done and she needed somewhere to live, you thought it would be best that she moves in with you?" He raised his eyebrows.

"She had no one else. It was move in with me, or move into a halfway house with a bunch of junkies. She was better off with me."

"Do you really think that? Even now? After everything that's happened?"

I look down at the chipped table and shake my head.

"When did things start to go wrong?"

What can I say to that? I can't say that she never wanted to move in with me, that as soon as I'd heard of her impending release I had begged and pleaded and guilted her into changing her mind. I can't explain the haunted look in her eyes when all I wanted was for her to love me. No, I can't say any of that.

"I don't know. I noticed that she was starting to become more paranoid about a month or so ago. We had been living together for half a year by that time. She would lock herself in her room for days on end. I had to force her to shower, to eat. I

381

should have called someone, had her recommitted, but I didn't. I didn't want to betray her by sending her back."

In truth, she had been paranoid from the start, jumping when I entered the room, keeping to herself as much as possible. She didn't want to do all the mother daughter things I had planned for us. Going to dinner, movies, getting manicures. All she wanted to do was spend all of her time as far from me as she could get. I couldn't understand, couldn't get why she didn't like me.

"Did you ever get the feeling that she might be dangerous?"

"I did notice a knife missing from the kitchen, but I never thought she took it. I thought I'd misplaced it somehow."

Another lie. I noticed the missing knives almost immediately. At first I *did* think I'd misplaced them. Then I found one in her room, under her pillow and I broke down. I screamed and cried and accused and begged. But still I was met with that same timid expression. Like a little dog that's been kicked one too many times, but still does it's best not to anger it's master. She wouldn't tell me why she hated me, what she was so afraid of.

"What started the incident tonight?"

"I don't know. I just went into her room to tell her dinner was ready and caught her with the knife. I tried to take it from her, but she got aggressive."

The lies flow so smoothly from my lips now, I can hardly tell I'm talking. Both storylines run through my head, superimposed over one another. She hadn't spoken a word until I held the blade to my wrist, threatened to end it all. What hope could I have after all if even my mother couldn't love me? Then she'd moved toward me, taken my arm and led me to her bed. Sat me down and told me everything.

"How did you end up with the knife, Margaret?"

"I... we struggled... wrestled for it. Finally, I knocked her against the wall and the knife fell from her hand. I grabbed it before she could."

She told me about who I am, where I came from and what really happened that night so many years ago. As she spoke, memories flooded back to me. I was 7 years old and in the tiny bathroom my family shared. The walls were wet with steamy condensation and my little sister, Ellie, sat in the tub in her little bath chair. "I'll be right back, watch your sister," my mom said. Ellie was kicking, splashing, and laughing. Then I was staring at her face, gazing up at me as I held her under the water she was still kicking, still splashing, but not laughing anymore.

My brother, screaming as I chased him down the hall. Grabbing the knife I always kept hidden in my toy chest. Cornering him in his room and plunging it into his chest, over and over.

My other baby sister sleeping peacefully for once. My new mother lying beside her, snoring loudly as she got the first deep sleep in four months. My hand covering Emma's mouth and nose, my other hand holding her tiny body still as she tried to squirm. Not letting go until she was still.

"When she came at me again, I knew I had to use the knife. It was her or me."

I wipe the tears from my face and look up at the detective. I can see that he's not really satisfied with my story, but I know he has nothing on me.

"I think we are about done here, I've heard all I need to hear. I just have one last question."

I nod at him to continue, my head in my hands.

"Why do you remember everything that happened? It seems that your typical coping mechanism is to block out traumatic memories. So why do you remember this one?"

I look up and into his eyes. He's looking at me with compassion. None of the disgust and suspicion I had been imagining. And I tell my last lie of the night.

"I don't know."

***

Back in my apartment I collapse onto my couch, utterly exhausted. I will have to clean the spare bedroom soon, probably replace the carpet. I close my eyes and think about everything I've learned today. About my self, about my mother. About how she was picked up one night working the streets by a man who turned out to have a dismembered body in his backseat. How she had escaped before he could kill her, but not before he could rape her. How she thought about killing me when she found out she was pregnant, how she held out hope I was another man's child. She said as soon as I was born she could see him in my eyes. Could feel him in my soul. But she loved me anyway. Loved me enough to take the fall for the murder of her children. Loved me enough to spend 10 years locked away in a mental institution.

It's touching really. Makes her death that much harder. But once she started talking about therapy and working through our issues I knew I couldn't let her live. She would eventually let something slip to the wrong person. I will miss her, but I still have my adoptive parents. They will support me through the next few weeks. The investigation. The funeral.

And I'm sure they'll support my decision to find my birth dad, assuming he's still alive. I hope he'll be happy to hear from me. I have so much to learn.

NOBODY SWIMS AT 2 O'CLOCK

Jennifer Winters

"Mama, when are you coming?"

My youngest son's voice shook as he spoke. I listened to the voicemail one more time, then deleted it. My heart ached a bit from hearing the pain in his voice. I'd call him as soon as I finished my swim, and then look at the calendar for a good weekend to make the five-hour drive to see him, his brothers, and their dad ... my husband.

"Mommy needed a break," I murmured towards the mobile in my hand, noticing two women who were leaving the pool center as I walked towards its front doors give me a glance, and then look at each other with a knowing, disapproving nod.

This was a small town, if it could even be called a town, and it was well-known that I was the evil woman who had stayed behind when her husband had been transferred to Charlotte. I was the sorry excuse of a mother who'd let her four children go, the youngest only seven years old. And all because I needed a break.

Yes, I knew it was selfish. And, yes, I did read *Eat, Pray, Love* shortly before I made my decision to go my own way for a while.

My husband and I had married the summer after our sophomore year at Ole Miss. We'd had a clear vision of finishing up at the university while living in the housing for married students, with our part time jobs at fast food joints providing plenty of income when combined with our scholarships and grants. It had only taken one semester to show us how naïve we'd been. I ended up quitting school with the understanding that I would support both of us by working full time while my husband finished up his degree, and then I would go back to school as soon as he graduated and found work.

The second phase of the plan never happened.

I was already pregnant with our oldest boy just before my husband graduated with his engineering degree. He got a good job right away, and we decided that I would be a stay-at-home mom until the baby was big enough for Pre-K. Then came Babies 2, 3, and 4. Number 4 was a surprise. The child of my impending middle age. A new job for my husband that promised a high quality of living brought us to this small Kentucky town in between Babies 3 and 4. The folks here were generally warm and friendly, but there was a clear line between those who were From Here, and those who weren't.

I grew more and more frustrated with my lack of a life outside of motherhood and wifery, until it put me in a perpetual state of anger and resentment. I loved my children passionately, but I constantly dreamed about life as a single woman with no kids. "Is There Life Out There?" and all that.

So, earlier this year when my husband got a sudden, lucrative job offer in Charlotte, I encouraged him to take it, then informed him that I would be staying behind. Mommy needed a break. Truth be told, I was angry. Not at my husband and the boys, but at myself for feeling so trapped. For needing some time to not be a wife a mom. I was angry for saying "that's fine" too many times when it wasn't fine, and for not asking for help when I needed it. I was angry at myself for not feeling more guilt about what I was doing.

After my husband and children left for Charlotte, I got a job in a used book store, and answered an ad for a housemate. The placer of the ad turned out to be a ridiculously sexy man about fifteen years my junior. We'd been housemates for four months, and the sexual tension was thick as molasses; to me, anyway. Nothing had happened, yet, just mild-to-heavy flirtation that was steadily getting heavier. In fact, just this morning he'd suggested that I try out his Jacuzzi bathtub when I commented on being sore from yesterday's workout. (I'd begun working out in earnest when I decided that his seeing me naked was a possibility.)

My roomie's invitation was replaying in my brain as I walked through the front door of the pool center. More people exited as I entered. This was precisely why I chose to take my lunch break later than usual. The pool center was on a lovely wooded property about three miles down a country road that wound away from the single intersection in what we called "downtown." With membership just costing twelve dollars a month, it was no wonder that it was both run down and popular. The whole place was in need of repair, with missing tiles, showers with oxidized heads, and a sauna of worn, splintered wood. That said, it was usually crowded, with at least two swimmers to a lane. Just last week I'd smacked heads with a retiree who had decided to share my lane without letting me know.

It was around ten of two in the afternoon when I approached the front desk to sign in. Miss Annie, one of the matrons who had managed the pool center since we'd moved here eleven years ago, looked up, surprised.

"Hi, Andrea. What are you doing here?" She seemed genuinely perplexed at my presence.

"I'm going to get my laps in," I answered with a smile.

"But, it's almost two . . ." she seemed to be weighing her words, "Nobody swims at two o'clock."

I answered, "Yes, ma'am, I know. I've noticed that the pool generally clears out around now, so I figured that it was a good time to get a lane to myself."

Miss Annie removed her silver-rimmed glasses and looked at me hard; not unkindly, but as if she wanted to make sure I understood. "Andrea, nobody swims at two o'clock."

"Well . . .," I stammered, confused. "The pool is open at two, right?"

"Oh, yes. We're open from six in the morning until nine at night. Nobody swims at two o'clock." Miss Annie held my gaze, her head bobbing in a slight nod.

I smiled and told her that having the pool to myself sounded perfect. I went into the changing room, unlocked my locker, and quickly changed into my suit. After a quick, mandatory shower, I entered the pool room. The pool looked like any indoor pool: Olympic length, six lanes, in need of resurfacing. Some of the overhead lights were burned out, with one flickering. The other pool center manager, Miss Lyla, sat high on the lifeguard's seat, almost regally. I always wondered what she'd do if someone were to start drowning, given her advanced age.

"Andrea," she said. "Miss Annie told you that no one swims at 2 o'clock?"

"Yes, ma'am," I answered, feeling a bit annoyed and confused. "The pool is open, isn't it?"

"Oh, yes, it's open. But, nobody swims at this hour." Her face took on the matronly look of an older woman dispensing wisdom to a young girl, which I was not.

"Great," I answered.

I jumped into the water. The soreness from yesterday's workout eased a bit as soon as I hit the cool water. Twisting this way and that, I did a quick stretch, and decided to start with a backstroke. Checking the red numbers on the old digital clock that was mounted on the wall, I started timing myself at 1:59:00.

As I began my first lap, I let my mind wander. I thought of my boys. The oldest was plenty pissed at me, and the youngest missed me terribly. I missed them, too, despite my almost frantic need for "a break." And that's what it was, right? I still wanted to grow old with my husband, just not right now. My mind shifted to Sexy Housemate. Despite my lust for him, I had no desire for a real relationship. I just wanted to test the Jacuzzi, so to speak. Just one time, maybe two, and then I could seriously think about going to Charlotte.

By the time I finished my first length, the flickering of the defective overhead light was getting on my nerves and my arms and legs felt a bit heavy, so I flipped over to do a crawl. The clock was at 1:59:32. My thoughts went back to my boys: how much I missed them, despite enjoying some freedom after so many years. Could their dad forgive me? (My legs really are tired. Slow down a bit.) He says that he understands. Damn, what a good man. Always such a good man, down to his bones. (Legs are so tired, so heavy. Should I stop for a few seconds? Should I . . .?)

Something was wrong.

In my reverie, I had stopped swimming about halfway through the second length, aware that my arms and legs had simply ceased moving. Maybe I should change from a crawl to a breast stroke. I tried to bend my knees and press the soles of my feet together to get started. My legs didn't respond. Neither did my arms.

I was spread eagle, floating on top of the water. Beneath me, the light refracted, playing its usual tricks. I noticed that the flickering caused by the faulty light stopped, the light shining steadily, as it should. I needed to take a breath, but my head would not turn to the side. Too confused to feel afraid, I blew the air out of my lungs.

I immediately realized my mistake. Unable to move and now needing badly to inhale, I began to sink. I only heard the muffled roar of the pool pump, and nothing else. Not even my heartbeat. Where was Miss Lyla? Surely she could see that I was in trouble! Why couldn't I move? Was I having a stroke? The rising panic would have brought me to tears, had I been able to breathe.

As I watched the floor of the pool draw nearer, my thoughts turned to my children. How could I have let them go? They were all such *good* boys! I wanted to see them. And their daddy. My children may be permanently motherless because of my stupid soap opera fantasy.

I continued to slowly sink towards the bottom of the pool, my lungs now burning with the need to breathe.

"Mama, when are you coming?" My baby's voice in my head gave me a rush of determination. Fiercely, I willed my limbs to move, my legs to kick. Now!

Nothing moved.

My lungs didn't burn, anymore.

I reached the bottom of the pool, and kept sinking, down, down, and the floor of the pool was now a ceiling over my head, growing ever more distant.

***

Miss Lyla joined Miss Annie in the lobby. They didn't speak for a while. Andrea was gone. Not dead. Not alive. Just gone.

The security camera at the front door would provide footage showing her leave at around 2:45 PM, her hair wet and a towel in her hand, even though such a thing had never actually happened. The sheriff wouldn't call for an inquiry. He never did. The two o'clock swimmer would quickly fade from everyone's memory, as was always the case. Her husband would give up looking for her, much sooner than he probably should. The boys would grieve, and then, after a while, only vaguely remember that they'd had a mama named Andrea.

Miss Lyla would see to Andrea's car in a few minutes, before any three o'clock swimmers arrived.

When they did arrive, they would note the unbroken, perfect tiles and newly sealed pool surfaces with a detached approval. They would admire the new, soft lighting in the pool room. They would comment on how wonderful the new cedar sauna smelled, and moan in pleasure when they stood under the fancy, massaging shower heads that were now in place. It wouldn't occur to any of them to wonder how all of the improvements on the pool center were made in a single hour. It never, ever occurred to them to wonder at the two old ladies who had managed the pool center from as long as anyone could remember, even those who had been swimming there from kindergarten to geriatric care.

Miss Annie spoke, "That should do for a good long while." She paused, then continued, "I hate it when they have children. It's better when they're single, or old."

Miss Lyla just grunted.

"I know that she let her family leave," Miss Annie continued, "but she was alright. People get fed up. Especially the mamas, it seems. Pulled every which way, I think."

Miss Lyla grunted, again.

In the beginning, before there was even a town, when the pool was nothing more than a deep depression in a large stone, they came willingly. If not willingly, then with a sense of duty. Miss Annie didn't mind it so much, back then.

Miss Annie asked, as she did every few decades, "And all we can say is that people don't swim at two o'clock . . . not much of a warning. Why can't we get a hateful person to swim at two o'clock?"

Miss Lyla didn't answer for a moment. Finally, she turned and looked Miss Annie dead in the eye. "You know that's not how it works. Anyway, it wasn't a punishment for anything. It just worked out this way. This time."

Miss Annie nodded and rose from her stool, busying herself by setting out the clipboard with a new sign-in sheet for the three o'clock swimmers. Miss Lyla straightened up and went to the locker room to clean out Andrea's locker.

REINE

K. J. McDonald

"Oh, my *god*, Mom!" Lexi screamed when she opened her birthday card.

I screamed, too. I couldn't help it.

"*Mooom!*" She shrieked, "We're gonna see Reine!" Her eyes brimmed with tears as she held the two golden tickets out for everyone to see. Her friends seethed with jealousy.

"You can pick who goes with you, of course. I'll drive you kids." Every teenage girl in the room leaned forward.

"Obviously I want you to go, Mom! You've been a fan since you were a little girl."

I must admit, I savored the renewed looks of envy on their faces. Some seemed nearly sick with it. I smiled savagely at them. *C'mon girls*, I thought, *aren't you happy for us?* Of course, they weren't.

"Okay," I said, clapping my hands together, "Who wants cake?"

...

"How could she even afford those tickets?" I overheard one of my daughter's friends say as I passed out plates of birthday

396

cake. "My dad is worth like three times as much as her and he couldn't even get one for me."

"You know, Emily," I said, "Those tickets are actually exclusive to people who are willing to sign the waiver."

"Waiver?" Emily scoffed. "Waiver for what?"

"Well, Reine selects her dancers from her audiences, you know. You have to sign a waiver when you buy tickets, in case you – or your child – catch her eye."

"Oh, my god! Reine's dancers are amazing!" Squealed some nondescript adolescent whose name I can't remember.

Emily rolled her eyes, "Reine only picks new dancers once every dozen years or so… it's not like either of you are going to get picked… god, I don't see why dad wouldn't just sign it. It's a non-issue."

"Well, if she chooses you, you can't say no. That's what the waiver says. Your dad probably didn't like the thought of that. Reine's dancers tour with her non-stop. He'd probably never see you again, if she happened to chose you."

…

"I can't believe we're actually here," Lexi shouted over the din as she gazed around the amphitheater. "I don't think I've ever seen so many people in one place!"

"You ain't seen nothing yet!" I yelled, "We're two hours early!"

Already the drone of a thousand conversations was deafening. Lexi stood with me somewhere near the center of the main floor, gazing around at the balconies. People were already pushing and shoving, fighting to get the closest spot to the stage.

As her face was turned toward the ceiling, a girl about her age shoulder-checked Lexi, sending her sprawling. I grabbed the teen by the hair and flung her backwards. I helped my daughter to her feet as the girl disappeared under the shoes of the swarming crowd.

I wiped the blood from Lexi's mouth, "Watch out, baby!" I screamed "People are going to get crazy!"

She nodded vigorously, face pale with shock.

When the next concert-goer tried to shove her out of the way, she planted her feet and pushed back. The stranger bounced off her and disappeared into the throng behind us.

Finally the house lights dimmed and the masked dancers pirouetted onto the stage, spreading their arms simultaneously at the screen that hung behind them. They were identical, waif-like and perfect, every one of them. My eardrums buzzed painfully with the roar of the crowd. I gazed around me. *Where are the gladiators*, I thought. This audience was fit for them.

Colored laser lights swept the crowd as the montage began to play on the screen. Pictures of Reine in all her pale, black-haired glory elicited screams of exultation from every one of the tens of thousands of mouths.

A booming male voice came over the speakers, even louder, somehow, than the crowd.

"Reine has entertained the nations for more than 150 years," he began.

A video of Reine played. "And I'm still hot!" she proclaimed, gesturing to her obscenely proportioned body, her black mane shimmering.

The crowd erupted, a new decibel was surely defined.

"She is the *pinnacle* of pop culture," the booming voice continued, "The *definition* of art."

Another clip of Reine played, "It doesn't even have to be good," she cried, "Whatever I put out, you lap it up like dogs!" Her angelic face turned up and blistering cackles tore out of her red mouth.

The crowd shrieked again. Warm trickles of blood poured out of my ears.

"Without further ado," the voice shouted as digital music began to pound relentlessly from the speakers, "I give you... Reine!"

I looked at my daughter, she was jumping and panting as Reine exploded onto the stage out of a pillar of black smoke.

The insectile crowd around us began to surge. I grabbed Lexi's hand and pressed the long, sharp knife I'd brought into it. "You'll need this!" I screamed, but my words were long lost in the cacophony. She got the idea, though.

The beat dropped. I released her hand and she tore through the crowd with her weapon, like a cannonball. She left the ground wet and tacky behind her. I've never been so proud.

Reine's siren voice tore through the atmosphere.

Worship me, she sang.

Body like fire

Voice like desire.

I'm your queen.

Worship

Worship

Worship

Worship

I saw her hand reach up toward the stage, matted with the blood and hair of fallen fanatics. I knew it was her, even before Reine pulled her up onto the stage. *That's my girl*, I thought.

Tears poured out of my eyes, glittering like diamonds in the strobe lights.

Reine made a motion with her hands and the music stopped. My daughter, my Lexi, stood, trembling and laughing next to her on the stage.

"Silence!" She hissed, and was obeyed.

"What is your name, dear?" She asked.

"Lexi."

"I think I've found my new dancer, at last. What do you think about that, love?"

Lexi nodded emphatically as the crowd bellowed.

Reine's mouth fell open, impossibly wide. The music began again. The crowd shrieked with hysterical glee. A long, pronged tongue snaked out between her lips and latched around Lexi's throat. Her neck snapped back violently as she was drained of her lifeblood.

Reine glowed, even more impossibly beautiful than before as Lexi fell, pale and spent, between her feet.

One of the dancers jete'd to Reine's side and handed her a dancer's mask. Silver hooks snaked from the back of it and burrowed into Lexi's dead face.

She rose, elite, to join the rest.

THE ATTIC
P. Oxford

The moment we saw the padlocked door hidden behind a bookshelf in the attic of our new home, we knew something was off. We had been joking about how moving into a mansion in the countryside sounded like the beginning of a horror movie, but the story of the house was more risqué than scary. The previous owners – a retired hedge fund manager turned failed writer and his young wife – had seen their impending financial disaster coming, and they fled the country before the house of credit cards could come crashing down around them. The police looked, of course, but there are lots of beaches in Mexico.

"You ladies seem much nicer than that *other* couple," the aging waitress at the local diner had told us when she realized we were the ones to have bought the house. "We were not even surprised when they ran off, no ma'am. That man gallivanting all over town with whatever young innocent girl he could seduce. And that wife of his? Can't say if she didn't know or didn't care; she wasn't exactly the friendly sort. I never trusted either of them – too slick. And then they just leave, all their bills unpaid like the crooks they were."

Save for a few items of value that the bank had auctioned off separately, the house was left just as it had been when the previous owners left. We spent the first few days exploring the rooms, searching for treasures, and finding quite a few. There was something eerie about sorting through the clothes and personal items, and more than once I jumped at the unfamiliar sounds of the old house.

Eventually our search made it to the attic. It was there we found the heavy wooden bookshelf we decided to repurpose for the kitchen. When we went to move it, we saw the door. The large padlock wasn't the only thing holding the door closed; wooden boards were nailed across it. A piece of wood had been chopped off the bottom of the door. The space was about ten centimetres high and twenty centimetres long, with rough edges like it had been done with a hammer. Linda and I exchanged a quiet, wide eyed look before I got down on all fours and shone my flashlight inside.

"Looks like a bedroom."

"That's fucking creepy."

"Wanna open it?"

"Damn right I do!" Linda said, crowbar already in hand. Within five minutes she had the door open.

We were met by a musty smell that made me cough. The room was beautifully furnished, with a four-poster bed, a large fireplace, a comfy chair and a thick carpet. A small skylight exposed the grey sky and made the room glow with the weak light that seeped through the clouds. Linda opened the wardrobe, and I sat down on the bed. There was a notebook on the nightstand, and I picked it up and flipped through it. The first part was mostly snippets of writing: ideas for stories, the occasional writing exercise, and every once in a while, a line or two about the day, or the week, or even the month. Towards the end, the tone changed, the number of diary entries increased, and it got ... weird.

"Listen to this," I said, and started reading it out loud.

I am still not feeling great. I don't know what it is I've contracted, but the missus insists I spend some nights in the guestroom in the attic. I remember when she decided to furnish this little room I thought she was being silly, but now I'm glad I indulged her little whims. The room is pretty nice, and, frankly, she's probably right not to want me in her bed.

Poor thing, sometimes I feel bad for her. She doesn't know about S, and I have no intention of changing that. The way she looked at me today, I thought for a moment she might have realized, but of course she hasn't. She's not the suspicious type, and it's not like she ever found out about A, or any of the others. Damn, I miss A. She was quite the firecracker.

~

I was going to write today, I promised myself. But my head feels so woozy, I can't focus. Hopefully a few days of rest and the dry attic air will make me all better.

~

I feel even worse today. I haven't been out of bed the whole day. Ginny brings me food, but I can't say I'm very hungry. I forced myself to take some bites anyway, and drank the whole smoothie she made me. I didn't even try to write anything real, this is all I can muster, and it's not exactly a literary masterpiece. Ginny is so lovely to me, it really has been a long time since we talked like this. It feels more like it did when we first met. Maybe I should end things with S. Well, I guess things are ended until I get out of this bed, and I don't feel like doing that any time soon.

~

Still feeling the same, i.e. bad. I asked Ginny if she would take me to the doctor, but she just laughed at me and said I obviously have the flu, no point in wasting the doctors time. I haven't had the flu in years, but I seem to remember it feeling different. Maybe I'm just being a hypochondriac, though, I've always been a worrier when it comes to my health. Ginny is probably right. God, but this room is driving me crazy.

~

I had a fight with Ginny today. I told her I wanted to go for a walk, and she yelled at me to get back in bed and stay there until I got better. I didn't want to fight with her, but I got so angry. This room is driving me crazy. In the end my dizziness convinced me she was right, and I went back to bed. At least the food she's bringing me is delicious, and even though my head is still swimming, my appetite has come back a little.

~

That fucking bitch! Ginny was late with the food today, so I decided to go get some for myself. I couldn't open the door! That bitch fucking barricaded the door! She's trapped me in here!

I yelled at her, and when she came to the door, she told me it was for my own good. She didn't bring any food either. Somehow while I was napping, she got a piece off the bottom of the door and slid a tray under it. That psycho bitch. I yelled at her for hours, but she just repeated that it's for my own good and she doesn't want to catch what I have. I tried to break down the door but she has reinforced it somehow.

God, writing this shit down makes it look even worse. Little innocent Ginny has locked me in a room in the attic. Now that I'm thinking about it a little more calmly I am wondering if she's not right. I mean, Ginny wouldn't ever hurt me, she's too sweet. A little naïve, not the cleverest, but cruelty has never been her thing. Shit, now I don't know what to think.

406

~

Today I tried pleading with her to let me out. She started crying and told me not to ask her, she was doing it for both of us, and I shouldn't be mad at her. I still think she thinks she knows what she's doing, but I'm worried she's gone a little mad. If she was really so worried, she'd take me to a doctor, not lock me in the attic. I guess this is what I get for marrying the pretty blonde, isn't it.

Sorry God, should've gone for the brunette. Next time. But shit, I knew she was dumb, but I didn't know she was "being locked in the attic is good for you" dumb. Next time she brings me food I'll get her to let me out. I got her to marry me, I got her to believe all the dumb ass lies about the other girls, I can get her to let me out.

~

I can't get her to let me out. Pretty sure I've been in here for more than a week. If my head wasn't swimming all the time I bet I could've convinced her, but it's like whatever is wrong with me is slowing down my whole brain. I get that Ginny's afraid of contracting it, because it's really not getting any better, but I still feel like locking me in the attic was a bit over the top.

When I get better I might have to give her a piece of my mind, but for now I guess I'll just ride this latest of her crazy ideas out. Maybe she has it in her head to be a nurse again, like she wanted to before she met me. Maybe that's the issue, she's just play acting a nurse. Did she have to fucking pick Nurse Ratched though? Jeez.

Maybe I should let her go to nursing school after all. She's gonna get bored within the first semester, and then she'll go back to being my good little wife.

~

Unless I starve to death. That pretty little idiot forgot to feed me today. Maybe I won't let her go to nursing school, she'd obviously make a shitty one.

~

I'm not entirely sure how long I've been up here, but I am entirely sure that it's been way too long since I ate. It's like the hunger pangs are clearing up my brain a little, but I'm getting really worried.

~

I just had the most chilling thought. What if something happened to Ginny? What if she was in an accident, and is in the hospital – or worse? She doesn't have any friends anymore, so it's not like she'd have told anyone about locking me in here. On the bright side my hunger pangs have been replaced by a hazy fog of tiredness.

~

I've tried to get out of here for hours, but no use. I'm trapped. I'm gonna fucking die in here, and that's how it is. Shit. Wait, no, I figured it out! There is a way out, it's been staring me in the face this whole time! God, I'm an idiot.

"And then what?" Linda said.

"It's the last entry."

"Holy shit..."

"Do you think it's real?"

"It can't be, can it?"

"The boarded up door behind the bookshelf does kind of lend it some credence, don't you think?"

"Yeah," I responded, dumbstruck. "Do you think he made it?"

"He's not here, is he? And they all said the couple took off to get away from their financial problems. Or ... I guess they don't actually know that, people just assumed because they disappeared."

The silence hung heavy between us until she spoke again.

"Don't you think if he made it we'd have heard? I mean in a small town like this, it's not like this story would've gone unnoticed..."

"Shit," I said, staring into the fireplace. "Should we call the police?"

She didn't answer, and walked over to the large fireplace. "'It was staring me in the face'. Can I have the flashlight?"

I tossed it to her. She turned it on, stuck her head inside the fireplace, and looked up.

"Fuck," she croaked, jerking back. Before I could say anything Linda threw up all over the rug.

They hadn't run off to Mexico together. Well, Ginny might have made it, but her husband only made it halfway up the chimney.

THE CHANGELING TREE
AIB

I never put much stock in urban legends, especially ones enshrined in children's' rhymes. Growing up my town had one. It was one of those little, close-knitted villages where most everyone knew everyone else, and The Changeling Tree was passed down from mother to child in every generation. I never believed it was anything more than a cute poem children recited with handclaps or jumping ropes, but as was tradition I taught it to my little daughter.

> *Oh, don't go 'round the Changeling Tree,*
> *The willow in the wood.*
> *The Watcher Mother's waiting there*
> *To catch you if she could.*

There are more verses, of course, but over the years they became garbled and lost. Honestly, the beginning is creepy enough to hear a young child singing; I don't think it needs any more.

But you *will* hear young children singing it constantly, especially on the playground in the park. By the time my little

411

Molly was old enough to be taken to the park to play I'd gotten so used to hearing the rhyme. It was more background noise than anything else.

I was wrong. Some urban legends shouldn't be ignored.

That day, I took Molly to the park in the early afternoon. Most of the other mothers of young children took them there around the same time, so there was always someone for Molly to play with and someone for me to talk to. I sat on the bench on the side of the playground, chatting with two other women. My belly was swollen with my second child, so I was letting them feel my little boy kick.

Oh, don't go 'round the Changeling Tree

We'd been there for several hours already, and the baby was getting restless. I was sure Molly would be getting tired about then. It was time for snack. I pulled a baggie of crackers from my purse.

"Molly!" I called out. "Are you hungry? It's snack time!"

The prospect of food usually brought her running, but that day there was no response.

"Molly!" I tried again. "Honey, I have your crackers! Where are you?"

412

I could still hear the rhyme being chanted steadily, but Molly was nowhere to be found.

This was any mother's worst nightmare. I felt bile rising into my throat as I brushed aside the two other mothers and stood on my swollen ankles. I tottered over to the slides; no Molly. I checked the swings; no Molly. I stumbled to the see-saw; no Molly. Panic began to consume me. Where was my child?!

I heard her giggle.

My stomach dropped into my shoes as my head whipped around to find her. She had stepped off the playground, chasing a huge butterfly down the dirt path that lead into the woods.

"Molly! Stop!" I cried, mixed feelings of relief and frustration washing over me. "Don't go into the woods!"

"Come with me, Mommy!" Her voice carried faintly on the wind as I watched her little form disappear into the shade of the trees. My feet were already carrying me down the path. "Help me catch the butterfly!"

"Molly, come back here right now! Please, honey, it's dangerous!"

The wind answered in her stead, blowing out of the woods to tangle in my hair and send a shiver down my spine. I stepped into the shadows.

At once, all the sounds from the park seemed to fade. The sunlight that filtered through the trees was sparse; barely

413

enough to see the dirt path leading further in. I heard no birds, no animals; just a deafening, oppressive silence, punctured only by the occasional echo of her giggle somewhere ahead of me. I meant to call for her again, but the stifling pressure of quiet filled my lungs and I couldn't speak. My only choice was to follow.

My body felt heavy. I waded through thick, stale air, my footsteps echoing obscenely off the trees, which grew ever closer to the path. Her faint giggles carried hauntingly on the sparse breeze as I pushed forward with a mother's determination. There was a spark of light ahead; if I could just get there I would find her, I was sure.

The willow in the wood.

I didn't find her in that clearing. Instead, a monstrous willow tree stood square in the middle of the opening. The other trees grew in a ring around it, giving it a wide, respectful berth. The breeze stopped. The willow's weeping branches hung deathly still. A cold chill ran through me; the knotted grey bark formed eye-like protrusions that seemed to stare at me accusingly.

I heard Molly giggle again. As my eyes searched for her desperately I saw her. The huge butterfly she had been chasing flew behind the tree, out of my vision, and she followed. I saw her back disappear behind the willow.

I tried to call for her again, croaking out her name as I choked on the silence, but she did not reappear on the other side of the tree.

Mustering my strength, I tripped forward, touching the bark of the tree as I circled counter clockwise around its back.

Molly was not behind the tree.

The Watcher Mother's waiting there.

I was panicking again as I came around the other side. Molly wasn't there. Instead, everything had changed.

The trees that had crowded the path had been replaced by skeletal imitations of themselves. They let in far more light, but the light that poured in was red. Deep red, like the sky had become an open wound, dripping blood down from the heavens. The path I had walked to get to the tree was now covered in bright white pebbles that crunched angrily when I stepped on them. The only thing that remained was that horrible, strangling silence, and my continued inability to call for my daughter. Even the willow seemed much more menacing in the crimson hues; somehow angrier, more enraged.

415

She must've headed back to the playground, I reasoned. There was nowhere else to go but deeper into the woods, and I didn't hear her go that way.

I headed back the way I came. All the trees were gnarled, raking their finger-like branches across the slivers of sky I saw. The pebbles on the path made strange creaking noises, shrill, like a quiet scream. I had to get out of these woods. Despite my protesting ankles I ran. I ran down the shrieking rocks. I ran past the decaying trees. I ran until I burst from the treeline into what I can only describe as Hell itself.

The landscape stretched before me, drenched in crimson light. The white pebble path ended at the edge of the woods, and from there it was wasteland. Hot, arid wasteland. Dead grass swayed feebly in patches on the scorched Earth. The playground remained, but it was destroyed. Coated in rust and broken. The swings squealed on their hinges as the hot wind attempted to push them. Great holes gaped in the slides. The seesaws had fallen off their pivots and lay dejected beside them. A doghouse stood lonely to the side, a chain leading from a pole to inside the darkness aside an empty food bowl. Mounds of sand covered parts of the playground, pieces of something sharp sticking up from them like jagged teeth.

But the most horrific thing were the children. If they were children.

They stood in stark contrast to the burning hot landscape with their pale, blue-toned skin. They shambled like zombies around the playground, white faces turned to the ground. I watched one slowly make his way to the doghouse, a box of something in his hand. He knelt and began to fill the empty bowl with what I can only assume was dog food, reaching in to pull the chain.

The poor creature that slid out had been dead a long, long time.

The child patted its skeletal head soothingly, murmuring something to it, though his teeth chattered so loudly as he spoke I couldn't begin to figure out what it was.

The sight of these unnatural children made my skin crawl, but if anyone had seen my daughter they would've had to. I stepped forward, as close to one of the pale creatures as I dared, and cleared my throat. It came out as a strangled groan, and all the children's faces snapped forward to look at me, white skin gleaming in the red sun.

And then I realized they didn't have faces at all. I was looking at a playground full of porcelain-masked children. My breath caught in my throat. Smiles had been painted onto the masks, inhumanly big, stretching from ear to ear and painted with cherry red lips. I could see the children's eyes through the small holes. Despite the farcical smiles on their masks, their eyes were wells of deep despair, frozen as if on the verge of tears. Those eyes shone brightly as they looked at me, as if pleading for something only I could provide.

"Please, have you seen my daughter?" I whispered, trying to look at anything but the masked children. My eyes landed on a mound of sand. The jagged edge sticking up from the pile was porcelain white, like a mask. A small, palish-blue hand poked out helplessly from the base of the sand.

"Those were unhappy children," one of the masked ones, a girl, finally said, drawing my attention back to her. Click-clack. Her teeth chattered wildly, as if she were freezing. "Only happy children live here."

"My daughter's name is Molly," I said quickly, trying not to think too deeply about what exactly she meant. "I think she might come this way. Did you see her?"

She nodded and turned. She lifted an arm and slowly lifted it to point at the other end of the playground.

"Watcher Mother decides who can stay." Clack-clack.

My blood froze.

To catch you if she could.

My daughter stood at the other end of the playground. Her back was to me, but her head was turned up to look at the abnormally large butterfly she'd been chasing. It sat purchased on a long, spindly finger.

The Watcher Mother's finger.

She would have easily been eight feet tall had she been on her feet, but she was squatting down, attempting to be on Molly's level. Her body was bulky, fleshy skin, draped over oddly thin arms and legs. I could see her veins protruding from it even from so far away. A single eye sat centered in her hairless forehead, wide and unblinking, red like the sun. She had no mouth. Or, I thought she didn't, until it opened, splitting her neckless head open like a great gash, sharp teeth jutting out at bizarre angles.

A monster. The watcher mother was undoubtedly a monster.

"Tell me, child," she rasped, teeth glistening with saliva as her grey tongue caressed each word carefully. "Are you happy?"

"Mmhmm," Molly answered, nodding.

"Do you like other happy kids?"

"Yes…"

"Do you want to play with other happy kids?"

"Yeah!"

"Wonderful." She shifted, and the butterfly flew away. Her fingers reached toward my little girl, and a wave of nausea flooded me as I froze in fear. "Why don't you stay here with us? You can be happy forever, and play with other happy kids all day."

"But..." a note of uncertainty had crept into Molly's voice. "What about Mommy?"

"I'm your mommy now."

Those words snapped me out of whatever stupor I'd been in, and I screamed. The porcelain-faced children stared with their frozen eyes as I barreled forward, wrapping my arms around my child. I pulled her backwards, away from the monstrosity squatting before her.

"Mommy!" Molly cried out, clasping her little hands behind my neck as I picked her up and put her on my hip. "Mommy, I'm scared. I wanna go home."

The Watcher Mother roared, and I felt the ground shake beneath me. My legs trembled as I began stumbling backwards, eyes glued to the evil thing that had tried to trick my little girl. The single eye locked on me with such malice that it felt it like a punch to the throat. My unborn son kicked wildly in distress.

"Mine!" The Watcher Mother bellowed, lurching forward, stick like arms stretching forward as if to pull Molly away from me. "Unhappy children! I will make you happy! You belong to me! Stay! Stay forever!"

I'm not sure if it was me or Molly screaming; likely it was both. All I know is that instinct kicked in and I turned on my protesting ankle and ran. I didn't stop to see if she was chasing us. I wouldn't dare. All I knew was that I had to get back to the Changeling Tree and get us out of there. The Watcher Mother roared again somewhere behind me, anger palpable.

As I ran, the masked children began to chant, and I could hear them all the way back to the woods; the missing verses to the rhyme.

Oh, don't go 'round the Changeling Tree,
The willow in the wood.
The watcher Mother's Waiting there
To catch you if she could.

The tree leads to a reddened sky,
To hot and dying places
The Watcher keeps the children there
Smiles frozen on their faces

Oh, don't go 'round the Changeling Tree
Within the wood so wild.
The Watcher wants to keep you there
To be her happy child.

Those rhymes will be seared into my brain as long as I live. I could hear them echoing in my thoughts even as we reached the tree, and I stopped to catch my breath. I put Molly down and took her little hand. I didn't know if it would work, but I had no other ideas: I touched the bark of the Changeling Tree and went around the back of it clockwise.

I realized I had inadvertently closed my eyes as we came around the other side. I felt Molly tug on my hand.

"Mommy, look! We're back!"

I opened my eyes and let out a sob of relief. The trees were back to normal, only letting in small amounts of light to illuminate the dirt path. They crowded close, full of leaves and life. This time, I heard the twittering of birds and the distant sounds of children playing in the park. I took a deep breath and squeezed Molly's hand.

"Yes we are, baby. Let's go home."

***

Molly was unusually quiet on the ride home. I assumed she was still shaken up over the whole incident, and I was wondering what I'm the world I was going to tell my husband.

But the normalcy of driving well known roads was soothing to me, and she seemed content to start out the window.

The sun had begun up sink beyond the horizon as we pulled into the driveway. I shut off the engine and undid my seatbelt, reaching over to undo Molly's.

Her small hand stopped me.

Instead, she reached over and rubbed my belly, smiling up at me. Smiling a little too widely, with eyes that seemed a little too frozen.

"Mommy, when my brother is born let's take him to see the pretty tree. I'm sure it'd make him happy." Then she unbuckled herself and hopped out of the car. As I watched her head towards the house, something fell out of her hand into the gravel of the driveway.

I was frozen. My fingers were stiff over the seatbelt. The strange expression on her face stuck with me.

I shakily climbed out of the driver's seat, my knees feeling weak, and hesitantly went to see what Molly had dropped.

In the gravel was a broken piece of porcelain, white as snow. I picked it up, holding it away from my body as far as I could. Scrawled on the piece of broken mask in deep red letters were the words, "I am always watching."

As I watched the little girl opening the front door to my house and jumping into my husband's arms, my mouth hung open in shock and terror.

Who the hell came back with me from the Changeling Tree?

THE NOWHERE DOOR
Caitlin McGlynn

I used to love that house. Every summer my family would ride down to North Carolina and see it. An elegant old house standing against the sky. The sound of waves crashing down on the nearby beach providing the perfect soundtrack to my summer. I can still remember myself, and Elise and Ethan, running towards the house. The twins would be fighting with each other over who gets out the car first. The memory now tastes bittersweet. All because of the one summer where we messed with that door. The one we can't forget...even if we wanted to.

That summer started out normal enough. Long days spent on the beach. Campfires at night. It was just great, until the smell started. I was awoken one night by a terrible smell. This hasn't been the first time an awful stench had been in our house. However, it was never this bad. I almost gagged. I'm a very light sleeper and the terrible scent was more than enough to wake me. I marched to my parent's bedroom and informed them of the smell. My dad decided to investigate. I followed him up to where the smell seemed to be coming from.

"The attic. Of course it is." My dad grumbled. I cautiously walked behind him. While I hated the smell, I was type of kid who always wanted to feel like they were the boss. I followed him into the attic. I had never been there before so I was a bit nervous. My eyes widened when I saw what was inside.

The room was mostly bare with only a few old nick-nacks and clothes laying around. Mint colored wallpaper that was peeling off at the ends, covered the walls. I coughed from the thick layer of dust that seemed to cover everything. It seemed like any stereotypical old attic, expect for one thing.

At the very end of the of room stood a large door. Unlike the dark, hardwood floor, it seemed to made out of ashwood. It seemed worn down somehow. It was ajar just enough for me to see a wood wall unusually close behind it. At the very top I could see a bit of the night sky which just confused me more. I was pulled out of my thoughts by the smell becoming even stronger.

"Oh, found it." My dad called out. I stared in disgust as he pulled a dead rat off from the floor. "Guess we need to put out traps."

I cringed at the idea of rats being in the house. I knew I wouldn't be going back in the attic for a while. However, I still wanted to know more about the strange door. My curiosity got the better of me. "Hey, dad, what's with that door?"

Dad looked away from the rat and turned towards the door. A nostalgic smile appeared on his face. "The nowhere door. I honestly forgot it was up here."

"The nowhere door?" I was even more curious "Why do you call it that?"

Dad wore a smirk as he opened the door. I could now see the wall was literally right behind the door. He pushed on the wall and it fell down. As it fell the night sky was revealed. I expected it to fall onto our backyard below, but to my surprise it laid flat like diving board.

Dad chuckled at my bewildered expression. "Your Aunt Connie and I had the same expression on our faces when we first found it too. Grandma told me her father built it."

"Why?"

His expression grew a bit somber. "Well, he started building this the fall after Lola died. He probably needed something to keep his mind off it."

Oh. Lola. The great-aunt I never had the chance to met. I think every family has a Lola, a family member who died too young and will forever leave a scar that carries over to all future generations. Because of her all the children in my family are told to be wary of the ocean. Apparently Lola loved the ocean so much that she sneaked out to go night-swimming, but she never came out. One of my older cousins told me that they had to bury an empty casket because they never found her body.

My father soon disposed of the dead rat, and we went back down the ladder. All throughout the night I couldn't stop thinking about that weird door. Still, there was a chance for normalcy. That was until Elise and Ethan caught wind of the attic. The twins were always looking for new places to have their little make-believe games in. They couldn't resist the idea of having their own space.

"What are you guys doing?" I asked one day. I came up to the attic to investigate a ruckus, and Elise and Ethan were dressed up in crude, handmade pirate costumes. They were holding "swords" that were really used paper towel rolls.

Ethan smiled like he was extremely proud of himself "Me and Elise are pirates looking for buried treasure!"

"Yeah and then we're going to be the rulers of the pirate world!" Elise boasted.

I rolled my eyes. At ten most kids had outgrown playing pretend and all that stuff. Then again, most kids didn't have Ethan's huge imagination or Elsie's endless energy. Together they were always going on an imaginary adventure and/or getting trouble.

As (in my own opinion at that time) a very mature fourteen-year-old I just couldn't get it. "You two need to be more quiet. I could hear you all the way down stairs." I said in my patented *"I'm older so I know best"* voice.

Ethan looked a little embarrassed, but Elise just pouted. "Fine, *Mom.*" She said sarcastically. They tried to be more quiet after that, but they returned to being the loud the next day. It became a daily occurrence to hear laughing and running in attic.

One night it became louder than usual. Mom and dad were spending a romantic night at the beach, and figured we would be fine. It was barely a three minute walk away from the house after all. I was trying to sleep when the sound of feet pounding on the floor above me woke me up. I sighed angrily. I marched down the hallway to the ladder, ready to give them a piece of my mind.

As soon as I saw inside the attic, my mind stopped. All I could say was "What you doing!?"

The Nowhere door was opened wide, with Elise standing on the extended plank of wood. Ethan was right behind her, just about to join her on the plank.

"Sarah!" Ethan yelped. Elise quickly got off the plank. "Are Mom and Dad back?" Ethan asked nervously.

My initial shock was soon replaced with anger. "That's what you're worried about? That plank's been there since Grandma was kid! It could've broke at any time."

"W-well, we were playing pirates and we thought it'd be fun to the use the door as a-" Ethan began.

"I don't care." I interrupted. "You guys could have died! Now get away from there."

I went over to the door and pulled the plank up. "You always act like your boss of us when you're not!" Elise argued.

"Newsflash: when Mom and Dad are out, I *am* in charge." I grabbed her arm to pull her out of the attic. I went to get Ethan. I saw he had moved halfway into the space between the plank and the door, his hand ready to close it anytime.

"Ethan..." I growled.

"Y-you can't tell me what to do. I'm Captain Ethan Lindberg of the King Ed's Revenge." He seemed to gain confidence with every word.

I gave Ethan a flat look, while Elise smiled widely and gave him a thumbs up. I began to walk towards him so he wouldn't mess with that stupid door. Ethan quickly slammed the door shut, placing himself in that tiny space.

"Ethan!" I yelled. I ran towards the door and tried to force open. It wouldn't budge. "Open this door right now!"

"Yes! I have the bested the evil Queen Sarah!" Ethan boasted in an over-dramatic tone. Elise cheered and I turned to glare at her. "Now I have saved the kingdom and-" Ethan's delusions of grandeur suddenly stopped right in the middle.

Then he was quiet for a second. Eerily quiet. "Ethan? Very funny. Now open it." No response. "Ethan, stop messing around!" I suddenly got the horrible image of Ethan falling off the side of house. "Ethan...?" I repeated once more, fear creeping into my voice.

This time I get a response. "Sarah?" Ethan asked. There something off with his voice. He sounded very confused.

"Yeah, I'm here." I couldn't help but be relieved that he was okay. "Please just come out."

"I can't. When I try to twist the knob it won't move. And there's something weird with the closet... I don't think I'm in it anymore."

"Oh, really? Are you in Narnia now?" I was being to get annoyed again. Elise crept closer and seemed to be genuinely concerned.

"Where are you?" She asked.

"I don't know. It's really dark but, I can tell it's bigger than the closet. It's also smells really bad. The floor is made of dirt. I think it might be a cave..." Ethan voice then became frightened. "Guys, I think I saw something. Please open the door."

"I'm trying but it won't open. Unlock it."

"I didn't lock it!" Ethan yelled. "Please just-" Suddenly he yelped. "It's coming closer." The door began to shake like Ethan was banging his body against it.

At first I thought Ethan was just pulling my leg, but the fear in his voice didn't seem fake. Plus, I doubt he would started pounding on the door that hard if he didn't think he was in danger. Another thing occurred to me. I had never seen the nowhere door completely closed before. Considering how old the door was, the locks might be broken.

"Elise, go get Mom and Dad. I'll try to open the door." Elise hesitated. She probably didn't want to leave Ethan. However, she did hurry out the attic and down the stairs. "Ethan, I'm going to pull the knob while you push on the other side, okay?"

Ethan whimpered. "Okay." He sounded like he was about to cry. We began our a little plan but, it wasn't working. A minute into it Ethan stopped.

"S-s-Sarah..." Ethan voice was shaking. "It's coming closer..."

"Don't worry, Ethan. Mom and Dad are going to be here soon." I was trying to comfort myself as much as I was trying comfort Ethan. My heart was beating so fast I thought it was going to explode.

"But Sarah, it's-" Ethan's scream cut through the air. "*It's here! It's here!*" He began banging on the door faster, and more frantically, than before.

I pulled as hard as I could until my knuckles were white and hands were burning from pain. Nothing seemed to work.

Then, out of nowhere, the door suddenly opened. Since it was so sudden, and I was pulling so hard, I fell onto the floor.

"Ethan? Sarah? What's going on?" I could hear my Dad's voice call. I could also hear his and Mom's footsteps coming up the stairs.

I smiled widely, happy that everything was going to be okay. "Ethan and Elise were playing in the attic and I went to-" The words died on my tongue.

I looked to the door expecting to see a freaked out, but safe, Ethan. Instead, all I saw was the empty space between the door and plank.

My family was devastated, obviously. Mom and Dad called the police when they realized Ethan was nowhere to be seen. Of course, no one really thought mine and Elise's story was real. Hell, I wasn't even sure it was real. Mom and Dad were downstairs talking and trying comforting each other. I was laying in bed the next night, unable to sleep. I nearly jumped out of bed when I heard footsteps coming down the hallway. I peeked out the door to see Elise walking towards the attic.

"What are you doing?" I hissed.

Elise flinched. She turned to me and I could see her face was extremely pale. Her eyes were red from crying. "Sarah, I saw Ethan."

"What? Really? We have to tell Mom and Dad!" I felt like I had some hope again. However, Elise shook her head.

"No, I saw him in a dream." She hesitated. "Well, nightmare. Ethan was hiding under behind a dead tree. Weird...things were looking for him. Ethan looked so scared..." Elise almost started crying but stopped herself. "Then he turned to me. He looked shocked at first and I knew he could see me too. Ethan mouthed something to me. *Open the door.* Then I woke up."

Elise finished her story and looked at me with pleading eyes. "We need to go up there and try to open it. Mom and Dad wouldn't believe me. But you were there. You know."

I sighed, "Elise, that was just a dream. You're worried about Ethan and you were freaked out by...whatever...happened last night. That's why you had that dream. Besides, Mom and Dad don't want us going in the attic without them."

Elise grabbed my shirt and pulled on it. "I know it was real! This might be the only way to get Ethan back!" She spoke passion, her voice rising with every word. "If we don't Ethan...Ethan might..."

Elise began crying. She buried her face into my chest. I tried to soothe her as best as I could. She was taking Ethan's disappearance the hardest.

"Okay." I said reluctantly. "But at the first time of trouble, we're getting mom and dad."

Elise's eyes lit up and she quickly nodded her head. We headed up the ladder and into the attic. All the miscellaneous items that had been moved out earlier in an attempt to find any sign of Ethan. The attic felt so much bigger when it was empty. Elise and I carefully made our way to door. It was closed, probably by one of our parents, just in case we tried to mess with it. Like we were about to do. I wasn't sure what we were going to do after we got to it. Elise already had a plan, however.

She knocked on the door and called out "Ethan?" There was no reply for a minute. I was about to suggest we go back to bed, when I heard a familiar voice from the other side of the door.

"Elise, is that you?" Ethan asked. His voice sounded so worn out and scared. No ten year old should ever sound like that.

"Yeah, it's me and Sarah. Are you doing okay?" Elise said quickly.

"I hid from the things behind a tree. Everything here is almost the same as back in town but, it's all run down and the sky's red. And the things...they kinda look like people but,they they're all...wrong. They never say anything and they walk on _"

"I thought you said you were in a cave?" I interrupted.

"That's the thing. Things around me keep on changing! I close my eyes for second, then everything different!"

"Okay, okay." I was still skeptical but, I was just glad I knew where he was. "We're going to go get mom and dad. Just stay there."

"No!" Ethan yelled. "They'll find me by then. They're probably almost here. Please just open the door."

"Sarah, he's right. We can't just leave him there." Elise agreed. I admit, I was scared by the idea on those *things* Ethan kept describing, coming out and attacking us when we opened the door. Also, Ethan's story was starting to make less and less sense the more he told us about it. Either he was lying or this situation was even stranger than I first thought. Which was saying *a lot*.

Still, the terror is my siblings' voices convinced to help Elise in trying to open the nowhere door. We pulled and pulled and pulled but, the door just wouldn't budge.

"Things are changing again." Ethan said, his voice shaky. "Promise me you'll come back soon."

"We promise." Scared as I might be I wasn't going to abandon my little brother.

"We'll definitely come again." Elise said with confidence. However, Ethan didn't say anything back. Elise knocked on the door again. "Ethan?"

"What are you doing?" Someone replied but, that voice wasn't Ethan's. Elise and I both gave small shrieks and flinched back.

Mom was peeking through the opening to the attic. Her worried expression quickly turned into a scowl. "Girls, we said to stay out of here."

"Sorry Mom, we just..." I tried to think of some kind of explanation, but Mom just sighed. She went up to us and pulled us into a tight embrace.

"I know you guys are worried about Ethan. I am too. But you need to keep calm and listen us. Okay?"

"Okay." I mumbled back. I looked to Elise. Elise gave me an uncertain stare. I nodded just enough for her to notice, never breaking eye contact. She then gave me a slight nod back.

"Okay." Elise said slowly. But I knew she wasn't talking to mom. We were going back to the attic tomorrow. Our brother needed our help and we were going try our hardest to save him.

We had to wait for Mom and Dad go to sleep the next night. They were up late talking police. I heard that a story about Ethan was going to be on the news soon. Eventually, they ended up going to sleep around 2:00 AM. Elise and I slowly crept down the hallway, careful not to wake them. After we got to the attic, we closed the hatch to the attic and locked it.

Elise went to the door and knocked on it. "Ethan?" She asked.

A few seconds went by before Ethan replied. "Yeah." He said weakly. He sounded like he was sick. It briefly occurred to me that Ethan probably hadn't eaten anything in two days. I thought it was strange that he didn't mention being hungry at all.

"Ethan, we're going pull as hard as we can while you push hard on the other side. Can you do that?" I asked.

Ethan hesitated for a second. "I'll try."

Elise and I put both our hands on the knob. We pulled so hard our knuckles turned white. Ethan was doing his part, pushing so hard I thought the door was going to crack. Suddenly a ray of hope appeared. I could feel the door start to slowly. I smiled brightly. I was finally going to get my brother back.

Then it all went wrong. The door opened just a bit. The door still was unnaturally hard to open all the way but, it was still something. Then, the arm came through from the other side of door.

It was horribly emaciated, with it's skin mottled and possibly rotting. The fingers were unnaturally long and spider-like. More than that, the skin on the arm began to burn away almost immediately. Before me and Elise could scream an inhuman shriek came from the other side of the door. The arm quickly went back to the other side. Elise and I were so shocked from what we just saw, we accidently let go and the door closed once more.

"W-what happened?" Elise asked "Did one of those things get through while we were opening it?"

"No." Ethan answered. "I put my arm through and it started hurting a lot." He winced from pain. "Are you guys okay?"

My blood ran cold. "Ethan, can I ask you question? Do you know what you look like now?"

"I...I don't know. My head feels so cloudy. It's getting hard to remember things." He was quiet for a moment. Ethan seemed to have came to the same realization I just had. "I can't come back, can I?" His voice cracked on the last words.

Tears sprung from my eyes. I tried to say something, but words just wouldn't come. Elise was processing what Ethan said. She then shook her head frantically. "No, you're coming back. You have to!" She was crying too. Ethan ignored her.

"Sarah, tell Mom and Dad that I'm sorry I didn't listen to their rules. Tell them that I love them so much." Ethan began. "Sarah, even if I call you bossy sometimes, I always knew you were the best big sister. Elise, you're my best friend and the best pirate captain ever." One last pause, and a shaking breathe. "I love you guys. Goodbye."

Me and Elise sat in shocked, devastated silence for second. Then Elise's entire body began shaking. "No...no, no, no, NO!" Elise ran to the door and opened it.

"Elise, no!" I cried. But I didn't need to worry about anything. The only thing on the other side was the night sky. When our parents finally forced opened the hatch hours later they found me and Elise hugging each other, sobbing, while the sun rose behind us.

My parents searched for months and months for Ethan. They never found him. After a year, they finally stopped looking. We had to bury an empty casket. I never felt so empty as when I saw it lowered in the ground. I wonder if that's how Grandma felt when they buried Lola. Sometimes, I wonder if Lola had the same fate as Ethan or if my great-grandfather had something to do with whatever horrible place my brother got trapped in. I guess I'll never really know. There are a lot things I'll never know. And it still kills me.

Elise never recovered from the loss of Ethan. She lost apart of herself that day. I know she still has terrible nightmares about Ethan. I don't know if she still has a link to him or if it's just from the trauma. That's why I didn't tell her about what I'm planning to do this summer. My dad's going to sell the house

440

next fall. He offered to take us one more time to the house. I'm the only one who took the offer. I'm not going for nostalgia's sake though. I'm going to nail the nowhere door shut and knock the knob off. I already failed to keep my little brother. I'm not letting that door take anyone else.

TAKEN TO THE BRINK

Wynne F. Winters

I'd never seen the tattoo parlor there before. It must've popped up, I thought, in the middle of the night. After all, I walked this way to the train every day—how could I have missed it?

The parlor sat between a used bookstore and an indie café, the storefront reflective black with gold lettering which read: "BrInk Tattoo Parlor" in flowing calligraphy. It was quite lovely, but uninformative, and I probably wouldn't have bothered if it wasn't literally on my way home. To tell the truth, I'd been toying with the idea of getting a tattoo ever since I transitioned—a symbol of my new life, I guess. I even had an image picked out. I'd just never really, you know, *gotten around* to actually *visiting* a tattoo artist.

When I stepped inside BrInk, I wasn't planning on getting a tattoo that day. I thought I'd look around, talk to the staff, get a price, then give it some more thought. After all, I could always stop by on my day off to get the actual inking done.

The inside of the shop was small, appearing even smaller courtesy of the black walls and ceiling. Framed artwork hung above a black counter, beyond which stretched a dimly lighted hall. There wasn't a single person in sight.

I looked for a bell or buzzer to announce my presence, but found none. Instead, I leaned over and shouted down the hall: "Hello? Is there anyone there?"

"Oh!" I heard scuffling, followed by a bright female voice calling, "Sorry, sorry! I'll be right there!"

I stood patiently, drumming my fingers absently on the countertop as more thumping and thudding emitted from the hallway. Figuring this could take a while, I glanced up at the artwork.

There were three large pictures framed in thin black plastic and hung asymmetrically. They were all abstract, white objects on white backgrounds, defined only by shadow. The first was filled with jagged lines like shattered glass, images of birds rising from the pieces. The second was filled with drips like rain, the shapes of waves crashing into the margins. The last was filled with cutouts like mountains, though at first I couldn't make out the secondary image. I stared at it harder, my eye catching on the contrasting lines. Gradually, I began to make out a silhouette: a face, half-turned to look over its shoulder, eyes downturned. A woman's face...

"Thanks for waiting!"

I blinked and found a young woman beaming at me from behind the counter. Her hair was pixie short and bright pink, a silver stud winking from her nose. She wore a sleeveless shirt despite the winter weather, revealing colorful images down both arms and across her collarbone.

"Sorry about that," she said. "We're still moving in—haven't quite got everything settled yet."

"It's fine," I said. "Um. So, to be honest, I'm not exactly sure how this all works."

"Oh, a virgin!" she said, then clapped a hand to her mouth. "Sorry! That wasn't very nice. I mean, this is your first time?"

"Ye-es," I said. Had I made a mistake coming in here? "In fact, I'm not sure if I really want to get one, yet. I'm just sort of...shopping around."

"Ah, okay, got it! Well, first thing is to figure out what you want and how big. We charge for size and complexity—once we know what you're looking at, we can give you an estimate." She reached under the counter and pulled out an enormous book, which she started flipping through. It was filled with sketches and photos of finished tattoos. "Then you'll want to decide where to put it. Once that's all settled, Brian will draw it up—Brian is our resident artist—and make sure it looks the way you want. Then we just print it onto a temporary, slap it on you, and he'll go to work." She grinned and leaned across the open book, hand outstretched. "I'm Lisa, by the way. Sometimes I forget my manners."

I looked at the offered hand, the nails sporting chipped, black paint, then shook it firmly. "Elle," I said.

"Elle? That's a pretty name." A tall man with long, dark hair emerged from the dark hallway. His expression was cheerful in contrast to his black, skull-depicting shirt. "I'm Brian. Pleasure to meet you."

"Pleasure to meet you, too," I said, transferring my handshake.

"Well, I'm sure Lisa's chatted your ear off," said Brian. "She gets a little excited when she meets someone new."

Lisa beamed, apparently unoffended. "I was just showing her some of your previous work."

"I see that," Brian said, glancing down at the open book. "Let me ask this: do you have an idea what design you'd like? If you do, I can show you some similar things I've done."

I considered this. Lisa's fountain of enthusiasm had been a little too much for my already hesitant visit, but Brian's calm, collected approach was reassuring. Their pairing was quite a good match for business, I thought. "I've always wanted an ankh," I said, testing to see if he was familiar with the symbol. He nodded.

"I've done a few of those," he said, flipping through the book. The relevant pages showed several appropriate tattoos: a shape much like a cross, but with a loop at the top, creating the ancient Egyptian symbol of life. "Do you know what style you'd like?"

"Really simple," I said. The photos ranged from intricately realistic stone to deconstructed geometric shapes. "Like, just black lines. Nothing else."

"Okay." Brian pulled a blank piece of paper and pencil from behind the counter and began to sketch. "Like that?"

I took a look. "Maybe the cross part can be a little flared on the ends? And the loop can be slightly longer."

He drew it again, and this time it was perfect. I was astounded by how quickly it happened. I'd only set foot in the shop a few minutes before, and now I was staring at my dream tattoo. I told Brian so.

"I'm glad to hear it," he said, smiling. "So now Lisa can scan that into the computer and get it sized, and we'll give you the price. Then we can set up an appointment for you to get inked."

I chewed my lip. This was all happening very fast. A part of me was starting to panic now that my years-long daydream was becoming a reality. But, another part of me argued, if I didn't do this now, I was never going to—and this *was* something I wanted, badly enough to actually be here, right now. Right?

"Actually," I said as Lisa fired up the scanner. "I was wondering . . . do you have any openings this evening?"

Brian's smile broadened. "Sure do. Got every slot open, in fact."

I smiled back. "Guess it's my lucky day."

***

The pain wasn't as bad as I'd thought it would be. The whole process was quick as well—it felt like I'd just sat down when the buzzing of the tattoo gun halted and Brian announced that we were done.

I was immensely happy with the result: a simple black ankh, about three inches long, on the inside of my wrist. My eyes traced the crisp edges, marveling at the that fact that this work of art was now a *part* of me.

Brian bandaged me up and gave me a list of aftercare instructions, along with a business card. "Don't pick at it," he warned me as I tucked everything into my purse. "It'll itch like hell as it heals, but if you pick off the scab, the ink'll come with it."

I thanked him for his advice and wonderful work, and returned Lisa's enthusiastic wave on my way out. I paused halfway to the door, looking at the art behind her. "You alright?" she asked, still smiling.

"Yeah," I said. "Yeah, I'm fine. Thank you again."

447

"No problem. See you around!"

I exited the parlor and headed home, the bandage bulky beneath my sleeve. It was probably only a trick of the eye, a queer consequence of the abstract nature of the piece, but I could've sworn that the last picture was slightly different. It seemed, upon my last glance, like the silhouetted woman's eyes were no longer downcast, but looking straight-on, directly at me.

***

Once home, I followed Brian's care instructions, then applied a fresh bandage for the night. The next day, I wore my loosest clothing and removed the bandage to give my newly minted artistry some breathing room. But my anticipation turned to dismay as I beheld the ink beneath: it had begun to leak, feathering out into my skin.

For a moment, I just stared, disbelieving. My next move was to wash my wrist, illogically thinking perhaps it was only excess ink which had oozed from the open wound, as Brian had warned me may happen. But it didn't wash away—it was, very firmly, beneath my skin.

Panicking, I tried calling the tattoo parlor, but no one picked up. That was understandable—it was very early, and they likely hadn't opened yet. My initial resource rendered bunk, I turned to the internet.

I got some results for feathering tattoos and blowouts, but nothing as extreme as I had. The tendrils of ink leaking from the thick black ankh were nearly an inch long, and numbered nearly a dozen. Frustrated, I turned to tattoo forums, searching desperately for some sort of answer—was this fixable? What had caused it? Had I just spent two hundred dollars for some guy with greasy hair to fuck up my arm?

I was deep into the archives of the world wide web when I happened to look up and curse. I was late for work. Instead of heading to the subway, which would undoubtedly exacerbate my lateness, I opted to Uber and rushed to get ready, knowing this was just the start of what promised to be a thoroughly shitty day.

***

At lunch, I tried calling the parlor again. A busy signal buzzed in my ear. With a sigh, I ended the call, thinking I'd try again later. Maybe they were out to lunch?

"Hey Elle!" Calvin, my coworker, slid into the booth, a bag of Taco Bell in his hand. He was a cheery guy who had the cubicle across from mine, the friendly type who seemed to know everyone's name and favorite sports team. As he looked at me, a flash of concern crossed his face. "You alright?"

"Yeah, yeah," I said, sliding my phone into my pocket. I picked up my fork and started picking at my cobb salad, though anxiety had dulled my appetite. "Just...trying to make an appointment, but I can't seem to get through."

"Oh, I hate that," said Calvin, nodding knowingly. He took a bite of his burrito, hot sauce oozing from the tortilla. He narrowed his eyes suddenly. "Hey, what happened to you hand? Was your pen leaking?"

Confused, I glanced down.

Thin tendrils of ink peeked from beneath my sleeve, staining the back of my hand. I stared.

"I, uh," I said. "I have to—" I stood up, fumbling with my purse. "Sorry, I'm not feeling well. Have a good lunch, okay?"

"Sure," said Calvin. "Hope you feel better!" he called after my hurrying back.

I headed to the bathroom, dizzy with panic. I shut myself in a stall and jerked my sleeve back, telling myself I was overreacting, that it wasn't going to be as bad as I feared.

The ink had spread, wrapping nearly around my wrist and inching up the back of my hand. The ankh was completely lost, swallowed by the spreading black blob.

What was going on? How was this possible?

I tried to call the parlor again, on the verge of tears. This time, I was met with an automated message: "The number you have dialed has been disconnected . . ."

I could've screamed. What the Hell was happening? What the fuck kind of con-men had I met yesterday?

Enough was enough, I decided. I was marching straight to the parlor after work and *demanding* they fix this—or I'd sue. Yeah. That's what I'd do.

Having a plan calmed me. I took a few deep breaths, then took out my phone again, snapping a few pictures of the mess those assholes had made of my arm. They wouldn't get away with this—if this was irreparable, I was going to make their lives hell.

***

The subway ride home felt like it took forever. I found myself tapping my fingers, the sound muted by my gloves. I'd been wearing them since lunch, worried that someone else would notice the ink.

Once above ground, I stomped down the street, rehearsing the confrontation in my head. No one had mentioned this kind of side effect, neither had it been mentioned in the paperwork they'd had me sign. That *had* to be some kind of violation—I

451

could get their license suspended. I could sell my story to the local paper. I could post it all over the internet and ruin them for good—

I stopped.

I'd arrived at my destination, I was sure of it—and yet I was completely lost.

There was no tattoo parlor.

It wasn't that the parlor was closed, or abandoned. It was simply gone. To the left was the used bookstore, its displayed volumes as dusty as ever, and to the right was the indie café with its weird wind-flute music piped out over the patio. Their brick walls met seamlessly, with not so much as an alley in between. There was no space, no room for a parlor with reflective black windows and gold calligraphy.

Everything seemed to come unmoored. I felt sick. It was difficult to breathe. Only half-aware, I turned and started to stagger home, overwhelmed and unsure what else to do.

With some effort, I managed to get back to my apartment, only to stand shell-shocked in the entranceway. Had I hallucinated everything? Had there ever been a shop there? I looked down at my black-gloved hands. If it'd all been an illusion, then what had Calvin seen at lunch? Had I really just had a leaky pen and invented the rest?

There was only one way to find out.

I gripped my left glove with my right hand and began to peel it off. It was strangely difficult—the glove clung to my skin, and seemed damp, though it hadn't been wet outside.

Underneath, my skin was black. The ink had spread completely around my wrist, with tendrils heading toward my elbow. Both the front and back of my hand were black, as were my fingers. I'd just gotten the glove over my third knuckles when they seemed to catch on something. I paused, worried, but I reasoned that I needed to see the extent of the damage. So I grit my teeth and pulled the fabric away, feeling whatever it was give way.

It'd been my nails.

I stared in horror at the little plates of keratin sticking to the inside of the glove fingers, glistening black and dripping. My hand was even more horrifying: the soft pads that had housed my nails were oozing a viscous black liquid that stank of rotting blood and ink.

The world tilted and I leaned against the wall to remain upright. This was wrong. Very, very wrong. I must've—they must've given me something. A flesh-eating bacteria or—I needed help. Medical help.

I fumbled for my phone one-handed, my left arm held out in front of me. I struggled to unlock my phone, right hand still gloved, my gazed locked on my grotesque left arm, unable to look away.

9-1-1...they'd send someone...the hospital, I needed...

Beneath my skin, an inky black tendril flexed.

I screamed and dropped my phone. It hit the laminate with a clunk that would've made me wince any other time, but all my attention was locked on this—this *thing* infecting my arm. As I watched, the black tendril pressed upward, bulging against my skin, and began to creep toward my elbow...

I had to get it out. I couldn't let it infect the rest of me.

Driven by this singular thought, I rushed to the kitchen, tripping and bruising myself on walls in my mad dash. I crashed into the counter, panting, and fumbled at the knife block resting there. In my haste, I knocked the whole thing over, sending it crashing to the floor, knives scattering everywhere.

I dropped to my knees, frantic, and grabbed the first handle I reached: a wide, stainless steel chef's knife.

Swiping the other knives carelessly aside, I slammed my hand against the laminate, fingers splayed and still oozing that awful mixture of blood and ink. For a split second, I came back to myself. What the hell was I doing? This was insane! I needed to calm down, think this through . . .

As I struggled to think logically, the skin on my forearm bulged, like a blister. I stared in horror as other bulges formed, rippling and bubbling. I couldn't feel any of it, and that, too, scared me — shouldn't I be in pain? Was my arm so septic it'd killed even the nerves?

The bulges swelled, rippled — then burst. Black tendrils squirmed from the open sores, covered in that same stinking mixture of blood and ink. I screamed and brought the chef's knife down.

It took only a few swift, frantic hacks, and my arm lay on the kitchen floor, black and oozing, the tendrils still wriggling over my blackened skin. Pain seared through me, blood pumping from the stump where my arm used to be. It soaked my clothes and the hot, metallic scent turned my stomach.

A tourniquet, I thought, my mind already hazy. *I need a tourniquet.*

A towel hung from the oven handle a few feet away. My vision swimming, I started to crawl toward it, every second taking me further and further from reality. At last I collapsed, my head striking the floor. I lay for a moment, telling myself to get up, but my body unresponsive. As the darkness of unconscious began to swallow my vision, I thought I saw something creeping across the kitchen — something black and oozing, dozens of inky tentacles pulling it closer.

***

I woke with a headache and the taste of blood in my mouth. For a moment I was confused, wondering why I was cold and aching, before I realized I was on the floor. As it all came rushing back, I jerked upright, my body screaming in protest, and collapsed into a sitting position against the cabinets. The last thing I remembered was bleeding to death. Which begged the question: why wasn't I dead?

The kitchen was still littered with knives, glinting dangerously against the faux wood laminate. There was no arm, black or otherwise, to be seen. Instead, a trail of dark, thick blood crossed the floor, a few knives pushed aside, as though something had been dragged through the mess. It cut a straight line...to where I'd previously lay.

A terrible feeling of freefall overtook me as I looked down to my stump.

The arm was there, as grotesque as ever. It'd reattached itself, black ink tendrils pulsing between it and my ragged elbow. The blackness had spread, disappearing into my sleeve.

Panicking, I ripped off my shirt, desperate to see just how far the abomination had spread.

Inky tendrils curled over my shoulder and down my chest, tracing my ribs. As I watched, the tendrils stretched further, their darkness transforming me. I realized I couldn't feel my shoulder at all, and sensation was vanishing from my torso.

I began to cry. *I need to get help*, I thought. But even if I could manage to crawl to the front door and retrieve my phone, who could help me? Whatever this was, it was no simple bacteria or virus—it was sentient, and determined to consume me.

It did so quickly. It spread down into my legs at a rapid pace, rendering them heavy and numb. I sat silently weeping as the inky numbness infiltrated my body, turning my blood sluggish. All hunger vanished as it consumed my stomach; all need for air retreated as it subsumed my lungs. My heart shuddered and ground to a halt as liquid tentacles filled my aorta, soaking into my ventricles until my hardiest muscle was only a sodden lump of meat and ink.

The terror grew unbearable as the numbness crept up my throat, tracing the edge of my jaw, and cradled the back of my head. The taste of ink filled my mouth as the blackness took my tongue, my lips, my teeth. A final shiver rippled through me as ink sunk into my eyes, covering them like a film, rendering my world completely black.

And then, from the darkness, emerged a shape.

In the flexing, writhing blackness, I could make out the silhouette of a woman, her back to me. As I watched, she turned her head, glancing over her shoulder, and smiled.

She seemed oddly familiar, though I couldn't quite place her.

Unable to look away, I watched as she turned fully toward me, her hair flowing, her eyes bright and gleaming. She grinned at me, her lips stretched too wide, her teeth too numerous, and then she opened her mouth wide, then wider, and wider, and then...

THE BEGGAR

Blair Daniels

"Please, ma'am, could you spare some change?"

The homeless woman was bundled up head-to-toe in dark clothes, leaned up against the wall. All that peeked out was a sliver of pale skin and brown eyes.

"I'm sorry. I don't have any cash."

I walked away from her. With every step, my pockets jingled, betraying my words.

I made a left, then a right. My tired legs ached underneath me. It was an awful day at the office – fourteen straight hours of hell. I sighed, sucked in a breath of icy cold air, and made a left onto 10th Street.

But it wasn't long before the jingle of coins rang through the air again. And there, sitting under the awning of a closed restaurant, was another beggar. Or maybe it was the same one? It was hard to tell, in the dim light.

"Please, could you spare some change?"

"No, I'm sorry."

"Even just a dollar would help," she said, softly jingling her cup. "Please. I'm so hungry."

My anger suddenly flared. The exhaustion of the day, the pain in my feet, all came lashing out of my mouth. "I'm sorry, but, no. I work hard for my money. I just spent more than fourteen hours in the office, working for a shitty boss, with a splitting headache. Want money? Go get a job. There's plenty to do in this city."

Her brown eyes looked at me sadly.

I turned on my heel and took off. I could feel her staring at me as I went, but I didn't care. I was too tired, too hungry, too angry.

I took a right onto Maple Ave

The streets were desolate at this hour. Amber lights flickered from the lampposts, casting the sidewalk in jittery shadows. The silence was only broken by the occasional car, rolling across the pavement. Motor thrumming, snatches of music dissipating into the cold air. All else was silent.

I approached the intersection. I pulled out my phone – **2:21 AM. No new messages.**

I idly scrolled through my texts. *Hey Britney! Are you free right now?* A text from Alex, sent days ago. Probably wanted to ask me if I'd put her resume in front of my boss yet. *Give me a call! I have exciting news!* From Danielle. Probably wanted money for some new crazy business venture, as always, that would crash and burn in a few weeks' time.

They weren't worth it.

If there's one thing I've learned in life, it's that *everyone* is looking to use you for something. Connections. Money. If it's a guy, probably sex. They're all bloodsuckers, looking for how much they can get.

I came to the intersection.

Ching, ching.

The familiar jingle of coins against a plastic cup, coming from around the corner. *Another one?* I thought. *At this hour?*

I turned the corner.

A bundle of clothing leaned against the building, scarf fluttering in the icy wind. All covered up, except for a sliver of pale skin. Deep brown eyes.

"Could you spare some change?"

It was the same woman.

The same brown eyes, pale skin, bundled clothes. I was sure this time. "Are you *following* me?!" I yelled, leaping back from the sidewalk.

"Please, could you spare some change?"

"I told you, no! I'm not going to give you any money!"

I turned around and quickened my pace. *What if she mugs me? Or attacks me?* I ran down the crosswalk, my heart pounding. *Three blocks to go. Just three blocks...*

Click, click. A slapping noise on the pavement behind me.

461

I glanced back.

The woman had gotten up off the ground. She lumbered after me, her shadow swaying over the sidewalk.

Dammit.

I pulled out my cell phone. *Police?* No. That would be an overreaction. *Mom?* No, she's over a thousand miles away. *Alex?* Maybe. She only lived a few blocks from here; she could pick me up.

After three rings, she picked up.

"Alex! Hey, can you come pick me up?"

"What? It's almost 3 AM."

"But someone is –"

"Britney, I haven't heard from you in weeks. Where have you been?"

"I've been busy, uh –"

"Look, call me sometime tomorrow, okay?" she said, with some bite in her voice. "I have to get to bed. I have an interview tomorrow."

The call disconnected. I stared at it for a second. Then I glanced behind me. The sidewalk was desolate; the woman was gone.

I breathed a sigh of relief and stepped into the crosswalk. *Only two more blocks to go.* I took a deep, shuddering breath, and raced across the pavement. *Two more blocks. Two more –*

Ching, ching.

A soft jingling sound. I froze in the middle of the crosswalk, my heart pounding.

There – in the shadows.

Her blocky, bundled silhouette. Scarf wrapped over her face. Hat pulled down low. Brown eyes peering out at me.

"It's you," I choked. "Why are you following me? Why?"

She stared silently back at me.

I sprinted away from her. Down the block. My lungs stung in the cold air. My eyes watered, and the city scene – of red traffic lights and amber streetlamps – melted into a blur.

One more block to go…

Half a block to go…

There.

The door to my apartment building.

I hurriedly pressed my fob against the door. *Beep. Click.* I yanked the door open and watched it shut behind me. Made sure no one followed me in.

I was never so happy to smell that familiar, musty smell. Never so happy to press the elevator button and wait for the outdated thing to reach me. The warmth returned to my fingertips; my pulse slowed. *I'm safe. I'm safe.*

Ding. The doors whooshed open.

She was in the elevator.

463

The homeless woman was just standing there. In my elevator. Black clothes swaddled around her, brown eyes wild.

"What – what do you want? Money? Here!" I emptied my pockets. Several coins clinked against the floor. "Just leave me alone!"

She slowly, silently, shook her head.

"How did you get in here?"

Her hand reached into her coat. She pulled out a set of keys – with my building's fob attached.

"You live here?" I choked.

She nodded.

Then, slowly, she reached her hands up to the scarf wrapped around her face. With a smile in her eyes, she yanked it down.

No.

I was looking into my own face.

The pointed chin. The small nose. The loose curls of dark hair. She looked several years older than me – thin wrinkles cut her cheeks, her eyes – but it was unmistakably *my* face.

"How – what –" I choked.

"I'm you," she said, taking a few steps towards me. "I'm Britney Hayworth."

"I don't understand."

"You will, in a few years." She took a step towards me. "When things suddenly stop going right for you. When, suddenly, *you* need something... and find everyone has turned on you."

She walked up to me, until her face was inches from mine. I froze, my heart pounding.

Then she briskly walked past me. The door swung open, and she disappeared into the night.

CHOCOLATE CHIP COOKIES

Adelaide Hagen

I'd never been that into baking, but when I inherited this house I knew I'd have to keep up the tradition.

The house in question belonged to my grandmother. It was small and cozy, exactly the kind of place you'd expect a grandmother to live. The only thing that wasn't adorable and quaint about the house was the forest that bordered it, which loomed intimidatingly over the tiny thing, almost threatening to devour it.

Every year when it started to get cold, or "on the first frost" as my grandmother said, she would bake chocolate chip cookies. Not just any chocolate chip cookies though, the recipe for these was very precise. It's was most important, she always told us, to have all of the right ingredients. Even the little things like cinnamon, and salt.

In the end all of this precision would pay off, as the cookies were always delicious. But we couldn't eat all of them. Four cookies would always be left outside, "so that winter goes easy on this poor old house."

I inherited the house a couple years ago when my grandmother passed away. However, I was in college at the time and didn't move in until just a few months ago. It was summer when I first started living here, but it didn't take long for the trees to shed their leaves. Today I woke up to a dusty coating of frost on the windows.

Luckily, years of watching my grandmother make these cookies meant that I knew the recipe by heart. So I got to work; assembling the ingredients and mixing the dough. Despite not usually being interested in baking, the nostalgia and sense of tradition made it enjoyable.

However, I failed to notice that I was out of one ingredient until the recipe was nearly done. Right before plopping the mixture onto the pan, I attempted to sprinkle on just a little salt. But nothing came out of the salt shaker. For a moment I felt my heart drop, remembering with a tinge of fear how much my grandmother had stressed the importance of having all the ingredients, but then the rational part of my brain took over.

That was obviously just something she did to make remembering the recipe more fun for us as children. It was impossible that neglecting to include a single ingredient could do anything more than simply make the cookies a little less tasty. Satisfied with my decision I put the cookies into the oven to bake, then I waited.

Soon the delicious smell of chocolate chip cookies began to waft through the house, and I decided it must be time to take them out of the oven. While they cooled on the countertop I looked out the window. It must have been windy, as the dark tree branches swayed back and forth, eerily silhouetted in the frost covered glass.

As always, after eating as many cookies as humanly possible, I made sure to put four aside on a paper plate. When I opened the door to put them outside I was surprised by the biting cold, as it was only late autumn. It felt like the middle of winter.

That night I went to be bed with a feeling of unease in the back of my mind. There was something uncomfortable about breaking such an old tradition, and something unsettling about the way the tree's scrawny limbs bent and swayed outside my window.

I woke up to the sound of footsteps crunching in the dry leaves. Someone was outside. I sat up and clutched the blanket around my shoulders, it was bitterly cold. On the window were what must have been a dozen handprints of varying sizes, some as small as a penny and others as wide as a dinner plate, but none the size of a normal human's. A shiver ran down my spine, but I couldn't tell whether it was from the cold or fear.

I got out of bed, but I wasn't sure what to do. After thinking a bit I decided I should start a fire in the fireplace. Sure, I could go down to the basement to check why the boiler wasn't turning on, but I wasn't planning to end up like a stereotypical horror movie protagonist.

The house looked different in the flickering firelight, devoid of the quaint charm it usually had. For a while I sat by the fire, wrapped in a blanket. My grandma had always kept a rifle above the fireplace, but only now did it occur to me how strange it was considering that she didn't hunt.

At some point I must have drifted off. I don't remember when, but I do remember being awoken to the sound of footsteps. My heart skipped a beat. They weren't the sound of crunching footsteps on dried leaves, these ones were coming from above. Something was on the roof. Or multiple somethings, I realized, listening closer. I clutched my blanket tighter. The sound moved back and forth, almost as though they were looking for a way in.

Swallowing my fear, I stood up and took the rifle as carefully as I could. Never having used a gun before, I had no idea how to tell if it was loaded or not. I just clutched it for dear life and hoped that I wouldn't need to find out.

Sitting here in the dimming firelight, listening to whatever those things are trying to find a way in, it occurs to me that maybe salt was the one ingredient that actually mattered.

NANNY
Melody Grace

Everyone has that one terrifying nightmare from their childhood they still remember, but what happens when they find out that it was real?

When my brother James and I were growing up, our family lived in an old Victorian Style home located in Massachusetts. It was a beautiful tribute to the profound craftsmanship of the early twenties; picture a life size rustic dollhouse with an absolutely stunning part glazed, timber framed porch. It was also very secluded, with our nearest neighbor being maybe a mile away.

We would spend most of our days outside, in the treehouse our father built, as we made up stories of pirates and treasures. I was always Blackbeard while James would be Calico, we were the unstoppable duo of the high seas. There was a special hole in the middle of the tree where we would hide our stolen treasures. James had noticed it the very first day after the fort was built.

As exciting as our tree house was though, I would have to say the best part about our home was our nanny. She was so thoughtful and fun, the best nanny any child could ask for, really.

At night, we would hear a soft humming sound that echoed throughout our whole room. It would lull us to sleep, enveloping our minds with such a calmness that we barely had any dreams, only that soft sweet hum from *nanny.*

Some nights though, James and I would startle awake, both having had the same nightmare. Frequently it involved not being able to breathe, as if someone had placed a bag over our heads, or shut off our air supply some how. We would always wake up right before we died, hands on our throats, as we coughed away the night terror.

The mornings after these episodes, we would wake up to find nanny had left us a note. We couldn't quite make out all the scribbles, but I was sure I caught the word "sorry." We always knew she wanted us to be happy and forget about the terrible shadows that haunted our minds.

We would often tell our parents about *nanny*, and how she was so kind, leaving us notes in the night. They would usually comment on how feverish our imaginations were, also adding in how we needed to stop getting into the craft bin without asking. Honestly, I think they were just jealous that we were both so fond of nanny, she had quickly become our favorite person over the years.

James and I eventually grew up and moved out of our family abode, leaving poor nanny behind. We could feel her sadness as we packed our bags, on what would be our last night home. We both took the time to each write nanny a goodbye letter that we placed on each of our nightstands, we knew she would appreciate that later.

We had found an apartment together in the city, and boy, was it different. We both received full rides to Boston University, each taking on a different major. I had decided I wanted to be a teacher, while James dove into Engineering, he was more interested in getting his hands dirty I guess. The school work was time-consuming, but we never forgot about *nanny.*

Years later, I was going to write my college thesis on my childhood, and how I was basically raised by a nanny. While looking up our family home, I stumbled across an article online, written about the original family that lived there in 1915. A mother and father, two little ones, and their nanny. Wait, *our* nanny.

My head began to spin as I inspected the article more thoroughly. Was this really the same woman? How is that possible? I was confused, but I guess a little excited to learn all I could about the woman, or I guess spirit, who had helped raise both my brother and myself. I nostalgically thought to myself, *maybe she missed the kiddos from the previous family and that's why she took such good care of us!*

I could not have been more wrong.

The word "murderer" caught my eye and I quickly scanned further down the article, mortified at what I was reading. A lump began to form in the back of my throat, as my heart sank deep into my chest.

The article reported how the nanny had lost both of her children due to the negligence of a drunk driver in 1913. Never having been able to properly cope with their deaths, she actively searched for the monster that had stolen her babies lives. That is when she became employed by the Dobson's.

On her journey for revenge, she had taken her time, caring for the monster's children as if they were her own. Until that dreadful night when she murdered the two sleeping babes. She had smothered them with a pillow, most likely singing to them ever so sweetly, as she always did.

After they had died, the article stated that the nanny had written what appeared to be a suicide letter and left it next to their bodies. She then killed herself.

At the very bottom, was a photo of the backyard in which my brother and I used to play. In the middle, was the tree our fort had been built upon. As I looked closer I noticed our treasure hole, only, it looked different. It was covered in a deep crimson red that made my own blood run cold.

Next to the tree was the lifeless body of our Nanny, gun still in hand.

Made in the USA
Middletown, DE
10 May 2019